T0367938

Because I Want To:

Her Side

Because I Want To:

Her Side

MATIESHA C. BURLEY

ARCHWAY
PUBLISHING

Archway Publishing books may be ordered through booksellers or by contacting:

Archway Publishing
1663 Liberty Drive
Bloomington, IN 47403
www.archwaypublishing.com
844-669-3957

ISBN: 978-1-6657-5718-8 (sc)
ISBN: 978-1-6657-5719-5 (e)

Library of Congress Control Number: 2024903783

Print information available on the last page.

Archway Publishing rev. date: 02/23/2024

Chapter One

I hate Mondays. I mean, deep down...from the bottom of my soul... cross my heart and hope to die, kind of hate. They're always the same. People rushing, trying to make it to their destinations. Driving like fools because they had way too much fun over the weekend and are having way too hard of a time switching back to work mode. *Or,* like me, they did absolutely *nothing* over the weekend and got way too comfortable sleeping past seven in the morning. Only climbing out of bed when they felt like it.

Now that Monday morning is here responsibility has taken the place of laziness. Only problem is, the energy that comes along with responsibility *just...isn't...quite* kicked in yet. So, when the alarm goes off at five thirty, like me, they hit the snooze button. Five forty-five...snooze. Six a.m... snooze. Finally at six fifteen, they sigh, stare blindly into the early morning darkness that blankets the ceiling and silently begin reciting the days to do list. Marveling at how much more comfortable...and soft...and warm their comforter suddenly now feels. Comparing it to the warmth of the sun, after a record-breaking winter season.

Then at six forty-five the alarm screams, filling the space of their room with the sounds of farm roosters. Snatching them away from calm blue skies and salty breezes of their beachy dreams. Though they try their best to turn off the alarm and call their boss and inform them that they have a terrible, *horrible*...**life threatening** cold...some unseen force rolls them over on their side. Nudge their unwilling legs and feet to the floor, then boot them out of bed. Down the hallway, into the bathroom and into the shower. Even the unnecessarily chipper morning host from the bathroom radio show can't perk them up. The warm water of the shower, the slight touches of facial make-up. Not even the fresh spritz of cocoa butter body spray or thin, soothing layer of cocoa butter body lotion could perk them up.

Or maybe it's just me. Maybe that's just how my weekend went. Which is the reason I'm now almost an hour and a half late to work, *but* still standing in this coffee shop. Silently willing the young counter assistant or "coffee-*mate*", as they call them in this particular shop, to quit bragging about her "*super-hot*" boyfriend and the "*super-hot*" weekend they shared together. Oh...the things he said and the things they did... yadda, yadda, yadda. I keep looking at my wrist, watching the time tick tock closer and closer to eight thirty. All the while wanting to shout to her that, *'the one she brags to is most likely the one that's sleeping with him behind her back. Now shut up and bring me my cappuccino.'* But I don't. I just stand there and wait somewhat patiently frustrated.

In the meantime, my cell phone is ringing and, of course, I have way too many things in my hands. Why I brought my work bag in with me instead of just grabbing my wallet like I normally do, I have no idea. Somehow, without checking the caller's I.D., I manage to answer...and grab my coffee from the coffee-mate. Speaking into the phone, I immediately realized that *not* checking the caller's I.D. was a big mistake.

"Good morning, beautiful."

It's my ex that doesn't want to accept the fact that he's my *ex*-boyfriend, Eric. If I had paid attention to the name, I wouldn't have answered. Right now, I'm just not in the mood to be a human record player. Repeating myself over and over again. I've tried and tried to explain as best I could, mind you...without being rude, that it's just not going to work.

"Good morning." I echo sighing to myself.

"Wow Ayo, could you sound any less excited to hear my voice?"

"Eric..." I say half distracted, half wanting to just blurt out the truth that I haven't had the courage to tell him.

"I don't get it Ayo. One minute we're doing just fine and the next we're over. Just like that. No explanation, no conversation. You just stop taking my calls. What's going on with you?"

"Come on Eric." Nodding thank you to the cashier, I try my best to balance the phone to my ear with my shoulder. I grip my cappuccino with one hand and stuff the change she's handed me into the tip jar next to the cash register.

"I thought we covered this already. It didn't work out. And I didn't *just quit* talking to you."

Turning to leave, I remove my phone from my shoulder with my free hand intending on switching ears. Instead, without looking, I run face first into a brick wall of a man who's standing directly behind me.

"Oh!" I gasped.

My shoulder bag slips from my arm, my glasses flip from my face. My cell phone, though I try to save it, drops like a lead brick to the ground. I don't even want to think about how bad the screen looks. No case or cover, no protective film over the screen. I'm pretty sure it's done for. On a happier note, and this point is what I'm most proud of...I manage to not spill a drop of my cappuccino. Or fall backwards for that matter. That's partially because he was standing awfully close to me, so I slammed into him pretty good, and partially because he's extra *extra* tall. That's when I realized he's still holding me by my shoulders.

"Whoa," he says, "are you okay?"

His voice rumbles low from his throat, and the words quietly escape from his lips which is surrounded by the most fantastic full beard I've seen face to face. I want to touch it, but I've learned in life that certain things are rude and just shouldn't be done. Randomly touching peoples' hair is one of them, I should know. So, I restrain myself.

"I'll manage." I say, quite composed I must admit. "How's your chest?"

"I'll manage." he chuckles. His eyes wrinkle in the corners and his mustache slightly curls upward indicating a small smile. Releasing my shoulders, he bends to pick up my glasses and phone.

"Thank you." I take them and drop them in my bag, readjusting it back to my shoulder.

"You're welcome."

I'm sure I should walk away but I don't think I can move. I like looking at his face and for some reason it makes me smile...big, and I'm pretty sure I probably look stupid. *Okay, I should leave now.*

"Thanks again." I mutter brushing past him. "And sorry I crashed into your chest."

"You're welcome again." He turns with me as I walk away, smiling just a little bit more.

"And don't worry, if I have any issues, I'll send you my bill."

Now I'm smiling bigger.

"Okay, you do that." I say. *Turn around dufus before you run into something else.*

Stopping outside the coffee shop I take a couple of cleansing breaths. Electrifying as this brief encounter was, I need to take it easy. If I don't slow down, my day is going to go straight down the shit tube. And there goes my phone ringing again. Maybe it's not as bad as I thought.

"Hello?" I snap after fishing it out of my bag.

"Ayo, what happened?"

Shit, it's Eric again. I really should start screening my calls better.

"Eric," I say sipping my cappuccino, "*really* not a good time right now. I'm having a rough start to my day. I'm late for work..."

"You're not at work yet???" He, a-k-a, Captain Obvious asks.

"No Eric," I sigh, glancing into the coffee shop window. Mr. Concrete Chest has made his way to the lady's room and is standing outside the door waiting. His girlfriend must be inside. Oh well, it was cute while it lasted.

"Eric, I gotta go." I say making my way down the street. "I need to get focused on my day and you're not helping at all calling like you do."

"Ayo listen," he begins to say, but I don't want to listen. I want this 'situation' ended and over with.

"I gotta go Eric." And with that, I hung up.

It's long... this situation has been drug out for far too long. It's one of the reasons I walked away in the first place. Eric could discuss something to the point that there are no more aspects in which the conversation could be had. He never lets things go, and it got old having the same conversation over and over again. Sometimes he would ask the same question, only using different words, and I would look at him dumb-founded, like, how else can I answer that question without repeating what I've just said. Even so, I only have myself to blame. I don't want to be rude to him, but I probably shouldn't be answering his calls. Or returning them for that matter.

At first, I felt like I owed him some kind of explanation seeing as how I am the one who ended things. Now it's like, *God,* get it already Eric! It's irritating and makes me question why I never noticed before how whiny and needy he is.

"Can you help me?" A small voice whimpers, pulling me from my thoughts.

"Excuse me?" I ask, stepping back a couple of steps towards the tiny old woman. I was walking so fast I practically walked right past her be-fore she even completed her sentence. She was this tiny shell of a woman standing in front of me looking greatly confused.

"I was wondering if you could help me?" she asked again, reaching for my hand.

Her voice is quivering, and her fingers are freezing. As an instinct of any veteran nurse, I remove the cup from the hand she's touching and place it on one of the outdoor dining tables in front of the deli where we're stopped. Then cover her hand with my free hand trying to create some kind of warmth for her.

"Sure, I can help you." I want to ask her what she needs but clearly, she's confused. To what degree I don't know, and I don't want to bom-bard her with a bunch of questions that might overwhelm her even more. So, I wait, watching her as she quickly scans her eyes up and down the street. It's obvious she has no idea where she is. My nursing skills are kicking in.

"What's your name?" I ask.

"Emma," she responds, "Emma Apollo." It's as though she's made a minor discovery.

"Well Emma," I say smiling down at her, "do you know where you are?"

My question brings her attention to my eyes. Eye contact is good. Now that she's focused, I can't tell if it's the cataracts that are making her eyes glossy or if she's just on the verge of crying.

"No." she squeaks growing more and more uncomfortable. Her hands are shaking, and she is afraid now, which makes my heart strings tighten for her. Why is this woman out by herself?

"I came from…" She points her bony finger in one direction, but her eyes shift the other way. Mumbling to herself, it seems she no longer acknowledges my presence.

"I was looking for…" She begins and stops in the middle of her sentence.

She turns and I notice that her shoes are all wrong for her. She should have on something more comfortable. Something that'll allow better blood circulation.

"I'll tell you what, Emma." I say soothing small circles over the slight hump of her back.

"How about we walk in this direction until we see something that's familiar to you?"

She nods her head in agreement, and we slowly began to walk, with her hand in the crook of my arm and my hand covering hers. She's relieved and tells me thank you over and over again. Though she makes me smile, and is very sweet, I really need her to stay focused.

"Were you with anyone?" I ask distracting her from her thank yous.

"My son?" She remembers almost shouting.

'Her son.' Does this prick not even realize he's lost his mom? Probably not, *and* he's probably an idiot.

"Mom!" A voice booms. We both look up at the man rushing toward us. 'Mr. Concrete Chest?' How in the world did this tiny, *tiny* woman produce this giant of a man?

Look at him with his fine chiseled muscles, and his t-shirt clinging to his ribcage. His smooth, long legs stride around the outdoor chairs of the coffee shop. 'Look away, Ayo.' I think to myself, 'Don't stare into the light'.

"Mom, where did you go? I couldn't find you. I stood outside of the lady's bathroom, but you never came out?" He bends down on one knee wrapping her up in his massive, fantastically sculpted arms for a surprisingly tender embrace.

Hug me next.' my heart whispers...*'SHUT UP!'* my brain shouts.

"I waited outside the bathroom for you, but you weren't there." Relief plagues his face and oozes from his voice, as he hugs her close again. Okay so he's not an idiot.

"I'm okay now." She tells him comforting his back. "I'm okay, son."

It's all very sweet, how she ends up being the one to comfort his worried soul. He kisses her cheek, and she pats his face running her fingers through his beard.

"When are you going to shave? You have such a lovely face."

"One day, I guess." He smiles.

'No,' my brain shouts, *'don't shave.'*

"I'm okay, son." She repeats, "I got a little turned around is all. This sweet girl helped me."

Now they see me.

"Oh, did she?" he asks, looking at me with his rich chestnut eyes.

Hmmm, those...eyes could stop a train on its tracks.

"Mom, do you mind sitting here for a second while I talk to this nice lady?" He pulls a chair out for her, "I'll only be a minute."

She takes her seat and places her purse in her lap as he stands straight up, way...way up, and slowly strides over to me. Seriously, how tall is this man? I mean, I'm six foot three in my Converses and he *towers* over me. Goodness gracious he's tall.

"Thank you." He tells me extending his hand out for me to shake. Damn those eyes.

"You're very welcome." I speak. Silently giving myself two points for holding my composure and not drooling all down my chin. "It's what I do." I'm bragging but it's okay, he seems to be amused. His mahogany mustache slightly curls into a half smile, and I must say it is very attractive. "She made it as far as the deli."

I slip my hand from his giant paw and point my thumb over my shoulder. "She asked me for help, and I couldn't just leave her standing there." I mentally urge myself to look away from him because those pools of chocolate he calls eyes are drowning me where I stand. But I can't, I simply just can't.

"She was in the lady's room." His eye contact breaks to glance back at her, then his hands slide into the pockets of his loose-fitting slacks. In the meantime, I mentally smack myself in the back of the head because I truly believe I stared way too long in that... 'area', where his zipper is.

"After a while, when she didn't come out, I asked a waitress to check on her for me. She left her purse on the sink." He looks back at me, worry still etched in his eyes. "This never happened before."

I can tell that he loves his mother dearly, and in my line of work, for as long as I've worked in healthcare, and with all the dead-beat children I've crossed paths with. It's refreshing to see.

"She was fine." I reassure him, "Like she said, just got a little turned around is all." His shoulders rise and fall as he exhales deeply.

"Thank you again."

Again, he offers his hand and I take it fully intending on a two-pump handshake. Until he steps closer, placing his free hand on my right elbow and leans in quicker and smoother than I'm ready for. I don't know why...I have no idea what made him lean his soft, mahogany face forest against my cheek planting a small, caressing but noticeable kiss on my cheek. What's even more 'funny', I have no clue why my first reaction wasn't to step away from this stranger but to lean in and light weight snuggle my face closer to his. Yes...I said *snuggle*. His beard smelled...I don't know...foresty. It was soft and thick and firm all at the same time. Sigh...my hand even ended up on his side somehow.

I have no clue what the hell just happened, but I **really** like it. I'm hot under the collar and I'm wearing scrubs, which have no collar. Then to make it worse he's directly in my right ear with his rich, low toned voice thanking me, again. The hairs stand up on the back of my neck and tingles shoot down my side...my right side. Which is my 'good' side. That side that shivers and tickles in a good way when things start stirring in a hot situation. Only we aren't in a 'hot situation'. We are in broad daylight, standing outside of a coffee shop, on the middle of the sidewalk with his mother sitting less than fifteen feet away from us. Definitely not my idea of a hot situation, but still I'm stirring anyway.

Again, I give myself major points for composure. Because by the grace of something divine, I manage to maintain a controlled half smile the entire time. At six foot three, I usually have to lean down to accept a kiss from anyone. For once without having to think about it or feel awkward in any way, I get to just stand there and accept it. Brief as it was it still got to me, and that's worth about a hundred points just for keeping my cool.

"It wasn't a problem, really." I tell him, readjusting my bag over my shoulder. "But you're very welcome."

My eyes are on his, but I still notice his shift to one side. Casually, I step to my right beside one of the tables and stride around Mr. Concrete Chest, over to where Emma is sitting. I stoop down and place my hand over her hand focusing on her eyes. The gloss is gone so her cataracts weren't the problem, she must have really been scared. It makes me wonder how many people walked past and ignored her before I came along. Now that I have a chance to look at her, she's very well kept. Her clothes are nicely pressed, and she clearly goes to a great beautician.

"Mrs. Apollo?" I say softly to get her attention. "It was very nice to meet you and thank you for the walk. It was very lovely."

"Oh, you're welcome, dear." Her smile is soft and sweet as she kissed my cheek gently on the same side as her son. "We can go anytime you like." Her smile widens and she pats my hand with her soft, well-manicured bony fingers. She really is a sweetheart of a woman.

"Thank you, Mrs. Apollo." I say returning her gentle smile.

"Call me Emma." she instructs, "Mrs. Apollo was my mother-in-law."

"Yes ma'am."

"And do me a favor dear." she asks, completely catching me off guard.

"Anything." I promise her growing more intrigued.

"Tell him to shave. He has such a lovely face."

An involuntary chuckle escapes my glossed lips. It's such an unexpected thing for her to say that I find myself wondering who this woman thinks I am. I look back at her son, who, and I'm pretty sure I'd be correct in saying, hasn't taken his eyes off me.

"I don't know, Emma." I say standing and slowly walking toward him. Casually studying his face. The way his beard is groomed around his cheeks, full but still outlining his strong jawbone. All the way up blending with his sideburns, on into his carefully knotted chestnut man bun. I stop directly in front of him, at a respectable distance, of course. Though I may want to get closer, I won't. I only just met the man this morning...and there he goes sliding those massive hands into his pockets again.

I'm sorry Emma,' I think, *'I can't agree with you.'*

"The beards kinda working for me."

His mustache, though it blends with his beard, is clipped so that it noticeably curls up into subtle points at each corner, is now curled around his bottom lip. Which is neatly tucked beneath his top row of teeth. He's trying to hide his smile from me, but his attempt is a failure because his eyes tell it all. I need to go, there's not much more I can do here and if I stay any longer not only will I have a no call no show at work, but I'll also end up flirting endlessly with this man and falling head over heels for his mother.

"I gotta go to work Emma." I say glancing over my shoulder.

"Goodbye, dear."

I turn away and give him one last look as he takes a couple of steps back in order to let me pass. "Have a good day." He says to my eyes as I walk by.

"You have a good day yourself." I tell him winking and smiling. That's worth about a hundred more composure points, plus another fifty for walking away without looking back. I don't need one last look, the only other place I'll probably see this guy is in my daydreams...and night dreams...and mid-day dreams and every other time I must think.

I reach my car and stop immediately in my tracks eyeballing the parking ticket flapping from underneath my windshield wiper. Instantly my smile fades. **FUCKING MONDAYS, MAN!** I snatched it out and stuffed it in my bag. I don't need to read it to know it's for the big ass fire hydrant that is barely even beside my back bumper. I pull into traffic checking my rearview mirror just in time to watch myself drive away from the cappuccino I left sitting outside the deli. Swear words automatically glide from my mouth. It's going to be an extra shitty Monday.

Chapter Two

"You're late." Mary, my RN supervisor announces as I round the nurse's station.

"Yeah, yeah." I say placing my bag and other items down. "It's been one of those mornings."

"Tell me about it." She says tapping away at the computer keyboard with one hand and handing over my med-cart keys with the other.

"You don't want to know." I say arranging my cart for my medicine count.

"Oh, but I really do." She laughs, "You're never late, ever. Not in the six years that you've been working here. I'm very interested in what could have you, of all people, delayed."

She smirks then laughs and I automatically know she's up to something sneaky, but I tell her anyway. Making sure to leave out a few key details or two...or three.

"So," I say opening my med-pass book, "I was already off to a slow start this morning in the first place. Way too much sleep this weekend I guess, I don't know, anyway. I stop at that coffee shop that I like, you know, the one on Madison."

"And you didn't even bring me anything." Mary said, still looking at her computer screen.

"Yeah yeah, anyway, first off I have to suffer through the coffee mates extremely long, obnoxious details about her and her super-hot boyfriends weekend."

"Of course." Mary laughs.

"Once that torture is finally over, my phone rings and I don't even bother checking to see who the caller is, and of course…"

"It's Eric??" Mary guessed, finally turning her full attention to me.

"It's Eric." I confirm.

"That guy never gives up." She laughs and continues with the note she's typing.

"Anyway. As if that's not enough, I'm trying to hold my phone and my cup of coffee without dropping anything and as I'm turning to leave. I run dead smack into some dude that is for some reason standing way too close to my personal space."

The image of his eyes and how deep they seem to peer into my soul flash before mine.

"I drop my phone, which after one last phone call from Eric, shows nothing but a black screen."

"So, wait…" Mary blurts out, "Does this mean you finally have to trade that dinosaur in?"

"Yes Mary, I'm ordering a new phone on my lunch break. Which reminds me, I'm gonna need to use your phone."

"Thank you, Jesus."

"Whatever Mary, my phone was fine."

"Yeah, for a dinosaur."

"Anyway." I continued, "I'm headed to my car trying to get rid of Eric, when this tiny little woman, that kind reminds me of Gertie, stops me and asked if I could help her."

"Was she old?" Mary asks.

"Yes. She's old, she's tiny, her shoes are completely wrong for blood circulation because they're very swollen and puffing over the tops."

"Where did she come from?"

"I had no idea at that time. Poor thing was so small I didn't even see her at first. I had to double back to see where the voice came from."

"What was her name?" Mary says, turning from her computer.

"Emma and come to find out, she was in the same coffee shop I was in, supposedly using the lady's room, but ended up wandering outside of the store and getting turned around."

"How in the world did this woman happen to leave the store without being noticed? Why was she even there? Was she with anyone?"

"Turns out she was."

"Asshole." Mary blurts out, "How could they not be paying attention."

"Because a certain nurse slammed into him while he was waiting in line to buy his coffee. He missed her leaving the store because he was too busy helping me pick up the few things that I dropped."

"Her husband?" Mary laughs. "You ran over her husband?"

"Her son." I say correcting her.

"Was he cute?" She asked smiling.

"Meh," I smirk remembering those eyes and the smell of his beard cologne when he kissed my cheek, "he was okay."

"Just, okay?" She mumbles, "I'd like to see what your idea of "*okay*" is."

"She's clearly in early stages of Alzheimer's." I say, changing the subject away from Mr. Concrete Chest, "She got confused and teared up trying to figure which direction she came from."

"So, where'd she end up going? How'd you find out that the guy from the store was her son?"

"I decided to walk her back in the direction that I came from, and he was there looking for her all in a panic."

"I hope she's okay." Mary says shaking her head and pouring a cup of water for a resident that had been waiting.

"She's fine," I chuckle locking my narcotics drawer. "Just got turned around is all."

"What's so funny?" Mary asks.

"Nothing." I'm not about to give her any more details about Mr. You Know Who or how handsome he looked half smiling at me when I recited those same words to him.

"On top of all of that," I continue, "I got a fucking parking ticket for *barely* parking in front of a fire hydrant."

"Congratulations," Mary laughs, "it's probably a first for that too."

"Aw thanks," I say laughing, "You're too kind."

"Don't thank me yet." She warns, "Your day's about to get worse. So," she continues ignoring my eye roll. "You have two new residents admitted this weekend. I was trying to finish up the paperwork on that, but...there's been a fall and we're sending Aurther out. He may have a broken hip."

I drop my head in my hands and groan loudly, suddenly missing that cappuccino that got left behind. "That's just perfect."

"It gets worse." She continues.

Looking up I notice she's holding a disciplinary action form. I tilt my head to the side giving her a look she's familiar with.

"What's that for?"

"Frances wants me to write you up."

"For what, being late for the first time in six years?"

"Yes." she says flatly.

"Fuck Frances." I say, laughing, wishing for my drink even more. "And I'm not signing that."

"I know, that's why I'm prepared to offer an ultimatum."

Shaking my head, I watched her tear the form into pieces, not uttering a word. I'm more interested in what she has to say. Before I say yes, of course.

"You have to attend the Alzheimer's banquet tomorrow at the Babbits, in the facilities honor."

"There's no way I'm going to that boring ass luncheon."

"You have to. Frances can't go because she'll be here working."

"Here for what? My vacation starts tomorrow."

"She's covering for Jackie because of her surgery."

"Bullshit, she could go, you go!" I say. I'm making a fuss, but I know I'm going to go. As a matter of fact there's quite a few reasons why I'm going to go. One, I finally get the opportunity to dress up for something formal. Two, I like Frances, she's actually a pretty decent boss. And three, which is the most important reason. Ever since New Years Day I've been playing a little game. I call it 'Say Yes'. Anytime I'm asked a question as a favor...I say no. But if I'm given a direct command or no choice, I have to say yes. Mary didn't *ask* me to attend the banquet in the facilities honor she told me I "had to". She doesn't know I'm playing this game. In fact, no one knows. That's what makes it so much fun for me.

"I can't go, Bob finally wants some alone time."

"Whatever," I say secretly enjoying myself. "What time is it?"

"It's from six until whenever, but you don't have to stay for the entire event."

"About time you showed up." Frances calls from down the hall.

"Frances, come here and give me a kiss." I say spreading my arms open.

"Why? No." She answers, walking closer.

"Because I like a little fore play after I'm fucked." I mouth the last word since she's close enough to read my lips.

"Oh, shut up." She laughs nudging past me, "You don't have to stay the whole time. Sign in, show your face then leave. Or...they've rented out the bar for the night so stay and enjoy drinks on them."

"Fine," I sigh. "I'll go."

"Yes!" Frances whispers, throwing her fist in the air. "You're going to be so bored. Whew!"

"Bite me, Frances." I say dropping a pain pill into a cup. "Come with me so I can take this woman's pain pill."

"Also, before I forget," Frances tells Mary who waves her off as she's answering the phone, "The printer's down so we'll have to fax the face sheet from Arthurs' medical chart."

"I'm sorry," Mary says, looking at me and deliberately speaking louder to get my attention, "You're wanting to speak to Ayo Mitchell?"

"Dammit Eric." I say out loud, knowing full well he's the only person that calls me at work.

Only Mary shakes her head. She's familiar with Eric's voice so she would know if it's him or not. "I gotta give this lady her pill." I say walking away. It only takes a few minutes, so Frances and I are back at the desk in no time.

"Do you have your badge and name tag?"

"No." I say, "I lost it this morning somewhere between my car and the coffee shop."

"Yes sir, I'll be glad to do that." Mary speaks into the phone, "He says to tell you, he's found it and would like to return it to you."

"Okay, so tell him to stop by today and leave it at the receptionist's desk." I go to another resident's room with their medication in hand. When I return to the desk Mary is still on the phone.

"Here she is," she says, but I waved her off before she could hand me the receiver. "I'm sorry, Sir. She's tending to a resident; can I give her another message?"

She pauses, then nods her head.

"He says he's sorry but today isn't a good day and he'd like to give it to you personally. What day would be good for you?" She stops talking and looks at me smiling, expectantly.

I look at Frances, who is waving her arms in the air to get my attention and informs me that I need my name tag to attend the banquet since my presence counts towards in-service credits. Not just for myself but for every nurse that works my shift.

Fuck...this person could be any lunatic on the planet.

"Ask him where'd he find it." I told her.

"I see." Mary responds without asking my question. "He said, and I've been instructed to quote this verbatim. As a matter of fact, I've been instructed to tell you that *he* wants you to know that I'm quoting him..."

"Okay." I say confused.

"Interesting." Frances says smiling as she leans on the desk with her arms folded across her chest.

"Where'd he get my name tag?"

"He said, and remember I'm quoting this, 'I found it by my mothers' feet where you dropped it earlier this morning. Also, Emma says *hi* by the way.'"

The involuntary smile that spreads across my face, against my will mind you, mirrors the smile that's spreading across Frances' face. Or maybe her smile is a mirror of mine. What makes it worse is the excitement that's bubbling around the sound of Frances voice.

"Who's Emma?" she asked, looking back and forth between me and Mary, "Who's on the phone?"

"Hmph, tell him I said to tell her *hi* right back."

"She said to tell her *hi*." Mary repeated.

"No." I say laughing at Frances expression, "Tell him verbatim."

"She said to tell her hi right back, and that's verbatim." She pauses for a few seconds, then shakes her head smiling, "How's your morning going?"

"It just got a little better."

"It just got a little better." She repeated sitting back in the chair and crossing her legs.

"Who's Emma and who's on the phone?" Frances asks again.

"That's very good to hear." Mary tells me. She fans her face with a folder from the desk. "He has a nice voice." She tells me.

"Tell him thank you for holding on to my badge for me and if he likes he can meet me at The Pennington inside the Babbits Hotel tomorrow at six thirty."

"Oh, he'll be there, six thirty sharp." She repeats after a brief pause.

"I'll be wearing red and black so he can recognize me."

After relaying my message and listening to his, her mouth drops, and her cheeks flushed crimson.

"He said, and remember this is verbatim, *how could anyone ever forget what you look like?*" Mary's head falls back, and Frances loses any cool she ever had.

"Holy hell." Frances laughs clapping her hands.

I shake my head unable to hide my smile from my coworkers.

"Tell him I'll see him tomorrow." I say laughing at how childish Mary and Frances are acting. This man so far has drawn a reaction from me that feels a bit effortless.

"He said he's looking forward to seeing you." Mary tells me. She looks directly at me and starts describing the smiling expression on my face into the phone. "Oh, it was my pleasure. You have a great rest of your day also." She tells him right before hanging up.

"Who the freak was that?" Frances whispered loudly. I'm pretty sure if the nursing station didn't have residents sitting around waiting for their medicine, she would have been much louder.

"And why haven't we heard anything about him until now?" Mary chimed in just as enthusiastic as Frances.

I have no answers for them. I wouldn't even know where to start. Telling my personal business or opening up to people that I don't feel close to isn't really my strongest suit. Never has been. Even when I was a kid the idea of over sharing to fit in didn't really make sense to me. The things that typical girls would sit around and talk about didn't really relate to me. Now that I'm an adult...not just an adult but an adult woman, with no husband, no children and no boyfriend in sight, seems like I have even less to talk about. My life is dull and even if I wanted to, there's just not much to talk about.

"How long has this been going on?" Frances asked, fanning herself with a manilla folder she picked up from the desk.

"There's really nothing to tell." I say handing medicine to a resident, "It's not at all like what you think."

"What are the odds of him finding your name tag?" Mary said, "Wait." she said just as she was about to unlock her med-cart, "He said he found it by his *mothers'* feet." She stopped, "Emma is the little old woman you helped this morning? *That* was the son you ran into?"

"What little old woman? What happened this morning?" Frances asked lightweight frantically. "See this is why I don't like sitting in my office all day. I miss out on all the dishing."

"You really didn't miss out on anything." I confess, "I helped a woman find her way back to the coffee shop where she accidentally ended up wandering away from."

"Oh really?" Frances scoffed jokingly, "So you just met him this morning?"

"Never met him ever before?" Mary asked.

"Nope...never."

"Then what in the world was that just now on the phone?" Mary blushed, "Because I'm a bit hot under the collar after the heat that was steaming between the two of you."

It was a bit chemical, the heat between the two of us. I felt it earlier when I very literally ran into him in the coffee shop as he held me strong, and firm. His eyes peered into mine with such dedicated conviction, making it impossible for me to look away at first. I felt it a few minutes ago when Mary mentioned his mother's name. The hairs on the back of my neck stood at the very idea of him finding me. I can't explain it or even tell you what it means, or why it happened but it did.

Along with a faint flutter of butterflies that lightly tickled the inside of my stomach. He could've easily left the name tag he found at the coffee shop or dropped it off at the front desk but he insisted on returning it personally. And who could refuse such a gentleman like gesture. Although I'm not one to swoon over a man just because he acts a bit interested in me, I'm also not one to ignore it when I recognize it.

"That," I say walking away from the cart, pill in hand ready for the next patient, "was unexpected."

As I'm walking away from my coworkers, I can hear Mary joking about needing to make a call to her husband Bob as soon as possible. I couldn't help but laugh. No matter who we are or how old we get, there will always be that little girl inside of us that is dying to hear the juiciest of all details when it comes to boys. Even if there really aren't any details to be told. Lucky for me, we had a ton of work to distract us from our teenage fantasy of dishing our girl talk, over root beer floats and an old-fashioned game of *BOY CRAZY*.

From the med pass to the new resident admission, to the resident that fell out of bed and needed to be sent to the hospital. To the nursing assistant that had to be written up for neglecting to return the bed to the lowest position or raising the bed rail. Which would have allowed that particular resident to brace themselves as they transferred from the bed to wheelchair. Hell, it would have at least allowed that particular resident's feet to touch the ground.

In this business of medical HIPPA contracts, levels of abuse, and ambulance chasing lawsuits. Neither of us that pledge to give the utmost care, to the best of our ability, for people who can no longer provide that for themselves. Can afford to rush or dismiss any of the small details that make the residents day go smoother. I didn't want to, but a write-up had to be done. At this stage in that resident's life, a fall like that could literally mean life or death.

It could mean that some family member who may or may not be ready, would have come to terms with the fact that life is nearing the end for their loved one. A life that could be a very magical story to tell, could come to an accidental end and that family would have to readjust to terms that they may or may not have accepted. I don't want anyone that I work with to have to suffer that burden, so it was necessary to point out the mistake and allow that aide to come to terms with the steps that *cannot* be skipped.

With that being said, I welcomed all of today's duties with open arms. Not only did it make my day go by a shit ton faster, but it also took away any opportunity I might have had to think about seeing Mr. Concrete Chest tomorrow. I'm not exactly nervous, I mean let's be honest, the chemistry was undeniable. Even Mary and Frances recognized it. But isn't that how things always start off? You both meet...you both smile and flirt a little. You both talk a little and realize just how much you have in common, and things go really good for a time. Be it a few weeks, a few months, maybe even a few years. Then the next thing you know, you're both bumping heads and arguing. You may not even be able to stand the sight of each other. The things that used to be cute turn out to be the things that aggravate you the most.

No, I'm not nervous about that at all. In my opinion the only reason things like that happen is because one, if not both, people are over thinking. I don't have time for that. I'm either going to do something, or I'm not. I won't feel nervous about it, and I won't bother with giving up any of my precious time trying to figure out how anyone feels. Or what they're thinking. If I can't be told, then it wasn't meant for me to know, and I'll remove myself from the situation. If it's not working out, then there's no point in holding on to something that's turning into a train wreck.

So, the way I see it, there's no reason for me to send my brain into hyper think mode over a guy that I only met once. Besides, as far as I know, he may just be a nice guy. That gentle kiss could have been something he would do for anyone that was kind enough to help his mother out. The chemistry that was so undeniable, could be something that exists between anyone that he's having a conversation with. Nothing special.

But then again, walking over to him right before I said my goodbyes and have a nice day, I saw him looking. His eyes took that long journey from my eyes, all the way down and back up again. He drank more than his fair share of me in, and he loved every sip. His face may be covered by a forest of well-groomed whiskers, but his eyes aren't, and they were very telling. The thing is, I've been through the events that come behind that look before. You meet someone and think the signs are all there, only to find out later down the line that you were wrong. That the person you thought you knew isn't really who they are, and until it's over the confidence level that's usually so high, even for me, begins to plummet.

Suddenly, in my case, I start to feel every inch of my six-foot three height becoming a problem. As far as I know, this guy could want just what he said...to return my name tag. So, with that being said, I must put this guy out of my mind and focus on what I know for sure...nothing. Except those eyes. Those pools of chocolate that burned into my own grey irises.

The rest of the day did it's best to live up to my fucked-up standards of a typical Monday, but my brain just wouldn't let it. I kept thinking about him and this morning. By the time I actually paid attention to the clock, it was well past time to go. All my work was completed, including the write up and intervention meeting for the CNA that neglected to lower the bed and raise the bed railings. The resident's family was called along with his primary physician.

I got chewed out four times. Once by a family member that was in town visiting a resident and wasn't satisfied with the amount of clothing, or lack thereof, that the resident owned. And three times by three different residents that...well actually, those three residents are just angry people in general and aren't really kind to anyone. But still, I managed to take it *and* make it through my day with a smile on my face. The nurse that was my relief actually showed up on time bright eyed and bushy tailed, ready to count the medicines on my cart and take a report about my day. By the end of it all, I was more than ready to turn over my keys and take my exit. I looked around, said goodbye to everyone that was around, threw up a peace sign and made my way to the time clock... ready to start my much-needed vacation.

Chapter Three

Within the span of almost two hours, I manage to make it in and out of the grocery store, and my favorite music shop for a pack of blank sheet music before I actually made it home. It's September, so even at five thirty in the evening it's still daylight. Which means, though I've been gone most of the day, I still feel like there's some day left to properly relax. I pull my car around to the back of the house, as I normally do, and enter through the back door.

Mindlessly, I place the groceries on the counter and begin removing my nursing home infested clothes. Starting with the shoes which I place on a shoe tree next to my washing machine. My socks, pants and panties, which I layer inside the machine, along with my scrub shirt and bra adding to the last four work outfits that were waiting to be cleaned. Then I add detergent, color safe brightener and drop in a fabric softener ball, and set the cycle settings. I put the groceries in their correct places and head through my house towards the shower.

The best part of being a woman that lives alone is being able to walk around the house completely naked without any care in the world. With that being said, the worst part of being a single woman that lives alone and can walk around naked without any care in the world, is not having anyone around to enjoy the view.

Chapter Four

I don't know if it's because I slept until ten in the morning or if it's because I don't have to go to work for the next seven days, but I woke up feeling absolutely magnificent. So magnificent that I stayed in bed watching every talk show and game show that I could on television. Only getting up to use the bathroom and make myself a healthy breakfast of oatmeal and fruit. At about noon, I finally got out of my comfortable queen-sized bed and worked out in my home gym for as long as I wanted to, going as slow as I wanted to.

The music was blasting, and I watched myself stretch and bend in every direction my long, lean body and limbs would allow. I was even able to manage more than a couple of solos on my eleven-piece drum kit, *and* my favorite guitar. It felt great. Hell, I felt great, banging out sounds that any veteran drummer would consider probably be very elementary. It felt so great that by midafternoon, I was stretched across the bed making no real attempt to fight the nap that was creeping up on me. The kind of nap that I am not ashamed to say was about to feel awesome. So awesome that I set my alarm for later on, so I don't accidentally sleep through the convention. Although that wouldn't be a bad thing.

There's a reason Mary and Frances cooked up that stupid scheme to trick me into going. Because *they* didn't want to go. It's the single most boring thing anyone could ever attend, but it's only one night, once a year and it's in-service points for every nurse that works at the same facility. As long as they work the same shift as the unfortunate nurse that is chosen to attend. Full time or part time only. Last year I volunteered to go and ended up listening to some doctor talk for eight hours about *fibromyalgia,* or something to that effect. Ever since that long... long day, I like to brag to people about that being the day I learned how to get a full seven and a half hours of sleep with my eyes wide open.

Time passed and I find myself sitting in front of the mirror of my vanity admiring the natural tones of my makeup, pleased with the final touches and realizing that anything more would be too much. I look just how I like...enhanced...like myself with just a touch more to bring out my natural tones and features and blend beautifully. I checked the time and it's close to five thirty, almost the exact time that I wanted to put on my clothes. Just enough time for me to take a couple of puffs from the already rolled joint resting in the ashtray. Not enough to get stoned, just enough to mellow out my nerves. Not that I needed it for my nerves but what the hell, I'm on vacation, why not.

The black halter pencil dress with vertical red pinstripes hugged my curves perfectly, as if it missed them. Final touches, black pearls for my ears, neck and wrists. A black clutch purse, black t-strap heels, a sweater wrap and I'm off to the boring fest to suffer in a style that most of us in the medical field would consider some form of abuse.

The bar itself, because of the banquet, is probably more crowded than it normally would be on a Tuesday. People are sitting at the lavishly set dining tables and booths quietly chatting about whatever people quietly chat about when they make a little free time for themselves and choose to enjoy every second of it. There's a dance floor, which is, not surprisingly, empty and a live band is set up on stage singing cover songs from various artists and decades, and sounding quite good if I might add. All in all, it's a very elegant place, and I make a mental note to maybe, one day in the future, to come back and see what the regular crowd is like.

Right now, I must be honest, sitting here at this bar, listening to whatever this guy said his name was, talking about whatever it was he said he did for a living, is getting a bit tedious and quite frankly is bringing my high down a bit. He doesn't even notice that I'm not paying him any attention. I just keep saying things like... "*interesting*" and "*now what does that involve?*" and he'd be off again. Talking about whatever it is he's talking about. His eyes tell me he's probably had a bit too much to drink, which may be contributing to his chattiness. But what the hell, the moment I can, I'm going to excuse myself from his company anyway.

I notice very subtle movements over his shoulder and glance, then double glance and automatically correct my posture. Before now, I was slouching, uninterested. Well now, Mr. Concrete Chest has shown up and most definitely, from the looks of it shown out. What's his name may as well not even be standing here, because every ounce of my attention is on the person sitting behind him. A portion of his chin length hair is pulled back into a bun while the rest dangles at the back of his neck. His beard is trimmed a little revealing more of his bottom lip. Maybe I could kiss it, just a little. A small one, like he gave me yesterday.

I watch him speak to the bartender who in turn nods his head. Turns to the assortment of bottles, fills one double shot of tequila, with just a little more than a splash of cranberry, just like I like it. He prepares a second glass, then a third. Offers on to Mr. Chest then the second and third to me and what's his name. His eyes are on mine as he raises his glass in a long-distance cheers.

"Compliments of the gentleman sitting over there." The bartender tells us. He taps the bar then moves on to assist the other patrons. What's his face no longer oblivious to it, turns towards the man sitting behind him, then back towards me and decides he's unwelcome and excuses himself. Raising his glass to Mr. Chest in a silent thank you, or maybe even a *you won* gesture. It doesn't matter, either way, he's gone and there's nothing between me and the man who wanted to personally return my property, but space...and opportunity.

He stands with his drink in his hand and strolls easily towards me closing the two-barstool gap between us, and allowing me the opportunity, which I take wholeheartedly, to drink him in. Black dress slacks, black button-down shirt with the sleeves casually rolled to a three-quarter length. Showing off his tattooed forearms. Red suspenders with a matching bowtie. We match...quite nicely I might add.

"Good evening, Ayo." He said stopping in front of me, "Can I sit?"

"By all means." I say watching as he situates himself on the stool next to me.

"Oh, before I forget." He fishes into his pants pocket and pulls out my name tag offering it to me.

"Thank you for bringing it all this way." I say slipping it into my clutch.

"It's my pleasure." He sips from his drink, "I wanted to see you again."

What's this now??? Pure honesty from a man without having to guess or dig for it. *'Alright, Mr. Concrete Chest, you're starting this game. Let's see how long you're willing to play."*

"So... it's not just me?" I ask. I can't help wondering if I'm playing the right hand with this guy, but it all feels so natural. I almost can't help myself.

"What do you mean?" He asks leaning in closer to me, straining to hear over the chatter and loud music.

"Well," I pause sipping from my drink and lean towards him so my lips are directly at his ear. "It honestly seems like it would take more energy fighting what might be happening naturally, then it would just letting it happen."

There, what do you have to say to that handsome?

"I completely agree." He smiles, nodding his head and placing his hand on his thigh. "You look stunning."

"Thank you," I say smiling, "so do you."

"Thank you." He tells me, capturing my eyes and holding them hostage as he leans back away from me. "I try."

"You succeed." I say straightening my posture.

"Dance with me." It was more of a command than a question as he stood up holding out his massive hand. I take it and carefully stand. The front of my body presses into the front of his, because he doesn't even attempt to take a step back and allow me any space. In these heels I'm standing at the top of his shoulders, and I know for a fact that if

I laid my head down, my face would fit perfectly into his neck. A rare luxury for me.

The band switched songs picking up the pace with a cover of my favorite Lou Begga song, so I have to lean up to his ear in order for him to hear me. But he takes it a step further. Wrapping his right arm around my waist and placing his hand at the lower part of my back, he pulls me full press into his chiseled body. Then he holds his head down so that his ear hovers in front of my mouth. I don't have to shout, I don't have to bend, I don't even have to stretch. I can just...speak, and for once in a very long time, perhaps for the first time, it's effortless and not at all awkward. Another luxury I'm not always privileged to have.

"There's a banquet here at the hotel that I have to attend...for work." I didn't realize I'd wrapped my fingers around his suspenders until he turned his face closer to my ear, on the *good side*. His beard tickled my neck and teased my ear, while his voice caressed my ear drum sending chills down my neck to my fingertips.

"How long will it take?" I realized then that my fingers are caressing the material of his suspenders. He doesn't complain, so I don't stop.

"I'm not sure." I say, "Sometimes these things can take hours and sometimes all I have to do is sign in and show my face. Then I'm free."

He angles his body and tilts his head so that he's looking into my eyes...or maybe he's looking at my lips. Maybe I'm looking at his lips. He removes his hand from my back and the warmth is gone from that spot.

"I'll wait for you here." He says in my ear. Now it's my turn to command his eye contact.

"Or you can just go with me." His mustache curls in the corners and I know that's a yes, "Besides, it's going to be super boring, so I would appreciate the company."

"Let's go." He stands and places my hand in the crook of his arm and slides both hands into his pockets. It's so easy and carefree walking next to him. I can't imagine anyone else fitting as perfectly as I do.

"You know," I say once we're passing the coat check area, "I don't even know your name."

"No?" He asked, sounding maybe a little puzzled, "With all of the excitement yesterday, I must've forgotten."

"Must have." I agree.

"Ayo," He begins, "My name is Eros Apollo. No middle name, *first* of his name, son to a mother you've already had the pleasure of meeting."

"Such a formal introduction." I say laughing as he bends low and kisses the top of my hand, tickling my knuckles with his beard. "How very Game of Thrones of you."

"Winter is coming." he says so close to my face that I swear he's going to kiss me.

"The north remembers." I reply as they do in the show. He smiles...a nice white toothy smile. "I love that you know that quote." I say softly. I can't help but smile. Right now, I'm at a good equal balance of goofy, sexy and nerdy, and for once I'm in good company for it.

"I've read the books twice." He tells me quite proud of himself. I'm surprised and impressed. I've seen those books and the shows which are all great and well written. So, I know it's a long... long interesting read.

"I'm impressed." I say softly clapping my hands.

We continue walking towards the end of the hall where two women are seated behind a long table organized with pamphlets and brochures on almost any and everything a person needs to know about Alzheimer's. I produce my name tag and wait for them to finish gawking at the two giant people towering over their table and tape the *'Hello my name is...'* sticker label to myself and offer one to Eros.

Side bar...I really enjoy him watching me.

We get a few of the brochures and some of the other things for Eros to read over. With his mother being in the early stages, he will need to keep up on all the latest information.

"Ready?" I ask reaching for the conference room door. Eros stops me by placing his hand on the flat of my stomach, then opens the door for me.

"My lady." He says nonchalantly waving his arm.

"Thank you." I said hoping he didn't notice me blushing as I brushed past him.

"No, thank you." He responds by grabbing my hand and lightly kissing my knuckles again.

His hand is at the small of my back as we enter the room, and it fits so well. If this guy is for real, everything about him...fits so well. So far.

"Welcome." A small man, well smaller than us, walks up with his hand extended out to me. "My names Tom, thanks for coming to our Alzheimer's conference, Ayo." He read from my sticker, switching hands from me to Eros, "and *Guess?* Guess, is it?"

'Guess?' I frowned, 'Did he just say Guess?'

"Hum, Guess. That's a unique name." Tom continues. I look from Tom to Eros, then back to Tom wondering why he couldn't see the humor in Eros' face. Maybe his expression looks different from another angle. I step next to Tom and stare into Eros' face smiling at the wink he gives me. Nope, he looks the same, very pleased with the fact that he scribbled the word *"Guess"* in the box of his name sticker.

I'm baffled! Who thinks of doing that? Oh, this night just got interesting. So, Eros has a sense of humor.

"You're not pulling my leg, are you?" Tom asks, looking at Eros then me.

"That's really his name." I say with a, what can you do kind of look.

"Wow," Tom gasps, chuckling. I want to laugh so badly but all I can do is smile. This guy is earning himself some major cool points.

"Well," Tom says glancing over his shoulder, "There's refreshments over in the corner. Booths are set up all over the place, with all kinds of information, as you can see. Help yourself to whatever you find interesting. There are attendants at every station just waiting to answer any questions you may have."

"Thanks Tom." I say shaking his hand once more.

We walk further into the room, moving from booth to booth. Listening to various explanations on various aspects of this incurable disease. It all sounds very textbook and uniform, but I know from experience that it most definitely is not as simple and easy as these *attendants* are making it seem. No one talked about the horrors of trying to redirect a *sundowning* elderly person who now has their days and nights mixed up. Trying to keep them up all day so that they can get back on track with sleeping at night. They made no mention of what to do if someone's sweet elderly mother, who never raised a hand to strike anyone, now wants to chin check you every chance she gets just because she doesn't understand that you're trying to help her go to the toilet.

They left out the pain in seeing your usually stoic grandfather cry profusely because his brain reminds him every single day of the death of his wife. The pain that comes along with that memory feeling so fresh, seems as though the loss of that person happened just the day before.

Or how, someone who suffered from the disease for so long, can't take another day living locked inside of their own mind. Or how it feels for the family, that was built on the sheer strength of this person, to have to witness them die a horrible death of starvation because they either *can't* or *won't* eat another bite. These are just a small portion of what could happen when dealing with this terrible disease and I don't know if Eros knows about what could happen in the days, or years for that matter, to come. Maybe if the right moment presents itself, we can sit down and talk about the truth that no one seems to want to mention.

Of course, right now isn't that moment. I am thoroughly entertained by the highlight of the evening, which is every one of the conference marveling over Eros' *name*. I am thoroughly entertained. One lady even started throwing out different names as if trying to guess and inviting people over to join in the mystery. John. Michael. Peter. Richard. Name after name after name, even though we kept telling them that his name is *"Guess."* She finally gave up and even had the class to apologize for the misunderstanding. At one point, I excused myself for the restroom. My intention was to say our goodbyes after I was done, but I found myself almost cornered by Tom and his wife, whom he introduced as Nora.

They weren't talking about anything. Mostly about my friend Guess and what stages I thought his mom may be in, which was something he must've mentioned to them. I drag my attention away from Tom and the misses and find Eros standing in front of a booth conversing with a representative. I'm too far away to hear what he's saying, but I sure like watching him say it. Tom asks me a question and I answer as best I can, but I'm not paying attention. To them I may seem engaged in the conversation, but really, I'm focused on Eros slowly making his way over to me. Stopping at every booth that he approaches, picking up random pamphlets or pieces of paper, peering his eyes over the top in a very James Bondish type of way.

Judging by his creative introduction of himself, it wouldn't surprise me one bit if he wasn't humming some spy tune to himself in his head. Luckly, after what seems to be more than the brief moment that it was, Tom sets his eyesight on a group of people just entering the room, offers me his hand to shake and excuses himself with a slight shout of the same welcoming greeting Eros and I received when we first arrived. Now that I'm alone, Eros abandons his booth and strides over to where I'm standing.

"Are you ready?" I asked, walking to meet him halfway. He doesn't say a word, instead, pulls his name tag from his shirt, prompting me to do the same. Together we turn to find Tom so we can say our *good-byes* and *nice to meet yous*, then we set ourselves free of this necessary mondain-ness.

Whew, we did good, it's only going on about eight o'clock, so we stayed for just under an hour. Our walk back to The Pennington was a lot slower and funnier. Listening to Eros' explanation of his made-up name, which was simply to make the event more fun for me, made no sense at all. And yet, all the sense in the world, and he's right. Everyone in that conference room is going to be around their dinner table one Sunday telling their families about the guy they met named *Guess*. We reach the bar and this time I don't reach for the door. My daddy always said, if a man wants to be a gentleman, you step back and let him.

"Let's get a drink." He suggests with his hand back in its spot on my back. Now that I've accomplished what I was supposed to do for our in-service points, I can get comfortable and enjoy myself.

"I need to go to coat check first." I tell him.

Once there, I turn over my cardigan wrap and clutch purse along with the goodie bag Eros collected. Soon as everything is checked in, I take my return ticket and turn to find Eros with his hands in his pockets and his coco dream eyes blazing at me. Scanning the tattoos that decorate my caramel skin. I can't help the half smile curling at the corner of my mouth. He likes it... he likes it a lot, and he's not even trying to hide it.

I must admit, it's refreshing not having to guess or question the atmosphere. The truth is, I'm too grown up, we're all too grown up to have to wonder if someone likes what they see or not. I don't like having to try and figure it out. I want to know the true facts, no games. No questions. With this man, there's an attraction between the two of us and it's thick as pea soup...as my momma would say.

"Come on." Eros says softly offering me the crook of his arm. We walk over to the bar, and I order the same drink as before. Eros takes a seat on one of the stools, places his hand on my lower back and pulls me as close as I can get without standing in his lap.

"To guys named Guess." He says clinking the rim of our glasses. We engaged there for I don't know how long so I'm going to say...three drinks, and a whole lot of hugs disguised as giggling on both our parts, later.

"Well sir," I say finally putting my drink down, "I do believe I promised you a dance."

"Yes, you did." He takes my hand and leads me out to the dance floor.

The lighting in this area is different, slightly dimmer with softer colors creating a more romantic mood, not that we needed the help.

"I'll be right back." he says, putting his finger up for me to wait. I watch him stroll casually to the stage and speak to the singer. Who in response nods his head, leans in to hear Eros over the digital music that's blasting from the speakers, then nods again and shakes Eros' hand. I'm no dummy, that was a song request. My eyes never leave Eros as he walks toward me.

"Ladies and gentlemen." The singer says into the mic, "We've got a special request going out to Ayo."

I smile at Eros and take his outstretched hand and allow him to gently pull me into his embrace. His hand is in its place, and my left-hand rests on his bicep. I place my head on his shoulder with my face towards his neck, and just like I thought, it fits perfectly. He kisses the knuckles of my right hand and guides me from side-to-side in a sway. The singer slowly, rhythmically and smoothly covers the words to a beautiful song about a man being at ease in the arms of a woman. A song I know very well. Finally, I get to lean into him...breath in his subtle woodsy scent. No words are spoken. Neither of us make a sound...I don't even think we're breathing. We don't need to do anything but enjoy the feel of each other, until the song is over.

To our surprise, everyone around clapped softly for us. I hadn't realized that we were the only ones still dancing, until other couples began to crowd the dance floor. We both take a mocking bow for those still watching, then join for another dance...and another, and more after that. Fast songs, slow songs...songs that had us doing our best version of the robot dance, which was awfully funny and ridiculous looking, but we didn't care. We were having fun. I was having fun. More fun than I'd had in a very long time.

I can't tell you how much time passed, but I will say, when Eros asked if I wanted to take a break another slow song began to play. My feet were damn near numb. And though I do try and workout almost every day, my thighs were burning more than they ever had. I shake my head and hold my arms out for one more slow dance. Truth be told, I just want to be close to him again. Touch him, feel his muscles press through his shirt. Feel his breath brush my shoulder every time he exhales. I mean seriously, I couldn't be anymore content than I am right now, at this moment. But I'm getting tired, and I find myself stifling a yawn more than once, while we dance.

"I don't want this night to end." I say to Eros.

"Are you getting tired?" He asks, sensing the real meaning behind my words. I nod my head against his shoulder and stifle another yawn.

"Come on." He said kissing my forehead, "Let's get you home."

I follow him off the dance floor to the bar so we can settle our tab. Then over to coat check.

"Did you drive?" he asked, holding my sweater out for me to slip my arms through.

"No," I tell him fully yawning this time. "I used a car service."

"Can I drive you home?" He asks. Honestly, the manners of this man is extremely touching.

"Please." I say leaning into his chest, breathing in his earthy scent, "I don't think I have the patience to wait for a driver to get to me."

"Where do you live?" He asks once we're in his SUV.

"It's not far." I say, talking through a yawn. "I don't know why I'm yawning so much, I'm not even sleepy for real."

"Do you have to work in the morning?" He asks.

"No, actually I started my vacation today." I don't know if he's going to mention it or not, but just in case...I've made up my mind that he can stay if he wants to. Why not, we had a great night, we're both adults. One-night stands can totally be a mutual choice that both people are okay with.

In what seems like no time at all, we are walking side by side up the steps to my front door with me holding on to his arm.

"This is you?" He asks, referring to my house.

"This is me."

"Nice."

"Thanks." I say fishing my key from my clutch.

"I really enjoyed being with you." He confesses as I unlock the door and drop my keys on the side table.

"Thank you." I tell him. His eyes are holding on strong to mine, "For everything."

Finally, there's no one else around but him and me, and the door frame that separates us. He reaches over and pulls me into the warmest hug I can imagine.

"Will I see you again?" I asked in his ear.

"Absolutely."

"Tomorrow?" I ask hopefully...I don't know, maybe even a little skeptical.

I don't usually second guess my actions, but I could be coming off a bit eager. If I was, he doesn't seem to care. He looks down, uses his thumb and index finger to tilt my chin up bringing my lips to his. His tongue is warm, and skilled. His hands are soothing as they caress my back. I want to tell him to stay, but that *would* be eager.

"Tomorrow." He agrees, pulling his lips away from mine, "I'll be back tomorrow."

He presses a soft kiss on my forehead one last time, then turns to leave.

"Good night, Eros." I speak. My lips felt puckered and swollen from his kiss, that I didn't want to end.

"Good night, Ayo." He repeats over his shoulder.

I stand and watch him get in his truck and pull off, and didn't close my door until he's clear around the corner.

Goodness gracious, what a night. By the time I undress, shower and style my hair in two chunky size braids, it's been almost about, an hour and a half later. Just after midnight and I'm no longer as sleepy as I was when we left the bar.

I flop across my huge, empty bed flipping through the plethora of channels, puffing on a joint that I had left over in the ashtray. Nothing is on but I continue puffing and pressing the channel up button hoping to find something interesting enough to either get Eros off my mind. Or boring enough to put me to sleep. Either one will be welcome right now. Way more welcome than whoever is on my porch ringing my doorbell. I don't even bother putting on my robe to cover up. Whoever is wanting my attention at this hour is just going to have to get an eyeful given what little bit of clothing I'm wearing. Hell, at this hour, I don't even feel the need to rush seeing as how whomever it is didn't even have the decency to call first.

I slowly stroll out of the room as the doorbell rings again. Down the hallway, doorbell again. Into the dining room past my dining table, over to the door and peek through the peephole...and freeze. Eros is back, and for some reason, the first thing I think about is Emma. But of course, if it was Emma, he wouldn't be here. Not to mention, he's too casual. I peep through the hole again and he's leaning on the door frame swiveling his key ring around his index finger. I unlock the door and open it with slow, careful movements. This is it.

"Hello." I say looking up at him.

"Hello." He whispers. He's wearing a T-shirt and sweats. His chin length hair is hanging loose, framing his face highlighting the flames burning in his eyes. "It's tomorrow." he says softly, stepping in and locking the door behind him, then turning to face me. His back is leaning against the door and he's staring at me up and down. Oh, I like this look...a lot.

There's no question about what he wants, and right now I'm more than willing to give it to him. But I'm in the mood to play a little bit first. I want to make him really want it.

"Would you like a drink?" I ask. He shakes his head slightly. This brings my half smile back.

"Hum." I say, turning away from him and slowly retracing my steps through the dining room. Stopping in the door frame, I turn around and as I expect, he's still watching me. My feet are crossed at my ankles and my hands are clasped behind my back.

"Maybe there's something on t.v." I say.

"Maybe." He agrees, cutting his eyes at the television to his left, then finally making his way towards me. I continue towards my bedroom, slowly walking backwards. "But no."

Once we're in my bedroom, he closes the door and I pick up my tablet and scroll through my music app for the perfect song. And once again he's leaning against the door with his hands in his pockets watching me. I plug the auxiliary cord into my tablet connecting it to the mini surround speakers mounted around my walls.

"How about another dance then." I don't need him to say yes, the answer is all in his eyes. I select the song and put it on repeat. A soft, slow beat fills the room as I step in tune to the rhythm, until I'm moving my body directly in front of him. My hands go up around his neck, and his find their place on my back pulling me in as close as he could get me. I start rotating my hips against his, moving seductively to the rhythm.

Encouraging him to dance with me. My fingers glide across his shoulders and down his arm past his sleeves. Still dancing and gently grinding his pelvis as I run my hands up his chest, removing his shirt as I go.

Dropping it to the floor, I lightly brush my fingertips from the base of his throat down his tattooed arms. A low, approving hum surfaces from his chest. His hands have found their way up the back of my shirt, and his fingers are skimming the bumpy trail of my spine. Goosebumps prickle on my skin from his soft gentle touch.

"I knew you were soft." He whispers between the kisses he's trailing from my collar bone and shoulder to my neck and ear lobe. His left-hand travels slowly south and finds its way to the corresponding side of my ass as he pulls my still grinding and rotating hips closer into his groin. I want to touch it. Actually, I want to do a lot of things to it, but I'm not finished with my seduction yet. Plus, I need to slow him down or else this is going to be over with way too soon.

"I really like this." I say walking my fingers through the mahogany carpet that covers his chest. It's smooth and thick, and soft and silky to my fingers. Just as he's reaching his hands down my sleeping shorts to my bare pantyless cheeks, I trail my hands down his arms and remove his hands backing away from him at the same time. Giving him a look of *not yet*.

Silently he chuckles, drops his arms to his sides and watches me sway my body, skimming my hands over my skin. My eyes are on his, but his eyes are watching my hands as they drag from my hips to my shirt as I pull it over my head and drop it on the floor. He steps out of his shoes and kicks them to the side. All the while watching my hands skim over my belly up to my breast. The smile on his face as he nods his head to the rhythm tells me that he is...loving this. He steps towards me, and I let him get close enough to touch me as I slowly begin to circle around him. Stopping at his back, which is also fully tattooed. I wonder who has the most body ink, him...or me.

My fingertips glide down his sides and his body slightly shivers as I move them up his back...over his shoulder blades and across his neck. He seems to be enjoying this so much, that I retrace my steps this time using only the tips of my nails, feathering them down his sides then around to his firm stomach. I step closer and lightly kiss his shoulder blades, one at a time trailing my fingers beneath the band of his boxer briefs, rubbing them around the area where hair should be growing. A slight sound of air hisses through his teeth as he turns to face me.

Stepping into me, he grips both of my thighs and lifts me very carefully to the bed. Trying his best to take control. Since this is my house, we play by my rules and my rules say I can do whatever I want to do. Sitting up, which is new for me seeing as how I'm taller than the average man and usually have to bend really...really low, I lean forward and run my tongue across the bottom of his belly, removing his pants and boxers. I adjust myself so that I'm lying on my back giving him time to step out of his pants. Just as he was about to climb onto the bed, I stopped him with the ball of my foot. He grips my hips and pulls my bottom closer to the edge of the bed into his groin. Fixing me in a 90-degree angle... my back on the bed, my butt to his groin and my legs straight up in the air crossed at the ankles.

His hands and lips are rubbing and skimming kisses up and down my legs and I am enjoying every second of it. If I didn't enjoy watching him enjoy himself so much, I would close my eyes and just allow myself to feel the magic that was happening. But I can't, I'm like Aerosmith right now...I don't want to miss a thing. I walk the balls of my feet up his chest slightly lifting my butt from the bed allowing him to remove my shorts and toss them aside. He places his massive, warm hands on my thighs and brush his fingers up to my ankles. I slowly scissor my legs allowing him to kiss a warm trail down the inside of my tattooed thigh all the way down to what my mother used to call my *lady parts*.

Just as his lips get near the crease dividing my inner thigh from my vagina, I brace my foot on his shoulder and push myself away from his mouth and towards the head of my bed. He looks at me with a smokey smile. I do believe he likes this game of sensual seduction. I lean up and balance my weight on my outstretched arms and hands, watching him crawl onto my bed, over my legs kissing them on his way up to my smiling face.

"Are you running from me?" He asks kissing me just below my ear lobe.

"Not at all." I whisper, twisting my head so he can continue kissing my neck.

"You're loving this aren't you?" His lips are brushing mine as he speaks.

"Aren't you?" I say pressing my lips to his, tenderly sucking his outstretched tongue.

"Yes ma'am, I am." He places his hand between my breast and guides me with ease onto my back, hovering his body over me. My left knee is up, and my fingers skim the muscles of his side down to his waist and up his back to his shoulders.

His lips and teeth and tongue toy with my earlobe and my neck and my throat on to my other ear. The ear I like to call the *good ear*, because for some reason to this ear and this ear alone, the slightest touch can send an eruption of chills down my spine. I gather my senses as he continues kissing my chin, my neck, my chest on over to my breast. Cupping it with his hand, he licks his tongue softly across my nipple, nibbling it with his teeth. Slightly sucking it stretching it in his mouth. When he's had his fill of fun he moves on to my other breast and gives it the same treatment. Teasing and taunting my senses as I grind his erection, he shoves my nipple further into his mouth. I groan from my throat and grind my wetness on whatever part of his body is close enough to rub it on.

I'm supposed to be the one seducing him, making him eager for me and somehow the tables are turning. I am slowly but surely losing the upper hand in this situation. His kisses are slowly making their way down the permanently inked drawings on my belly towards the bottom where he leaves tiny wet marks from his tongue. I raise my head and my eyes meet his just as he takes one...long... moist lap of my clitoris, gently sucking me like a baby sucks a pacifier. My eyes roll and my eyebrows knit together and a small moan slide from my lips. I lay my head back, lock my fingers in his hair with one hand, cup and knead my breast with the other as I circle my hips to the rhythm of his tongue.

This...man...has *skills*. He's got my inside voice talking...or should I say *thinking* in a fake New York accent. All that keeps running through my mind is...'*Yo son! Ssss...yo son! Fuuuck me, he needs to STOP!*'

And as if on cue, he sits up, leaving the junction between my legs more than moist and throbbing for more.

"Time to change the pace." He tells me climbing off the bed and moving away from my wanting body, forcing me to shiver from the absence of his warmth. I watch him, somehow gracefully scoop up his sweats from the floor, remove his phone and judging by the sound of the crinkling plastic wrapper, what could only be a condom. I'm sure I'm right in assuming that he knew exactly how this night would end seeing as how he came prepared. I tenderly toy with my nipples as he unplugs the auxiliary cord from my tablet, sets it to the side on the dresser, and plugs in his own phone. Scrolling through the selections with his thumb until he finds what must be the right song for him...then rips the tiny package, compared to the size of his hand, then smiles at me from the foot of the bed as he rolls the condom down his erection.

"You know," I say in a low, almost whispering tone, "I can't allow you to come into my home, and think that it's that easy to take control, just like that."

"Is that right." He whispers climbing back onto the bed and up my long-limbed body, kissing my clitoris long and tender on his way up. "If it makes you feel any better..." I rake my nails through his hair and down his back as his lips brush against my belly and nipples. "I don't think it's that easy at all."

The rhythm of the song he chose is hard and the base line rumbles from the speakers. The background voices are almost soft while the lead vocalist has almost a gravely tone. It's a very hypnotic combo.

"Good," I say pulling his hair away from his face so I can kiss him better, "As long as we understand each other."

The song finishes just as Eros begins to tenderly return my kiss. His hand strokes his erection, and I can feel my moist body stretch to the size of him only slipping in the head. Waiting those brief seconds for the song to begin again. The quiet space of the room is once again filled with the beat of the song as he lifts my foot to his mouth and softly kisses the arch of my foot and just as softly sucks on my toes one by one. Not once taking his eyes off mine.

I've never felt so empowered and yet so submissive all at once. I've never...ever been touched in such a way that boosted my confidence to a higher level than it already is. And yet, allow me to relax my body, close my eyes and enjoy the rhythm of the song by silently snapping my fingers and rotating my hips in small circles around the head of his dick. Patiently waiting for whatever he wants to do next. Just as I'm about to speak, the beat drops and he thrusts himself all...the...way inside and holds it there...deep.

A loud gasp and moan escape my mouth, and he pulls back and thrusts once again, holding it there just as before and again I can't stop the moan that bursts from my mouth. He does it a third time holding it deep, then letting my foot drop and leaning his weight into me. Thrust a fourth time. This time, instead of holding it deep like before, which allowed me to at least catch my breath, he continues thrusting... watching my face as I lose all control of how my body feels. Although I'm trying my best, I'm not sure how much longer I'm going to be able to hold out. He leans his face onto the side of my face hissing the word, "ssshhhiiittt...", through clenched teeth over and over again. My arms are draped around his neck and my legs are around his back crossed at the ankles. My entire body is wrapped around his matching his movements, thrust for thrust.

"Come here." He whispers, gripping my thighs and without breaking stride, lifts me to his lap allowing me the ultimate pleasure of a riding position that I've only tried once before. And because of my height, or maybe the other person's lack of...well put it this way, it was in no way as enjoyable as this. Or easy. We somehow fit each other so well. My head rolls backward into the palm of his hand. His free hand taps the side of my butt lightly to the rhythm, as I grind his thrust that is deep enough to touch that soft spot with every rock of our bodies.

'Oh my-fucking-goodness.' My movements become quicker, and he picks up the pace with me flawlessly. His hands are on me...his lips are kissing me, his beard and body hair are tickling and teasing my senses in all the right places. His voice in my good ear sending shivers down my spine and chills through my scalp, is taking me exactly where I want to go. This train has taken off and my destination is in sight…

"I can feel you trembling." He whispers, "Yess, it's right there. Let me get it."

He says that last part gripping my shoulders, holding me down on his erection so that I can't move and begins grinding…and thrusting…and grinding…and thrusting…touching that soft spot until I squeal.

"There it is." He moans, then he's off again, thrusting into that soft spot. One thrust…*soft spot*…two thrusts…*soft spot*…three thrusts…*soft spot* and I'm done, down for the count. Exploding over…and over…and over…and over…and over. His hands are around my back clutching my shoulders from behind and my arms are squeezing his trembling body close to mine. We sit like this quietly breathing into each other's space, neither of us moving as we allow our bodies to drift back down to earth's surface.

Finally, after God knows how long, I loosen my arms from around his broad shoulders, smiling at the kisses he's carelessly planting on my right shoulder. I lean back and look down at his smoldering mocha eyes and all I can think to do is whisper the words…

"What…the…fuck!"

I'm done…we both erupt into uncontrollable, hysterical laughter. I mean tears rolling, and stomach tightening laughter. We kept trying to pull it together and act like grownups that just finished having good sex. But instead, we just keep giggling like two high school virgins that just figured out how to do it for the first time. Even when he finally stood up and disconnected his phone from the aux cord, the giggling continued. I mean, damn…who the hell was expecting that! Because I sure as shit wasn't.

"That's it." He says removing the condom, tying it off and dropping it into the wastebasket next to my vanity table, then climbing across the bed next to my stretched-out body, "We're getting married…tomorrow!"

I chuckle and yawn as I tease my fingers through his chin hairs. He's leaning over on his elbows looking down at me and my euphorically sleepy eyes.

"Eros." I whisper. I don't know why I say his name, it just feels right in this moment. I see him...all of him...and I think he's beautiful.

"Ayo." He whispers in return, tracing my bottom lip with his thumb.

"That was the absolute best." I say softly. I smile big at the way his mouth drops silently in mock surprise.

"Good job." He tells me holding his hand up for my responding high five. Yep...it's official...we're dorks.

He chuckles and settles onto his back wrapping his muscular arm around my body as I curl up close to him resting my head on his chest. Except for the sound of his beating heart against my ear, the room is quiet. All is still besides the feel of his fingertips brushing up and down my arm and side.

Chapter Five

"Hey you." Eros smiled, stretching his legs and arms out.

"Good morning." I say yawning. My mouth tastes like I swallowed a wad of cotton and I'm pretty sure the fumes that escape is toxic, so I cover my mouth with the edge of the sheet. Protecting him from the beast that resides inside there. The last thing that I want to do is to subject him to the results of whatever goes on in my mouth while I sleep.

"Why are you covering up?" He asks propping up on his elbow, turning his body on his side to face me.

"Morning breath." I say smiling behind the sheet.

"It's a little late for that." He said hooking his finger in my sheet and pulling it away from my exposed mouth, giving me the sweetest, most gentle kiss, I've tasted this time of morning in a very long time. "You blew that dragon all over my chest."

Despite my smile my jaw drops in mock surprise. At least his sense of humor hasn't changed. The entire time, while we were attending the conference and while at the bar, I found myself laughing out loud and extremely hard at some of the silly things he would say. True they were a bit corny, but they were funny...and I like corny...a lot.

"Look," He tells me, lifting his chin and pointing to a spot on his chest, "Some of my chest hairs are missing." For a second, I stared at his chest focusing my eyes on the spot he's talking about. Then I realized what he was saying, and his actual words registered. "Singed off." He laughs.

Without even thinking about it, I remembered the dumbest game on earth that my brothers used to play when we were kids. Any time someone was caught slipping with their head up leaving their throat unguarded, the person that was lucky enough to notice had to seize the moment and give the unguarded throat a swift chop. Sometimes the person caught slipping caught their mistake and dropped their chin to protect their neck before they could receive their chop. And sometimes they found themselves violently gasping for air...or spitting up whatever drink they were enjoying (which was the most obvious opportunity). This game had no name. There were no rules to this game outside of *don't get caught slipping*. There was no start to this game. No conversation about how to play or anything. One day they just started jabbing each other in the throat and chasing each other around for revenge...and they've been doing it ever since.

I don't even know when or why I was included in this *game*; I just remember being about seven or eight years old. I was going through my jazzercise faze so I was working out to my *Get in Shape Girl* workout tape, dressed in a full, head to toe *Get in Shape Girl* aerobics outfit... complete with leg warmers and sweatbands. I got thirsty so I went to the fridge to get a glass of juice. I was standing with the ice box door open with my Walkman headphones on listening to music, so I didn't hear my brother walk up behind me.

Next thing I know, I'm violently coughing and spitting up grape juice all over the refrigerator shelves and the floor. Once I caught my breath, I realized it didn't hurt as much as I thought it did, but the moment I heard my mother's voice scolding my brother for 'hitting me...a girl', I played it up. Academy award style. My brother got in trouble, I got treated with special treatment by my mother. And from that day forward, or at least until summer ended and school started, I was the target of every prank they could think of.

It was a game I hated but with Eros' chin pointed upward and his neck totally left open, I couldn't resist the opportunity. With a quick jab, I got a clear shot and he gasped loudly, pushing away and coughing until he cleared his throat.

"Are you serious!?" He managed to say. "Did you really just do that to me???"

"You left your throat open." I said chuckling.

"You just chopped me in the throat!"

"You left your throat open." I repeated laughing. The look in his eyes reflected a bit of disbelief...maybe a little bit of shock...mixed with some humor. "You can't leave your throat open; those are the rules."

As I'm talking, I notice him slowly circling the bed moving closer to the side that I'm on. Growing up in my family, survival and tactical escapes turned out to be my greatest skill when it came to my brothers. Right now, my natural instincts are to fake a stretch and roll over to the opposite side of the bed.

"Where you think you're going?" He asks noticing my sly maneuver.

"I'm not going anywhere," I say moving again to the side that he's not standing on.

"Stop running." He said laughing, "You choked me..."

"I *chopped* you..." I said correcting him and snatching my foot away from his grab.

"You choked me..." He said pretending to lunge on the bed, "so I'm gonna choke you back."

"You're so funny, Eros." I joke, smiling, "Don't threaten me with a good time."

I stand up and stretch my long body, laughing at his smiling face, not at all ashamed of my nakedness. Shame has never been a part of my personality. I was always taught to love myself first, no matter what. '*Confidence is key,*' is what my mother likes to say.

"I'm glad you came back." I say adjusting my superman sleeping shorts around my waist and reaching for the matching shirt. I notice the smile on his face but as he's lying on the bed, I realize that he doesn't respond, and my first instinct is to assume that I've played the wrong hand and should've waited. After all, this could still be a case of a one-night stand...which would be a shame.

He climbed from the bed and walked around to his bundle of underwear and sweatpants. I can't be wrong about him. *He* came to me.

He could have stayed home, but he didn't. Instead, he came here...to my home...made spectacular love to me in my bed, and later shared my sleeping space. I'm not wrong in this. Even now, he's watching me, watch him pull his pants over his boxer briefs with the same smoldering look in his eyes. He still feels it too, I know he does.

"Come here." He tells me, but I don't move until he folds one arm across his chest, tucking his hand in his armpit and wiggles his finger indicating for me to come to him. It's cute...he's cute and I have no idea why I'm smiling.

Okay screw it, I'm just going to go to him. It's not like I don't want to. But I don't see why I have to be so close for him to confess to this being just a one-night stand. Folding my arms at the wrist behind my back, I slowly, one step at a time, cross the very short distance into his waiting arms.

"I'm glad I came back too." He tells me, which is nothing new to me. "But here's the thing." He continues.

"What thing?"

"I tend to fall very hard, very fast and the idea of what that could mean usually scares women off quick. I don't want to scare you off." He stops and searches my eyes for any indication of...I don't know, fear maybe. He's out of luck in that department.

My eyebrows knit together in confusion. I'm pretty sure I haven't shown him any negative feelings indicating that I didn't want what he was offering. I inhale and exhale deeply, smiling once again, at how adorable it is to see someone be so honest about what's on their mind.

"So," I say running my fingers through his beard and relaxing my side into his body. "Here's the thing for me. I'm not afraid of any of that. Everything you just said sounds like music to my ears." He gazes at me with his big brown, dreamboat eyes. "I don't want you to hold back. I want you to be yourself. If you want to love me...then love me. Be it hard and fast or soft and slow, or a combination of all four, it doesn't matter to me. I deserve it all. I want it all." Pressing my hand to his chest, I pause and breathe deeply.

Though it doesn't feel like it, this could all be a big mistake, but what the hell. Mistakes are nothing but lessons to be learned, and my best…most valued lessons are those that came from making mistakes… not avoiding them.

"Yes, I know society tells us we're supposed to wait. Find out if it's the right thing to do or not. Give it time to see if it's what we both want…if both of us can be trusted or not. Is one of us living some kind of secret life or not. But the truth is, those are all things that we'll find out no matter what. It doesn't really matter how long we wait, the truth of who both of us really are will come to light no matter how hard we try to hide it. So…you want to know what I have to say to that?"

"What's that?" He asks toying with the hem of my shorts.

"Fuck society."

"Fuck society?" He repeats, flashing his white teeth and biting his bottom lip. "So, what happens if time passes and one of us realizes things about the other that we won't or can't deal with?"

"Well," I say, smiling at the gentle feel of his fingers on my thigh, "If we come across something that one of us just don't like or feel like it's something that just can't be compromised on, then we mutually agree to go our separate ways with no hard feelings."

"Just like that?" He asks gazing into my eyes.

"I don't know if it'll be as easy as *just like that*, especially when real feelings get involved, but yes…in a sense, just like that."

He nods his head smiling slightly, still holding on to my gaze, "So what does all this mean?" he asks looking down at his fingers as they continue to skim my thigh. And there it is…I see it as plain as day. Eros is shy. Bashful as all get out, and I can't help wondering if there's something else, he's not saying.

"Well, Eros." I sigh, "This means whatever we want it to mean. I guess for some people it makes sense to have negative thoughts about whether things move too fast or not, but I don't." I pause because I realize that I'm being vague and not really answering his question. "What do *you* want it to mean?" His eyebrows shoot up to his hairline at the question. Maybe I caught him off guard, I don't know, but he seems to be torn for some reason. "What do you want it to mean?" I ask again.

"We just met." He says softly, but I can tell it's not what he wants to say.

"So." I whisper. I step away from his embrace and stand a few feet away from him, giving him room to think. Gazing at him, challenging him to speak his true mind.

"You really want me to tell you what I want?" He asks, lacing his arms across his chest and crossing his legs at the ankles.

"I really want you to tell me," I answer, trying my best to ignore just how gorgeous of a man he is right now.

He takes a deep breath and exhales through his nose, "I want us to give in to this attraction we feel without overthinking it or being afraid of it. Annnd, I want to fall in love with you knowing that you're falling in love with me too." He finishes with a sigh and a 'there you have it' expression on his face.

And there it is...the sexiest quality a man can possess. It's the one quality that enhances all other qualities...pure unadulterated honesty. It's to die for, and at this moment nothing else could make me happier.

"Okay," I say smiling my half smile. He nods his head and does a very poor job of holding back his smile.

"Okay?" He asks walking his shirtless body towards me. I take careful steps backwards until my back is pressed against the wall next to my door. My heart is racing. He is intoxicating and my body comes to life with every step he takes. Images of his hands caressing my legs, and his lips kissing my skin. His tongue tasting the sweet, sweet spot between my legs. The sound of his voice and the shivers it sent down my spine.

He stops in front of me and put both of his hands on either side of my face. He's toying with me, positioning his face in different angles as if he's going to kiss me. I tilt my face up to his expecting a kiss but instead he pulls back keeping his lips just out of reach of mine. So, it seems this is the game he's going to play...keep away. Poor thing doesn't even know I can do this all day. I tilt my head up smiling at him just for him to pull back again.

"So, what are you gonna do today?" He asks. I think *he* thinks he's slick. Standing here pressing his hips into mine. He wants me to react and get all flustered by him. Well, honestly, mission accomplished...only I'm not going to let him see that just yet.

"Well, I'd like to shower first."

"Okay." His face is close to mine as he nuzzles against my neck, speaking so that his lips brush against my cheek and collar bone. "Then what?"

"Then I'd like to go and see Emma." I say slipping my thumbs into the waistband of my shorts, shift them around my hips and let them fall to my feet.

"Is that right?" he asks, looking at my shorts on the floor. I smile because his voice is softer, and his attention has drifted to my exposed hips and thighs.

"I did promise to see her again."

"Yes, you did." He comments. He's not even paying any attention. He's too busy tracing the assortment of music notes that are tattooed on my hip and thigh.

"I like this." He says looking at me.

"Why thank you." I tell him, bringing my lips up to his, not only because I want to kiss him, but because I want to see if he's still playing this tit-for-tat game. And of course, he keeps his lips just out of reach of mine.

'*Okay, fine.*' I think smiling to myself...maybe not so much to myself.

"Keep away?" I say, "Is that the game we're playing today?"

"I think so." He smiles, curling his mustache up in one corner.

I sigh and step underneath the arm that's outstretched beside my head and stroll over to my laundry basket.

"Just so you know," I turn and face him, pleased that he's still watching me. Smiling, I grab the hem of my shirt and pull it over my head, then drop it in the basket. "I'm going to enjoy this." I pull my towel from its hook screwed into the back of my closet. Then delicately pull it around my body, tucking the corner in at my breast. He's seen enough for now.

"What are you going to do now?" he asks, finally after picking up his jaw.

"Take a shower." I say brushing past him.

"Do you want some company?" He asks following me out into the hall.

"Um," I say turning towards him but still walking backwards away from him. "I think I'll be okay."

His mouth is slightly open, and his bottom lip is tucked just under his teeth. Oh, that look is quickly becoming my favorite. Well, at least one of them. I open the bathroom door and wink at him just before slipping inside. I wait a few minutes to see if he's going to follow me. When he doesn't, I chuckle to myself. This guy is unbelievable. And so far, fun as hell. I remove my towel and hang it on the hook next to the mirror looking at myself as I always do. I give myself a *who are you kidding* look. If he would've kissed me back, I would have caved...hard.

I don't know why I'm smiling so hard, but I do know that I need to be slapped so I can be snapped back into reality. I think from the time I woke up until now, I've probably racked up about 300 composure points. Lord have mercy, this man has rattled my spirit to the core.

"Ayo?" Eros calls softly from outside the bathroom door. My mouth drops and I look around for something to distract me. I snatch a bandana hanging over the back of the toilet and quickly adjust it around the back of my head.

"Yes, come in." I say composing my face.

I'm standing at the sink adjusting the knot of my bandana in the back of my head while looking at his reflection in the mirror and doing my best to hide my half smile, of course I fail. It thrills me that his eyes briefly closed when he saw my naked backside. And I'm more than excited that he now leans into the doorway having completely gathered his wits.

"I got a call from the Social worker at Emma's home."

"Is everything okay?" I ask forgetting the game.

"No, she's fine," He assures me, with a slight wave of his hand, "It's about her wardrobe. I asked her to give me some advice on what I should buy."

"I see." I said turning my attention to the hot and cold knobs of the shower. "That's good."

"You think so?" he asks, stepping over the threshold of the door into the bathroom.

I've been living in this house for six years, and I've owned it for about five and a half, almost six. The very first thing that I noticed, is the same thing I've noticed about houses since I was fifteen years old...door frames are not designed for people standing over six foot one inches tall, and if you're not careful you could end up banging your head each and every time you enter or leave a room.

We've all been through it, it's not fun, no it's not something we just get used to. Which is the main reason why, before I could comfortably live in this house, I had every door frame, of every room redesigned to stand six foot five inches. It would have never occurred to me that there would be someone in my house that *still* had to duck his head to enter a room.

"I usually buy her clothes, but I usually get help on what to buy."

"I'm impressed." I say waving my fingers through the water, testing the temperature. "Not very many men would even try."

"Really?"

"Trust me," I say pinning my plaits to the side of my head, making sure they don't dangle over my shoulders when I'm standing in the water of what is about to be a very refreshing experience. "Not very many men would even try. Ask her about shoes that support circulation."

"Okay, will that help with her feet swelling?"

"It can. At any rate at the very least make it worse."

"Um got it. Okay, so I left the address on your dresser. It's not far from where I live so I'm gonna go home and shower first."

"That's a good idea," I say laughing, "Don't want to go with last night to still on you."

"Oh, it's all in here." He tells me tapping his finger against his temple and joining my laughter. "Meet me there when you finish up here."

It was a command, but it was so gentle that I still feel like I have a choice to say no, which of course I won't. It's been a very long time since someone made a decision for me. Most guys that I've dated always seemed to try and Jedi mind trick me into volunteering my own invitation. Which automatically made me feel unwelcome, and I always ended up saying to almost all of them, *"If you want my time all you have to do is say something."* I mean honestly, I know women can do anything. But we're not mind readers no matter how much we pretend, so it's nice to see that he doesn't mind taking some control over the decisions. Even for something so small.

"Which one is she at?" I ask as I sprinkle my fingers away from the water, so they don't drip all over the floor.

"Golden Heights." he answered, sliding his hands in the pockets of his sweatpants, pulling the waistband down a little as he moves in closer to me. "I tried to put my number in your phone, but it must've died overnight because I couldn't turn it on, so I just wrote my number on the back of an envelope on your dresser."

"Oh yeah," I said remembering that my phone was killed in an unfortunate accident yesterday and reminding myself to get online and order a new one. "My phone stopped working sometime yesterday after I dropped it. I'll have to put the address in my GPS. As soon as I figure out how to use it."

"Do you want me to put the address in for you?" He asks. If this was a contest on who could stay focused the longest, I would have won minutes ago. He has completely given up on looking me in my eyes and is looking in the mirror behind me. Probably at the reflection of my ass.

"That would be nice."

"Well, I don't want to hold you up any longer, your water might get cold." Before I can respond, his hand is around the small of my back and I'm being drawn into a brief but deeply passionate kiss and embrace.

For as much as I was trying to hold it together and remain a player in this game of keep away that I thought we were playing only a few minutes ago, I could all but feel the bonus coins that I was just giving myself dropping from between my legs to the floor between my feet.

"My keys are on the table next to the front door. My car is in the backyard."

"Okay," He tells me, releasing me from his massive arms. "I'll put them back and lock the door when I'm done." He turns and is careful about ducking his head before walking through the door. "See you then." And with that, he disappears down the hall towards the front door.

Chapter Six

Almost two hours later I'm pulling into the parking lot of Golden Heights Retirement Community, having no trouble finding a parking spot. Working in a similar environment, I know the procedure is to sign in at the front desk as a guest of whomever I'm visiting before I just roam around freely.

The facility itself isn't as big as its grounds. The walkway leading to the front door is lined with various flowers and an occasional park bench and table. Trees are scattered across the grounds, and I can see painted bird houses hanging from random branches. It's all very beautiful and inviting, so I can see why he chose this place for his mother. It's almost as good as living in any of the gated communities in town. After signing in, I'm told that by the receptionist that Emma is in the activity hall listening to a guest singer. When I find her, she's sitting at a table, resting her head on the back of her chair resting her eyes and tapping her fingers along to a cover of *Blue Moon*.

"Hello Emma," I say stooping down next to her. "Remember me, I'm Ayo. We went for a walk the other morning."

"Of course, I remember you, Dear," she chuckles, patting the seat next to her, "I only put on for my sons' sake sometimes. He seems to feel more helpful if he thinks I can't do things for myself."

"O-kay, that sounds a bit patronizing." I say laughing slightly, settling into the chair.

"Oh no not at all," she tells me as she straightens her shirt collar, "He's always been that way. Very quick to want to help. It's the very reason why he became the man he is. But I'm sure you didn't come here to have *that* type of small talk."

"Actually," I say thinking over her words, "those are the kind of things I would love to talk about."

Laughing, she stands on her feet, "Well then, we best get started. There's not much time left."

"What does that mean?" I ask as I follow her out of the dining room. For such a tiny little lady, she sure moves fast, and I have to pick up my pace a little just to keep up with her. I notice that she's wearing a lovely blue blouse with white polka dots. The collar comes up high around her neck, but the sleeves are almost sheer and probably wouldn't be very protective against the unusual September wind. It's almost too warm for me and the off the shoulder sweater I'm wearing, but for her it could be different.

"Would you like to get a sweater or a cover up for your arms before we go?" I ask catching up to her and slowing my stride to match hers, "It's a bit windy out."

"Oh of course," she giggles, "If I don't Eros will never let me hear the end of it."

She snakes her hand around the crook of my arm, just like the other day.

"So," I say as we walk, "I'm very anxious to hear some of your stories about your son."

"And I'm anxious to tell them." She pats my hand blinking her brown glossy eyes up at me, "So where should we start."

"Hello Emma." A blond-haired woman calls to us as we stand waiting in front of the elevator. "How's your day going?"

'*Very good. Very good indeed.*' I thought to myself. Good staff never let your residents walk out with a strange person.

"My day is going a little bit better, thank you for asking, and yours."

Emma's tone had gone from very pleasant and upbeat with me, to bleak and sarcastic towards this woman.

"It's not so bad, thanks for asking." She responds pushing the elevator button again, "Who's this you have here with you?" For some reason she felt the need to look me up and down as if I weren't standing about two feet taller than her own height. For reasons that are not at all foreign to me, I felt the need to smile as pleasantly as I could.

"This is my daughter-in-law." The woman's smile fades and her eyes dart to mine.

"I'm Ayo." I say holding my hand out, "We're just going to take a walk around the grounds."

"That sounds nice." The woman manages from behind a tight-lipped smile.

"When you see my son," Emma tells her as the elevator doors open and we step on, "will you tell him that I'll be out by the pond...with his wife, please."

The woman's eyes flash at me once again but her tight smile never cracks. She may even be biting her tongue. If she's not, I am. Emma is more than within her wits. She's downright mischievous, and I can clearly see where Eros, or shall I say *Mr. Guess,* gets it from.

"Of course, I will." she says as the doors begin to close.

"Oh!" I blurt, sticking my hand out to stop the doors, "Is there a way we could maybe get some bread slices?"

"Of course." She tells me, "Just stop by the kitchen on your way out and they should be able to give you whatever you ask for."

"Thank you." I say sweetly, removing my hand and letting the elevator doors close.

Emma and I make our way towards her room as she introduces me, her *daughter-in-law,* to everyone that comes across our path. The nurses that provide her medicine, the nursing aides that provide her daily care. The same type of people that I work with every day. Different faces, different personalities but the same goals and wants for their residents.

We make our way to her room for the sweater, then back downstairs. Making a quick stop for the bread and we're on our way.

"It's such a beautiful day." Emma commented as we exited the building.

"Yes, it is." I agree as we stroll along slowly, in no hurry to get anywhere.

"Do you get the chance to get out and enjoy the weather much?" I ask, looking around the grounds.

"About as much as we can. Of course, Eros takes me out whenever I'm up to it." She admits. "But it's no secret that our staff is limited, so it really depends on if there's anyone on the schedule they can spare." I nod my head in agreement.

"It's like that for a lot of places, my own facility included."

"There's not always someone available so beautiful days like this can go in passing, as if they never happened."

"Hum…" I say in understanding. "Um, Emma?"

"Yes?"

"*Wife?*" I asked, snickering. We approach a pair of benches and I watch as Emma coo and calls to the ducks and ducklings paddling in the water.

"I don't care for her that much. She's always asking after Eros. Always questioning me about how he's doing, or when he's coming back for a visit." Emma finally answers, to which I respond with a giggle. Protective mothers are all the same no matter who they are, and she sounds exactly like my own mother when it comes to my brothers.

"She's not very pretty…"

"*Emma.*" I say laughing slightly.

"Well, she's not, dear, you saw her. Her face is as tight as leather, and it's a wonder her skin didn't crack just now when she was smiling. Not to mention she smokes like a freight train." This time I laughed out loud as I handed her a few slices of bread.

"Those are not very nice things to say." I light heartedly tell her as I toss small bits of bread to the ducklings.

"Pssh." She scoffs, "If you think that then you should hear some of the things the aides and nurses say about her."

"I can imagine." I say, laughing still.

"Much worse than anything I could ever say."

"I can imagine that too."

"My son must like you a lot." She tells me, catching me completely off guard, and peaking every ounce of my interest. This tiny woman is perfect in every way. She has a very specific way of telling it like it is, and I love it.

"Why do you say that?" I ask.

"Well, you're here aren't you." She tells me, in sort of a sing-song kind of tone. Her eyes were bright with humor, and she seemed to be enjoying herself. To what degree I can't quite figure out. "Do you think he brings every woman he meets here to meet me?"

I gaze into her eyes as she speaks. They are like his, and I see the same truth in her that I saw in her son just hours ago.

"His most prized possession, my words not his." She looked away from me and tossed more bread at the ducks, and watched quietly as they paddled in the direction of each floating piece. Bobbing their heads up and down, then swimming back towards her waiting and squawking impatiently for more.

"I'm all he has left so he keeps me very well protected from anyone whose intentions may, to him, seem less than...honest."

"Anyone that might think getting close to you was the way to his heart." I say catching on to what she was hinting around to.

"It is the way to his heart, and to leave you alone with me." She tells me, tossing her last piece of bread, "He must trust you."

"Either that," I say handing her more bread, "or he knows I don't really like you."

Unexpectedly, she erupted into a contagious half laughing, half slightly coughing spell. Which instantly made me think I should've remembered to bring some water out for her.

"You know," she said, catching her breath, "That nurse's breath usually stinks too." I couldn't help but lean my head back and join her in her laughing spell. "It does," she continued, "Like a soggy ashtray, and spearmint gum. No but seriously." She tells me turning to face me, "The main thing you should know about my son is, if he says he's gonna do it...then you can set your clock to it. You can trust him." She held my eyes as she nodded her tiny head, confirming her words.

"Well now." I say kissing her forehead tenderly. "Who can argue with that."

"Look at the two of you." A voice call from behind us. I know it's Eros from the sound of his voice, but I'm not prepared for what I see when I turn around. He's casually strolling towards us in dark whiskered denim jeans, fitting and hanging just right around his waist. With small cuffs that sit on top of brown casual sneakers. I wasn't prepared for the way the cream thermal shirt, unbuttoned at the top with the sleeves partially pulled up his forearms, hugged his very well-formed chest muscles. Complimenting his shoulders and biceps very nicely.

"Hey momma," he greets, kissing her on her cheek. At some point, I guess I'm going to pick up my jaw and regain my composure, but not before he smiles at me and kisses me on the same side of my face as earlier.

"Wassup Ayo." He says, smiling, then whispers in my ear, "You look beautiful."

Oh, he does not play fair. He makes himself comfortable on the bench, on Emma's opposite side, slightly facing into her.

"We're feeding the ducks." His mother tells him.

"I see. They seem to like it."

"And having girl talk," she confesses.

"I see that too." He reaches for the bread, that I'm handing him from behind the bench, gently caressing my fingers in the process.

Oh, he really does not play fair, at all, got me blushing in front of his momma.

"Thank you." He speaks. It's just like when we first met, *and* when we were at the bar last night. Electrical.

I wonder what he's thinking as his eyes hold mine, seemingly pleased with the look that I'm giving him in return. We sit there with Emma listening to all of the stories about Eros that she can think to tell. Stories that he didn't want to hear again but didn't mind listening to. She talked about his elementary school days. The school plays he was involved in. The peewee league football team he used to play on and the friends he made on that team. All the teammates he had, that used to hang out at their house, and the appetites they brought along with them. Anything that she could think of to talk about, and I enjoyed every bit of it.

He, on the other hand, objected the entire time she talked, but didn't put up much of a fight for her silence. He even corrected her and filled in for the parts that she couldn't remember. When she had her fun with story time, she fed the ducks more bread and named all seven of them. Laughing at the way two of the smaller ones fought over a small bite of lunch. Pretty soon, her laughter and chatter died down and we sat in silence enjoying the quiet of the afternoon. It was obvious that she was getting tired, so without any objections to her request, we escorted her back to her room and helped her get settled in. She sat in a small chair next to her bed and he gave her a jumbo letter crossword book, a pencil, her glasses and the remote control for her television.

"Do you need anything else, momma?" Eros asked as he gently laid a throw blanket across her legs.

"No son," she responds softly patting his hands, "You two go out and enjoy yourselves. I'll be fine."

"Alright." He sighs, once again kissing her on her cheek.

"It was good to see you again, Emma." I say quietly, "I really enjoyed myself."

"I'm happy I got to see you too, dear." She looked her soft weary eyes over at mine and smiled quietly, "Will you come back tomorrow... we're going for a ride."

"Of course. I'll come back tomorrow." Confused, I kiss her cheek and look up to Eros who nods his head, answering my unasked question. I wonder where he's taking her.

Side stepping out of his way, I ease into the unit hallway, quietly closing the door behind me. Being as discrete as I possibly can without being obvious, I softly exhale. Internally trying to gather my wits, and check my emotions all at the same time. *What in the world* is going on in the universe right now? I can feel in the marrow of my bones that something different is happening. Forget about the fact that by midmorning, because of the words of a sweet little old lady, I ended up being the wife; to a man I just met *yesterday*. At least that's what the staff now believes.

Judging by the smiles and side glances, they most definitely believe they have no reason to doubt Emma's words. To which *I* will not be the one to shed light on *any* false truths.

Besides, I'm not anything, if not honest with myself and I *must* admit, the looks I'm getting are making me feel some type of way. And I *like* it. Not speaking like I want to get married right away or anything like that. I'm just saying, if I had to lie or pretend like I was married to anyone, I can think of worse people than him. Hell, his momma already gave her blessing.

The door opens behind me, so I take a step, allowing him the space to quietly close the door behind him. I can't help noticing his eyes, slightly reddened around the rims. If he hadn't been crying, he most definitely teared up.

"You, okay?" I asked, moving alongside his stride to the elevator. His body language isn't off putting, but it isn't exactly inviting either. It's only three levels to this building, so the ride to the ground floor was a smooth decline, decorated with deafening silence. His, because of whatever is on his mind, and mines because I can tell there's something on his mind. "You want to talk about it?" I ask, slipping my arm around his.

"Hum." He grunts quietly.

"It's okay if you don't want to. I'd understand." I assured him. I can't pretend like I don't understand what it's like to have something on your mind, but not exactly a clear way to express it into words.

"Thank you for being here." He tells me quietly, pressing a furry kiss on my temple as we stroll through the small parking lot.

"I really like her," I say looking up at him, "and I love how you two are with each other."

"Do you?"

We stop casually by my car, and he pulls me into a soft warm embrace, which is a complete contrast with how firm his biceps and shoulder muscles are.

"Of course, I do." I say against his chest, "It tells me a lot about your character." I rub my hands over his sleeves until my arms are around his neck, returning the squeeze of his embrace. It's an amazing feeling not having to bend to embrace someone. Though I don't want to let him go, he pulls back, and just for a few seconds I miss the feel his body next to mine. I want to continue smelling his earthy scent and feel his hands smoothing the surface of my back. And I want to feel his lips against mine so without thinking, I place my hand on the side of his bearded jaw and pull his mouth closer.

At this moment, it's exactly what I want. His warm tongue exploring my mouth, flirting with my tongue. His hand on my side pulling me deeper into his body. His other hand resting on the curve of the lower part of my back, gently clutching the hem of my sweater. My entire spirit is relaxed beyond recognition, and I love how it feels. I love him... at least, I'm positive I'm going to easily fall in love with him. And if what we're trying to have doesn't work out, then at least I know, on my part it wasn't for nothing.

'Girl stop.' I think reluctantly, as I pull away from his lips and his gentle grip. Quietly exhaling.

"Wowzah." He says smiling. I'm starting to really enjoy it when he looks in my eyes. They seem to ask silent questions and search for the answers at the same time.

"Anything special you want to do today?" he asked, looking down at me. Unsnapping my clutch, I retrieve my key remembering that I scheduled this vacation with the intentions of doing absolutely nothing at...all. Every day that I'm off.

"I haven't made any plans at all." I say shaking my head.

"Good." He responds, almost to himself. "I have something planned." He offers me his hand, palm up and holds it there until I figure out what he's waiting for.

"What is it?" The smile on my face is uncontrollable as I drop my keys in his hand.

"It's nothing big." He assures me, as he keys the lock to my driver's side door. "Did you see my note I left for you."

"You mean the note stuck to my front door with the instructions to bring an overnight bag?"

"That would be the one darlin." He opens the door and steps back.

"I did, and it's in the trunk." I say stepping closer to him, lightly pressing the front of my body against his. "What did you plan?"

"I told you...it's nothing big."

"Well, it's the thought that counts, *darlin.*" I say sweetly, emphasizing on the last word. "Always the thought."

"Come on." He nudges his head indicating for me to get in the car. "Follow me."

With or without the beard, his shy smile reached beyond his eyes, which gleamed with pride. He was obviously very happy with himself. *Which* is a completely different vibe than what it was a few minutes ago.

"Do you want to make any stops when we leave here?"

"Do I need to?" I asked, almost caught off guard.

"No."

I don't know what could've changed his mind so quickly, or if he's just allowing himself to be distracted. But it's working. What I do know is how it feels to need a distraction. To want to talk, but not want to bring up anything that's going to end up with me saying...I'm sorry, I'm just venting. I know how it feels, to just want to be in the presence of a person, that seems like they are completely comfortable in my presence.

This might be one of those times for him, so I think what I'm going to do, is...I'm just going to get out of his way and let him enjoy himself. Because those moments do not come along for most of us that often. I think I might just enjoy this my damn self.

"I have a feeling," I say as I settle into the driver's seat. "I should probably tell you thank you ahead of time."

"Aw it's no problem." He tells, me closing my door, then leaning into the window, "anything for my wife."

"Oh...no." I utter, absolutely caught off guard. "That was your mother's idea." My eyes pop and my jaw dramatically drop in a loud gasp, and a slight chuckle. I completely forgot about Emma's little joke, at that nurse's expense. I can't do anything but laugh and watch him make his way towards his car.

Chapter Seven

It took about five minutes, but we finally pulled out of the parking lot. About fifteen minutes later, I'm following Eros into a u-shaped driveway in front of a huge but practical cottage style house. It's dark red brick, with beautiful blue shutters enclosed around windows that rest above rectangular flower buckets. It's beautiful and cozy, and I instantly love it. It doesn't seem like the house that a single man would come home to.

"Welcome to my home." He tells me opening my car door.

"Eros, it's beautiful." I say, "It's not quite the bachelor pad I expected."

"You had expectations?" he asked, pulling my bag from the trunk.

"I wondered."

His eyebrow arches shot up as he chuckles, "Don't speak too soon." he says, closing the trunk.

"Really?" I laugh. I'm starting to pleasantly amaze myself at how comfortable I am around this man. I feel so natural, and organic. Everything that I'm doing is happening so easily with him. That half smile that I think he likes so much. My laugh when I think he says something funny. I can feel my womanly sensuality waking up and dusting itself off, doing a little dance in the process. I don't feel like I'm intimidating him, which *has* been a problem in the past. At this point in my life, having these feelings is refreshing. Kind of like the difference between having a cold glass of Sunny-D versus fresh squeezed orange juice.

Eros wraps his right arm around my shoulder so that his hand dangles in the air. Stepping into his body I lace the fingers of my right hand through his and wrap my free arm around his waist. Loving the feel of his thumb caressing the inside of my palm. At the door, instead of him dropping the arm of the hand that I'm holding. He sets my bag down and unlocks the door.

"You ready?" he asks, smiling.

"Wait." I say laughing. "What kind of bachelor pad are we talking about? Like, bean bag sofas and wicker chairs?"

"No," He laughs, "It's a little more than that."

I laughed and step in, leaving him to tend to my overnight bag. I can hear him behind me, closing and locking the door, as I look around and take in the entire scene.

"A *little* more, huh?" I say walking down the three steps that lead into a large carpeted open floor plan. The ceiling is high with rustic mahogany beam's angling in a steeple slash cabin like fashion. To my left is a gigantic fireplace with a dark red brick border and mantle, matching the outside structure of the house.

The sofa is designed so that it's a wide half-moon shaped arch complimenting the fireplace area. Much like the seating arrangement at an outdoor amphitheater.

"What do you think?" he asks, walking around me and over to the half-moon sofa where he places my bag. Completely at ease with himself.

"I think it's fantastic." I say, noticing the tall, bar style dining table that served as the focal point that divided the living room and dining areas from the kitchen.

"How long have you lived here."

"Eleven years now, maybe. There's more downstairs." He's made his way into the kitchen area tossing his keys on the surface of the island counter.

"There's more?" I asked, walking towards the kitchen to join him.

"Um-hum. It's what made me buy it. I had it remodeled after my first super bowl win."

His casual way of saying his last words pulled my attention in his direction and I nodded my head, agreeing to the bottle of IPA he's holding suspended in the air waiting for my response.

"I was wondering," I say, nodding my head to the beer, "when we would get around to that."

"Get *around* to it," He holds out a glass in the same manner as the beer, and I shake my head, turning it down, "you already knew about that?"

"Honestly Ero." It's hard not to blush at the way he's trying to hide his look of what…. shock? Truth is, I think I gave up hours ago on accomplishing that, because at this point, I don't even try anymore. "You may be the most modest man I've ever met in my life. It's very refreshing." I reach for the bottle and clink the bottom of mine against the bottom of his, for my first taste of imported style ale.

"So," He began, smacking his lips at the taste, and forming them around each word, "when I told you my name, you already knew who I was?"

"Sort of." I confess. I was already standing with my back against the island counter, so it only felt natural that I leaned my weight back on my elbow, as I took another drink. "I knew your name; knew you played in the league…"

I paused long enough to take a drink and wipe my mouth…then I caught his eye. "I knew about your injury. I also knew about your retirement. But I didn't know you." I take another drink. "I know quite a bit about sport ball, but you have to understand, I am not a fan of *any* sport ball." His eyebrows knit together in confusion, and I continue to explain. "You see I have six brothers and no sisters, and as a kid, for the longest time I had to do whatever they did. For the most part, all they did was play football, talked football or watched football. And, once they became adults, they volunteered to coach football. At some point, I had to kind of become dedicated to the sport by proxy. But I don't like it."

I leaned over the counter and pulled a napkin from the holder, fold it and used it as a coaster for my bottle. "With that being said. I am, however, a huge fan of your career." I say to him in a casual matter of fact kind of way, "You've done well for yourself in the league. Also, my family are huge Chicago Bears fans. So, there's that."

I pause my movements, as he steps closer to me and places his bottle on the counter next to mine. He did it in a way that forced me to stand full length in front of him balancing my butt on the edge of the island. Loosely gripping the sides with my fingertips.

"I guess I figure, you know I'm a nurse, right?"

"Um-hum." He responds, removing the brown plaid pageboy hat from my head.

"Well, nursing isn't all I'm about."

"Right." He agrees, while I watch him trace his finger along the rim of my sweater, just beneath my collar bone. Leaving a tickle of his touch trailing behind his fingers.

"I just automatically assumed that football isn't all that you're about."

His eyes shift from the activity of his index finger that's now tracing from my jawline to my chin leaving another trail of his touch.

"And." He asked. His eyes reflect the content that I'm feeling and once again, I find myself drinking in his bedroom gaze. Did I mention I love how he looks at me.

"And what?" I asked, lifting my chin higher to his face, allowing his finger to trace the length of my neck.

"What do you think about what you know so far?"

"It's working for me." I say smiling at his chuckle.

"Good." He whispers.

"Very." I say mouthing silently.

"Yessss!" He hisses through his teeth, with a quick fist pump. It's not the dorkiest thing he's done all day, but I instantly get the giggles anyway. "It feels kinda good, right...I mean, it's kinda weird that it's only been a little over twenty-four hours since we first met. But I'm okay with how I'm feeling so far."

He said the second part so fast that it left me no room to answer the first. I did however, noticed him trying to sidestep in a way that most guys only do when they're trying to adjust themselves. He played it off smoothly, but I still noticed.

"You think it's weird?" I ask, watching him wipe the moisture from the sides of the bottles.

"A little bit," He responds, "don't you?"

"Not really." I say, "I will say I'm surprised, pleasantly of course, but still surprised."

"Really?" he asked, stepping towards the wall of sliding glass doors. Clicking the door unlocked with his finger, he tilts his chin for me to follow.

"Absolutely." I assure him, "I'm excited about whatever this is that's happening between us."

"So, it doesn't bother you in any way, that we just met?"

I step past him through the doorway leading to his backyard, and it's marvelous. The greenery lining the perimeter of the yard along the privacy fence. The flat stoneware is elegantly placed stretching the length of the yard, branching off in the direction of the underground pool and the outdoor kitchen area. The grass, however, was as green as green can get. It's the kind green that reminds me of the grass in my parents' yard. The kind of grass that calls to me, urging me to feel it between my toes, and beneath my feet.

"Not at all." I say standing on the top step of his porch, looking out at the plush goodness. "Side bar:" I explain, "I can't help myself, I'm about to take these boots off and walk around barefoot."

I turn and sit on the edge of one of the plush lounge chairs and carefully pull off my knee high boots and place them on the deck floor beside where I sit. I step off the deck and run my feet through the thick blades of grass.

"The thing is." I say, getting back to the subject at hand, "I'm excited because there's so much more for us to learn about each other." He doesn't speak right away, but that doesn't bother me at all. I'm too busy smiling at the tickle sensation that washes over me starting from my feet.

This is what I love. What I've always loved since I was a child. The purity of nature...the smell of how clean earth can be. The greenery lining the fence is some kind of leafy flower. I'm not good at knowing the names of things like that, but it has never stopped me from enjoying the feeling that swells within me whenever I'm surrounded by the outdoors.

"You are so beautiful." Eros says from back on the deck, drawing my attention to where he's standing. And it occurs to me, as he gazes down, that he's been watching me the entire time. Watching my every move.

Anybody can say things like that. Anyone can give a compliment, if not for anything other than making that person feel good about themselves. But right now, how he leans against the support beam, dangling his foot over the first step leading from the deck. Both beers in one hand while the other hand loosely grips the support beam overhead...I believe him.

Right now, his especially chocolate eyes have captured mine and refuses to let them go, making it hard for me to look away. Well, I can, but I don't want to. The honesty that I see there is too much and not enough all at the same time. I watch him descend the steps and stroll over to me slowly. Hooping his arms around my backside, he lifts me against his body at a level slightly above his head. It's all just...intoxicating, and the memory of his thrust from the night before echoes through my head.

"Thank you." I say softly. Smiling at the feeling of myself blushing.

"You are most welcome, Ayo." He whispers. My body is already alive in his arms. He seems to be at ease carrying me, so I'm at ease letting him.

"Are you hungry?" He asks, still carrying me, moving with absolutely no urgency.

"Famished." I reply, kissing the outside corner of his eyebrow, then tracing it with my fingertip.

"What are we having?" I asked, kissing him again. Just barely touching my lips to his ear lobe.

I close my eyes as I breathe in his woodsy cologne. I need to find out what it is, because he should never run out of it...ever.

"Nachos." he says, halting my next kiss in mid-air. I can feel his smile against my hand, and his erection against my body as he slides me down, returning my feet to the grassy ground. He lifts his eyebrows and basically points his head with a nod, urging me to turn around. I noticed the picnic table before, while taking my boots off, but paid no attention to how it was set up. I noticed the brick enclosure that houses a four isle gas range, an oven, a large gas grill. Along with a small sink and minifridge completing an appliance set, that would even impress my brothers.

Not so much because they are exceptional chefs or anything like that, more so because they greatly appreciate gadgets and appliances that make them feel and look like they are.

"Have a seat." He tells me, placing his hand on my back, and stepping around me, lightly brushing his hand across my butt. Giving it a light pat.

"You're cooking?" I say, easing myself into one of the chairs.

"I am." He responds, opening both bottles and handing me one.

"You nervous?" he asks, sitting in one of the chairs and removing his shoes then socks.

"Not yet." I say, drinking from my bottle, smiling at the drop of his mouth.

"Don't be nervous." He tells me, leaning into my body. He leans into my chair, hovering his face over mine, supporting his weight on his arms by gripping both arm rest.

Then it dawns on me...he's still toying with me. This entire day has been about his seduction of me, and goodness gracious it's been working. The subtle hand touches, the brushes against my body. The soft kisses, his fingertip tracing my skin, down to carrying me to this area. All of it was to set my body on fire, and man is my body burning.

I reach up to rub the hair that frames his bottom lip and instead of allowing me to touch it he kisses my thumb, catching me off guard.

"Emma taught me well." he says, smiling, kissing my thumb once more. All I can manage is a half-smile. *'His house, his rules.'* I think to myself. He leans in and nuzzles his face into my neck. The hair tickles, and his tongue tastes my skin between small kisses leading up to my ear.

Images of his eyes as this same tongue laps the surface of my lady bits, flash through my mind. He closes his mouth around my lobe and the ghost from the feeling of him gently sucking my clit shutters through me and I clench my thighs, gasping slightly. He's got me...*dammit,* he's got me. This damn man has beaten me at my own game.

"I'm fading away here." I say absolutely *not* convincing at all, and he knows it, which is why he's smiling.

"Yes ma'am." he says softly. He stands up, and just as I raise my bottle to my lips for another drink, *he,* mind you still not taking his eyes off mine.

Side bar: Did I tell you that I love how he looks at me.

Anyway, he grips the area of his thermal shirt where the tag is and pulls it over his head. I can't even stop the smile on my face. Or the way my eyebrows shift upwards at the sight of his nicely sculpted shoulder muscles flexing as he removes his shirt. And there goes that handsome half smile. He knows he's getting to me, and he is enjoying every minute of it. Good, I'm glad he can see it.

He turns to the fridge and removes a package of chicken and ground beef, along with the other ingredients. Obviously, he is very comfortable in the kitchen. Cutting peppers, dicing chicken, even adding seasoning. All that good stuff, which makes it a real joy watching how relaxed he is.

"So," I say, picking at the blades of grass with my toes, "This is what you had planned?"

"Part of it." He admits, turning towards me holding up a green pepper. "Do you like peppers?"

"Yes." I confirm, waiting for him to continue. I watch him pull a wooden cutting board out from underneath the counter. "Can I help?"

"No but thank you." He responds, slicing the pepper into strips, then dicing them into small chunks.

Slowly, I get up from the table where I'm sitting and move to one of the bar stools, opposite the counter where he's chopping.

"So earlier," he began, "you mentioned having six brothers?" He finished up with the green pepper and used his knife to split a yellow pepper in half and began seeding it.

"Yep, six." I say, pushing my empty bottle off to the side of the island.

"Older or younger?"

"Older." I say.

"*All* of them?" he asks, surprised, looking up from his partially diced yellow pepper.

"Yes," I say, chuckling, "and it was awful."

"*Awful.*" He uses the blade of his knife to pick up the peppers and drops them in the bowl with the green ones. Then moves on to splitting a red pepper in half.

I noticed, as he was splitting and seeding the previous peppers, that he placed the seeds on napkins in two separate piles. Keeping up with the same theme, he seeded the red pepper onto another napkin. Then folded each one up, placed them in small zip lock baggies, and used a sharpie to label each bag with the appropriate color name.

"I'm thinking about growing my own veggies." He explained, as he plucked a bulb of garlic from a hanging basket next to the mini fridge and peeled a single clove from the body.

"So, how could having six brothers be awful?" He asked, placing the flat of the blade on top of the garlic, and smashing the skin away from the flesh. "Your father must have been crazy about you." With quick skill, he made light work out of dicing and mushing the clove up into a thick paste.

"You would think so, but nope." I say laughing, as he removes a frying pan from one of the cabinets and places it on the stove.

"So, you weren't a daddy's girl?" He asks laughing, as he dumps in the garlic, and begins peeling and dicing an onion that he grabbed from the fridge. Adding that with the garlic.

"Honestly," I tell him, laughing, "Up until I was twelve, I think he thought I was a boy."

Stirring the onions and garlic in the pan, he quickly washes his hands, and pulls two glasses from another cabinet, along with a bottle of wine from the fridge. Moving quickly, he pulls open a drawer, finds a corkscrew and easily twists the bottle free from its stopper.

"Six brothers sound awesome." He tells me, tossing our empty beer bottles into the trash and pouring a glass for the both of us, then handing one to me.

"It probably *would* sound awesome to you," I say, picking up my glass, smiling at the way his fingers brush over mine, then raising my glass to his lifted toast. "You're a boy." I say, sipping my wine. "You would love the things they did. I'm a girl, *and* the youngest. If I wanted to go outside...I had to go with them."

"Really?" He smiles, pulling a thick pack of bacon from the fridge. "Your dad's idea?"

"Nope," I say, smacking on the wine I'd just sipped, "My moms... she called me birth control." I tell him laughing.

"Really?"

"Anything they did, I had to do."

He laughs, and the sound is joyful to hear. All of this is a part of his plan...his own unique way of learning about me.

Now, I am very much aware that there are men that exist out here, who do these types of things on a regular. Until now, I have never crossed paths with any of them. It's fun, and so far, every second of it is turning out to be a moment that I don't expect to forget any time soon. I also know for a fact that I like being here with him like this.

Relaxed and comfortable, unaware of what the rest of the world is doing, simultaneously wondering what the rest of the night will bring. For every question he asks, I want him to ask another, and for every answer that I give, I want to tell him more. So that the feeling of this moment can last that much longer.

"Like what?" He asks, snapping me away from my thoughts and, finally turning the flame on low under the skillet.

"What kinds of things would you have to do?"

"All kinds of things." I giggle.

"Like what?" He repeats, puncturing the bacon package and slicing it open.

"Like wrestling with them." I say between sips of wine. "They would always want me to let them practice WWF moves on me."

"And did you?" he asks, laughing, as he cut the strips of bacon into chunks.

"Every single time." I say, laughing with him, "It would be fun at first, then I'd get tired of getting pinned and cry."

"Why would you cry?" He asks, tossing the bacon into the warm pan with the other ingredients. "Would it hurt?"

"No, it didn't hurt." I admit. "I just knew that if I simply *asked* them to stop, they wouldn't. So, I'd conjured up a few crocodile tears loud enough for my mother to hear, and then *she* could tell them to stop."

Once again, we find ourselves laughing in unison. Our voice tones, in no way harmonizing with one another. His tone, a low base vibrating from his chest, and mine...well let's just say I've never been ashamed of my loud cackle; besides the sounds we make are like music to my ears.

"So did they ever do anything you wanted to do?"

"Sometimes." I say, nodding my head, "But it was rare."

"What kind of things did you wanna do?"

He stirred the bacon with the onions and garlic, which filled the September air with a thick smell of goodness.

"Well, when I was younger, I liked the typical girly things. Playing with my Barbies, having tea parties and things like that."

"They didn't mind doing those things?" He removed the chicken breast from the package and was rinsing the meat in the sink.

"At first," I say, standing and reaching for the wine bottle, helping myself to another glass. "They didn't mind. I guess because I was so young, and they didn't want to upset me. But as I got older, they stopped wanting to play."

"So, you were a Barbie girl?"

"I still am a Barbie girl." I say smiling, "Only I play dress up with myself."

"I've noticed." Eros comments, stirring the bacon and sipping his wine.

Oh, he's hot tonight. He shifts the bacon around by shaking the skillet back and forth. The muscles in his back shift with every push and pull.

"So how old were you when you decided to do your own thing?"

"Well, really..." I start, after another sip from my glass, "I always had my own interest. So as long as it was productive, my parents didn't care."

"Well, that's good." He said turning the fire off underneath the skillet and pulling the bowl from the cabinet and lining it with paper towels. "So, what were your interests?"

He pours the bacon mixture into a strainer that he propped over the bowl, allowing the grease to drain to the bottom. I don't think I've ever been asked that question outside of a job that I was interviewing for. It makes me smile that he seems to be enjoying himself. I mean genuinely pleased. It's all in his eyes, his laughter, even in his body language. Every chance he got to pause in between his task of chefery, he would lean on the counter to focus on me and the things that I say more closely.

"Music was one." I tell him, smiling, knowing he's going to get a kick out of this topic.

"Music?" he asks, tossing the chicken into the same skillet he cooked the bacon in. "What kind of music?"

"All kinds." I say, sipping more of my drink, "I started off playing drums at six."

"At six?" He repeats, "How? Did you have lessons?"

"No, not at first." I say, watching him season the chicken with what could only be a blend of Mexican flavors, then add the peppers and onions medley. "Music was my dad's first love, but after he married my mom he realized, music didn't really pay the bills. So, he worked for the post office for about fifty years, and played gigs with his buddies whenever he could."

"Okay." He smiles, spooning the chicken into a dish, "But how'd you get started?" He places the bowl into a warmer with the bacon, then turns to the sink to wash the skillet.

"I don't really remember." I say trying to think back. "All the band equipment was kept in our house, which is where they practiced. My dad likes to tell the story about how he came home from work one day, and I was just...playing."

His head whipped around so fast; I almost didn't see it turn. "What do you mean playing? Like...a song?"

"I guess I was." I say laughing into my glass, "I just played the same sounds that I heard them playing."

"You played them by ear?!"

"Well...I couldn't quite read yet." I say, laughing at the way his mouth dropped, "Eros, you seem to be really enjoying yourself right now."

"Oh Ayo, you have no idea." He drops the raw hamburger into the now warmed skillet, adding the same seasonings as the chicken chunks. "And just so you know, the fun started three days ago." And then he winks his eye at me! Everything I'm doing pauses, and I mentally go down a checklist...

Breathing stopped...*check.*

Slow heartbeat...*check.*

Eyebrows jacked up to my hairline...*check.*

Mouth open...*check.*

Wine glass suspended in the air, hovering over my lips...*check.*

Smile on my face...definite, *check.*

"Do you play anything else?" he asks, smiling behind his glass.

It's at this moment that I realize, no other woman on this good green earth deserves anything that this man has to offer, *except* me...no questions asked.

"As a matter of fact," I say, taking another sip then sitting my glass down, "I play nine instruments."

"*Nine?!*" He asks, mixing the bacon and garlic with the hamburger, after draining the grease, then turning the heat down low.

"Nine."

"Fluently?" He asks, taking the previous dish from the warmer.

"Yes," I admit, smiling at his gleaming eyes, "Fluently."

He's staring just below my nose, so naturally, I moisten my bottom lip by slightly biting it.

"Um-hum." He half smiles, breathing deeply through his nose.

Wiping his hands across his apron, I watch him pull another bowl from the cabinet, then spoon the ground beef in. Carefully wiping the sides of any droplets.

"Want some help?" I ask again.

"Nope, but thanks." He tells me, as he passes by to place the bowls on the table I previously occupied.

He walks back and forth, placing each bowl on the table, one by one in a sort of family style order. On each turn, as he passes by where I'm sitting at the outside island counter, he grazes his fingertips across my thigh.

Dragging them slowly down the length to my knee, or vice versa for that matter, depending on which way he's going. The last of the bowls contained four different kinds of salsa...Pico de Gallo, mild, spicy and salsa Verde'. The latter being my favorite which goes very well with the white queso he has placed on the table, along with everything else. Which included, ground beef and bacon, sauteed chicken and peppers, sour cream and chives, both kinds of olives. Last but not least, two bowls of tortillas, the ones that shape like scoops and the deep-fried triangle shaped ones...both being my favorite.

After placing the last of the dinnerware, a newly opened bottle of wine and the glasses we were using on the table, he placed the chair I was using before closer and patted the seat from where he stood behind it.

"This is your seat." He tells me standing behind the chair. Smiling, I take the few steps necessary, and just before I take my seat, he stops me by placing his hands on my hips.

"Wait, don't sit down yet."

I don't know if it's the wine kicking in, or if being in his presence puts me in a natural euphoric state of mind, but his hands on my hips and his soft, low toned voice trickled through my ear canal, down to the drum, and is sending vibrations that can't be stopped. It's a complete fire starter, igniting all my senses from his mouth, that's positioned next to my ear, down to the spot where he pats my hip twice.

He walks around the island and finds a small speaker with an auxiliary cord and connects it to his phone. A two-note piano melody fills the air, and I know the exact song. The volume is low, but I'd know this young man's voice anywhere, and if there's anyone out there who doesn't know the song, "Love Faces", I challenge you to find it, and download it today. Put it on repeat and tell your significant other that it's time for some one-on-one time. I guarantee they'll be some love faces being made before the night ends and the morning sun rises. It's a must have in the rotation.

"Okay, now you can have a seat."

He's in my ear again and his hand is grazing from my back to the curve of my backside, and the vibrations from the fire follows the trail of his hand as I settle in my chair. I look at the spread laid out in front of me, with this song playing as background music.

Chapter Eight

*Damn...*this man really knows how to set the mood.

"I hope you brought your appetite." He tells me, as he takes his own seat.

"If it's one thing you need to know about me, it's that I don't ever leave my appetite behind."

A small chuckle escapes my lips, and I'm instantly thankful for the spread of food. My level of tipsy needs to be slowed down a bit, and food is always a good treatment for that condition.

"So how did you know?" I ask him, as he pours more wine in our glasses.

"Know what?" he asks, removing his apron.

"That nachos are my favorite snack food."

"I didn't." He tells me, smiling, obviously *further* pleased with himself. "Is it your favorite?"

"One of them." I say, clinking my glass to his.

"Aw snap, bonus points. That's good to know." He smiles, laughing at his own joke and offering me a plate. "Nah I'm just kidding; I saw it on your fridge circled on a menu."

Automatically I know what he's talking about. My freezer has a multitude of menus from close by restaurants that deliver in my area. Although I'm not a creature of habit, I do have my select favorites from certain places that are automatic go to's circled. He starts spooning different ingredients onto my plate for me, making sure to put a little of everything.

"I'm impressed." I say nodding my head to the bacon bits he's offering.

"So," he starts, spooning the same ingredients onto a plate for himself. "You were telling me about instruments you play."

"I was, wasn't I." I popped an overstuffed scooped chip in my mouth. Closing my eyes savoring the combination of flavors. Salty, from the olives and bacon. Crunchy, from the chips. Mildly spicy, from the salsa Verde, meaty from the chicken and beef. A fragrant aroma, from the garlic and peppers fills my mouth, marrying my revived taste buds with my already alive senses.

"Oh my god." I say putting my hand on Eros' knee. "Oh. My. God."

"What?" He asks, but I hold my hand up halting all the possible questions he may ask. I look at him through slitted eyes, and smile at the way his mustache is curled upward on one side.

"I think I just had a food orgasm...a *foodgasm*." I sip my wine and close my eyes, smiling behind my glass at the way the flavors of my drink blend with the flavors of my food. "I had a foodgasm."

His eyes gleamed, the way they smoldered as he gazed into mine. Damn those bedroom eyes of his. Damn the way he grips my belly length necklace and urges me forward, stopping my face a breath's distance from his.

"That's not the only orgasm you're going to have tonight."

My mouth drops and before I can really even process his words, he's softly cleaning away the wet trace of wine from my top lip with his mouth! I...am done and done. Caramel left on the dashboard of a hot car doesn't spread the way I am right now. As bad as I want to feel his beard tickle my face, he pulls himself away from me, so my window of opportunity has closed before it fully even opened.

Taking a long deep breath, I exhale as slowly as my body will allow.

"You are killing me." I whisper, tasting the moisture he left behind on my lips.

"Exactly." He comments, as he adjusts the napkin across his thigh. "I'm glad you like it though, because I do too."

"Instruments," I say, chuckling, piecing myself back together. God knows this man is a natural distraction for me and seeing as how it's still quite early...pacing myself would be a great benefit for me tonight. "Alright, so, I play lead and bass guitar. Slide trombone and trumpet. The violin, cello, piano and flute. And my personal favorite...drums." I put another chip in my mouth, smiling at how impressed he looked.

"All by ear?" He asks between chews, referring back to the answer to a question he asked earlier.

"Um-hum, all except the trumpet and trombone. I learned those in band class and eventually learned to read sheet music to them all."

"Do you still play?" He asks behind his wine glass."

"Yeah.' I tell him, dusting my mouth with my napkin. "I have all of my instruments at my house in my music studio."

"Music studio? There's a music studio in your house?"

"Yes." I laugh. He seems genuinely surprised and impressed at the same time.

"So, when's the last time you played?"

"Yesterday morning."

Really?" He asked, even more surprised, "Have you ever recorded anything?"

"I've recorded plenty of times, but it's for my own personal use. I've never had anything played on the radio or anything like that."

"So, I'm not going to turn over an album or CD and see your face on the back of the cover?"

"Nooo," I say laughing again, "Nothing like that."

"Why is that?"

"Well," for a moment, I sit in silence contemplating his question. Once again, something I've never been asked in casual conversation before...in any conversation actually, "music has always been my own personal way of meditating. If there's going to be an audience, it's usually only my family."

"Hum. So will I ever get a chance to hear you play?"

"Maybe," I say stuffing my mouth with another bite. "If you stick around long enough."

"Oh okay," He chews what's in his mouth, then wipes with his napkin. "Which brings me to my next question."

"Ask away." I say sipping my wine.

"Well, it's more of a statement then it is a question."

"Okay." At this point, I am more than intrigued. Our conversation, up until now, has jumped around so much there's no telling what will be said next. We've gone from, his career, to my brothers, to my next orgasm.

"What we talked about this morning?"

"Which part?"

"Relationships." He confirmed, sitting back in his chair, "How serious were you?"

"What do you mean?"

"Just that. It's been more than a few hours since then and you've had time to think about it and maybe even change your mind." He held his glass in his hand for a few seconds before speaking again, "How serious were you?"

His gentle eyes pierce mine, and the truth is all I can give him.

"When I said, fuck society and their rules, I absolutely meant it. Societies rules might be the most *popular* rules to go by...nobody ever said they were the *only* rules."

"No, they didn't." He agreed. "What about everything else? You still think it's a good idea to jump, headfirst into a relationship, no questions asked?" He nervously scrapped the food around his plate, not hesitant in asking, but hesitant in hearing my answer.

"Are you asking because you want to know if it's okay for you to get comfortable...or because maybe you've changed *your* mind?"

"I most definitely haven't changed my mind."

"Neither have I." I say, "No matter how long we wait, we're going to be finding new things out about each other for a long time. Some things we like, some things maybe not so much. My theory is, maybe those things will be more interesting when there's a foundation of commitment to stand on."

"I completely agree." It's all he says. It's all he needs to say.

The way he's watching me right now, ultimately relaxed. Shirtless, slouching back in his chair, one arm draped over the arm of the chair with his hand dangling in his lap. His other hand casually twisting the corner of his mustache, as soundless words escape his mouth...reciting the words to the soft background song.

'Don't it feel good when I touch on it...wouldn't it be nice if all night I was in you...'. I should go to him right now and straddle his lap and give him the lap dance of his life.

"Let's go for a swim." He suggests, unknowingly, putting a halt to my plans.

He's not asking me, he's telling me. It's a challenge, and I wholeheartedly accept. I stand up facing him and remove my sweater then drape it on the back of my chair. Then peel my jeans down my long legs until they're around my ankles. He's no longer looking at my eyes, instead, he's skimming my belly, down my thighs, stopping at my ankles.

Sitting forward, using the strength of his arms, still not looking up to meet my eyes. I watch him, watch himself lift my right foot upward. Delicately rub the palm of his hand up the length of the bottom of my foot. Then kiss it ever so softly. Resting that foot on his knee, he drops his hand and signals for me to repeat the same process with my left foot. I make no effort to stop him, mostly because I am way too intrigued and just plain and simply turned on to deny him anything at this point. With my feet in each of his hands, he places them together ankle to ankle and uses his legs to adjust his seating. Positioning himself further back and more upright in his chair. Then feather lightly, kiss the balls of both feet, pulling both pant legs simultaneously.

Next, I watched him slide everything I pushed to my ankles, over my feet and off my legs simultaneously. Folding the pants and stuffing my panties in the pocket of my jeans, then gently placing my feet on the ground. Before I can adjust my seating, he's on his feet and gazing into my eyes. I return his gaze until his arms move, drawing my attention away from his face and down to his fly. *Now this is a show I want to see,* and he seems to be in the mood to give it to me. His hands are taking careful time undoing each button, and for some reason I already know that I don't need to look up to see that he's watching me. I can feel the heat from his stare, and I'm okay with that. I just want the rest of his show.

And there it is... just glorious. Mentally I applaud his performance while he steps out of his pants. Finally, I let my eyes travel up his abyss to his pecks then his neck muscle, to his lip poking through his beard and the oozing chocolate in his eyes.

That is, it. I want to touch him, so I hold my hand out to him, for help up. I remove my necklace and bracelet and place them on the table. I remove my strapless bra and step around him grazing my hand across his stomach and back, heading toward the edge of the pool. Until the palm of one hand squeezes my ass cheek, and the hand on the flat of my belly pulls me backwards into his body, so he can graze a quick kiss on my neck and lightly squeeze the other side of my butt. Then just like that, as quick as all that happens, he's diving into the pool, leaving me to brave the slippery steps alone.

The cool but refreshing water instantly dissolved the harsh September night, removing the sticky film that seemed to have built up and covered my skin throughout the day. It wasn't particularly *hot*, but it was much too warm for the sweater I chose to wear. I would've been better off wearing a T-shirt with a jacket. At least I would've been able to take the jacket off and let some air circulate. A pair of low-cut sneakers would have been more appropriate, but at least, at some point, I was able to take those knee-high boots off completely.

That's always been a problem of mine. Even when I was younger, I never really got a good grasp on the whole weather thing. After school, when it was time to go home, I was always that kid with their winter coat tied around their waist, because it was too hot to wear it. So tonight, when Eros suggested we go swimming, I didn't hesitate to agree. Challenge or not, I would've done it simply because I was ready to get out of these clothes. By then, the jeans I was wearing had already started to stick to me in places that I didn't want denim clinging to.

I walked around the low end of the water long enough to disappear beneath and resurface on the other side of the pool. Refreshed and relaxed, weightlessly floating across the surface, slowly swaying my arms and legs back and forth keeping my body afloat. This is nice...I could get very used to this.

"I hope you do." I heard Eros say.

"You hope I do what?" I asked as I flip my body to face him just in time to see him toss a miniature basketball in a hoop adjusted to the edge of the pool.

"Get used to this." The ball floated my way, so I scooped it up and floated it back towards him. "You said you could get used to this."

"I said that out loud?"

"Yes." He laughed, "We all heard it." He waved his arms around as if indicating to the imaginary crowd of people standing behind him.

"I'm sorry," I say, laughing as I float across the water on my back. "I'm so used to either being by myself, or nobody paying attention that I tend to forget not to talk to myself out loud when other people are around. I'm not crazy...I promise."

"That remains to be seen." He laughs.

Actually, we both laugh, but I think for two very different reasons. Me, because it sounds like something my brothers would say, and him, because he tends to laugh at his own jokes. I noticed that fact earlier when he was showing off his nacho cooking skills. Normally, laughing at your own jokes can come off as a bit obnoxious, but with him, it just comes off as goofy. As a matter of fact, the more comfortable he seems to get the more nerd vibes he starts giving off. It's beginning to be a very cute personality trait, and that's the opposite of what meets the eye.

Just by looking at him it would be easy to see him as some muscle-bound, giant-sized playboy. But watching him now, shooting water hoops as if it's a full press basketball game...against *himself* as the players *as well as* the commentator. He's calling every spin and turn. Every pump fake and fake block, gets called as the greatest move...in the greatest one-man water basketball game ever. And all I can do is laugh, and float across the pool cheering him on.

Every now and then I float across the goal and block his shot, only for him to call a foul or illegal play. He eventually caught on to my tactics, so after that, every time I floated past the goal, he aggressively dunked on me. Rolling across my body, splashing me around...copping a feel every chance he got. By the time the game was over, every shot that I made had a penalty called, and every shot that he missed was because of some made up pool rule that I unknowingly broke.

Eventually we agreed to fight about the outcome of this game for the rest of our lives and to never let each other forget it. We spent the rest of the time skimming around and floating, dipping under the water only to resurface from a different spot. All the while casually brushing past him, ruffling the water, brushing his skin with my wrinkled fingertips. Answering whatever questions, he has for me and of course, throwing in a few of my own. By the time my wrinkled feet matched my fingers, I was standing in five feet, adjusting my hair into the best messy bun I could manage. If I've learned anything throughout my life, it's that, once my hair is wet it's best to manage it right away or else when it dries it'll be a bitch to handle. Even now, with it all sopping wet, I still can't manage to keep it pulled tight.

"Leave it out?" Eros says as he swims up behind me. Although it's a statement, it's more in an asking tone, so I turn and there he is. Almost black, chestnut hair slick down the back of his neck. The beard slick down his face, bearing into my soul through my eyes.

"That's just crazy talk." I tell him as I accept the scrunchie that he's offering me. "If I don't get some control over this mess now, then tomorrow it's gonna take me hours just to detangle it."

"Not hours." He said laughing.

"Yes...hours...upon hours." I said finally bundling my hair to my head. "There's a process to all this shit."

"To detangling, how hard can it be?"

My eyebrows shot up, "How hard can it be? Put it like this, there have been times when I felt like just cutting it all off and saying to hell with every strand."

"It can't be that bad." He spoke. The reflection of his hands on either side of my waist waver with the water, "I could comb it for you."

"Oh, you think so, huh?" I say, smiling at his sureness, "Have you ever even touched a black woman's' hair, let alone *comb* it?"

"Well, no, but you could teach me." He smiled, "Besides, in my defense, I was always told that black women don't like people touching their hair unless they give them permission."

It's not necessarily what he's saying that's making me laugh so hard, and believe me...I'm laughing way too hard, it's more about *how* he said it. The water is just barely touching his stomach and his arms are folded across his chest, but his head is nodding up and down and he has this goofy looking grin on his face as if he's truly proud of himself.

"Yeah see," He said stepping closer to me, reading my thoughts through my eyes, "I know a little bit about some things."

"I see, I'm impressed." I say still chuckling a bit.

The sun has gone down and the night air is not quite in the stage of cooling down at night. It is still just as hot in the dark of night as it was when the sun was high in the sky. The only difference between then and now is the slight breeze that brushes over my shoulders.

"You ready to go in?" He asks, caressing his hands on my sides.

"Absolutely."

"Wait here," he tells me as he brushes past, "I'll get some towels." His hand slowly dragged across the low...*low* part of my belly. And his fingers...well let's just say, they brush a *tad* bit lower than that. And I like it. Finally, someone that's not afraid to just *'do it'*. No overthinking, no second guessing...no half-steppin it. Just going for it.

In all fairness, it would be a shame if I didn't take the same initiative. I reach out as he passes and palms a handful of his fantastically firm ass cheek. He didn't seem to mind judging by the, *'touch it if you want'*, smirk on his face as he looked over his shoulder. I watch him take the steps then walk the edge of the pool brushing water from his chest and erect penis. Glancing at me just as his hand skims his parts. I smile at his eyes, needing him to see that I enjoy the sight of him. I mean let's be honest, with his physic, most women would. He stops near a short cabinet where the towels were kept and begins to dry himself, cupping his erection with one end of the towel, and drying his stomach and chest.

His smile fades and he watch me watch him as he travels back around the edge towards where I still stand in the pool. I look away from him long enough for me to climb the stairs, brushing excess water from my breast and stomach and thighs. By the time I look up he's right there wearing a towel around his waist doing nothing to hide his *excitement,* holding a second towel in his hands waiting to dry me off. I stop in front of him and he wastes no time, softly but effectively drying my body. Starting with my back. Then my shoulders, and arms. Sides and... oh my lord, this man is squeezing then lifting and separating my cheeks. He is being very casual, stepping in front of me like he didn't just open my crack.

I'm watching his face, searching for his reaction up close and personal. Wondering if he is just as riled up as I am. I mean, I know he has an erection, but let's face it, the wind can shift in the opposite direction and a man can get a stiffy. This guy's face has become a vault for his emotions, revealing nothing of his thoughts. His eyes have become these smoldering pots of steaming chocolate, but I don't shy away, because I want to see what touching my body does to him. He seems to be enjoying himself. Concentrating on every surface his toweled hands touch. It's fascinating the way he studies each surface of my body.

The way he lifts his eyes to mine, knowing full well that I'm not going to look away. He's not giving a damn about my heavy breathing as he dries between my legs. He bites his bottom lip as I begin rotating my hips on his hand.

"You ready for me to kiss you yet?" He asks, abandoning his task and wrapping the towel around my chest, tucking it in at the corner.

"You've been playing some kind of keep away game this entire day..."

"Have I?" He chuckled.

"Yes, you have." I say, tucking my towel in tighter as I fall in step behind his long, toweled stroll.

"Keep away, huh?" he said, turning around and walking backwards, watching my every step as I moved towards him. "That sounds like a kid's game."

"It is." I tell him.

"Hum..." he grunts, stopping in his tracks waiting for me to take the last few steps towards him, reaching his arm out for me to grab his hand. "I'm sure you know by now, I'm a grown ass man."

Chapter Nine

"You tired of hearing this song yet?" He asked, turning towards the open wide framed door.

"Absolutely not." I say entering the room behind him.

"Good. Here," he says, commanding my attention from the extra-large bed in front of me. "You can use this to dry your hair."

I automatically reach for the towel he's handing me and start drying my hair when I realize I'm using the towel from his waist.

"Oh," I say softly, but loud enough for him to hear. "Oh, you gotta pay back coming Frank." I speak.

"Well, if you ain't first you're last." He says, laughing, at my Ricky Bobby reference.

"You're overdressed." He smiles, slips his finger around the tucked corner of my towel and removes it from my body, then moves to the closet door and drapes it over the top.

"Before now," He being as he makes his way towards me, "This song was only background music."

"And now?" I ask, grazing my fingers down the thick, smooth hairs of his chest towards his belly. I haven't touched him nearly enough today, so I lean into his body and kiss his chest right above his nipple twice.

"Now not so much." he says, pulling my attention to his beautiful, brown eyes.

I lift my hands to his wrist as he steps into my body, caressing his thumbs along my jaw on both sides. "You still with me in this?"

"Of course, I am." I tell him, moving and swaying with his step.

"You wanna dance with me?" he asks, tucking my hand into his chest and sliding his other down to the small of my back.

"It feels like we already are." I say laying my face into his neck. My other hand skims the surface of his back feeling how his muscles shift and lift with the swaying movement of his body. His fingers are resting on the top of my butt and are tapping to the beat.

Holy smokes...I *finally* get it. I *finally* understand what almost every woman has been talking about. The comfort level...the feeling of security. I don't know, maybe it's just me but at my height, I don't get this feeling that often. In fact...I don't get this feeling at all. I've never been able to rest my head on someone's shoulder as we danced. Hell, the closest I've ever come to being able to do so, is when we were laying down, or curled up on the couch watching a movie. And that goes for every...single past relationship I've ever been in. This feeling here...this is a much welcome...and a *fantastically* needed feeling. I guess my mother was right, life is always going to give you what you need...even when you're not looking for it.

"How tall are you?" He asks in between the tender kisses he's placing on my shoulder and fingers.

"Six-three."

"That's so perfect." He whispers, mostly to himself, as he glides my arms up and around his neck. His hands slowly slide down my arms, my back, over my butt and to my thighs. "You feel so soft, I love touching you."

He's in my ear again and the vibrations from that mixed with the friction of his rubbing hands are, for lack of better words, heating me the hell up. The song stops and starts over, and he changes the pace by dancing me backwards. When we stop, he bends and grips his strong hands around my thighs and easily lifts me over the foot of the bed.

"Are you okay?" he asks as he climbs onto the bed then hovers over my face.

"Fantastic." I say.

He straddles my hips and I watch his hands glide across my belly and up my chest. Then he closes the space between us caressing my face with his eyes and his thumb.

"I wanna kiss you." He tells me. *Finally!* After waiting all night for him to kiss me, he finally makes his move. First his lips press against both of my cheeks, then the tip of my nose, then both of my eyes.

*Wait...*It becomes obvious, as he's kissing his way across my arms and chest, that he intends to kiss my entire body! I watch him meticulously taste each one of my fingers, then kiss my palm, on both hands while grazing his fingertips up and down my arms. I've seen enough. He is clearly working at his own pace, which just to be honest is a pace a woman like me can get used to.

Being able to sit back and enjoy the feel of my body as this man, or any man for that matter goes on a kissing journey exploring as he pleases, is an absolute new experience. That I wouldn't trade for nothing...in any world...ever. He kisses my side down to my pelvis and a slight moan betrays me by escaping my mouth as I squirm beneath the tickle of his beard. It leaves behind a tingling path of kisses as he crosses the bottom of my belly to the inside of my lifted thigh.

'Oh, I have to see this.'

I watch the top of his head make its way up my long leg to my feet. His eyes are on me now, but I'm only interested in him kissing the heel of my foot. Then the instep...the pad of my big toe. I gasp and moan, involuntarily mind you, at the sight of my toes disappearing into his mouth, as he sucks on each. One by one, as if they're cheese fingers fresh out of a Cheetos bag.

My face is going to permanently freeze in this half smile. He is slowly but surely claiming this body as his own, and right now I am more than willing to give up possession of it. I bite my lips and squirm at the feel of his 'not-so-hostile' takeover of my body. A couple of times I even found myself giggling at his delicate touch. I'm not normally a ticklish person but my body is so alive right now, every little thing he does sparks tiny little flames throughout my entire system. I am completely unraveled and more importantly greedy for whatever else he's going to give me.

This is his show, and I am his one-woman audience. Enjoying every minute. Every touch. Every sensation he is creating. Until he has had his fair share and is working his way back to the top.

My hand travels up to his neck and jaw, and I stretch my neck so he can kiss his way to my *good ear*, to which I have every intention of letting him have his fill of that too.

"You've been teasing me with that ear since day one." I close my eyes and enjoy the feel of his tongue and lips licking and probing my lobe.

"Have I?" His voice travels through my ear and out my mouth disguised as a moan that sounds a lot like... "Yes."

"Since day one?" He asks. I'm vaguely aware, but I'm sure he's watching my face. I can feel his eyes caressing my expressions. I try to answer him, but the fire is spreading now and what was meant to be *'um-hum'*, comes out as... "Mmmm."

A very enthusiastic *'mmmm!'*.

"Oh my god." He moans. I feel his beard before I feel his lips, and then they're there. Massaging my lips and tongue...and then they're gone.

"Turn over." He tells me. His straddled body is adjusted so that I can turn without him actually having to get up.

Once on my stomach the bed shifts briefly and seconds later Eros is oiling down my shoulders. Needing them right at the tip of my spine out to my left shoulder and back down to my lower back and across. His slick fingers gliding up my back to my right shoulder.

"Are you okay?" I hear in my left ear. This time I can actually get something out.

"I'm okay." It's breathy but it's English.

"Interesting." I hear him say, but I'm too far gone to wonder why. "Turn your head."

Then kneading and gliding down my right shoulder and out to my hands, lacing his fingers through mine. I can feel his body pressing into my back. My body is grinding him in total anticipation. I want him *bad*.

"I want to put it in you so bad." I heard him say to my good ear, and again I spit his voice back out as a moan. My hips have joined in a circular motion with his. "That's the reaction I'm looking for."

Gripping the sheets, I stop rotating in midair and let him grind my backside. I can hear the air escape his mouth in a hiss, so I pick back up with his rotating rhythm flawlessly. He leans his body weight back and guides my pelvis back into the mattress by placing both hands on my cheeks and firm but gently massaging my hips flat. His hands are oiled again, and I stop moving because having my butt groped and lifted and jiggled and separated is creating an open and close sensation in the front. I open my mouth to moan but only silence comes out.

"Ayo, you are so beautiful." He whispers. The fire has now spread to every surface of my body, and I am so ready. Beyond ready, past ready. Now his fingers are skimming from the back to the front through my legs and into my opening. Rotating two fingers in and out.

"Ayo." The air he's hissing out evaporating into my ear and out of my mouth. "Oh, my goodness…"

"Eros…" I moaned, and moan again.

"Come here, love." I barely understand his words but being rolled over and feeling my body stretch to his girth, along with the tingle from the sweet spot has me right there on the edge of orgasm.

"Shiiittt…" He whispers, pausing deep within me. Closing his eyes to the feel of my slick wetness. He is completely gone. His…in-out…in-out…in-out…rhythm is magic.

"Don't it feel good." He whispers musically in my good ear in tune with the words of the song.

At this point, I am no longer interested in his strokes. I pick up the pace on my own and he groans and groans, and groans. It's the in…out…in…out…in…out….in…out, that I'm living for right now. *And* that sweet spot that's blossoming and growing…and expanding.

"It's there." I say, breathless.

"Right there?" he asks, shifting himself directly on the spot.

"Yes!" I half groan slash half moan. "Oh yes…that's it."

"I feel it." He confirms. "Hold still." I hear him say, "Let me get it for you."

So, I do. My arms snake under his arms to his shoulders and I bury my nose in his beard.

His rhythm deepens and quickens. I'm lost even further into bliss, and I can no longer control my vocals or my body. He has completely taken over, so I manage to close my eyes and open my mouth for...the... most musical, and mangled moan and groaning organism duet I've ever almost heard.

And it feels...fucking glorious!

"Come here, babe." Eros whispers, as he cradles me straddled across his chest, kissing my face.

My breath shutters across his chest as one last trimmer vibrates through my body. Laying there with my eyes closed, I breath in and out of my nose, effectively bringing my heart rate back to normal.

"You, okay?" He whispers into my hair.

"Oh," I whisper chuckling through my slight smile, "Fan-fuckin-tastic." He settles his arms around my waist and squeezes.

"I mean honestly, Eros." I say leaning back to look at him, "What... the...actual...fuck."

Shrugging his shoulders, he smiles that shy smile that I've noticed so many times now.

"I could ask why you are single, but the truth is, I don't care. It's better for me." I prop myself on his chest and finger my way through the curls of his beard.

"How so?" He asks sinking more comfortably into the mattress and bringing his knees up behind me.

Does he really want my answer to that question? I search his face for a hint. His eyes show comfort, content, and wonder, and strength. He reaches up and strokes my face with the back of his fingers, searching my eyes for something of his own. Fuck it. He wouldn't ask if he didn't want to know the truth...at least he *shouldn't* ask. Well...at least don't ask me. Besides, I do remember telling him not to hold back, it's only fair that I do the same. Even still, I like this guy and I want him to know how I feel. How he makes me feel whenever he so much as looks at me.

"Nobody deserves you like I do."

"Is that so?" he asks, smiling. "Nobody?"

"Nobody." I repeat. "You cooked me nachos, so it's kind of a done deal."

"Really?" He asks, lifting his body and shifting me on my side. I settle onto my stomach propping a pillow under my head. Closing my eyes to the soft touch of his finger tracing up and down my spine.

"Really." I say crossing my legs at the ankle. His hand glides down my back and the length of my leg. "Look at you." I continue, "I don't know how it was being with you for other women, but I love you touching me."

His hand stops in mid-rub as he readjusts himself next to me on his side. "You enjoy my body like no man ever has, and I love watching you enjoy me." I close my eye as he tucks a piece of my hair, which at some point slipped from what I thought was a secure bun, behind my ear. Which doesn't stay because it's already frizzy from pool water and magnificent love making. When I blinked open again, a look of worry clouded his chocolate pools that passed for eyes.

"You look like you want to say something but…" Then I stop and think about the number of times I just said the word love, then sigh. "Is this starting to be too much?" I ask softly. The last thing I want is for this to be over with so soon.

"Too much?" He whispers, shock replacing the worry in his eyes, "No. Hell, I'm trying to come to terms with the fact that I can't get enough."

"Is that why you look so worried?" I ask, shifting to my side, facing him."

"I look worried because every minute I spend with you I'm finding it harder and harder to contain myself."

"Why do you want to contain yourself?" I ask knowing the answer, or at least I think I do. Maybe he's used to being the only one falling hard and fast. The idea of someone falling with him may be a scary thought for him, maybe even unbelievable.

"Because I tend to get…intense."

"What's wrong with intensity?"

"It can be intimidating."

"That's true." I say exhaling deeply. I know what he means. I completely understand the accidental art of intimidating someone you like. He's uncomfortable. He needs to do things at his own pace, and I need to show him that whatever he is feeling is welcome.

Maybe I'm being too intense and should pace myself...*sigh*...but that's not me. I except how I feel, when I feel it...and who I feel it for. In this case it's the *who* that makes the *how* and *when* so much more of an adventure.

"Do you need some space?" I ask, searching is eyes, hoping to find the answer no. "I could go home and give you the time to think." I can feel the quiver in my chest rising to my throat, but I swallow it back down.

"Is that what you think?" He asks, creasing his eyebrows and dipping his head backwards.

"That I want you to go?"

"I don't want to make you feel uncomfortable." I have to stop talking or my disappointment is going to leak through my eyes. And that's just going to look stupid.

"Don't go." He tells me, "I just don't want to..."

"You're not scaring me, Eros." I assure him. And that's it, that's his problem. He said as much earlier, or yesterday actually. "You don't scare me. Whatever has you worried...doesn't scare me. How you feel doesn't scare me. Not even a little bit." I pause to make sure my words are getting through to him, "And, just so you know, you don't intimidate me either. I just want you to be yourself. Whatever that means to you, because, so far it's working for me." His answering smile warms me, and I can see him relaxing more. Maybe he just needs reassuring. I can do that...I can do that all day.

"We did make a *fuck society* pact." He remembers snuggling next to me.

"We did." I say cozying into his arms, and finger raking his beard.

"I don't want to break that." He tells me offering me his chin, closing his eyes at the feel of my fingers.

"Good, neither do I." I say lightly scratching his jawline.

His head is tilted back giving me full access, to which I take note of his enjoyment. The way his eyebrows slightly lift when I move further up his jaw.

"I'm falling for you." He whispers. And I stopped all beard play. His eyes open and shift down at me before his head actually shift with it. Is that what has him worried? Falling for me?

"Actually," He continues, "I can honestly say I have completely skipped over *falling and* went straight to loving you."

Fuck me...yes. Honesty is his best quality.

"And that scares you?" I ask. My fingers trail down to his waist.

"Not saying it scares me more."

"I'll tell you what. Say what you feel whenever you feel it." I say watching my fingers trace his side, "Even though, after today, it kind of shows."

"Ya think." He chuckles shaking his head, beaming his amazed eyes down at me. "So," he says pushing my afro away from my face. His thumb and index finger lift my chin up to his.

His eyes scan my face. They're not searching now but admiring me. "In the spirit of *fucking society.*" His tongue smoothed over his lip and nodding his head. "I've loved every minute, of every day since you had the courtesy of running into me Monday morning."

I want to speak but his eyes and thumb caressing my cheek have me momentarily speechless.

"I love watching you." He continues, "And touching you...and talking to you..."

I wasn't wrong about him. He's telling me everything I've already figured out for myself. I lift my fingers back to his beard and caress his mustache smiling at the kisses that touch my fingers.

"Your smile, your hair, your skin and tattoos."

I lean up and softly kiss his lips.

"I love how tall you are." He continues. I kiss him again, rewarding the bravery of speaking his mind, "I love how soft you are." I kiss him again, and his mustache curls in the corner. "I love how you watch me." Another kiss, this time my tongue grazes his closed lips.

"What else." I ask curling my leg around his side. I watch him bite his lip as he drops his eyes to my thigh. Gripping it to pull himself closer to my body. "I love touching you." He's not paying attention anymore, he's too busy watching his hand caress my thigh and calf.

"You said that already." I whisper, arching my back as his hand travels to my ass.

"Did I." He whispers. My hips start to move to the circular motion of his hand. "Some things are worth repeating." He says into my neck. I close my eyes and rub my hand up his biceps. Then inhale softly as he enters me.

"That's it." He whispers softly. His hand is on my thigh as he pulls out and in again, "Just feel it."

A small moan escapes my mouth, and he swallows it with his. "I love how I fit inside of you." His thrust is getting deeper as his erection grows inside me. Delicately touching that spot. Over and over and over until the feeling of small fires spark throughout my body. His moans and words echo throughout my ear adding fuel to the flames of his thrust.

"I love how you respond to me."

We're laying on our sides so every sound he makes. Every word he speaks travels through my body from my ear. With every thrust we make, moans quietly spill over my lips. Every sound he makes causes my body to move to a rhythm that he matches, push for pull.

"Okay." I moan, not being able to think of any other word.

"Yeah?" He responds in my ear.

"Okay." I say again.

"Where is it?" He asks gripping my thigh tighter and speeding up. "Is it here?" He rotates in a different direction, "Or here?" Switching up yet again, refusing to abandon that spot.

"Oh!" I squeal softly.

"There it is." He moans rhythmically, "There it is."

He speaks...I spark.

I spark...I moan.

I moan...he thrust.

"I got it, baby." He moans, "I'll get it for you."

fuuuccckkk…

He speaks…I spark.

I spark…I moan.

I moan…he thrust.

"You ready?" He groans, "Because I'm fucking ready."

And that does it.

He speaks…I spark.

I spark…I shout.

I shout…he explodes.

He explodes…WE ERUPT!

Heavy breathing. Wet kisses. Gasping, and after shock moans.

"Oh, my goodness." I gasp rolling my eyes and reclaiming my leg from his side.

I look over and he's still panting with his knee lifted. His left hand is behind his head and his right is resting on the flat of my belly. By no means am I a virgin. I've had experiences, boyfriends, and an occasional one-night stand. I went into each situation knowing exactly what it was, and what it wouldn't be. This, whatever it is with him. This connection that we have is very much mutual. This feeling that I have is the very first time, out of all my previous situations, that I've felt like he deserves me and all that I am. I place my hand on top of his and he gazes over at me. I can't speak at first. His eyes have me trapped in the truth that I see there, and all of a sudden, every word to every romantic song I've ever heard makes sense. More sense than it's ever made before.

"I love you too." I whisper smiling. His face melts and splits into the furriest grin I've seen on him yet.

The arches of his eyebrows are pointed upward. His hair cascades in waves cropping his face around his jawline.

"Put your eyebrows down." I laugh reaching for his face and placing my index and middle finger on each brow point.

"I can't." He laughs, taking my hand and kissing my palm. "You know this is going to be…" He breathes in through his nose deeply then yawns.

"Yeah, I know." I say, catching his contagiousness.

"Come here." He commands, scooting me over so that he's in the center of the bed. I straddle his hips and he engulf my back in his strong arms pulling my body into his. I rest my face into his neck and breathe deeply...earth, and me and chlorine fill my nose. He squeezes his arms around me and circles his hands on my back before sliding his hands down to cup both butt cheeks.

"This is how I want to sleep." Is the last thing I hear him say. The rubbing and kneading of my ass is the last thing I feel.

Chapter Ten

What the hell? I open my eyes blinking. The room is completely dark. The soft intake and puff of Eros' breathing is the only sound I hear. That and the chirp of a dying battery somewhere. I tried to sit up only to find my arm pinned down by Eros' body. One of us must have shifted at some point. I slowly ease my arm out from under his heavy body, without waking him, then slowly climb from the bed.

Success...he didn't budge. The chirp from the dying battery lights up the screen from his phone, as I make my way over to it. I'm still naked and very much aware that I need to find a bathroom, and fast or my bladder is going to pop. Grabbing his phone, I unplug the auxiliary cord and use it for a flashlight as I search for the closet door where my towel is hanging. I find it and wrap it around me and I'm out the door in search of the facilities. Lucky me I don't have to search hard since it's the first door on the left from the bedroom, and it's huge. The tub can fit at least five people. The shower, which is separate from the tub, is large enough to fit about the same amount. Once I finish, I stand at the sink washing my hands, frowning at my reflection.

My hair looks like a Pterodactyls nest all over my head. It's going to be a bitch to handle. I search the cabinets under the double sided, his and hers sinks, only to find and, not to my surprise, men shampoos and conditioners, and sprays, and... beard oil. I open the small bottle and smell the wonderful woodsy scent that is my favorite '*Eros*' scent. In fact, that's what it's called, '*Woodsy Beard Oil.*' I'll have to google it and find out where he orders it from. I don't find any suitable shampoo or conditioner for myself, but I do come across an elastic hair tie and some bobby pins.

Sending silent shout outs to the man buns all over the world. I do my best to attempt at some kind of '*lady bun*'. Stray stands escape at the back of my neck and along my hair line and sideburns, it's a mess, but a much better mess than before. Now, a charger. His phone is an android so I can plug it into mine since I have no idea where his would be. I search through my overnight bag that's still sitting on the halfmoon shaped sofa, find it, attach it and pause...fawning at the screen saver photo of Emma and myself sitting on the park bench by the pond. SMH, this guy is something else. Refocusing I leave it on the fireplace mantle. It's not as early or as late as I thought it might be. The time on the phone reads 9a.m., which makes me wonder what time we actually got to sleep. I make my way to the kitchen and find a jug of orange juice, and as a habit drink straight from the jug. Smacking my lips as I finish. It's cold, refreshing and just what I needed. Not only because I'm thirsty, but also because I burned off a lot of energy last night...or this morning. I need to replenish.

Last night...was, for lack of better words, a complete pleasure. I've never had someone put so much thought into making me happy. I don't have a best friend to talk to, but if I did, I wouldn't even know where to start. So much has happened since Monday, it would be hard to explain. What would I say? I met a guy four days ago...we hit it off and now we love each other. Normal people wouldn't understand that kind of emotional and mental freedom. They're too stuck on sociological rules and regulations. What's right, what's wrong. When to go, when to stop. When to wait, when not to wait. They spend too much time '*thinking*' about the possibilities of an outcome, instead of the actions that actually make the outcome positive. In other words, they know what they want... just not a lot on how to go about getting it.

And don't get me started on all the atrocious '*social networks*' that's starting to float around the world wide web. Looking at that, humanity is bound to fail. The backyard is just as beautiful now as it was last night, and just as it did last night, the grass calls to me. Adjusting my towel, I make my way to the outdoor kitchen dreading the mess we left behind. And as I expected it is a mess.

This is going to take some focus, so I return to the house and find my tablet that has 96% battery power and plug it into the outdoor outlet by the sink. I select my music app, create a playlist of all jazz and big bands and set to it. Scraping bowls in the trash. Wiping this, wiping that. Then I stopped to adjust my towel yet again. Screw it, I pull it off and find my sweater laying on the back of the chair where I left it. Something's not quite right. I look around at what still needs to be done and realize it's the music. It's too slow and sad, and it more than contradicts how I feel right now. So, I turn it off and select a more upbeat station and start moving and singing quietly along to the words to an indie song from the early two thousands.

This is much better. Some guy banging away at the drums is enough to get me going. Before I know it, I'm finished cleaning and have gathered Eros' pants, boxers, shoes and socks. My jeans with my panties in the pocket, my boots where I left them by the deck and packed them all in the house. I dropped my things by the sofa and Eros' in the dirty hamper that I saw in his bathroom. Back in the living room I find a pair of dark denim skinny jeans, a zip up gray hoodie and lay them to the side for maybe later. With this guy, who knows where the day might lead.

For now, I grab the pair of Star Wars lady boxer briefs that I packed, an off the shoulder t-shirt and whatever else I need for a shower. Without shampoo the most I can do is wet my hair, comb through it and hope for the best. The water is warm and firm on my muscles and feels magical. Pretty soon I'm lost in the steam and singing along to another pop song from the nineties, when I hear the toilet flush. Simultaneously the once warm water goes freezing...I scream and jump back trying to avoid the stream.

"I'm so sorry!" Eros shouts, "I didn't know that would happen."

I find that hard to believe seeing as how he can't stop laughing. I slide open the shower door and step out, all soapy and wet. Laughing despite myself.

"You did that on purpose." I say, gathering my hair so it doesn't drip on the floor too much.

"I didn't...I promise I didn't." He chuckles, "I don't usually flush when I'm in the shower."

"I'll just bet you don't." I pout in mock anger. "Good morning."

"Good morning." He tells me. "I really am sorry."

"It's okay." I tell him, "If I wasn't awake, I am now."

"I'll bet." He's giving me that look-at-you-all-soapy-and-wet look, then leans in for the first kiss of the day.

"I need to rinse off." I tell him in between kisses. Reluctantly he groans and smacks my butt as I step through the shower door.

"Leave it on when you're done." He says with the toothbrush in his mouth. "Did you find everything you needed?"

"Everything but towels." I say stepping out of the shower. I watch him leave the bathroom and re-enter with two towels, one for my hair and one for my body. I wrap myself, top and bottom, then brush my teeth in the second sink. Then pull my razor and shave cream from my toiletries bag and touch up my arm pits, singing along to the end of the pop song playing through my tablet.

"So, what are your plans for the day?" he asks, using the scissors from his shave kit to trim his beard.

"Absolutely nothing." I say around the bristles of my toothbrush, "Vacation...you?"

"This is about it."

"That sounds like a pretty chill day to me." I say catching his smiling eyes in the mirror. Just as I was probably going to say something else, another oldie but goodie that I haven't heard since I was about fourteen, starts playing from my phone. Naturally my first instincts are to take a few moments...and enjoy.

"I'm sorry," I say, smiling as I turn the volume up. I lather my leg with shave cream singing along.

"I was walking down the street when out the corner of my eye I saw a pretty little thing approaching me." I rinse my razor and keep singing, looking at Eros, who's watching me holding his beard trimmers suspended in the air. "She said, I never seen a man who look so all alone, could you use a little company?"

He turns and faces me with pure humor on his face. I've never been shy about making a spectacle of myself and now is no exception. Besides, it's what I always do. True I'm usually alone, but he's either going to see me this way now...or later. "If you pay the right price, your evening could be nice," I continue walking the beat to him and ruffling his chest hair. He is thoroughly amused now, but I'm not finished. "And you can go and send me on my way."

"I said, you're such a sweet young thing, why you do this to yourself? She looked at me and this is what she said."

I walk back to my side of the sink and shave another strip up my leg continuing the song, "Oh there ain't no rest for the wicked. Money don't grow on trees. I got bills to pay, I got mouths to feed, there ain't nothing in this world for free. Oh no I can't slow down; I can't hold back. Though you know...I wish...I could. Oh no there ain't no rest for the wicked, until we close our eyes for good." I continue shaving and singing and dancing like an idiot who just doesn't give a damn. Laughing, because by the time the song is over Eros is singing and dancing right along with me. Like McDonald's, right now, I'm loving it...every split second of it. As if I didn't know this already about Mr.... "Guess", he's just as goofy as I am.

The song finishes with me looking in the mirror shooting imaginary pistols at myself. Eros erupts igniting my own laughter.

"I told you," He says, wrapping his arms around me, "Fun." I'm still wearing my towel, so when he lets go, I have to hurry and clutch it before it drops.

"Where do these go when I'm done?" I ask referring to the towels, as I pack up my toiletries bag. His mustache is curled upward on one side and he's biting his bottom lip. "Laundry basket." He tells me, dropping the basketball shorts he's wearing to his ankles. He's watching me. Watching my reaction. To which I don't disappoint. My eyebrows lift and my mouth drops in a gasp. I'm going to have to get used to him just dropping his pants all the time...I'm sure I probably won't though.

Okay Ayo, you've had your fill now get yourself together.

"Nice." I say, nodding my head, removing my towels and dropping them in the basket, then walking out without a look back, making a mental note to explore his tattoos later.

By the time Eros finishes in the bathroom, I've finished oiling my body with coco-butter, and have managed to yank and pull my hair back into a bun and is sitting at the far end of the bar table searching the web for his brand of beard oil while eating a bowl of cereal. The thing is, I'm sitting here, minding my own business...when *he* walks in with a towel draped over his shoulder drying his hair with one hand. I sit back in the bar stool styled chair and just take a moment to observe.

First of all, the calf length pants that he's wearing should be illegal. Not to mention, they're sweatpants material, which in my opinion, are some sort of payback to women for wearing sun dresses. The way they fit around his waist, only partially exposing the band of his underwear, should be enough to charge him with unnecessary sexiness...or something. His back is completely covered with one intricately detailed black, gray and highlighted scene. The top of his back just below his neck, from shoulder to shoulder are storm clouds that float mid-way down his back fading into the background. From rib cage to rib cage, is the most fantastically detailed three sail wooden ship, braving the choppy storm waters of the sea. At the bottom of the water, a masterfully blended anchor and compass. On the lower back are the words...'*Lost but still grounded*', neatly scrolled.

I watch the way his back muscles stretch and pull as he trades the box of cereal that I left on the counter for a different brand, then pours his milk. The water and the ship actually look as though they're moving... navigating its way through the sea storm engraved in his skin. Even the tiny little silhouetted sailor seems to be anxiously fighting for a safe return home. I don't even bother diverting my attention, or looking away when he turns around. Hell, how can I... his front is even more captivating. His left arm is a full sleeve covering from shoulder to wrist of an angel wing. Each feather is individually detailed.

I am fully aware that he's watching me, so I stuff my spoon in my mouth, shake my head and finally look up at his eyes. Which are lit up with humor.

"Well?" He asks, pouring more cereal. I pick up my bowl, drink the milk from it and walk over next to him and wash it and my spoon.

"It's working for me." I say smiling, as I dry my bowl.

"What else is working for you?" He asks. I look back and he's leaning on the island counter. When he notices that I'm done with my task, he takes the couple of steps over to the sink. Dump the rest of his cereal down the disposal then wash his bowl.

The part that has me smiling is, I was not in his way...what-so-ever, but that didn't stop him from placing his gentle touching hand on my hip and sliding me between him and the sink, from one side to the other.

"Excuse me." He says softly, proudly wearing his half-smile. He dries his bowl, places it in the cupboard, then spots his spoon on the other side of me. "Excuse me again." He says, replacing his hand on my backside, squeezing it and pulling me into his groin before sliding me over.

I can't control my smile. This man just has a way of pulling it out of me. He stretches over me and drops the spoon in the dish drain, looking down at me the entire time. I can smell his fragrant beard oil and it's intoxicating and hypnotic.

"I love you." He whispers after sweetly planting a kiss on my nose.

"Oh, that's definitely working for me." I say smiling bigger.

"You like that, huh?" He asks, humor still in his face but also genuine curiosity.

"Absolutely." I tell him, stepping over to the island and hoisting myself on top of the surface. I'm eye to eye with him now, because I want him to see the same truth in me, that I see in him. I need him to see that. I reach my hand out for him and pull him between my legs, resting my arms loosely around his shoulders. Grazing my fingers through the hair at the nape of his neck.

"Love," I begin, gazing into his eyes, "Is the purest form of human emotion we have. So many other emotions try to imitate and disguise themselves as love, but at the end of the day it won't hold a candle, because it'll eventually be exposed for what it truly is." I pause to see if he's following me. When I'm sure of it I continue. "Some people aren't capable of loving because they are too caught up in the formality of things. They have a hard time accepting that *this is it*. They get so infatuated with how things are *supposed* to be, that they lose focus on how they *want* things to be."

I pause a second time, hoping I'm making sense and trying to find my next words. "People like us are selfish enough to know exactly what we want, how we want to go about getting it, and we're smart enough to recognize when we have it. The problem is people like us seem to always come across those that make us feel that words like '*intense*' and '*intimidating*' are bad words. Well to me, intense is just another word for '*strong*' or '*powerful*', and intimidating is just a weapon others try and use when they don't take the time to understand the person that's standing right in front of them."

"You know...I've heard people say, '*he makes me feel ten feet tall*'...or '*she makes me feel like I can touch the sky*'. Well, I don't know what those kinds of things feel like. And though I've never had any confidence problems or complexes, I am very happy and confident in saying, you make me feel like I'm six foot three."

He smiles at me as he rubs his tailored nails up and down my bare thighs. "I'm not walking away from this, because I *want* to keep feeling like this, and I want *you* specifically to make me feel this way."

"Wow." He says after a few minutes of silence.

"I know." I say looking away from his eyes, "I tend to get long winded at times. You'll have to stop me when I do."

"Stop you?" He repeated, returning the squeeze around his neck with a squeeze around my waist. "If I didn't know it came off the top of your head, I would ask you to repeat it."

"Well," I say leaning back, "Love...is...a... pure???" And I crack up at his, '*is she really going to do it?* -face. "Nah, I'm just playing, I can't do it." I laugh, wrapping my arms around his neck, leaning my forehead into his, "But I do mean it, though. I mean every single word of it. The only reason I'm thrilled about you loving me is because I'm pretty sure you deserve all the love that I can give in return."

"Is that right?" He said, removing his arms and crossing them over his chest, "Just so you know, I may need to hear that again from time to time."

"Don't worry about it," I say, sliding off the counter. "I got you."

"Do you?" He asks, planting both hands on either side of my hips, and rubbing his junk on the print of my vag wedgie, that I'm trying to pull out. I have no idea what his face looks like, but I can imagine. In my mind he's sucking on his bottom lip, with his eyebrows dipped in the center. A look of seduction and concentration all mixed up into one. A look that I've come to adore in the last few days. I, on the other hand, am too focused on the fact that in order to rub me...where he's rubbing me, he only had to adjust his height a little lower.

'Humm.' I think to myself. I'm pretty sure I packed a pair of four inch, 'just in case we get dressed up and step out' heels and I'm pretty sure I stuffed them in the bottom of my bag. I wonder if I was to put my heels on, how much would he have to adjust his height.

"What?" He asks, sensing my distraction.

"Excuse me sir." I say, pressing my fingertips into his chest to nudge him backwards.

"What is it?" He asks again, stepping to follow me.

"Don't move." I say pointing at him. I found my shoes in the bottom of my bag where I thought they might be, and walked back to the kitchen.

"Are you...okay?" Eros shouts. The tone of his voice drops a few octaves on the last word as I reenter the kitchen, and his eyes drop to the shoes in my hand.

"I just want to see something." I say positioning myself back between him and the island. I place my hand on his bare side and lift my foot to my shoe, then drop it and do the same to the other. "Look at that." I say looking down at our groins. "Look at how perfect we line up."

He may be looking, I don't know, but I am. I watch his hips move back and forth into my vag-print and can imagine him sliding in and out of me. As curious as I am, I want to take this little experiment of mine a step further. I drop my shorts and spread my legs slightly apart, stepping my shoes on the outside of his bare feet. Now that I'm in position, I pull his joggers and boxers down just below his junk and watch myself tenderly slide my middle finger between my "lips down under' down to the hole.

I'm very ready. "Look at that." I say softly. The wetness swallows my finger greedily, and I hiss looking up at this magnificent man staring down at me with the most pleasant look of bewilderment that I have ever seen.

"I want to try something else." I say sucking my juices off my finger. His mouth opens as he licks his lips.

Wrapping my fingers around his erection, I begin to slowly stroke back and forth, watching him unfold. I'm throbbing at the feeling of him getting harder in my hand and at the sound of air hissing in his teeth. He likes it. He doesn't need to say it, but I want him to

"Is this working for you?" I whisper, still stroking. The kiss on my shoulder confirms his yes. I'm stroking him with my right hand, so I place my left hand on his side to stop his slow back and forth movement.

Still stroking, I look down and watch myself, rub the head of his penis between my lips and over my clit, moistening it with my wetness. *Oh, he needs to see this.*

"Look at us." I whisper, breathy, allowing a small moan as I lean back to give him a full view at what I'm doing. I rub myself a couple more times, then open my fist and allow his manhood the privilege of a full stroke, but not allowing him to enter me yet. I close my fist again and commence to rubbing my clit. His face dips down to my lips, but he doesn't kiss me.

"I'm going to tell you when to go, and when to stop. Okay?"

He nods, unable to speak. I position him inside of me, just enough to allow the tip to disappear, then move my hips from side to side.

"Go once." I whisper. And he does, but he holds it there a little longer than I expected, so I use my left hand to push him back, collapsing my hand around 'it', as he pulls out. He is juicy with my wetness and I like the feel of me using the head to rub a circular sensation that is beginning to spread throughout my body. I make the tip disappear again, marveling at the perfect way we line up.

"Go again…three times." I instruct and he fulfills.

"Fuuuck." He whispers on the third pump.

"Stop."

I pleasure myself with his head watching him, watch my hand movement.

"You ready, love." I ask, lining up our body parts.

"How many times?" he asks, biting my bottom lip.

I balance my weight with my arms by gripping the edge of the island and wrap my right leg around his waist.

"I want it all." I say, looking into his eyes. He places his hand on my thigh, helping me balance. I relax my head back revealing at the jumping and twitching of his length inside of me, just as his beard, lips and tongue touch my neck.

"Go." I say, and smile at the feeling and the sound of our love.

"Those are my new favorite shoes." Eros states, with his face still buried in my neck. "Anytime you feel like trying something, you just let me know."

"Will do sir," I laugh, stepping out of my shoes and picking up my shorts. "So what time are we going to see Emma?" I say.

I ask this as I'm on my way to the half-moon sofa, smiling to myself. I just treated him like a piece of meat, and he liked it, *and* it was awesome. Jeez, even a little 'afternoon delight' is mind blowing with him.

"We're not." I hear him say as he's walking into the dining area where I started my breakfast. "Thursdays are her spa days. I found this place that will go and pamper some of the ladies. So, all morning she'll be getting her hair washed and curled and whatever else goes on in beauty spas."

He's sitting on one of the stool chairs with his bare feet propped up on the chair railings. His back is leaning onto the table and his left arm is resting on the high back.

"Eros, that's pretty awesome." I say shifting my shoes to the bottom of the bag.

"It's a lot easier this way." He tells me. I pull on my lady boxer briefs and sit cross legged on the floor.

"On Fridays, there's a restaurant that comes in and caters dinner for those that can make it to the dining room. It's a tax write off for them, so they pull out all the stops. They have menus and a wine list, and a cover band and all."

"So, Thursdays is *spa day,* and Friday is date night?" I say swooning on the inside, smiling at such a romantic idea. Golden Heights isn't a long-term nursing facility in the same sense as a facility like mine, where a majority of our residents are disabled in some way or living life with the changes of dementia. It's a retirement community, so a lot of the residents still get around well and still do most things for themselves. So being able to do something that they've done their entire lives is pretty major.

"Some of the men will even get up and have a dance with their wives...or dates, for that matter."

"Dates?"

"Yeah. Some of them have lost their significant others so they're back on the market."

"Aww." I swoon, stretching out on the carpet and rubbing my hands through its softness. "So, what do you usually do on Thursdays and Fridays?"

I watch him walk around the sofa and flop down, half sitting and half laying. "Thursdays I usually do whatever. But Fridays I usually have dinner with Emma."

I'm lying on the floor with my eyes closed making snow angles in the soft fluffy carpet and freeze mid-motion.

'*Did he just...?*'

"So..." I say turning my head to see him better, "So every Friday you take your mom to dinner and dancing."

"Um-hum." he says, nodding his head casually. Then he just sits there like this is something all sons do. I get on all four and crawl over to his side and hover over his face. He pulls his hand forward and coils his finger around the loose hair of my sideburn.

"That's the sweetest thing I've ever heard." I say leaning into his touch. His eyes are looking over my face, then rest on my lips. He wants to kiss me, I can tell. His tongue skims his bottom lip leaving it slightly moist.

I lean closer to him and notice his breathing increase, but he doesn't move up to meet me, so I move closer to him and press my kiss to his lips. His hand is on the nape of my neck caressing it lightly. I kiss him again, slightly opening my mouth so our tongues can play. Roping and snaking and pressing into each other. We sit there, him lying on the sofa, me sitting on the floor beside him on my knees. Leaning over his face...making out. I haven't done anything like this since high school. He even successfully makes it to second base...*under* the shirt. Twisting and teasing my nipple, pressing my mouth closer to his. I'm not usually into nipple play because it's more of a visual thing for me. I enjoy watching it, seeing as how I don't usually feel anything from it. But I guess, with all the kissing and him caressing my neck, it's getting to me. His passion is getting deeper, and his caress is getting firmer...so I pull back.

"You keep that up and I might let you get to third base." I say smiling into his eyes. His mouth pops open in mock surprise.

"You want to go dancing with me tomorrow?" he asks, skimming the skin of my arm. His voice is quieter, and I wonder if he thinks I would say no.

"I would love to." I tell him, smiling at the way his eyes light up. I have to say, I really hope I never get used to Eros being shy. It's adorable and such a contradiction to how his touch feels. "Except, I don't have a date. You already have a dance partner."

"I think I can find you someone worthy." Now it's my turn to drop my mouth, feigning surprise.

"You're going to loan me out?" I say laughing, "Pimp me out?"

"Don't worry we'll get top dollar for you." He laughs blocking my playful smack to his chest.

I like this...hanging out...goofing off. The only other guys I've ever done this with were my brothers. Well...not exactly like this. His finger rubs my lips and I give it a quick kiss, then an even quicker bite. He gasps then pulls his finger back.

"You bit me." He tells me, looking from his finger then back at me. I gasped, shocked and appalled at his accusation.

"I'm so sorry." I say kissing the hairless part of his neck tenderly. Running my fingers over each kiss mark. Then biting the flesh of his chest. Not a hard bite. It was more playful than anything. He gasps and moves to an upright position.

"You bit me again." He says pointing at the place on his neck. Trying unsuccessfully to be stern. His face is firm but slowly the curl of his mustache twists upward on one side. I position myself on my knees in between his legs.

"You should apologize to me...now."

Oh, I can get used to this kind of foreplay. He tilts his head back giving me access to the area I just assaulted.

"I'm very sorry for biting you." I say sweetly, smiling at how a simple kiss on a finger has turned into a game of teasing.

"You should also kiss it and make it better." He demands, pointing to the spot.

I brace my hands on his thighs, lean into his neck and kiss the finger he's pointing with. Which is the same finger I bit before. I glance up at his eyes then slide my mouth all the way down the base of his knuckle and back up. Making a slurping sound on the tip of his finger. His forehead creases and his mouth drop open, just a tad. My half smile is back...kudos to mister concrete chest. Two hundred and fifty points for keeping his composure. Then, I kiss the spot he's pointing at.

"I'm sorry." I whisper again, parting my lips and lightly sucking. His hand curls around my ass and squeezes, then I delicately giggle.

"Um...good girl." He tells me musically. I smile against his skin... then bite him again.

"Ah!" He gasps.

I collapse into him laughing, then scream through my laughter. He's way too quick for me. Before I know it, I'm being jolted down on the soft fluffy carpet where I was just making snow angels. He's leaning on me poking my side with his finger, or at least trying to. For the most part, I keep batting his hands away.

"We don't bite people." He says, poking me with every word laughing at me squirming. I try to fight him, but I'm way too ticklish and I'm laughing too hard, so he succeeds at pulling my shirt up. Exposing my belly and blowing raspberries into my stomach, over and over.

I scream with laughter. My father's never even done that. He does it again, but this time I flip my body over and try to get away.

"Stop." I shout through my laughing and squealing.

"Where you going?" He laughs, straddling me and pinning me down with my hands beside my head. I've been through this before with my brothers, but it was never this much fun.

"You can't get away." He tells me to grind my butt. He leans into my body, close to my good ear. I really must stop leaving that ear exposed.

"I love touching you." He hisses sucking my ear lobe into his mouth. A purr escapes my throat. Oh, he has discovered a new toy and I think he likes it. My hips start rotating with his grind.

"This ear is my favorite body part of yours."

The fires are starting to ignite and once again I try and move, feeding off his still playful spirit, but he holds me down tight.

"Where you going?" he asks again, taking a long, rotating grind. His voice travels straight to where his erection is pressing into me. "Hum? You can't get away."

Side bar: His almost dirty talk in my ear is becoming my favorite thing about him.

I moan and arch my back. My clit is once again throbbing, and begging for some friction, but even so, feeling quite delicious. It's a struggle but I manage to turn over beneath him.

"Um." He growls, looking down at himself poking my vagina through my briefs.

He looks up leaning in to kiss me, mimicking his thrust...one kiss for each thrust. Nibbling and finding his way to my ear.

"I bet you're wet right now."

"Stop." I moan, hissing out the 'ssss', like my teacher taught me when I learned what sound *S* made.

"Stop?" He says, "Let's see if you really want me to." His body weight shifts, and he cups my breast under my shirt. Then wraps his warm mouth around my nipple and gently sucks making a smacking sound.

"Sssstop." I moan, squirming under him, still rotating with his grind. I moan a loud gasp at the feel of his mouth on my ear.

"Don't you wish I was in you? Touching that spot that makes you squeal." He says each part as a match to his thrust, fueling my desire.

Side bar: Back in my younger days people would call this *'clothes burning'*.

Fuck this man. My body is on fire, aching for more of him...all of him. But this game of stop, but you better not stop, is fun and exciting.

"Eros, stop." I moan musically, smiling at the feeling. Yes, yes yes...I like his idea of *intensity*.

"You want me to stop?" He asks again, kissing my chin. I don't respond so he leans beside my ear, "Do you want me to stop?" He asks again.

This man has trailed his hand down my belly and is inside my briefs rubbing circles into my clit, slowly easing two fingers inside. My eyes are blazing at him, as I begin to grind his fingers. My half smile is back and once again I whisper *stop*. Then suck air into my mouth, slowly moving my hips to match his finger rotation. Oh, I am lost on this pleasure trip.

"You don't want me to stop, do you?" I try to say no, but a wickedly weird moan comes out instead. And out again...and again.

Was that the doorbell?

His hand immediately stops, and his eyes grow wider than I've ever seen them.

And there's that fucking doorbell again.

"But no!" I say whining and holding his hand in place. I mean, whining like a three-year-old toddler that's about to have her favorite doll taken. His eyes are alive with humor. He is enjoying this way too much. "Keep going." I urge, or at least I try.

"Someone's at the door." He laughs, looking quickly at the door then back at me.

"But I was right *there*!" I say pouting and purring at the gliding sensation of his fingers exiting me. Then I watch his fingers disappear into his mouth, then slowly appear.

"Get the eff outta here!" I say, growling through squeezed thighs and gritted teeth. And when I say I growled...I mean I *growled*...deep from the bottom of my throat growl. Which couldn't be too intimidating because Eros erupts into laughter.

"Come on, dear." He tells me, "We've got company."

Chapter Eleven

I reach for his outstretched arms and use him as a brace to pull myself up.

And there it goes again...dumbass doorbell.

"That's okay." I say matter-of-factly, playfully snatching my bag up. "I'm about to go finish myself." His arms drop to his side, his chin slumps to the ground, I think pulling his head down a little with it.

Doorbell again.

By the time he glances in that direction and back at me I have my middle finger in my mouth lightly sucking it. Sliding it in and out of my mouth. Smiling as deviously as I possibly can.

"You better not." Eros says, pointing his massive finger in my direction. I wave my fingers at him and turn to sway down the hall. The last thing I hear is him whisper shouting my name chuckling, then cursing the doorbell, before I disappear into the bathroom.

I imagine him stomping his foot and crossing his arms over his chest. And for that...fifty points taken from you...and given to me. In the mirror I smooth out my hair, retwist my bun and splash water on my face. I reach into my bag and use my rag and towel from before, give my lady parts a quick wipe down, then pull on a pair of jeans and give myself one last glance. Welp...there's not too much more that I can do to myself. His words of, 'We've got company', keep wanting to ring out in my head, but I won't let it. Although it *was* really sweet of him to consider me as more than just a guest in his home. Really, if I think about...no. I won't think about it, because it makes sense. We already love each other. His mother already tells people I'm his wife. Oh, fuck it. It is what it is. His house is mine and my house is his.

'Okay Ayo, let's go meet your new friends.'

I leave the bathroom, drop my bag off in his room and head down the hall giving my hair one last smooth pat around the edges. Then I freeze.

"I just thought this was like any other time." It's a woman's voice speaking. "You know? You say it's over, then I show up and we talk it out."

"Why didn't you call?" Eros asks.

"I did." She responds, "Your phone went to voicemail." *Voicemail?* I plugged his phone up this morning. It must've died and he didn't bother turning it back on.

"Stop." I hear him say, sounding nothing like he did just moments ago. "Carrie...stop." Eros says again. "You need to leave."

I turn around and go back to his room, grab my bag and my keys from the side pocket, swallow the lump in my throat and walk back to the front room.

"Listen E." She coos. "We always…" And then she stops. Her hands are on his chest...*my* chest. She's toe to toe with him looking up into his face staring into those eyes that bleed chocolate. She's not the right height for him. She's way too short. Her eyes are on me, and she can't tear them away. Then he turns his entire body towards where I'm standing.

So many emotions plague his face, all at once and I can't tell which comes first. There's guilt, and I'm guessing it's because she's here, but there's no need to be guilty about that. He had no idea she was coming over...I hope. Then there's sympathy, and again...no need to apologize. I know all about unaccepting exes, that just aren't ready to say goodbye for good. I also see confusion. That's definitely because I have my bag and my keys in my hand, and now clarity. He's figured out that I'm leaving, and his eyes are pleading now, probably because he thinks I'm leaving for good. To be honest...I'm not really sure what I'm doing. All I know is that the atmosphere is thick and uncomfortable in the most awkward way... and I gotta get away from it. Seeing as how we just met, the thing that he hasn't yet had the chance to learn about me is that other women aren't something that gets under my skin. So, he has nothing to worry about.

Mainly because, one...I don't really like competing for someone's attention. And two...it always turns out being a huge waste of time. If I can't be seen for who I am, then I don't really want to be seen.

"Hello." I say with my hand out towards her. "I'm Ayo."

She's stumped. She can't even speak, and it clearly takes her a minute to gather her thoughts.

"I'm sorry..." She finally says, taking my hand in hers, "I'm..."

"Carrey." I say, "I know I heard." I look at Eros and his hands are in the pockets of his sweats, and he's looking at me with...*really? Humor*...now?

Look at this, Eros wants to play. Well...usually I'm game, but this isn't the time and he has unfinished business to handle.

"Actually," Miss Thing says, perking up. "I'm his girlfriend."

She leans into his side and places her hand on the flat of his belly. Honestly, it's kind of cute how she's trying to intimidate me by staking her claim. She's so short, she hasn't even noticed that he hasn't taken his eyes off me. I don't even have to look at him to know that. I can feel his eyes all over me. My half smile is involuntary, and my voice to me is the kind of sweet my mother used to have with me when I used to ask her if I could go and live in the woods behind our house. That tone that aunties use when they say, 'bless your heart.' Of course, I was six...this poor woman is an adult and still has no clue.

"Actually, sweetheart, you're not."

She...is...appalled! She can't believe what's happening here. Or why Eros, her *boyfriend*, is following me to the door, leaving her standing there to watch.

"Don't leave." He tells me. His eyes are drawing me completely in. Pleading me. Begging maybe.

"I'm not leaving, I'm just going home." I tell him. "You need some space here." Just as I did on day one when saying goodbye to his mom, I lean around him and say my goodbyes to his *friend*. But this time, I place my fingers in his chest hair, leaning more into him...then around.

His hands find what seems to have become their place...one at the curve of my hip and the other on the small of my back. "It was nice meeting you, Carrey." Aww...poor thing, she has tears.

Wait...that's actually pretty sad. But, as always, I'm way too selfish to care. She had her chance; she may have blown it.

Maybe...maybe not.

I look at Eros, sigh, lean up and tenderly kiss his lips. He squeezes my hip and grip his fingertips into my back and breathes in deeply through his nose.

"I won't be long." He says into my eyes.

"Take all the time you need." I tell him.

"I love you." He whispers.

Why is he whispering?

"I know." I say swallowing that lump again. I turn to leave but he holds me tight, refusing to look away.

Jeeze, I get it...stop looking into my eyes...

"I love you." He tells me again, this time louder. His eyes are urging me again, pleading. They look almost painful.

Goodness gracious...this man, this man, this man.

"I love you too." I say. I want to look away from him, but I can't, at least not before that one damn tear skates down my cheek. Fuck, now I look just as pitiful as she does.

He caresses my face with his thumb drying my tear.

Leave now, Ayo...go! I turn my head away from him, and then the rest of my body. Go down the steps, Ayo. Don't you dare look back! I coach myself all the way home...well at least that's what my plan is. The time on my dash says 2:45 p.m..... I wonder how long he's going to be?

No! No! No! I need to change the subject of my thoughts.

What do I feel like eating tonight?

I feel like some Sushi.

Do I have Sushi ingredients? Actually, I do.

Enough for two people?

No... I might not need it for two.

What if he doesn't come?

Dammit Ayo, **stop it**!

I reach over and switch the radio on. Music. My single most appreciated sanctuary. Music has never let me down. Sometimes I have to go through a bunch of songs before that *one* is found. The one that expresses my feelings exactly or enhances my mood. Or like this one that just came on. Talking about loving somebody like she's gonna lose them. Holding somebody like they're saying goodbye, because they'll never know when they'll run out of time.

'*Son-of-a-bitch*!' I think to myself, actually more like I'm scolding myself. '*Your cocky...overconfident...way too conceited ass just walked out on your heart. Left him in the hands of another woman. Another woman that loves him just like you do.*'

Wait a minute...love him? Like I do? Not possible. If she did, she would never have gone a day without showing him or telling him. There would've never been enough space between them for me to fit in. Or any woman, for that matter. What if she realizes what she lost...what if he realizes that he still wants to be with her.

No! I hate this 'what if' shit! It's fucking torture. So, here's what I'm going to do. I'm going to the supermarket for more Sushi ingredients... for two. Why...because I fucking want to. There's no other reason good enough. Then, I'm going home, I'm going to shower...wash my hair. Then jam...jam for as long as I need to. I'll deal with my feelings when he shows up...if he shows up.

I named all of those things like it helped. Going to the grocery store didn't miraculously speed time up or anything like that. By the time I finished, it was only five minutes after four. Knowing that, only made me wonder about how much time he was going to need. I mean, he said he wasn't going to be long, but how long...is long? I'll never admit it outloud, but I'm finding myself walking a little faster through the store, lightweight rushing to get home. Just in case he shows up and I'm not there.

There I go again...*shut up, Ayo.* What if he still wants what they had? Shampoo couldn't wash those thoughts out of my head, no matter how hard I scrubbed. What if she's comforting him right now, all because I walked out?

Images of him looking at her the same way he looks at me. That look he gives me right before he kisses me. Argh...I must stop this. It's madness! I need a real distraction, and blow drying my hair into its full length afro ain't helping one bit. For a split second, I think i might be losing my mind, because I think for that same split second, I could've sworn I heard the doorbell. I even pause with the blow dryer in one hand suspended in the air, and a pick partially pulled through my hair... listening. And there it goes again. This time I'm sure I'm not tripping, and automatically, I damn near throw the dryer in the sink, and rush to the front door. Pausing just before I reach the top of the stairs. Cursing myself for acting like a twelve-year-old little girl running to see the boy she's secretly crushing on.

Taking a deep breath, I head down the stairs casually making my way to the front door. Only to find that it's just my older brother Franky.

"Well...look at that fro."

"Not today, Franky. I say walking away, leaving him to close the door behind himself. He's been here before so he's definitely not a guest.

"Not today?" Franky stops in his tracks, "We've been planning this for months."

Planning what? I take two beer cans from the fridge and toss one to my brother. He's the one right above me, and though I'd never tell him, he's my most favorite.

"*Oh shit.*" I say, now I remember. Frank had an idea for a song. Our plan was to order food and spend the day putting the puzzle pieces together. I told him today, because I wanted to take a few days to myself. This may be just what I need. A major distraction.

"I'm sorry." I admit, "I got distracted, but we're good."

"We're good?" He confirms.

"Yeah." I nodded, noticing that the front door was locked. Franky locked it behind himself, so I reach around him, and casually unlock it. He might show up. He might not. "We're good."

"Good, because I think it's going to be great when it comes together. Plus, I was gone fuck you up."

He is oblivious of my mood. Rattling on and on about...something, I don't know. On the way to the studio listening to his idea, I'm becoming intrigued and anxious to get started. Building a beat takes focus and I'm in need of that right now. Some good old fashion *focus*. We discuss sounds and rhythms and everything else that make up a song. Then we get started on the next thing...the instruments that make up the sounds he wants to hear. Then we put our brains together and try to figure out where to place those sounds. At what speed, and...

"What the hell is on your mind?" Franky asks, stopping the music we've already worked on.

"What're you talking about?" I ask. Hell, I thought I was doing pretty good. I seem to be focusing...engaging in conversation...showing initiative and doing a good job at it.

He doesn't even have to say anything, he just gives me that, *'girl please'* look.

"I'm fine." I tell him, avoiding his disbelieving eyes. He's going to get the truth out of me but judging by the size of the knot in my throat, a few more moments of stalling will do me some good. "I'm just waiting on someone, that's all." I'm standing behind my keyboard, soundlessly fingering the notes to that part of the music.

"And we all know how you and waiting *don't* get along." He looks at me from behind my drum set, "I mean you've only looked at the door seventeen times."

"Have I? I don't think that's true."

"Oh, it's true." He tells me, leaning his back against the wall. "So, what is it about the person you're waiting on?"

"He's a guy I ran into Monday." I tell him smiling to myself about how literally that statement is.

"Are you waiting for him to *call*...or...*come over?*"

"Yes."

"What?" My brother asked blankly. "What does that mean?"

"Franky, can we just get back to work?"

"Sure. We can do whatever you want to do?" He replied, tilting his head slightly to the side, "Can you get focused?"

Sighing heavily, I roll my eyes and nod my head.

"*Girl no, nun-uh*." Frank said, stepping from behind the drums, and motioning me to follow him to the couch. "You *are not* about to put your stanky vibes all over my dope ass track. Come here, come sit with me."

I reluctantly drop my head and slump my way to the love seat where Franky is now sitting.

"Oh, my goodness girl, look at you." He tells me, handing me a box of tissues from the small coffee table, "You are a mess. Do you not want him here?"

"No, that's not it." I say blinking away a tear. Franky always asks the wrong *and* right questions. "I do want him here."

"Okay...alright." My brother says, nodding his head. "Now we're getting somewhere. Tell me about him."

Sighing again, I wipe away the tear that has escaped and is rolling down my cheek. Franky wants to know about him, so I tell him. Every detail, sparing him the explicit details but still being transparent.

"So let me ask you this..." He says when I'm done, "Did you feel good about your decision to leave?"

"I did at first..." I admit, wiping another tear, "Now, not so much."

"*Not so much??*" He repeated, reaching for his drink on the table. I'm just going to shake my head no, because if I speak now, the floodgates will open completely.

"Listen Sis. You've made it this far in life not second guessing yourself. Don't start now."

It's the simplest advice anyone can give, and it makes so much sense.

"Do you love him?" Franky asks.

"Yes." I admit, "Is that weird?"

"What, that you love him only after a few days of meeting him?"

"Well, yeah." I say, clearing my throat.

"For you...no, it's not weird at all." He tells me laughing, "And judging by the parents that raised you...hell raised us, it makes perfect sense. Does he love you?"

"Yes." I say, taking a deep breath, remembering his eyes from earlier on his porch.

"How do you know?"

"He's told me so." I say, leaning onto the back of the chair, suddenly feeling ridiculously stupid as hell.

"Then that's all that matters." Franky says matter of factly. "So, you can clear the tears...quit being a punk. I taught you better than that. If he shows up, he shows up. If he don't...then that's on him. But, trust me, if he's anything like you say. He'll be here."

He's so straight to the point, like me, that's why we get along the best. He knows exactly when to give it to me straight with no chaser, and it's always on time.

"Now," He says, dusting off my somber mood, "Can we get back to work." And with that, my head is in the game. Focus is my first name. Before I know it, the room is full of the sweetest melody and rhythm I have ever had the pleasure of listening to. Everything about the song is complete except the drum beat. At this point all we have to do is sit back and just listen, and I must say, everything came together nicely. Once I got focused, I could see exactly where Frank was trying to go with his idea. And man let me tell you, it went to a nice, comfortable place.

I'm sitting behind my drums eating a slice of the pizza we ordered, smiling at the results of our focus. Aside from being excited about what he wants to do with the drum line, listening to my brother's voice puts me in the mind of how the love child of Michael McDonald and Rick Astley may sound. He has a perfect mashup of the smooth tone, richness and control, paired with a rhythmic beat. The melody makes you want to sit back and just lightly sway your head. I'm behind my drum set with my back up against the wall, and my foot propped up on the rim of my bass drum and my head is resting on the wall. I'm so proud of our hard work, and I'm even more proud that it was all done in my very own studio.

This is my sanctuary space. Right here in this room. When I'm in here I don't have to do anything else but think about music. See music, hear music...love music. It's what I understand the most, the sense of freedom that comes over me, and how I can completely get lost in it. I fell in love with it many, many years ago. So being able to still play and get lost in it teaches me how to just...breath. Because sometimes...for some reason, I actually forget how to do the one thing that seems to be the simplest.

Franky gives me a thumbs up signaling that it was time to get started on the part that is my most favorite part of any song...the drum beat. My first love. The only thing that just comes out of me on its own. I put my pizza down and pick up my sticks smiling at how excited I still get right before I play. I look at Frank and freeze...he's here. I exhale what seems to be the entire oxygen contents of my lungs, which is kind of funny seeing as how I didn't even realize that I was holding my breath.

He's just standing there with his hands in the pockets of his sweatpants. Super casual like he's been standing there the entire time. I can't look away from him. His eyes just...paralyze me. Then the fucker winks at me, smiling, but just slightly. I want to go to him, but Franky is here, so it's best that I don't. Because I'm pretty sure that, when the time comes, I'm going to lose control in that man's arms...and it's going to be spectacular. I look at Franky just as he's turning back to me with this, what did I tell you, you look on his face.

I watch my brother get up and shake Eros' hand, say something in his ear. Then pat him on his back. He looks at me, using hand gestures, to politely tell me he's going to step out. I nod my head and laugh at how he's pretending to cover his genitals and bouncing from tip toe to tip toe. Indicating in the most not so subtle way, that he has to pee. I give two very sarcastic thumbs up. Thankfully the music was loud enough to drown out my voice when I call him a very subtle man. Laughing he puts his hand by his ear motioning me to repeat what I said, then waves me off in a 'never mind' kind of way. Then rushes out of the room towards the bathroom.

Not wasting any time, I slide from behind my drums and casually stroll over to him, step up to his body and look directly into his eyes. I must be cautious of the fact that my brother will be back any minute. Eros seems to be aware of the same thing because his vibe mimics mine.

I lean in to hear him talking into my good side. His hand is on the small of my back holding me close to him. It's a casual distance but it feels like anything but, for one, his voice is doing it's usual act on my senses.

"I got here as soon as I could."

I want to say okay, because now that he's here it's okay...only because of the fires that his voice on *that* side ignites...I can't. It'll only come out as a moan and judging by the way his face brightens up when he notices my stifled reaction, he knows it. I just nod my head trying to control my half smile and be composed about it, because on the inside I'm laughing a bubbly laugh. Catching me a little off my guard, he places his hands on my hips and leans his forehead into mine.

All I can do is lightly grip his wrist and breath in his woodsy beard oil and stand there...breathing. We're okay. Nothing else matters. Frank comes back into the room, and we separate. The music stops as the song ends, providing momentary silence.

"You ready?" Frank asks, taking advantage of the quiet.

"Let's get it done." I say, stretching my neck by rolling my head around, stretching myself as loose as possible. I need to feel limber, so I won't be so stiff. I stretch my arms over my head holding my stix in one hand. I cross them one at a time over my chest stretching my side slowly until I feel the light crack inside.

I take notice that Eros is stepping closer to where I'm standing, so I turn my back to him offering him my clasped fist. He knows this routine, he's an athlete so he doesn't need me to tell him what to do. He lifts my arms as high as they'll go and gives a slight bounce to my shoulder joints. It feels amazing. I haven't done yoga in a while, so the pain of muscles stretching is welcome.

As he plants his hand on my left hip for balance, he puts each foot outside of my feet for stability and his right thumb on my wrist with my first resting in his outstretched palm. Rather than shouting over the music that Franky has started over, he leans into my left ear and instructs me to inhale deeply and stretch my torso at the same time. I do, and the cracking of realignment that goes on at my lower spine is *ma-gi-cal*. Twisting my body in both directions then releasing me, Eros gives me a *how's that* face. I can't help smiling as I give myself a shake and a twist of the limbs. I give a quick stretch to my legs and bounce from foot to foot.

I feel great. Everything is great. He winks at me, then helps himself to the pizza as he sits next to Frank on the sofa, who is handing him a soda. I pick up the bottle of water I was drinking from the floor and take a couple of swallows.

'*Breath Ayo.*'

My drum butterflies are back in full effect. I separate my fro down the middle of the front, then bobby pin it back on both sides clearing my line of eyesight. I take a couple of deep breaths, steadying myself, give Frank the ok, then position my legs. I know when the music is going to start, so I have time to take another drink.

Alright.

Here it comes.

First beat.

My footing is wrong...or maybe my seating or something. Keeping with the rhythm, I adjust myself quickly until it feels right.

The rhythm that's coming out of me right now can't be stopped. Not even if I wanted to. Nothing matters but me...these drums...and the sounds that I'm banging and stomping into existence. Not Frank, not Eros, not Eric...damn for sure not Carrey. The song is building and so is the thought of how she looked when she touched him.

"*Actually, I'm his girlfriend.*"

The thought of the two of them and the doubt that I felt. The self-torture, and second guessing...none of that shit matters anymore.

Yeah...*this* is me. This is how I'm supposed to feel...free from any and every thought but music. That's what this room is for me...true, uncut freedom. The song comes to an end and I'm out of breath, but I'm composed because I feel relieved...and lighter.

Franks stops the music and though he is talking enthusiastically about the project and what we need to do next, the room is silent. Eros hasn't said a word yet.

"Alright, Sis." He finally says after helping me clean. "I'm taking the leftovers." I go to follow him out but he waves me off. "I know where the door is. Nice to meet you, Sir." He says kindly to Eros.

"Be safe." I call as he's leaving the room.

"Always." He calls back, "Don't forget about the anniversary. We need to talk about a gift."

"I actually did forget and since we're on the subject, I'm not going all out this year, Frank."

"You will if I say you will." He responds, "Bye, love you, Sissy."

"Love you too, Bubby." I can't stand Frank sometimes, but I love him to life. He's the closest thing to a sister I've ever had. Those are *his* words...not mine.

"I can't believe you just did that."

"Well." I say, hunching my shoulders, "This is me."

He pulls me close, guiding my arms around his neck, then smoothing his hands down my sides.

"I see you." He tells me. For the first time since I met him, his eyes can't hold mine. With his first finger and thumb he lifts my chin up towards him bringing my eyes to his.

"I want to see it again."

"What? Now?" I ask, thrown aback a little, but smiling at the slight nod of his head.

Fine by me.

He releases me and returns to his seat on the sofa. With Frank gone and the table moved back against the side wall, he can spread out more. He slouches in the chair stretching his legs out in front of him and crossing them at the ankle. Picking up my sticks, I sit on the stool and pull myself into position. Drinking from the bottle of water as I start the music and wait for my cue. The first few beats are from the bass, so my hands are free for the moment. He's watching me watch him. His arms are outstretched along the back of the sofa.

I roll my right drum stick through my knuckles, flipping it around my hand stopping it in time to catch the right beat on time. The air is thick, and I can feel him watching me. Every move I make commands his attention. I want his hands on me...I want my hands on him. I look at him sitting there, across from me. Way too far away from me. Damn these drums. I stop playing and place my sticks together across the snare. Once again, I don't run to him and jump in his arms...I savor him watching me. Removing my shirt and bra, I stand in front of him removing my pants, shoes and panties. Then wait for him to finish removing his clothes.

His erection is calling my moisture, but I prolong the anticipation by straddling his lap just as he leans up to brace me by putting his hands on my hips and thighs. He commands my eyes. Neither of us are smiling. We both know it's time to address the elephant in the room.

"Are you okay?" He asks in my ear. I turn my face into his beard and rub its softness into my cheek. His hands are caressing my butt, his mouth is on my ear kissing my lobe, and neck. And it's doing a proper job at starting the fires and all that good stuff, *but* right now, all I want is him inside me. I grip his erection and ease myself onto him, rocking my hips and moaning into his mouth, as he rewards me with the deepest kiss, I've felt from him yet.

He holds himself deep in me by gripping my hip almost firmly and slouches back into the sofa. Giving me a full view of him and his magnificent, tattooed body. My eyes hold his as the music starts up on repeat again. He's on the bottom this time...at my mercy. Because of the volume of the music, I can't tell him what I want him to do, so I'll have to show him. My eyes are on his as I move his hands down to my cheeks and start to move. He picks up on cue and begins to rock with me. The rhythm is evident in my movement. I'm controlling the pace... and he's losing control.

He can't hide in my neck or distract me by talking in my ear...which is exactly where I want him. His eyes roll back, and his head is turned to the side, away from me. I reach forward and turn his face towards me. Rocking my body, I lean forward, placing my hands beside his head, dipping my mouth to his so that our tongues can have a reunion. His hands are on my waist swaying with my rhythm and I lean next to his ear. He needs to see how it feels, he needs a taste of his own medicine. His earlobe is plump and soft in my mouth, as he groans.

"I love you, Eros." I whisper. He begins to move faster and deeper touching that spot. A moan escapes from him.

"Yes." He gasps, squeezing me tighter.

"I want to see you." I whisper to him. Sitting back, I use his arms to brace myself backwards sliding his hands down to my butt. I need him to balance me. Placing my hands on both of his knees, I lean my weight backwards and circle my hips.

Rather than hear him, I *see* him mouthing the words "fuck me" and can see that he's completely losing control. His hand is on my butt while his other hand is gripping the space between my other hip and thigh. He's watching my me, so I rotate my hips faster still rocking with the beat. His body is in a full wave rocking me up and down.

I want to get lost in it. Watching him, I start rocking with his wave... riding up and down as I move his hand from my butt to my mouth. His eyes open, as I slide his thumb over my tongue. His mouth opens and his forehead creases, as his eyes move with my hand, as I slide his thumb to my clit. He bites his lip as he rubs circles, matching my hip circles... and with that he's gone.

"Fuck me." He mouths again as I rock with him. He's touching that spot again and the circles are taking me there, so I don't stop.

Rocking...circling.

He's on his way with me. His grip is tighter...and I'm almost there. Leaning my head back, I cup my breast and knead them as I feel that spot begin to swell. My stomach muscles are twitching, and my mouth is open in a silent moan. Just as I look down, he leans up to cradle my body. I want to taste him, so I pull myself into his mouth, breathing my moans into his system. It's getting close and I need him to hear me...I need to hear him, so I place my good ear to his mouth, and my mouth to his ear.

"Get it for me." I whisper breathlessly.

"Yes ma'am." He moans sitting back, cradling my body to his chest. With ease he finds my spot, and I groan with pleasure.

"That's it, babe." He tells me, knowing exactly why I gave him my ear. "Rock with me." He tells me, "Rock with me."

He is rubbing that spot, and the effects are escaping through my mouth.

"I hear you." He tells me, "I know you love it...I love it too. I love you. Only you." His words are echoing through my body, intensifying every thrust, every throb...every spasm. For the first time in a very long time, I find myself at a moment in life, when I realize that I'm being told the exact words that I needed to hear. Even though I didn't even realize that I needed to hear them. It doesn't happen that often, seeing as how most people don't really pay attention to another person's needs. Unless that other person tells them what they specifically need. And even then, some people still just might not get it.

He is correct though; I do love it...every bit of it. So much so, I can no longer hold it in. I squeal his name and explode around his throbbing orgasm. I'm not trembling, I'm full out shaking, ridding my body of all the anxieties. All I want now is his arms on me.

"You okay." He asks, kissing my forehead.

"I'm okay." I say, nodding my head softly.

"You want to go upstairs?" He asks, gently rubbing my thighs and ass. I nod my head and move to get up. "Wait..." I hear him say, stopping me by putting my hands on my back. "I don't want to let you go." He confesses, standing himself up with ease, with me still straddling his waist.

Crossing my ankles behind his back, I loop my arms around his neck and rest my face next to his...cheek to cheek. A faint whiff of his cologne skims my nose, so I draw closer to him where the scent is stronger.

"Are you ok, love." He says as he's entering the room and easing me down on the bed.

"I could use some water." I say knowing full well that's not what he meant. I don't want to tell him that it was slight torture thinking about him alone with *her*. In all honesty, I don't know what to tell him and I'm pretty sure all I'm doing is just trying to stall time until I figure it out.

He comes back and I drink my water slowly as he climbs onto the bed propping his back against the wall.

"Come here." He tells me, taking the glass away once I've finished and sitting me across his lap. I bring my knee up next to his chest and rest my back against his knees so that we are facing each other.

"I'm okay." I tell him, no longer able to avoid his eyes.

"I'm sorry that happened." He tells me. "It was over eight months ago and..."

I hold my hand up, stopping him before he could finish his sentence. I don't need the details.

"You don't have to explain your past." I tell him. It's not his fault she showed up, no more than it would be my fault if Eric suddenly showed up at my doorstep. Which is highly possible. *Shit*, I better call him before that happens. Popping up is something he's very capable of. "I completely understand."

"Why did you leave?"

I don't know how to explain *why* without just saying what was on my mind. I've never been good at sugar coating things, so there's no point in starting now.

"Because I didn't want to feel like an intruder, so I thought that if I gave the two of you a bit of privacy, you'd have the space to handle things however you needed to." And that's about it in a nutshell...well almost, "It wasn't easy though." I say, almost to myself, "Seeing her hands on you."

"It wasn't easy watching you get in your car and drive away." He admits, "I kept thinking that you weren't going to want to see me again."

'What's this now?'

"That's a crushing thought, Ayo." He continues. "I tried to call when I was on my way, but you didn't answer."

Call??? I don't even know where my phone is at.

"I think my phone is in the other room." I say remembering that I never took it out of my bag. I sigh deeply and close my eyes to the feel of his hands grazing my hips. Savoring the moment of a situation ended... without either of us feeling the need to argue with the other.

"You sleepy?" He asks, tracing his finger down my nose as I shake my head no. "What's on your mind?"

I open my eyes and watch him watch his own finger trace around my nipple.

"I was relieved when I looked up and you were standing there." When he doesn't say anything, I continue. "Leaving seemed like a good idea at the time, but as I drove off, the thought of what choice you could make tortured my brain. Or rather I tortured myself." I want to look away, but I can't. It's all coming out now and I want him to know.

"What other choice was there?" He asks, coiling his finger around a lock of my hair.

"Her." I say softly.

"Aw Ayo," he says, soothing his knuckles over my jawline. "She was never an option. As a matter of fact." He continues, "There are no other options."

With that, I reposition myself so that I'm lying on my stomach pressed into his.

"You promise?"

"I promise." He chuckles. Sighing, I close my eyes, and smile at how much fun I had making up from an argument that didn't actually happen, listening to the faint sound of music floating in from the studio. *Oh shit!* I gasp and pop my head up from his chest.

"What is it?" Eros asks, meeting my eyes.

"I forgot to save and burn the track. Franky will kill me if I lose that song." I say, sliding from the bed, "It'll only take a second."

I pull on a pair of shorts, and slid my arms through a t-shirt, then head out of my room.

"Will you bring my clothes?" Eros calls after me but changes his mind quickly before I can agree. By the time I sit behind my computer, he is standing there adjusting his boxer briefs. I select the track, save it and place a disc in a burner. Eros is carefully picking up his pants. Why do men put so much crap in their pockets? He's up to something. He's fishing through his pockets and watching me the entire time.

He's found whatever he's looking for and is satisfied with it being in his pocket. I shake my head at the toothy grin he's giving me.... or actually he seems to be smiling to himself.

"What are you thinking about?" I ask him, removing the disc and labeling it.

"How worried we both were."

"All for nothing." I say turning the lights off and closing the door behind us. Eros wraps his arms around my shoulders and kisses my cheek as we walk down the hallway.

My insides are smiling. Although I don't want the night to end, I can't wait for whatever tomorrow will bring. We cross through the kitchen, and I remember the Sushi...for two.

"Are you hungry?" I ask, "I made Sushi."

"You made *Sushi?*" He asks, extra surprised. "When?"

"When I got home." I say. I start removing the ingredients and placing them on the table. There are trays with already prepared Sushi rolls on it.

"You did make Sushi." He's very enthusiastic about Sushi.

"Don't say this is your favorite snack food." I tell him smiling, as I organize everything on the snack tray.

"No," He laughs, "All food is my favorite food, snacks or otherwise."

"Really, all food?" I ask, offering him one of the trays. I grab the other and follow him to the living room.

He wants to sit on the floor and eat, which I was not expecting when I prepared all this stuff...happy bonus for me. He takes my tray and holds it until I'm curled up in front of him with my back to his chest. Then passes me the tray for me to sit in front of us. The other tray is on his left, so he pulls my body to the side so that my head is resting in the crook of his right arm.

"You made Sushi."

"You seem very excited about that." I say giggling.

"Do I?" He asks, trying to disguise his smile. Of course, he failed, but at least he tried. "It's just, I don't know anyone who would think of this."

"So, this is okay?" I say, opening my mouth for the bite he's feeding me.

"Are you kidding." He asks, handing me a small empty sauce bowl. Next, he dips a spoon into a jar of wasabi and adds a dollop to the bowl, drowning it in soy sauce. "Look how I get to have my midnight snack."

"Actually," I say watching him mix the wasabi and soy. "I can't take all the credit. Sitting on the floor was your idea." I dip a bite in his sauce and slide it in his open mouth, and except the one he's feeding me.

"You know," I say, feeding him another bite. "No one's ever seen me in my music room before. Except for my family, of course. But nobody I've ever dated."

"Really?" He asks, swallowing his mouthful. "Here, I want you to try this." He dips a bite into the wasabi and holds it for my reaction. I shut my eyes tight and open my mouth waiting. It's not bad, so I open my eyes. He's watching me smiling.

"I thought it was going to be hot." I say laughing.

"The soy cuts the heat." He tells me, "So why hasn't anyone ever been in your music room?"

"I don't know. I never really thought about it."

"Hum. Well thank you."

"For what?" I say, feeding him another bite.

"For letting me watch you play."

I can only smile. No one even asked me about my music bedsides him. I'm glad he was there.

"When I'm in there, I don't have to think about anything but music." I say refusing his next bite. "When I play, I can take whatever I'm feeling and get rid of it and never have to worry about it again."

"That's how I feel when I cook." I can see that being true. He was very focused yesterday, and really at ease. "I like seeing you there, you completely transform."

"Do I?" I say surprised.

"Um-hum." He dusts his hands on the napkin, then wipes my mouth. "Completely."

"Come on." I say lifting to get up, picking up the tray on the way. My carpet is not as forgiving on the ass as his is.

In the kitchen, we dish the leftovers into storage containers. Wash and dry the bowls and trays and put them away. I wait in the doorway leading to the back rooms as he checks the door locks. Clearly, he's a natural protector, and everyone that he loves he takes care of. In the bedroom, after giving myself two braids, I stand by the bed, remove my clothes and climb in. Waiting for him to remove his joggers and slide his warm body into the back of me.

"I need you to know something." He pulls me close, tucking me into his embrace. "There are no other options, there's only you." His fingers lock with mine, and he gives me a squeeze.

"You are my only option." He turns my body to face him. "Only you."

I don't need him to say it anymore, but I'm glad he does, and I intended on speaking and telling him as much, but his soft touch gliding across my face silence my words. I want to tell him, no... I *need* to tell him that, I think it's the only way to get it off of my chest. I had enough doubt for the both of us. I don't want him thinking that I'm slipping away. He needs assurance, and for once it dawns on me...maybe I do too.

"I know." I tell him, grazing my fingertips over his abs muscles. His eyes are hungry for more. "I can tell when you touch me. Or when I touch you." I skim my fingers through his chest hair, and trace my thumb around his nipple, watching it perk up. "I wanted to give you space to do whatever you needed to do. But..."

But *she* was so sad and pitiful standing there with her teary eyes.

"But what?" He asks. Oh damn, that lump is back.

"You didn't see her face when she saw us hug. She was crushed." I say softly, *oh damn*, that lump is back. "I don't want to be the one standing there all broken into pieces, watching the person I think I love embrace another woman."

There...I said it. Of course, I whispered it so my voice didn't betray me, but I said it.

"I especially don't want it to be because of a decision that I made." And that's it. That was the reason for all my previous anxiety. The fear that, my going home and him not knowing the reason why, could have made him believe that I didn't care. And, putting all cards on the table, I *really...really...really* do care. Especially now, as I stare into those eyes, those eyes...those eyes. I wonder if he was sad, would he cry chocolate tears. He's just watching me, absorbing my words...letting them soak in.

His hand stops grazing tingling trails up and down my arms, and cup my face just below my ear. Then he tilts my lips up to his for the softest kiss. I'm not even sure if his lips actually touched mine or not.

"You won't ever have to worry about that." He tells me, "I... am... yours." He continues, smiling a *check-out-my-new-teeth*, smile, with his eyebrows stretched up to his hairline. I place my fingers on the points of his eyebrows. Just as I did when I told him I loved him and pulled them down. Only for him to drop them in a mock angry face.

"Don't make that face." I say laughing, as he pokes his bottom lip out pouting.

Oh, I can't resist. I tilt my face up and softly suck it into my mouth. His hand squeezes my hip then slides around to my ass. I want more...so much more. Without missing a beat, I straddle his lap, moaning into his mouth. His hands are kneading and caressing my back, and shoulders and butt cheeks. He rocks his hips in mock thrust, so I rock back the same way I do when he's inside me. Needing to breath, I pull away from the kiss, still slowly rocking with his motion. He's such a beautiful man.

"So…" He sighs, "why hasn't anyone ever been in your music room?"

Well, it's not the question that I was expecting but, still a welcome change of subject. Not to mention, his mouth is all over my breast.

"Like I said earlier." I tell him, pushing my nipple further into his mouth. "They weren't interested, I guess."

"Well," he says, looking at me as he switches sides. I watch him suck my nipple into his mouth, only to let it pop back out with a sucking, smacking sound. "That sucks for them."

Great choice of words.

"Yes, it does." I say, grinding deeper into him. His hands slide around to my ass and down my thighs.

"Who was singing." He asks, kissing my shoulder.

"Franky." I tell him softly, lifting my shoulder into the tickle of his beard. I smooth my hands around his neck and rake my nails through his scalp. And he moans...actually moans.

Well, well, well...what's this, now? I skim my nails across the surface of his shoulders and watch goosebumps prickle his skin.

"Speaking of Franky," I say, kissing his neck under the beard where his skin is bare. It's smooth and firm, and his Adam's apple leaps as I cross over to the other side of his throat. Sucking and kissing everywhere my lips touch.

"My mother will be calling tomorrow." I run my nose through the soft curls of his beard up to his earlobe.

"You think so?" He asks, moaning from his throat, approving the feel of my lobe fondling.

"Baby," I say, rocking my hips...making sure to say that word in his ear. "You met Franklin Oliver Mitchell. By now, my entire family knows all about you."

"Oh really?" He asks, chuckling into my neck. "Are you okay with that?"

"Of course." I say laughing, but still rocking with his body, "You'll get to meet them when we go for my parent's anniversary party." I say this as though we've already discussed him going.

"When do we leave?" He asks, lifting my body up, sliding his hand around my butt cheeks to the back of my vagina and slipping a finger in.

"Friday." I say, moaning and arching my back allowing more of his finger to go in. "So, when my mom calls, I'll have her fix up the guest room on the main floor for Emma. It's next to the bathroom."

I stop rocking the moment I feel his finger freeze and lean back to look at his face.

"You wouldn't mind that?" He asks, I think he's even shocked... maybe. He slips his finger out and just as he's about to put it in his mouth, I stop him. Turn his hand towards me and let his moist finger disappear into my mouth. His lips pull back showing clenched teeth, as he hisses air into his mouth.

"You didn't think we were going to just leave her here by herself, did you?"

He grips the bed, then scoots over to the center, rising and falling with me on his lap.

"It's only an hour and a half drive, if she's up for it, she's welcome to come along." He slides his body down so that he's flat on the bed under me, rubbing circles into my thighs.

"I'll ask her if she's up for a road trip." I say, giving his neck attention from my mouth again. I love how his skin feels against my lips. How his nipples perk up against my kisses. The hair below his belly button isn't as thick as it is on his chest, so it's not a distraction when I kiss there.

Or suck there.

Or lightly rake my fingernails across there, kissing there again. Not at all ignoring his erection that's tapping my chin, every time it jumps. As if it's saying...*my turn*.

I tilted my chin down and let my tongue slide from the base to the tip. Then slowly circle the head making sure to get it good and moist. His hands, which are rubbing my arms, are gently squeezing them, holding them in place. Stopping me from using them in any way. Well, actually, I guess if I wanted to, I could. At the moment...I don't want to. Licking from the base to the tip again, I use my tongue to lift his head into my mouth.

He moans and squeezes my arms. His hips are slowly grinding back and forth, so I fix my lips in the shape of an 'O', and let him slide in and out, looking up to see his face. Every time he touches the back of my throat, I feel the moisture building. Every time he pulls out of my mouth, I hear a small throaty sound escape from deep within his belly. This makes me smile, because pleasing him is fun...for him and for me. And now that I've gotten his attention, it's time to quit playing around and get serious. I tighten my lips and push my mouth down as he thrust upward, then grind the tip with the back of my throat.

Now he's really thrusting, and my head is rocking back and forth as my hips would if I were riding him. My head is going back and forth...my tongue is going around and around. I'm moaning around a full mouth, as he's going in and out.

Through his teeth, he's hissing words like *"Shiiit..."* and *"Fuuuck"*, and tugging on the sheets. Meanwhile I'm about to explode. My nipples are about the size of pencil erasers, and he hasn't even touched me.

Without breaking stride, Eros sits up, stops my head from moving by holding both hands on each side of my head. Gazing at himself stroke in and out of my face. I look at him and smile because he's about to lose it.

"Can I come." He whispers, breathlessly. Since my mouth is full, I can't answer, so I just wink.

"Fuck." He hisses. Next thing I know, a small pop of moisture thumps the back of my throat. I can feel the vein underneath, begin to throb... releasing more and more every time until there's no more left. I back away swallowing as he escapes my lips, then smile as I watch him collapse back onto the bed. *That's right, Mr. Concrete Chest*...just bask in it.

Laying down beside him, I place my hands behind my head, cross my feet at the ankles and wait. Feeling pretty proud of myself. His response to my touch is inebriating. My eyes are closed, so I feel him, rather than see him, lean over to his favorite ear and tell me to open my legs. Keeping my eyes closed, I lift my knees apart and can feel him caressing me with his eyes. I want to see him and watch his every move, but the thrill of not knowing what's coming next is too stimulating.

"You look pretty proud of yourself." He's at my ear again, and despite the starting fires, my eyes pop open. "Oh yeah," He half smiles, "I'm going tit-for-tat on this one."

"Is that right?" I say, cocking my eyebrows up.

He leans forward and stuffs the pillow that's beside me under my head on top of the one I'm already laying on. They're pretty fluffy, so it stacks up pretty good.

"Now you can watch me." He says against my lips, sucking lightly on the top one.

"I love these lips." He tells me, switching to the bottom. His eyes are mocha title waves, invading my spirit. But I can't look away from him. I roll my eyes and tilt my neck, opening it up for his beard to tickle and mouth to suck on. My hips are moving as he stretches his body between my legs.

"I love your reaction when I talk right here." He whispers in my ear, then comes back to my mouth kissing away my moan. My nails are grazing up and down his back, caressing small circles. He works his way down from my mouth to my nipples, then my belly, even stopping to nip at my hip bone on the way, before stopping above my vagina, giving it a sweet little kiss. I can see everything he's doing. The way he flicks his tongue and dips his head. His hand is curled around my leg holding down the flat of my belly, and slightly pulling the skin so more of me is exposed to his tongue lashing.

And just as I think I can't take any more...he stops.

"No," I whine, lifting my hips, "No don't stop."

"I'm not stopping." He tells me as he slides my leg up to his shoulder, while rolling me from the pillows onto my side. He positions himself at the opening and slides full length into me. A breathy sound something like the word *oh* falls from my mouth as he taps that spot over, and over, and over again. "Not until I get what I want." And he continues stroking and grinding that spot.

His hands are at my hip and butt guiding my rhythm to match his movement, pulling me deeper onto him until I sigh...or moan, or whatever you would want to call it.

"Oh, my goodness, Eros." I start with my own movement pounding that fire, fueling...urging it to grow and spread, only to escape through my mouth.

"There it is." He whispers, leaning over me, driving himself deeper, "Come with me."

And I do. A deep, tsunami wave ripples through my body over and over. Until I'm absolutely spent, and still heaving when he lays behind me pulling me into his spooning body. Holding me firmly close, kissing the goose bumps that stretch across my shoulder blades until my breathing has become calm and less labored. Even with my eyes closed I can hear the click of the lamp, and see the room go dark.

Man-oh-man, aside from all the other wonderful things about him, Mr. Concrete Chest sure knows how to put a girl to sleep.

Chapter Twelve

You ever had one of those mornings, where you wake up and just automatically know...this is going to be a good day. Something about the way the gray daylight makes its way into the warmth of my bedroom through the window. Or how my feet, at some point during my slumber, found a warm corner to pocket themselves into. The covers are pulled up to my chin, and over Eros face. The time on the bedside clock reads 7:45a.m. and I smile...sigh, then close my eyes.

This is why vacations are so wonderful, staying up late...sleeping in in the morning. Paradise...just plain paradise. At least it is until someone decides to disturb the peace by ringing my damn doorbell. I groan but make no attempt to get up and see who it is. Maybe they'll think no one is home and go away. Or not...damnit, still there.

"I'll get it." Eros groans, just as I was about to move. Lucky me, once I've gotten up, I'll never be able to get this comfortable again. He climbs over my body. Very clumsy like, I might add, ruffling the covers over my face and mashing my head into the pillow.

"Quit it." I say laughing, swatting his hand away from my head. Minutes later he's back, climbing over my body to the spot where he slept, ruffling the covers and my face again. Grunting and laughing, I try and swat at him, but miss.

"Who was it?" I ask stretching my legs and yawning, pulling the covers closer into my chin.

"UPS." He tells me, flipping the small box over trying to find a clue. I completely forgot about dropping my phone.

"It's my new phone." I manage to breath out through a yawn, wiping my fingers over my eyes, rubbing the cobwebs away. I probably won't be going back to sleep, but I refuse to get out of bed so early.

I watch him open the box and remove the plastic wrapping from the disassembled items, then put them together.

"Now you can give 1992 its flip phone back." He joked, talking about my back-up piece of crap.

"Don't judge my phone." I say, accusingly, "I wouldn't have dropped it if *someone* hadn't put his concrete chest in my way...on purpose, so I can run into him."

"Shame on him." He replied, opening the handbook that was included in the box.

Is he really going to read the manual...who does that?

"Are you going to read that entire book?"

"Yes." He responds, flipping the cell over, looking at both sides like he didn't just put it together. Once he's satisfied with whatever he needs to find, he hands the phone over to me for my inspection.

Now...let's make note that it's about five minutes after eight, and it's about this time that everything in the universe...stops. The earth stops rotating. My ears stop listening to Eros' low toned voice, saying something about manuals, or pamphlets, or something. He may even be looking at me, seeing as how I'm stuck in mid motion, and haven't taken the cell from his hand yet. I was reaching for it, but, as I said...the universe has skidded to a complete halt.

"Say something."

I can hear him speaking. I even try and speak back, but for the moment I don't exactly remember how to use words. I've forgotten how to look at him, as beautiful as his eyes are to me, I can't shift my eyes over to him. I can't see anything but the simple emerald gemstone, embedded in the clutches of a small gold band. Which is fitted with clear diamonds halfway down each side of the band and encircling the base of my left ring finger.

Finally...finally I rip my eyes from this...what...engagement ring, I guess and up to his gaze, which is overwhelmed with worry. I can't believe it! I try to speak, once I'm able to prop myself up against the headboard, but I don't think I spoke any kind of English words. I think my words come out sputtering and slow, and I may have even drooled on myself. I probably look like I should be wearing a safety helmet and riding the short bus...but oh well. I twist my hand around, feeling around the band with my thumb.

It feels real enough. I even shake my hand vigorously as if I touched something hot. It still doesn't come off. Closing my eyes tight, I count for ten seconds then open them up. It's still there! A small delicate giggle ripples from my stomach, fluttering the butterflies that have taken up permanent residence there...on to my throat and out of my mouth...and it doesn't stop. Not when Eros pulls me close. Not when he pulls me onto his lap and wraps his arms around me. Of course, I hugged him back as I eyeball the ring over his shoulder...I think I'm so happy my eyesight is getting blurry. Plus, I can't stop giggling. Not until I realize he's brushing tears from my cheeks.

When did I start crying? And why is it, now that I know that I'm crying, the tears won't stop? I don't even bother drying my eyes or face. I just cradle my face into my fiancé's neck, twisting my engagement ring around my finger. He's rocking my back and forth, wiping my sniffling tears.

"Ayo?" I hear this man who has, in not even a week's time, exceeded all expectations I have ever had for any man, say. Hell, not even my father has cradled me in his arms and rocked me like a baby. I can even recall him flat out telling me, and I'm going to quote this verbatim.

"It's gonna take one hell of a man to put up with you."

Well...I can't say he was wrong. This here is one hell of a special man. I wipe the snot from my nose, sniffle and lean back to finally look at him. I mean...really see him. His messy bed hair, and ungroomed beard. His thick brown eyes searching mine. I still can't speak so I wait, really trying but completely giving up on trying to hide my smile.

"You gave me a ring." I say softly, finding my voice and what's left of my composure.

"I did." He tells me, nodding his head and smiling that bashful smile that curls up on one side of his mouth. Now *I'm* searching *his* eyes. How can this man that I allow to completely dominate my soul, be so...unknowing?

"You want to be my husband?" I ask, still smiling.

He adjusts his head so that he's looking at me straight in the face.

"I do." He responds. "Do you want to be my wife?"

Well, there's a question that I don't need to think about.

"I do." I think we just had the ceremony. I smile a bright...I can't help it even though my cheeks hurt...kind of smile. I caress his face, as he exhales deeply, "I promise I won't let you down."

"I do not doubt that Ayo." It's such a sweet moment, for sure one that I'll never forget.

Especially since the moment everything is quiet and I'm captivated by *my fiancé's* masterful kiss, my stomach releases a rumble that makes me wonder if it wasn't some kind of creature hiding in my belly. I groan a sound very similar to the sound Homer Simpson always makes... "Doh!"

"Hungry?" Eros asks, once we stop our giggling. I feel giddy and delicate, and feminine. Even more so than usual.

"Yes." I answer, wondering why my voice was so small. "But I wanna shower first."

"Okay." Eros smiles, "You shower...I'll cook." He moves to get up, but I wrap my arms around his waist holding him in place.

"Or" I say stretching my legs, "*we* shower...then you cook."

"Perfect." He smiles, "Let's go, wife to be." He scoops his arms around my waist and drags me from the bed, across the carpet out of the room. Down the hall with me laughing the entire way, not letting me go until we reached the bathroom.

Wife to be...ME! Shut the front *fucking* door. I can't stop staring at my hand, and the new ornament that now decorates it. It's so perfectly simple and elegant. Exactly what I would have picked out for myself, right down to the color. How strange can this be...how much more strange can things get? This precious little thing will be an heirloom and will get passed down to my son...if I happen to have one.

Well *damn*. Now there's a thought that's never crossed my mind before. *Me...* a mother? Do I even want kids? I must...the thought makes me smile.

"You look pleased." Eros says holding his hand out to me.

"Oh, you have *no* idea how pleased I am." I say placing my fingers in his. Just as I'm about to get up I snatch my hand back, stopping him from removing my ring.

"Just until we get out of the shower." He assured me, holding out his open palm. I make a face but give it to him, anyway, pouting at him.

The water feels awesome. My shower isn't as big as his but it's okay for the both of us. We can both wash and rinse at the same time. I can barely take my eyes off him, and his tattoos that seem to come to life as the water beats into his body.

"So, what's for breakfast?" He asks, rinsing his hair, as I apply soap to my face loofah.

"Oatmeal." I say with my eyes closed, exfoliating my cheeks and forehead.

"No." I hear him say. "Absolutely not." He places both hands and guide me so that my back is away from the water.

"What?" I gasp, rinsing my face, "You don't like oatmeal?"

"I love oatmeal." He tells me. Feeling pretty sure that my face is clear of any eye irritants, I open my eyes then smile at his brown beard and mustache, now fuzzy and white with shampoo.

He's right, it's our "anniversary day", at least it will be, come this time next year...something special is in order.

"Can you make eggs benedict?" I ask.

"You like eggs benedict?" He asks, surprised.

"I've never had it." I admit.

"Really?" He leans forward and rinses the suds from his lip and face carpet. "But you'll try it?" I nod my head and step out as he turns the water off. "I'll try anything twice." I hand him a towel and begin drying myself.

"Well, that depends." He tells me, watching me dry myself, "Do you have eggs?"

"Yes." I answer, drying my breast.

"Breakfast meat?" He asks, bringing his eyes up from everything that's below my neck. I made a promise to myself just before I fell asleep last night that I was going to behave myself today. Watching the fires burn in his eyes at this moment is making it really hard if he keeps looking at me this way.

Side bar repeat: I *love* when he looks at me this way. His eyes are an attractive combination of wanting and composed. Like he's trying to behave himself too.

"What kind of breakfast meat. There are a few choices to pick from." I haven't done this in a while, but one hundred composure points to me for not gobbling him up in my mouth when he dried his *man parts*. Fifty to him for maintaining eye contact with my hand as I dried between my legs.

"Okay." He tells me, wrapping the towel around his waist. "How about English muffins, lemon juice and olive oil?"

"Yes, on all three." I answer, spotting my ring on the sink beside the faucet. One false move and it could've fallen down the drainpipe. I'll have to remember to get a small soap dish or something to place it in from here on out.

"Eggs benedict it is then."

"Yes." I say, pumping my fist, smiling. I reach for my ring but move too slow, allowing him the time to pick it up first.

"Ayo," he says, stepping towards me and grabbing my left hand. "I'm not going to get on one knee, because there's a lot down there that I would love to kiss on right now."

'Oh, this half smile is going to be a permanent fixture on my face from here on out.'

"Although the calendar only says five days, I feel like we've been together for many lifetimes and just don't remember."

Oh dear Lord...*this* is my proposal.

Damn...where's a camera when I need one? I would love to capture his beauty at this moment. I'll have to remember to buy me one soon. So, I could watch this scene over and over again.

"Would you please do me the honor," He said stepping closer into my personal space, and dropping his voice down to a whisper, "and set my universe straight by saying yes?"

And *there it is.* Two things that combined creates the beauty that is his soul's foundation...truth and honesty. He really wants this, and he wants it with me. I smile and watch him slide my ring back to its rightful place at the base of my finger.

"Yes, I will." I say gushing, watching him kiss my ring then stretching my arms around his neck, pulling him close into my body. Loving the caress of his hands up and down my naked backside, and the tickle of his beard on my neck, and the sound of his exhale in my ear. This is really happening...and I'm going to behave.

"So," I say sitting at the island watching a shirtless Eros, who by the way is very much living up to the meaning of his name, gather the ingredients for our breakfast.

"Last night you said...all food is your favorite."

"Um-hum." He said, looking back from the fridge. His hair is hanging loose, and his gym shorts are stopped just below the vee shape of his lower belly. *I'm going to behave.* I'm really paying attention to his conversation, but I can't help getting a little hot under the collar. I want him, *but* I'll behave.

"So, there's nothing that you don't like?" I continue. I need a distraction or something. I'm already over the moon because of the engagement. Not to mention this perfect little ring that he picked out is working like an aphrodisiac. I should behave.

"Well," He said, putting a pot of water on the stove, "So far, I don't like hominy."

"Hominy?" I exclaimed, "That's it?"

"That's it." He laughed. He leaned against the island on his forearms gazing at me. The fragrant beard oil overcomes my senses, jump starting my heart rate. "What about you?" What don't you like?"

Not touching you...all the time.

"Food wise, or in general?" I'm starting to realize biting my lip does a hell of a good job keeping me from blurting things out.

"In general." He said after thinking it over, "*and* food wise."

"Peanut butter and wet socks." Twenty-five points per answer.

"*Peanut butter?*" He asks, making a face, leaning away from me. "Who doesn't like good'ol peanut butter?"

"*Me.*" I say laughing, "It's an evil invention."

"No not peanut butter." He laughs quietly, "It's one of my top favorites." He lifts my hand and kisses my knuckles. "This looks nice on your finger."

"It's very, very beautiful." I say leaning in to give him a kiss, smiling at the same tickle on my face as was on my knuckles. It's a sweet, tender kiss that doesn't last half as long as I want it to. I want to climb over the counter and give him something to hold on to. But I'm going to behave. Anyway, just as I decide to get carried away, I change my mind and pull back.

I think I like talking to my finance, so today that's what it's going to be about.

"Come here." He tells me, half smiling like he knows my game. "I need your help." I stand up and pad my bare feet over and stand next to his shirtless, I just had a shower and now my beard smells like a national forest, torso. Watching his chest rise and fall with every breath. "You don't have an egg poacher, so we're going to improvise." He pulls a potato masher from the utensil holder, then slides me between him and the stove, by placing his hand on my hip.

"Stand here." He tells me, looking down into my neck, making sure that I'm, what...paying attention? "Now, hold this here." He places the potato masher in the center of water that's now simmering, I guess is what you would call it,

He thinks he's slick. Reaching around me for an egg but making sure to hold his hand in place on my hip. Not to mention his, though not very erect, but very *very* noticeable groin resting into my lower back.

He bends both arms around me and cracks the egg with the back of a knife. Breathing over my neck and shoulder.

"And what was wrong with the side of the pot?" I ask, looking over at him. He is completely too preoccupied with his egg to even look at me.

"Nothing," He tells me, "But I don't want the egg to leak into the pot."

From the way he's trying to drop the egg in, I can tell that my arm is in the way. So, I reach down and place it around his thigh. Yes...I could have held onto the counter or the handle to the stove, but I want to touch him. This is the man I'm going to marry. I don't feel like I touch him quite enough.

"There." He said, dropping the egg in and looking at me. He kisses my cheek and moves to the refrigerator. Giving my backside two pats as he glides across. He removes a couple of the muffins, splits each one into two pieces and drops them in the toaster. Then returning to my backside, he removes the egg and adds another. "Do you like your yolk runny?" He asks.

"Yes."

"This one won't take as long then." His mouth is close to my ear.

"You don't like your eggs runny?"

"Not at all." He answers, removing the muffins. He places each of them on a plate then tops them with thin slices of the smoked salmon I had in the fridge.

Next, he spoons the eggs on one at a time. Sprinkles a pinch of salt on each, then smothered them both in the made from scratch hollandaise sauce.

"Eggs benedict." He says, smiling. It looks delicious. We sit at the dining table with my legs dangling over his thigh. Laughing at my reaction to how good it tastes. 'I mean, come on. Any man that cooks this well, looks delicious with *or* without a shirt on, and who is as sweet as pure sugar cane, itself, should be absolutely illegal. I mean, *really*. I silently give myself a shout-out and high-five for just being able to love him.

"Where did you grow up?" I ask him, taking a drink from my glass of milk.

"Right here in the city."

"Really?" I say between chews. "Have you ever lived anywhere else?"

"Not full time, no." He answers, "My dad passed away the summer before I went to college so that just left me and Emma."

"So, you made sure you were around to do the things your father would've done?"

"Exactly." He says, finishing his breakfast. "She's the reason why I went to the NFL."

"Seriously?" I say, taking another bite.

"Seriously." He confirmed. "As hard as she worked, she still came to every award ceremony. She was always there and never once complained...ever. I *had* to give something back to her."

"How excited was she when you got drafted?"

"Oh wow." He began, leaning back in his seat. "That night, after all the excitement was over, we went home and invited my best friend, T.K. and his family over for dinner. And just...talked."

"You just talked?" I asked. Who gets drafted into the NFL and celebrates by *just talking*. "You didn't go out? Have a party...nothing?" And there's that look again. Those honest eyes, and unkempt mustache curled up in the corner. What is he thinking?

"I've never really been much of a partier."

Hum...I find that hard to believe.

"Not even after a winning game?" I ask, hiding my skepticism with another bite. "Not even after the Super Bowl."

"Nope." His arm is propped over my knee and his hand is grazing the inside of my dangling leg. "Regular games...I usually went back to my room afterwards. After the Super Bowls, I showed my face at the team function for about an hour...then I left."

Well...just...wow.

"Why?" I asked between chews. He's holding my foot to his thigh and pushing his thumb up the instep, making small, full circles.

"Once you've been to one, you've been to them all." He states matter of factly. "How do you think I've read the Ice and Fire books twice?"

I shrug my shoulders, but honestly, I guess I just saw him out at some club or bar giving some lady a lethal dose of those chocolate grenades he calls eyes. Then again, no. That doesn't suit him at all. He's gentle, and soft.

"What did you talk about?"

"Draft night?" He asks, using both thumbs on my foot now. I can't remember ever having my feet rubbed by anyone that wasn't employed by some spa.

"Life. How it was about to change. My dad." That last part was spoken softer than the rest and I realize he's never mentioned him before.

"What was his name?"

"Henry." He tells me placing my foot on the floor.

"What was he like?" I ask, finishing my last bite.

"Tired." He recalls, opening his arms for me to sit on his lap. "He was a mechanic and worked twelve hour shifts four and five days a week. And somehow managed to make it to all my games." His voice is quieter. I can tell his dad is a soft spot for him, and I don't think I want to push that button too hard. At least not today. Henry will be a subject that I bring up in moderation.

"Your dad," I say, turning his face to mine, "would be very, *very* proud of the man you've become."

"Thank you." He tells me, against my kissing lips.

I wonder why the thought is just now occurring to me that he's going to need encouragement, too. I never realized how good it feels to make someone smile. His hand slides down my back to my butt and he squeezes, pulling me deeper into his kiss. My nails rake through the hair at the nape of his neck, and his groan vibrates into my mouth, straight to my tingling button.

'*No, Ayo, behave.*' I tell myself, pulling away from his mouth. "I'm going to wash the dishes." And with that I stand and head to the sink.

"So, tell me about your brothers."

"Well." I say, scraping plates into the disposal. "Jeffery's the oldest and is in management at the post office where my dad retired from."

"You've already met Frank, who's right above me. Then there's Daniel and Nathaniel, the twins above Frank. Then Phillip and Phelix the twins above Nate and Danny."

"Four of your brothers are twins?" He asks, surprised, once I nod my head.

"Phil and Phe," I say, referring to them by their nickname, "Are the attorneys, like my mother. Danny is an electrician, Nate owns a couple of grocery stores in town, nothing big, just a place where people can shop for their families without going for broke."

"Wow, really?" He asks, drying the glass that I offer him. "You're all very successful." He says this, and I can't help but chuckle.

"What?" He asks, mirroring my smile.

"When we go for my parent's anniversary, you will see that adult-hood and successful careers...do not...in any way, change six brothers and a sister they treat like a brother."

"When we're all home at the same time, it's like we're teenagers again. We don't use our cell phones because the internet service is a bit spotty where my parents live. And absolutely no work talk, unless it's in positive reference to the future."

"So, you all just...what?"

"Hang out." I say, "Get on my mom's nerves. You'll see. Speaking of."

I finish up the last dish, dry my hands, and go in search of my new phone. Eros follows me as far as the bathroom, and I continue to the room flopping across the bed. Positioning myself with my legs under the covers indian style and my back against the headboard.

Inhaling deeply, I ready myself to text my mother using my new cellular device. I send a quick 'good morning beautiful' message, then toss the phone on the bed next to my legs. It's only 10:45 in the morning, so all I have to do is sit back and wait.

"I'm back," Eros says, "and I have orange juice for you." He strolls in with two glasses, hands one to me, then stretches his long body across the foot of the bed.

We both adjust the pillows so that our heads are propped up, and I watch as he flips through the many channels...stopping on all the food channels. Just as he's commenting on a dish that is being presented to a panel of judges, my phone rings and I don't need to check it to know who's calling.

"Hello mother." I say, after putting the phone on speaker. One thing anyone should know about my mother is that no matter what, *she* is not the best candidate for being on speaker. There's no telling what she might say.

"Hey yourself." She said, somewhat distracted, "What're you doing? I've missed you."

"I'm watching t.v. right now, mommy. What are you doing?"

"Did you get to start your vacation on time?"

"I did...well, sort of. I picked up Monday though...I filled in for someone that had something to do. Anyway, what are you doing?"

"I'm hiding from your father, honey." She answered, sounding out of breath, "He's gotten bored, in his retirement. So, he finds activities for '*us*' to do. Today, it's building a birdhouse...from scratch."

"Why don't you want to help him build a birdhouse?" I ask laughing, tickling the bottom of Eros' foot.

"I'm not building no birdhouse. When I suggested that we do more things together...that's not what I had in mind." She replies flatly, scoffing, "Anyway," she sighs, "I'm hiding out in the boat shed...ain't that sad?"

"It's very sad, ma. Also, I have you on speaker." I say as I climb over Eros to lay stomach down in front of him.

"Are you still coming this weekend, honey? I really miss you." My mother may at times be a bit...straight to the point, for lack of better words, but she never ever let a moment go by without telling me how happy she was at having a baby girl. *Finally*...of course.

"Mommy, you know I'm staying the whole weekend. I wouldn't miss it for the world."

Not to mention, if I did...she'd never let me forget it...ever.

"Good, I can't wait to see you." Then hesitantly she adds, "and hopefully your new...*boyfriend*, for lack of better words." Eros' head pops over my face, with wide and humorous eyes.

"Yes momma, boyfriend is a good word to use." I smiled, giving him an *I told you so look*.

"Oh, and Momma, can you get a room ready? We were gonna bring his mother with us."

"Of course, honey." She said with pure excitement, "Do you want the downstairs room next to the bathroom? It still has that mechanical bed that your daddy had to use when he hurt his back."

"That's the one I was thinking of. Thank you, mommy." I close my eyes at the feel of Eros' finger trailing my thigh below the hem of my shorts.

"So, what's his name?" She said, in a sort of sing-song sort of voice.

"His name is Eros." I say counting the seconds on my fingers.

One...two...three...

"Eros?" She asked, very obviously amused, "As in the...Olympic god of sexual desire? High five, honey." She said, as I stifled a smile at Eros' dropped jaw.

"Oh no." She exclaimed, almost in a quiet stealthy tone.

"What is it, momma?"

"It's your father, he's coming to find me." Her voice is in a hushed tone, "Honey, I gotta go. The extra room will be ready when you get here...I can't wait to see you, and I can't wait to meet your new family... Oh no, he found me."

All her words came rushing out except for the last five, which drops a couple of octaves lower than her regular voice. Eros' is visually tickled but trying to maintain himself. My father is in the background asking my mother why she was hiding. Her answer...because she don't wanna build no stinking bird house. His response...well she shoulda just said that from the beginning. It ain't like she '*pacifically*' named something she *did* want to do, all she said was let's do something together.

Now, this type of *specifically* colorful verbal back and forth between my mother and father is something that I'm very much used to, but Eros on the other hand, is silently giggling his ass off. Especially after the last comment she made before the phone went dead. Her comment was...and I quote... "Maxwell! I was talking about having sex!" The phone goes dead, and my neck completely gives up on holding my head up right.

"They are funny." Was all Eros could say outside of laughing.

Chapter Thirteen

The rest of the morning was spent lounging around, relaxing. Laughing. Just plain good old-fashioned goofing off. Chasing each other around the house, tickling, touching...kissing, fondling, and teasing. Just good old-fashioned fun. The joint of *magic grass that* we smoked, most definitely helped lighten the mood more. As I seal off the ends and pass it to Eros to light, Frank calls. More than willing to talk about what he wanted to do for our parents' anniversary gift. After a very adamant and stern refusal...over and over again, on my part. And a very adamant and stern refusal to listen to anything I said, on Frank's part. I apprehensively agreed...to stand up in front of real live and breathing people and sing a song. Dedicated to my parents and the love they share.

Whatever. I absolutely, under every circumstance *hate* singing, especially singing in front of people. Family or not. I hate it and they know it. The conversation ended with Franky promising to come over tomorrow to *practice*. Again...*whatever*.

"What's the matter?" Eros asks, walking into the kitchen where I stand.

"Franky's coming over tomorrow." I tell him pouting. I open the freezer looking for...something...I don't know. Ice cream! I don't even bother with a bowl.

"You...look..." He hesitates. "Stressed? I think."

"So Frank has decided that he and I," I say, shoving a spoon of chocolate creaminess in my mouth, "are going to do a *duet* for my parents anniversary gift."

He's confused. I can tell by the way his head cocks to the side with one eyebrow jacked way up. **Side bar:** Confusion looks cute on him.

"I don't understand." He says, "He sings something...you play... something, right? No?"

I shove another hump of ice cream into my mouth, slowly shaking my head no. If only that were the case.

"He wants *me* to..." I can't even say it. The confusion on his face changes to poorly concealed humor.

"Sing?" He asks, watching me scarf down the cold treat. "Can you sing?"

"Not even a little bit." I tell him over a full mouth, as he takes the ice cream and store it back in the freezer.

"Tell him, you don't want to."

"It's no use." I said, leaning my body over at the waist, with my hands on my hips. "His mind is made up. And he's way more stubborn than I am."

I've already taken my hair out of yesterday's double twists, so my afro is as tame and wavy as an afro is allowed to be. In other words...it's all over my head.

"Look at you." He said, pulling me into his arms. "You're really nervous."

My forehead is pressed into his shoulder and my arms are wrapped around his waist.

"I have a feeling you'll do fine." He assures me. He smells fabulous. His oil has been refreshed and the scent is floating like ribbons around my brain. I don't know why it calms me, but it does. That, and his hands rubbing my back, brings me back to my relaxed state of mind.

"Are you going to go through with it?" He asks, freeing my eyelashes from an entangled strand of hair.

"Yeah," I tell him, rolling my eyes, "I'm going through with it."

His mouth pops open, genuinely shocked. Maybe even pleased. I shake my head and sigh, then immediately perk up. It's 4:30, which means I better start getting myself ready. I have a date tonight.

"What time is dinner?" I ask, no longer in the mood for pouting. He wraps his strong gentle arms around my waist again and lifts me off my feet.

"6:30." He confirms, "You have plenty of time."

An hour later my hair is in a loose bun, and I'm standing in front of the mirror giving myself one last look. I've decided on wearing an emerald green, floor length, chiffon maxi skirt complete with pockets. I'm wearing a basic V-neck black t-shirt and a black denim jacket. My signature natural tone make-up and nude glossy lips. I look good enough for dinner with an old guy. One last rub of lotion to my exposed forearms and hands and I'm ready to go.

Eros is in the living room watching the all sports channel, waiting, standing to greet me as I enter the room. I catch my breath the moment I see him. He's wearing a basic white button down with the top two buttons of his shirt undone. No tie, no belt, casual but very classy. I look down and chuckle at his choice of shoes, then lift the hem of my skirt to show him that I too opted to wear Converses. He chuckles, but does not abandon his grip on my eyes, or I on his. Not when he fishes his cell from his pocket, thumbs his way through whatever he's trying to find. Not when he selects his song or sits his phone on the table. Not even when he's standing directly in front of me.

Only when he leans in, just like he did when we first met, does my eyes close, embracing the feel of his hands at the small of my back. The joy of being on my tip toes to stretch my arms around his neck and nuzzle my nose against his woodsy face curls.

"Just in case," He whispers against my ear, smoothing his hand over my chiffon backside. "I want to have the first dance."

Oh lord, this man. My hand soothes over his shoulder and down to his jawline, where I hold his face to my neck as we sway and slowly two step side to side. I don't want it to end. The delicate feel of being in his arms and having him in mine. I can't help but smile. This doesn't have to end. This can go on forever. I'm his and he's mine, for now until forever.

"We need to go, love." I reluctantly say. I pull my hands to his face then smooth my thumbs over his mustache, lifting my face up to his incoming lips. "Just a small one," I say, stopping his mouth just as they brush my lips, "Right now, I'm very capable of getting carried away, and we have dates."

"Yes ma'am." He whispers, smiling sweetly, giving me the small kiss plus a little extra slip of the tongue.

'Oh, my goodness, we need to go.' I think to myself, shaking my head. I cannot be responsible for him standing his mother up.

Finally, he separates his body from my embrace inhaling deeply.

"One more?" He requests, holding up his index finger.

"Un-uh." I say, smiling as I retrieve his phone from the table and offer it to him. To which he grazes my hand in the process, prompting a bigger smile from me.

****

The ride to Golden Heights was quiet, except for the selected shuffle of music playing from Eros' phone through the car speakers. Songs we've listened to together in, shall I say...heated moments. Some we were listening to together for the first time, commenting on who's better and who will only be known as a one hit wonder. The short ride was peaceful and thick with the heat that had been building all day, especially just before we left. He steered the wheel with one hand and caressed my knuckles and ring with his thumb. As I sat memorizing his profile or listening to song after song with my eyes closed, remembering what he has done to me.

Or what I've done to him, or simply what I want to do to him and the other way around. So much has happened in the last week and yet... it's not enough. I don't think it'll ever be enough. Sigh...I want him, and if it wasn't such a short drive, and my skirt wasn't so long and frilly I would hike it up and straddle him while he drove. But I can't. I must behave just a little while longer.

Entering Golden Heights almost felt like prom night. All the residents that I saw were dressed in their brightest smiles and Sunday best. It's beautiful and sweet.

"I'll sign us in." I say, tilting my chin towards the front desk. Watching him, as he looks me up and down. I watch him walk away sliding his hands in his pockets, blushing but not looking away when he looks over his shoulder at me. I'm not a blusher, and yet my cheeks are on fire. Thank goodness for my brown skin.

"Mrs. Apollo?" Someone calls, just as I'm signing our name...*Mr. and Mrs. Apollo.* I look up and spot a twenty-something year old nurse headed my way with her hand out.

"Ayo." I say.

"Oh okay," She says, smiling, "So I heard you're having a date with one of my guys tonight."

Oh, I like her. She claims her residents as her own, as if they're family. That's a natural habit for any good healthcare worker.

"I am, if that's okay." I say, smiling back.

"It's absolutely okay. I wanted to give you a bit of a run down on him if you have a few minutes."

"Of course." I tell her, moving away from the desk.

"Okay, well his name is Joseph. He likes to go by Blind Joe."

"Is he blind?" I ask, then laugh when she tells me, no, that's just what he likes to go by. She tells me that my *husband* told her that I play guitar and that Blind Joe also plays the bass, electric and acoustic guitar, so that'll be good for conversation.

She also tells me to ask him about his time on the road with his band. She said he had some pretty awesome stories. Once she's done telling me everything, she thinks I should know, she asked if I had any questions, then excused herself to fetch my date. As I wait by the reception desk, politely thanking passing people on compliments for my outfit, or my hair. Or politely answering *six foot three* when they ask my height, and *no* when they asked if I played basketball. Not much longer, Emma, who is beautiful in her rose-colored cashmere sweater and black dress slacks.

Eros, who is...well, you know what I think about him. And my date, Blind Joe, who is surprising enough, probably only in his mid-seventies but still very youthful looking. He still held on to his very personal style of a sports jacket. A silk style button down (not tucked in mind you), with Hawaii style flowers decorating it and loose-fitting slacks. Oh, he's very much a musician, you can see it in his walk and in his smooth relaxed strides.

"Joe," Eros said, approaching, "This is Ayo. Ayo," he said, looking at me with those - *I'm about to take you eyes.* "This is Joe."

"It's very nice to meet you, Joe." I say, shaking his hand.

"Man, you a tall drink of whiskey, huh?" His voice is husky, and raspy. Probably from decades of belting out blues ballads.

"It all depends on who's standing next to me." I say, laughing.

"I guess that would be true." He responds, looking up at Eros.

"Good evening, Emma." I say, bending to kiss her cheek.

"It's really nice to see you too, Dear." She accepts my kiss and returns it with a kiss of her own, and a second on my other cheek. Her body seems tense. Not at all like the other day.

"Well, Ayo," Joe says, "Should we go see what these groceries taste like?"

"Please." I say, smiling. I can already tell, Emma's having an off day. The sooner we can eat, the sooner she can get back to her room and rest. We follow a staff member to a table set for four.

Eros is worried, I can tell by the frown lines on his brow line when he pulls Emma's chair out. I can also tell that Emma is tired by the way she semi-flops, slash sits in the awaiting seat.

"How's your day been, Emma?" I ask. I know she's tired, but hopefully she'll feel up to talking. Only then will I be able to tell what's making her so tired.

"I can't complain." She tells me, "It's just been a long one."

"I can understand that." Joe chimed in. "The cooler weather sure has a way of settling into your bones." For a second, I was confused by what he meant by *cooler*, but then I quickly figured out that he may have been referring to the air-conditioning.

"Yes, it does." Emma sighed. So, there it is. She's just plain tired. I look over at Eros, and mouth the words, "She's okay," to him wordlessly. Hoping to de-escalate his stress some.

"So, Joe, I heard you played in your own band."

More staff members come out, one pushing a tray with our dinner plates, and the other with our drinks.

"I did." He says, looking over his plate, "We called ourselves, 'The Nobodies'. I smile looking over at Emma who is commenting on how good everything looks even though Eros could have made better. To which he blushes, as though it's not a true statement. We spend as much of the dinner as allowed listening to either stories about Eros as a child or teenager, and how responsible he was. Or about Blind Joe's time on the road and how he got the name "Blind Joe". Apparently, it came from a woman Joe had dealings with back in Louisiana. He said, to him, she was the sweetest girl around. But his friends and bandmates liked to tease and say he must've been blind, because she was as ugly as a whooping stick. From then on out, they called him Blind Joe. Even after the two of them had married, had children and spent more than fifty years together.

That story made Emma laugh, and it was good to see her smile. She ate most of her food and drank a pretty decent amount of her water and iced tea. Which is good...a good appetite is a sign of good health. After a while, I notice Emma's eyes begin to drop, and I can tell she's fighting to stay awake. Just as I start to wonder why she doesn't just say she's tired, I notice the smile she musters up when Eros asks her if she wants dessert.

A ghost of his voice telling me how he couldn't remember a time where she ever complained of being tired, travels through my mind. Even now, no matter how she's feeling, she's still devoted to seeing him happy. It reminds me of every time I've ever heard my own parents say, "A mother's job is never done." Maybe, for the night, this mother's job has come to an end.

"Hey Emma," I say, grabbing my clutch, "Would you mind showing me where to find the ladies room?"

She smiles sweetly and politely agrees. Eros looks at me with gratitude and sadness in his eyes. It reminds me of when he discovered us walking outside of the coffee shop, the first time we bumped into each other. The same relief is on his face now, as it was then. Eros stands and pulls Emma's chair out, as I offer my hand for her to brace herself on as she moves around the chair. Her movement is slow, but no doubt still graceful. As I'm walking away Eros reaches for my hand and gently squeezes but doesn't speak.

"You'll keep Joe company until I get back?" I ask, patting my hand on his chest, "I won't be long, Joe." I say smiling at his crooked thumbs up.

"Take your time, Doll." He tells me.

I leave with Emma's hand in my arm, following her lead. Her mind is very much intact, but she is obviously tired enough to want to lay down.

"Emma?" I ask, hesitantly, "Would you rather just go up to your room and relax for a nap?"

"Thank you, Dear." She tells me, mirroring her son's gratitude as she pats my hand.

In her room, I help her to the restroom and into her sleeping gown. She washes her face, applies a moisture cream and drops her teeth into the waiting cup of water and a cleaning tablet.

"This is my Henry." She said, pointing to a picture of a young man standing on a paved driveway wearing a mechanics work jacket, smiling sweetly. Looking like I would imagine Eros looking without his facial hair. "He was the only man my heart would allow me to love." She said, stretching as much as her tiny body would allow her to, underneath what may have been about three blankets.

"I'm glad he has you." She confesses. "He's going to need you after I'm gone."

"After you're…"

"Now, now." She said, cutting me off before I could finish my objection. "I don't have much longer in this world. Correction, I don't want much longer."

I can't stop the tear that spills over the rim of my eye. What am I supposed to say?

"Don't cry, Dear." She tells me, "Now's not the time. Besides, I'm ready to go." She pats my face, and stares at me with her glossy eyes. "Be strong for him...he's not going to be ready no matter what." This is one strong woman, right down to the very end.

I pat my face drying under my eyes with one of the tissues from the box on her nightstand, taking a cleansing breath. She's right, he knew this woman when she was in her prime. Seeing her like this...small and tired beyond belief. He would probably blame himself. He wouldn't understand the peace a person finds when they're ready to move on from this life. I do. I see it all the time, just like I see it now.

"I will." I say, trying to smile.

Leaning in, I kiss both cheeks of this wonderful woman, pausing to allow the embrace of her tiny arms around my neck.

"You'll send my son up to say goodnight."

"Yes ma'am." I say standing to leave the room. Stopping outside the door, I look to a nearby Nurse and ask her for a bathroom.

Inside, I dust the moisture from my cheeks with my push-up make-up brush pausing to stare at myself in the mirror. *Be strong for him, Ayo, you promised.* I wash my hands and give myself one quick once over then make my way back to the dining room.

"I didn't take too long, did I?" I ask, walking up.

"Where's Momma?" Eros asks, standing up.

"She's laying down." I tell him, placing my hands on his arm.

"She's, okay?"

"It's just been a long day for her that's all." His chest rises with the breath he's inhaling. "She would like for you to come and say goodnight."

"Yeah?" He said, "Okay."

"I'll wait here with Joe." He nods his head and shakes hands with Joe thanking him for a nice dinner.

"That's quite a decent cat you have there." Joe comments after Eros walks off.

"He's something." I say smiling at Joe.

"Which do you rather?" Joe asked, "Gibson? Or Fender?"

"Fender." I tell him, "I like the feel of it." He's a musician, I don't need to explain more than that.

"You might know a thing or two." Joe smiles. He waves one of the staff members over and introduces me, then informs her that he's going up and he's bringing me with him.

I'm thoroughly confused, and the staff member is equally excited. What he meant didn't dawn on me until the staff member stood in front of the diners that were left and announced that she had a lovely treat for them. Joseph "Blind Joe" Gutierez was going to grace them with a song. Along with a special guest, Emma Apollos's daughter in law. I can't contain my shock. Or my smile. Joseph "Blind Joe" wants to jam with me.

"What do you say, kid?" He asks. He was already up and ready to go, with his arthritic hand out towards me.

"Of course." I say smiling. What else can I say? With all the stories this man told me tonight, all that he's lived through. I would be honored. I take his hand and follow him up to the area where the band is sitting.

Well now they're shuffling around for a stool for Joe and myself. A not so young, but still not old guitarist hands over his instrument to Joe, who passes it over to me.

"Young brother, I'm going to need a bass." He looks at me rubbing his gnarled hands together. "I hope you don't mind, Honey. These old fingers ain't been able to handle six strings for quite some time now."

"Not at all." I say, removing my jacket and handing it to a Nursing Assistant standing nearby.

"Now," Joe says, strumming a few strings, looking back at the man that loaned it to him, nodding his head in approval. "I'm gonna take the bottom beat, and when your fingers can't be still any longer, you start plucking."

I nod my head as his strumming takes the sound of a jazzier blues song. A tune starts to pick up in my head, so I start pulling it from the strings under my fingers. My left hand stayed in the same general area on the neck of the instrument, and fingers of my right-hand pulling string after string. I barely, just barely notice that Joe stops playing, giving me my very first solo in front of an audience. I keep playing but smile at the raspy voice praising me by telling me that I was *"too tall"*, for him. We play a few more chords, then end the song smiling at the applause awarded us by the diners, and a few staff members.

"Ladies and gentlemen," I heard Joe croak out, "Too Tall Ayo."

Too Tall Ayo, I have a blues name. I take my bow, return the guitar and say my thank you's and good-byes to Joe. Telling him how much of an honor it was to jam with him. Leaving him to prepare for the next set with the band. Repeating polite thank you's to the people complimenting as I make my way back to our table. Where I find my clutch, my jacket and Eros. The staff member must have given it to him when he returned. Which was...when?

"You are amazing." He tells me. There he goes, with those eyes...and there my cheeks go warming up again.

"I wasn't expecting that."

"Of course not." He said, "If Blind Joe asks you to play, you play."

"Is Emma asleep?" I ask, sliding my arms into the sleeves of my jacket he's holding out for me.

"Yes." He tells me. "I'm going to say bye to Joe." I watch him walk over, say something in Joe's ear. Who then, after shaking Eros' hand, raises his mouth to the microphone standing beside him, lifts his hand in my direction and says, "Ladies and gentlemen, one more time for Too Tall Ayo."

More applause...more smiles...more waves and thank you's and we're out. Eight thirty in the evening, and the rest of the night is ours...and I am finally free to abandon this ridiculous idea of behaving myself. His shuffle is back on in the SUV, but my attention is barely listening. One of my legs is crossed over the other with my skirt falling loosely over them. His hand is resting on my thigh and I'm running my fingers through the hair that joins at his sideburns and beard. Tracing my finger along the outline of his earlobe. Pretty soon we're pulling up next to my car. I watch him get out, stroll around the front of the truck, and open my door for me.

As soon as I'm out of the truck, Eros, the giant that he is, scoops me up in his arms. Just like I weighed nothing and carried me up to the porch. Into the house, after I unlock the door, and into the kitchen sitting me down on the island surface. Then leans his forehead into mines, with his eyes closed. He's still worried about his mom. No... he knows. Maybe she's told him that she's ready to move on and he can't do anything about it. Emma, in so many words, was right. Eros needs to feel needed. He needs to be able to give love and he chose me to give it to.

"Hey." I say cupping my hands around his face, so his eyes drag up to mine. "It's okay...she's okay." It's all I can say, it's not time for any other explanation.

He put his finger under my chin and lifted my lips to his. So much pain troubles his eyes, and I want to show him that he doesn't have to go through this alone anymore. This is right where we left off a couple of hours ago. Only this time we don't have to stop. We can get lost in each other. There's no one else in this world except me and him. I pull him closer by wrapping my legs around his waist and begin slowly undoing the buttons on his shirt. Tracing the details of his lion as I work my way down. By the time I have it open and untucked from his pants, he has me lifted in the same position around his waist and is carrying me down the hallway. I can't keep my lips off his, or my hands off of...well, him.

I want to touch him and kiss him...everywhere. I know I can't take away his sadness but maybe, I can take his mind off it. Even if only for a little while. In the room I unlock my legs from his waist and step, with ease, to the floor. He's so strong and carries my long body like it's nothing. It's the simplest thing to carry someone, but the problem is, not very many men have the stature to do such a thing. It takes a lot to make a woman like me feel even more delicate and light footed than I already think I am. And he does it, just by looking at me...the way he's looking at me now.

Composed, wanting, challenging. Needing. *Needing?* He needs me right now, and I know just what to do. My tablet is back at his house, which doesn't make a difference because I don't have anything that would suit this mood. This...make me forget my problems and sorrows, mood. Where every touch, every kiss, every caress is meant to be a release of any and all stresses weighing you down. I've known that feeling many...*many* times in my past. And I know from experience that the only thing that can make that feeling worse...is someone not paying attention to your vibe and making the experience all about them.

"I need your phone." I tell him. He doesn't on any level hesitate or ask any questions. He just hands it over proving he has nothing to hide. There's not even a lock code on it.

I'm not even sure what song it was, but I'm pretty sure of the singer, so I thumbed for his name. So far, I know every song that I scroll over, which means choosing the songs that I'm not familiar with is my best option. Lucky me, it's the correct one. Keeping with what is becoming our usual, I put it on repeat and place his phone on the charge station. Then I turn to him, standing, with his hands in his pockets. Watching me...wondering. I've been wanting him all day but it took just now for me to realize, he's probably never let anyone take care of him. It's entirely possible that no one has ever even tried. Well, he's going to be my husband and he needs to be loved right now.

I walk over to where he's standing and trail my fingers over the opening of his shirt. Skimming his skin as I slide it over his shoulders and down his arms. Kissing his chest and stomach, and sides as they become exposed. I want to take my time, so I fold his shirt and place it on the seat of my recliner. I circle his body softly touching his skin, tracing the muscles of his back and shoulders. Lightly kissing wherever my fingertips touch.

'That's right, my friend.' I think, as his chest rises and falls with his breathing, *'Just relax.'*

I walk him to the bed, sit him on the edge of the by lightly nudging the muscles of his stomach. Kissing his chest from one side to the other, leaving moist strands of hair in my trail. His thighs are firm and fit under the palms of my hands, but my focus is his feet. I sit crossed legged on the floor in front of him, arranging my skirt around my body so I'm not sitting on it, and begin untying the laces...one shoe at a time. I know he's watching me, but I wonder if he can *see* what I'm doing. After removing his socks, I reach for the body oil on my bedside table and saturate my hands.

He adjusts his seating and allows me to place his foot in my lap. My hands are firm, so I carefully rub my thumbs down the souls and up the instep.

"Close your eyes." I say half smiling, half wondering if he would... and he does. Then I rub small circles over the heel and ball of his foot.

"Just relax."

I even lace my fingers through his toes a few times, continuing with the other foot when I finish. After I'm satisfied that both feet are de-stressed, I lift my feet to his lap, from my sitting position, and he wastes no time undoing my laces and removing my shoes. He traces his fingers up to my ankle and back to my toes, but I don't give him that pleasure for too long... because it's not about me right now.

Using my legs, I stand in front of him and watch him...watch me pull my shirt over my head. His brows slightly dip and his bottom lip hides under his top teeth. I don't think he realized I wasn't wearing a bra today. I shudder at his soft touch following the outline of my breast. My skin prickles, but it's not about me tonight.

"My zipper please." I say softly, turning my hip to him. My skirt billows to the floor around my ankles. His hands caress my hips holding me firm to receive the small nibbles and sucks he gives my pelvis right above my panty line, and below my belly button. Though my eyes are closed, and my head is tilted back, I am still aware that he's slid his fingers into the waist of my panties and are sliding them down my thighs.

Slowly, he's trying to turn the tables, but I'm not ready for that yet. I lightly grab his bun and gently tug his head back.

"It's not my turn yet." I say softly, caressing the hair under his chin. Without a word I step out of my skirt and panties and pick them up... slowly. Allowing his fingers to graze my skin as I step away from him. I drop them on the same recliner as his shirt, grab a brush from my vanity, and climb on the bed behind him. Untying the stretchy band from his hair and gently brushing the tangles from his thick strands. His eyes are closed and his head tilts backwards as I rake my nails, starting from the lower part of his back. Tracing his spine up between his shoulder blades, up the back of his head.

Over his scalp from back to front. I work small, firm circles over the base of his roots. Kissing the back of his neck as I go. His body is there, finally. His chin is dipped into his chest, with his head hanging low. Now he's beginning to relax and de-stress.

"Take off your pants." I whisper in his ear. His movements are mildly slow and calculated, but his eyes are deliberate. Turning to look at me over his shoulder, then standing only stopping to watch me slide back further onto the bed. Only continuing when he's sure my eyes are on him, and his erection. *That* is the fruits of my touch.

I love looking at him, especially when he's watching me at the same time. I graze my hands up my stomach in a way that tickles my skin and perks my nipples, which are firm and begging me to twist and pull them to make them harder. He's licking his lips watching me, but he doesn't make a move towards me yet. He does, however, wrap his fist around his erection and begin to slowly stroke. Watching my fingers as I rub my slick wetness over my clitoris, and a moan slips from his mouth. I begin rotating my hips, grinding my own fingers, giving in to how good I feel.

Suddenly, he's hovering over me, kissing me, giving me a thorough mouth examination with his tongue. Showing no mercy, filling me with his groans. Not being shy about the fact that he's still pleasuring himself. I've been wanting that kiss all day from him, and now I don't want it to end. I reach down between our bodies and position his penis at my opening, while he shifts his weight to both arms, then moves my hand as he glides inside. Gasping at the slow, and very well enunciated, *"fuck... me"*, that slides from Eros' throat. He doesn't let me get the feel of the thrust. He just doesn't stop. Thrust after thrust, after thrust. Igniting a massive fire that flourishes over my entire body. And not the small, tiny ones that build as we reach our climax either. This one is a full out, full bodied, five alarm fire.

I try to separate our mouths so I can release my moans, but he smothers them, swallowing them. Taking in all my pleasure, all of my joy, all of my love, swallowing it down his throat and into his soul. And in return, I accept his pain, and his worry, and his fears...and I trap them into my spirit. Finally, he pulls away from my mouth and finds my ear.

"Do you feel that?" He asks. His voice is a raspy moan with every thrust. His hand slides down to my thigh, pulling it up into his side, driving himself deeper...and deeper...and deeper still. "Hum? Do you feel...*that?*"

That massive fire is becoming an asteroid, and I can't hold it back much longer. His voice enters my ear and exits my mouth in mangled, twisted pants of his name. And I love you's, and just sounds that I've never, ever heard myself make before.

"This is how you make me feel." He moans. Then his body convulses, and his voice somehow manages the words, "My Queen." To that, I can no longer hold back the asteroid, or the flood that comes along with it. My back arches, my mouth opens, and my voice goes up an octave. A couple of octaves, to be honest.

"Give it to me, love." He whispers groans, still thrusting. Gliding his hand up my arched belly, smoothly between my breasts then back down. Locking firmly on my hip and forcing me to flood the bed with my first female ejaculation. Before my body even has the chance to float back down from cloud nine, he releases a massive climax.

I wrap my legs and arms around his neck and waist and hold him until his breathing slows back to normal. Laying there with his head between my breast, his arms cradling my sides and his eyes closed... absorbing the feel of my fingers raking through his hair.

"Thank you."

"You're welcome." I say, assuming he was referring to his hair and wanted me to stop.

"Um-um." He spoke. His eyes were still closed, head was still cuddling with my breast. Body completely still, except for his arm darting up to grab my hand before I completely pull it away.

"No, not that." He said, returning my hand to his scalp. "I like that."

"Thank you for what?" I ask returning to my task, thoroughly confused now.

"For being you." He says, looking up at me.

Now I understand. This is a comment people say to each other all the time. Or at least I assume it is. I myself have been told this comment on, at the most, three different occasions. I didn't read too much into it then, just like I wouldn't have read too much into it this time except, Eros elaborated.

"Time stops when I'm with you." He stops talking long enough to position himself beside me on the pillow. Propping up on his elbow. "I've never seen anyone embrace living life the way you do."

"You're welcome." I say. Though it was a statement, it came out sounding like a confused question. I mean, what else can I say. I'm just being myself.

"Like now." He continues, tracing his finger down the bridge of my nose. "I don't want this night to end, but I can't wait to see what tomorrow brings."

"Hum," I say, leaning into his body, "You sure know how to make a girl smile."

"Do I... make you smile?" He asks, kissing my forehead.

"You're kidding right?" I say, smiling brighter, but still furrowing my eyebrows. "I haven't stopped smiling since Monday."

"You know," He said trailing his thumb softly across the curve of my cheek bone, "I've been trying to count your freckles since the first day I met you."

"Really?" I giggle. Which turns into a chuckle, then into a flat out laugh.

"What's so funny?" Eros wonders, echoing my laugh.

"Wait." I say, trying to control my giggles. "So, when I was in second grade, I guess I had to be about seven or eight maybe. Something like that, anyway. My teacher, Mrs. Thrift, around the last couple of days before Christmas break, started reading that book *Freckle Juice*. Remember it? Well, I used to get picked on and teased about my freckles..."

"What?" Eros says, leaning forward kissing the dots on my cheek. "But they're so cute."

"Yeah well, I didn't think so back then, and neither did any of my school mates. Anyway, that wasn't the problem."

He's scooting my body closer to his with that - *I'm here, and I'm listening but I'm focused on something else-* look.

"No? What was the problem?" He traced his finger from my shoulder down the length of my arm, gazing into my eyes. Attentively awaiting my answer.

"The problem was, we went on holiday before we could finish the book. So, I didn't know how it ended, *but* that didn't stop me from making my own *freckle juice.*"

"You made your own?" He asks, tracing the outline of the paper scroll tattooed on my rib cage.

"First of all," I tell him, sighing, bringing my arm above my head as his finger skims the surface of my ribcage. "With advice from Nate and Danny." Up my arm pit. "I used creek water." Up my arm to my fingertips, lacing his fingers through mine. "Mustard. Worcestershire sauce. Ketchup. Hot sauce." Using four of his fingers, he trails my palm and wrist. "Nutmeg. Salt. Pepper." Down my forearm, under arm. "Vinegar, and ginger."

Now he's kissing my fingertips, one at a time. "You're not paying attention, Eros." I say playfully, scolding him.

"Oh see," he says quietly. Kissing my shoulder bone. "That's not true. You have my full undivided attention." Then he kiss my lips just as tender as he kissed my shoulder and fingertips.

"What did you do with your juice?" He asks, tracing my jawline.

"I drank it."

"You didn't." He gasped, looking up from the bend of my neck.

"I did, and was sick as shit." I said, turning over on my stomach. He inhaled deeply and traced the bumps of my spine from my neck to the curve of my butt.

"Probably from the creek water." He says chuckling.

"That and the tadpole." I said nonchalantly.

"You ate a tadpole?" He asked looking up from the kisses he was tenderly spreading across my back.

"Actually," I tell him, blushing, again. "That was the second tadpole that I'd eaten."

I can't help the laugh that erupts from my belly. Eros' face transforms. His mouth drops, his eyes grow larger than I've ever seen them.

His eyebrows are well into his hairline, in a perfect blend of surprise and shock all over his face.

"You ate *two* tadpoles!?" He says, laughing with me.

I'm still laying on my stomach with my hands tucked under the pillow I'm lying on. So, I can only nod slightly.

"Why?" He asks. His attention is shifting again. I can only see his face. Well actually his side profile. Because he's busy watching the finger that I feel trailing down my back.

"The first time," over the curve of my butt. "was on a dare." Down my thigh to my ankle. "The second time was because," back up the inside of my calf, "it was in the cup when I scooped the water up."

Up the inside of my thigh and over the curve of my *cheek*. Stopping to palm and smack it so lightly it doesn't even make a sound. Then he has the nerve to look at me…as though his eyes never left mine.

"That's disgusting." He says nonchalantly, palming my ass the entire time.

"That's very distracting." I say, half smiling at the way his eyebrow lifts.

"What? This?" He asks, gripping my cheek and moving his hand like he's waving…slowly.

It's causing this open and close sensation between my legs igniting the first small fire.

"Do you want me to stop?" He asks, still watching himself *wave*.

"No." I say quietly. *Why is my voice so small?*

"Good." He breaths.

And there I go, throwing that ear up for sacrifice again. I didn't think about it until it was too late, and he was right there talking softly.

"Because I wasn't finished."

Now my eyebrows are touching my hairline, *has he started something?*

"Finished what?" I am thoroughly confused. Especially since he's up and off the bed and moving. *What's he doing?*

I turn over on my back and find him thumbing through his phone, then replace it on the charge station.

"My turn." He tells me, turning and walking towards the bed. *Anywhere* by 112 fills the air space of the bedroom.

"Um...come again now." I say watching him climb up my body, hovering over my stomach.

"A little while ago you stood in front of me and took off your shirt. I won't get into my thoughts when I realized you weren't wearing a bra all night." He shakes his head and closes his eyes. "I kissed you here."

I want to look at where "*here*" is, but I don't have to. I can feel where his thumb is caressing circles on my left pelvis. So, I hold his gaze, or rather, he holds mine.

"And here." He continues. I feel his fingers stretch across the flat of my belly and his thumb making circles around my belly button.

"Um-hum." He nods, as if agreeing with himself. I nod my head mirroring his head movements, hardly remembering what the question was.

"*And,*" He said, shifting to my right side, but still hovering and still holding my gaze.

Instead of pointing, he dropped his chin closer to my pelvis. Hovering close enough to trace circles on my skin using his beard. My mouth pops, at the tickle sensation, igniting fires in a circle pattern. Spreading with the fires around my navel, which have joined the other side of my hip.

"I can especially remember you kissing me here. Like this." Then I watch him dip his face to the circles his chin hair just made, and gasp at the feel of his tongue and lips...and kiss the same spot. "Remember?" He asks, looking back into my eyes. I nod as he lowers his body, resting his chin on his layered hands, that rest on my belly. I don't know where he's going with all this but he has my full attention. His hair has fallen around his face in thick silky strands. Reaching forward, I pull apart a lock and run it through my fingers.

"You stopped me."

My eyes flicker to his. "Your exact words were, and I quote," He lifts his head high enough to allow two fingers to form air quotes. "It's not your turn."

Those *are* my exact words verbatim. I can't believe it. He can't be serious. And yet his eyes are telling me exactly that, as I watch him climb over my body until he's hovering over my face.

"It's my turn now."

"Oh. Okay." I say finding my voice.

"Turn on your stomach." His body is hovering, so I have plenty of room to slowly turn myself under him.

Chapter Fourteen

"Now," I hear him say as he settles his weight over the back of my thighs. "Where were we? Oh yeah. You like eating tadpoles." I laugh despite my rising anticipation. I close my eyes, completely relying on my hearing and sense of touch.

"I don't like to eat them," I say. I can feel his mild erection resting on the bottom of my butt. "I thought it would help."

I arch my back and move side to side enough to feel his hardness twitch at the movement. His hand grazes my thigh up to my hip, then gently presses me back on the bed.

"Keep this still." He's gripping my cheek and waving it again. *Oh, that open and close sensation is nice.* I cross my legs at the ankles hoping to tame the growing sensitivity between my legs. The bed shifts as he moves his weight further down my body. I gasp a quiet sigh as his moist tongue slowly licks down my spine. Stopping only to palm and squeeze both cheeks kissing on both sides. Well…this is *very* new. I haven't had anyone passionately kiss my ass in like…*never*.

My head is absolutely spinning as I give in to his hands guiding my hips higher in the air. Kissing my ass more, I don't know…deeply. I hiss at his tongue brushing against my opening and hum a long sigh as he switches sides. Kissing the inside of my thigh. Palming and squeezing and waving both sides now. The open and close isn't my focus anymore. It's his flat, moist tongue grinding my clit in circles…from behind, mind you. I can't see him, but I can sure as hell imagine. I rotate my hips against his face accepting his tongue grinding. Absorbing it, moaning and humming. Welcoming the joining of all those small fires merging and becoming one huge blaze.

"You taste sweet." He tells me as I swallow air, licking my dry lips.

"Um." Is all I could get out.

It's all over for me. Every ounce of my control has been scorched and evaporated by the fires burning like a savage volcano ready to erupt.

"I know, babe." He tells me in his favorite soft tone.

"Ooh." I gasp as he uses the flat of his palm as a tunnel guide against my vagina for his thrust that slides up and down the length of me. Not yet entering me, and still from behind.

"Be still." He tells me, sucking air through his teeth. Is he *kidding*, even the sound he makes after saying that scorches my soul.

"I can't help it." I tell him, circling with his strokes. I just want him…and now. "Please." I moan, wiggling from side to side. This damn man has me *begging*.

"Okay, Ayo." I hear him say. Then almost simultaneously he slides himself in. Back out, then back in again.

"Oh…my…" Back out, then back in again. "Fuck." My moans are long and slow as I clutch the sheets. Back in again.

"Lay flat." I hear in my ear. My legs are urged close by his, but it doesn't stop me from grinding circles back into his grind. "That's it." I hear in my ear. He's matching circles now, rocking a rhythm into the bed that could make a ship captain seasick.

"Just like that, Ayo." I hear in my ear. "Just like that."

Shit…I can't stop trembling. He's so damn deep and I can't stop moaning and saying yes. Mainly because he asked me if I liked it, to which I whispered out *yes*…and kind of stayed stuck on it. And *that's* mostly because when I answered him, he chose that moment to thrust and change up to a faster pace. That spot is being obliterated, and I'm about to lose it.

"Please," I whine again, "Please go faster." I'm proudly begging… again.

"Faster." He said picking up the pace. "Like that?"

"Yes." I moan loudly, pausing at the feel of my beginning eruption. "Oh yes."

"Like that?" He asks again, stroking deeper...faster.

"Yes." I'm half squealing, half singing, half moaning all at once. "Oh...ssss...yes, baby yes."

"There it is." He groans into my neck.

"Yes." I moan again.

I can't move. Can't raise up. All I can do is circle my hips and enjoy his delicious strokes and thrust. Until I can't take it anymore and let go.

"Oh...my...God. I'm coming." I say just as the volcano that destroyed Pompeii ripples through me.

"Um. I'm coming with you." He grunts, and grunts. "Fuck." He whispers, exhaling into my back, shuttering at his aftershock. I'm breathing, well actually panting and whimpering. Basking in the afterglow. Eros' weight shifts and my backside feels the draft as he stretches his body beside me.

"Oh my god." I'm shaking my head as much as I can on my stomach. *I fucking love this man.*

"This man fucking loves you too." I hear. My eyes pop open, and he's gazing at me through sleep heavy eyes.

"How do you know what I was thinking?" I ask, closing my eyes again. Scooting closer into his strong warm arms.

"Because you said it out loud." Eros chuckles.

I yawn and stretch my body long, turning on my back. I really could use some yoga in my life, in the morning. Eros shifts his body over resting his head on my chest between my breasts. I wrap my arms around him cradling his face in my arms.

"You are the queen of my soul." He tells me.

＊＊＊＊＊＊＊＊＊＊＊＊＊＊

It's early the next morning when I awake, well rested and energetic. For a moment I lay there watching my husband-to-be sleep. His lashes spread out over his cheeks like a short fan. His mouth is open, and a small puddle of drool saturates the pillow under him. He's lovely even when he's unaware of himself. Briefly, I wonder how many women had an opportunity with this man, and how many women lost out only for me to run into him...literally. It doesn't matter, I have him now, and there's no way I'm letting him go. During my shower, my breakfast of pancakes, eggs and turkey sausage. During my drum session, (with the door closed, making the room completely soundproof) and now, during my yoga workout, I reflect on our relationship.

We met, dated, fell in love, almost broke up, got back together... then got engaged. All in a week's time. Aside from Franky spreading the news about him being the new guy in my life, we've been inside the small universe that only consists of us...and Emma, of course. And like two people, who happened to be at the right place at the right time, we're falling right in like two professionals. Fitting into each other's lives like we've been here since birth. Both of us want to be loved, both of us want to give love, and neither of us wants to have to wait for it. Why should we? I've always been pretty sure of my own mind, and he seems to be damn sure of his. Hell, at this point, I'm pretty committed to Eros. Not only because I want to be, but because he deserves the kind of devotion that I want to give. Besides, he seems to be, or more so, I feel like he is just as...if not more so, devoted to me. Everything has fallen into place. Like he said, the universe has been set right and will be made concrete when we say *I do.*

Which will be when? Whenever we want. That's how we've been getting on so far. Doing things our way, when and how we want. Why stop now? Most people wait years to find what we already have now. Why do we have to wait? I don't want to wait, but I will if he does.

Sheesh Ayo, you're getting married. I laugh at myself, not knowing exactly what's so funny. I feel...I don't know what word to use because words like love, and happiness. Or fantastic, or marvelous and every other adjective for those feelings just doesn't cut it. They don't hold enough value. I unfold myself from the floor bow pose and loosen my limbs, shaking my legs and arms. Instructing the blood to flow freely. Pick up my mat, towel and bottle of water then leave. Eros isn't in bed when I return my towel and mat to the closet, so I head to the kitchen.

And find him instead, sprawled across the couch watching ESPN and talking on the phone.

He's stretched way out, half sitting-half lying, one leg flat out to the end of the couch and the other bent upright, foot planted on the floor. His arm is propped behind his head highlighting and flexing every muscle from his biceps to his well chiseled rib cage and abs. He's not wearing a shirt and I guess this is his around the house look. -*Side bar*: I approve of this look! I also approve of his gym shorts that naturally seem to bunch up around his...well you know what I'm getting at. I think I stared at his junk too long, so I played it off by walking through the living room blowing him a kiss, smiling at his half smile. On my way past the couch, I tickle the bottom of his foot and giggle at the way he flinches.

Goodness gracious, all I need to do is refill this bottle and return it to the fridge. And now because of him, all I want to do is go over there, sit across his lap and grind. I cross over to the kitchen and fill the bottle, then turn to put it away and he's watching me. Well, I think he was watching my butt. Only because, when he noticed me watching him, he smiled that sheepish, '*Oh no! You caught me looking*' face.

"Alright," he says into the phone as I walk over to where he's, seemingly posing for some magazine centerfold, and sit. He's repositioned himself so that I'm able to lean back into his chest. "Alright then, bet, so let me know when you're done with everything, and I'll text you the address." He pauses a second, listening to the person on the other end, while handing me the t.v. remote. "Okay peace out." He hangs up then leans over me and tosses his phone on the coffee table.

"Good morning." He says, bear hugging my top half and kissing my cheek.

"Good morning to you." I respond, turning to face him, pulling my knees up and resting my arm on the arm of the couch, then leaning my weight on to my elbow. Accepting the kiss and squeeze to my thigh then butt.

"I invited T.K. over to watch football if that's okay."

"Of course, it's okay." I say, curling my finger around the corner of his mustache. "I'm going to be working with Franky anyway."

"Oh, that's right." He smiled, "Your big song." Groaning, I drop my head. "Are you ready?"

"No, but I guess I have to be." I say looking up at him.

He's not even looking at me, he's too busy watching his fingers pick at an imaginary piece of something on my hip.

"Can I watch?" He asks, finally finding my eyes.

"*No.*" I chuckled, smiling even though my eyebrows shot to my forehead. His mouth pops open, in for real shock this time.

"But I *love* to watch you play." Aww, look at him pouting his cute bottom lip at me.

"You can watch me *play* anytime you like." I say kissing his pouty lip, "*After* I finish rehearsing." His face cracks me up.

"Why not?" He asked, smiling, twisting his body so that he's sitting up right, though still slouching, with his bare feet propped on the table.

"You would be way too distracting." I say slowly, shaking my head. The surprised look on his face is completely priceless, but he holds my gaze none the less.

"I would distract you?" He asks, twinkling his eyes at me. Lord have mercy...he has no clue how cute he is.

"Yes." I say chuckling, "You're distracting me right now." It's funny how he doesn't know, and I can't help laughing. "In fact," I say, straightening my posture. "If we're going to do this." I wave my hand indicating all around us. "We're going to have to set some ground rules."

"Ground rules?" He laughs, "Okay, like what?"

"Like this for instance." I wave my hand in a circle in front of his torso and shorts area, "You can't walk around like this."

"What's wrong with this?" He waves his fingers up and down his chest, looking down briefly at himself.

"Nothing." I say looking down at him, not as briefly though. "That's the problem...it's too distracting."

"Ok so, let's start a list." He smiles, as he stuffs a pillow under his back, and shifts his pelvis.

I notice how he shifts himself slowly, lifting his hips, sliding my hips down so that my crotch is closer to his. Watching himself move the entire time. "So, I have to wear shirts." He leans his head against the back of the couch very casually.

"And socks." I say.

"Socks?" He laughs, "Okay, socks and a shirt."

"These shorts are out too." I say stretching the waist band. *Oh, my goodness,* he's not wearing underwear.

"What?" His eyes pop, "Okay, I'll wear my sweats."

"Um no," I say, shaking my head, vetoing that idea, "Not those joggers. I've seen those, they're out."

"Oh wow." He laughs, very casually leaning his head against the back of the sofa again. "Okay, I have one for you."

"For me?" I gasped. "What did *I* do?"

"You wear yoga pants very well." He reveals, running his hands up my thighs, "Yoga pants are out."

"Okay," I say, laughing and shaking my head, "No yoga pants."

"So off subject, but not really." He says, adjusting himself again, "What are we going to do about living arrangements?"

*Hum…*well there's something I haven't thought about. Not just in relationship with Eros, but ever. Not even when Eric and I were together and that *situationship* lasted off and on for 2…going on 3 years.

"Hum."

"I mean, how do we go about choosing where to live?"

"Well," I say, climbing from his lap and stretching out on the opposite end of the sofa, resting my feet on his knee.

"Why do we have to choose?" I ask, adjusting the pillow behind my back. "I've lived here for five years. I own this home. And my car. I've put a lot into this place. I don't want to sell."

"And you've been in your home for eleven years. Everything about that home is you. Hell, you have a kitchen in your backyard." I switch my feet from his lap to the back of the couch where his head is rested. Then use my toes to kick off my flats.

His eyes shift from mine to my feet then back to my eyes.

"See this," he said, turning, so that one leg is tucked under the other, and facing me. "This is on the list." My mouth…drops.

"What? My feet?" I asked, laughing, wiggling my toes by his face.

"Yes." He laughs, catching my painted toe between his fingers, "Your feet."

He lifts my foot and tenderly kisses the bottom. "You, putting them all in my lap, and wiggling your cute little painted toes by my face."

I laugh and roll my eyes but slide my feet from the back of the couch and pull them to the back of my thighs.

"So, keep my feet to myself." I say, playing sarcastic.

"Thank you." He said matter of factly.

"You're welcome." I say rolling my eyes playfully, "Anyway," I have to sit up, my legs are way too long to sit this way, so I'm up. Adjusting my pants, that have twisted around my waist. "I don't see why either of us should have to sell." I say dropping my knees indian style, leaning back on the chair arm behind me.

"Between the two of us there's a combined number of thirty years, of both the medical slash healthcare field and professional football league. After everything it took to accomplish that alone, for both of us, we deserve this. At least for right now."

"So, you think we should keep both houses?"

"You don't?" I watch him lift my legs and move them to the outside of his body one at a time.

Then he moves closer to me resting my right leg across his lap, and his back against my left.

"No." He said rubbing my thigh with one hand and flipping through channels with the other. "I think we should sell one or both and buy a place that we can make our own and start a family."

Hum...there's something else I've never thought about...*kids*. I mean, I've thought about it before, briefly.

"You want kids?" I say scooting my body down so the back of my neck is lying on the arm rest.

"Um-hum." He nods, looking down at me. I'm not watching him; I'm actually watching a chef on t.v. talk about what he plans on doing to the slab of baby back ribs he's dry rubbing. But I can feel his movements when he turns his head, and the warmth of his gaze.

"Do you?"

"Yeah, I want kids." I say, looking up at him. "But I think at this point, it's more of a question of *when.*"

"That's true." he says, leaning and turning his crotch into mine. "Can I do this? Is this on the list?"

"This is fine." I half smile, as I watch my hand glide down his chest, over his abs. Stopping at the waistband of his shorts, I remember that he's going commando and pull him closer between my legs, feeling the grind of his package.

"I really like these pants." He tells me gripping the waistband with both hands and tugging them down, "But they're on the list so they have to go."

"Your shorts are on the list too, you know." I tell him while lifting my bottom, helping him out.

He lifts himself up and slides his shorts off in one swipe, propping my long legs over his shoulder. His chest hair is so soft on the back of my thighs that I can't help moving them around to feel the thickness.

"So, when do you think, we should start trying?" he asked, while sliding himself into me slowly. He doesn't thrust...he doesn't stroke, or grind, or make any other movements except rubbing his hands on my thighs and hips. Breathing in and out through his nose.

"I think we already have." I say draping my hands over the armrest. "I mean we haven't exactly been trying to prevent it." I drop my hip slowly down his shaft and back up while he watches my movements still not thrusting.

"No, we haven't." He agrees, still looking down. I drop my hips a second time, and bring them up slowly, rocking back and forth.

I can feel his hands on my hips rocking with the motion, gently gripping as his bottom lip disappears under his top teeth. And there goes the thrust I've been waiting for, feeling it and watching for it to come is an image I hope to never forget. A whisper of a soft quiet gasp escapes my throat, just as I'm about to drop my hips. His eyes dart to mine, and he stops me, by holding me steady.

"Maybe it's already too late." There's no denying the passion or excitement in his eyes or his voice. Look at him, he wants to give me his *babies, aww*. Do I want this?? Hell…why not? The truth is, I'm 35 and getting older. It's either now or never.

"Maybe it is." I say, dropping my gaze to our joined mid-sections and watching myself slide down his shaft, then back up meeting his thrust.

I could be pregnant right now…hum. And if I'm not, okay. At least I know that if I do get knocked up, I'll be happy about it. I mean, at the end of the day, that's what drives my decisions. Whether the outcome makes me happy or not. Well, I guess from here on out, it's going to have to be whether it makes *us* happy or not.

"So, to make it official," he said, stopping my hips again. "We're in agreement, that if we have now…or should we in the future, near or far, make a tiny human together…we're okay with that?"

"As long as we do it together." I answer, dropping my hip watching his eyes warm up, "I mean no matter what. Me and you, as husband and wife, and mom and dad. None of that *baby momma*, or *baby daddy* bullshit."

"Absolutely." He agrees. I bring my hips up in short pumps, dropping all the way down after each pump. By the time I make it to the fourth pump, Eros, timing his own movement perfectly, meets me with a deep thrust and very thorough grind. His pubic hair, though semi-groomed, provides the most delicious friction against my clit. The moan that escapes my lips even sounds like some sort of beautiful seduction to me. And he knows it, because he's working that spot…grind after grind. Friction and more friction, at the same time approaching that spot with just the right amount of pressure.

Another moan escapes, and he thrusts again, this time I thrust back, matching his grind circle for slow circle. Adding just a tad more pressure to my clit. I've lifted my pelvis off the couch and he's supporting me with his thighs. Guiding it up and down with his hands but still not moving. I can't take it anymore and my willpower has completely given in to his hand's rhythm. I'm not even watching him anymore. My head is back, my eyes are closed.

Thrust...deep.

Moan...whine.

My mouth is slack, and I barely notice his hands caressing my hips. All I feel is his thrust. The long, deep thrust that he's driving into me. Over and over and over. Neither of us speaks. There's no sound except for our love making and our breathing. No music on repeat. No talking in my ear. No coaching me to *give it to him*. No begging him to get it for me. Nothing. Until our bodies erupt almost simultaneously, thriving in the feel of our own orgasm. I open my eyes and find that his half smile reflects the very same thought I'm having.

"Why are you smiling?" I ask, easing my body upright for his approaching kiss.

"Why are you?"

Am I smiling? I am.

"I was thinking," I began, picking my pants up from the floor. "We might have just made a crib midget."

"*Crib midget?*" Was all he could slip past his grin before he erupted into laughter.

The next couple of hours were easy going. We took showers, separately this time. Eros even offered to comb my hair. Apparently, he loves it. The color, the curls which are natural due to my mom being white and my dad being black. He's asking all kinds of questions. Do I dye it? Do I ever get it cut? Do I use anything to straighten it? To which I tell him I don't put any chemicals in it to straighten it. I like my wild, frizzy afro 90% of the time, the other ten percent, it doesn't like me. It took some convincing me, but I finally agreed to let him, telling him if he's going to comb it then he has to do it the right way. I gave him fair warning about having oily hands, but he was still willing. So, I showed him the few products that I do use and show him what to do with it. How to rub it in, how to separate it into sections making sure to oil from root to ends.

I give him my favorite spray bottle, because all of us natural hair folks have a favorite spray bottle and comb. Teach him how to work his way from end to roots, working his way up in sections. I thought he would lose interest, tap out and give up halfway through, but oddly enough, he seems to be enjoying himself. Delicately working his way through my strands until the very end. It was a rough start at first. I had to remind him that my hair was very much attached to my head, *but* if yanked hard enough, it would come out. After that it was smooth sailing and actually pretty pleasant. I love that his soft delicate touch isn't just limited to the bedroom. I love that he smells my hair as he's telling me about when he first saw me, and how the smell of cocoa-butter attracted him to me before he saw my face. I loved that when I asked him about us standing in front of the coffee shop and the kiss he gave me. His voice drops low. I can only imagine the bashful half smile that he's giving me.

"I don't know." He tells me, "I couldn't help it."

I don't know what to say to that, or how to stop blushing, so I don't say anything. I do, however, stand and turn to face him.

"What do you think?" I ask, offering him the opportunity to examine his handy work. I shake my head and roll my eyes at the super sexy, super casual way he's lounging. After his shower, he put on a pair of black sweats that are baggy enough to hang just right without showing anything. Not even the waistband of his boxers. He's wearing a black Yankees cap, and has it pulled low over his eyes. He's leaning with his back against the back of the sofa. Hands folded behind his head, biceps bulging. Chest hair spread out almost in a pattern over his abs and pecks. Giving the mane of his lion tattoo the illusion of real fur. He takes a deep breath and adjusts his cap to see me better.

"Nope." He says, "That's on the list."

"What...my hair?" I gasped, surprised, smiling and fluffing my fro on one side. "You can't put my hair on the list."

"Oh, it's on there." He's biting his lip and chewing on the straw from his breakfast drink.

"You can't put hair on the list." I say shaking my finger and placing my hand on my hip.

Dammit he's an eyeful.

"You put my bare feet on the list." He tells me, proudly pointing to his feet, that I notice are bare.

"You're breaking that rule right now." I say, reaching for my hair products that are scattered out across the table.

"Oh darling, I'm breaking multiple rules right now." His cap is pulled low over his eyes again, and his mouth is perked on one side as if implying he's a badass, "I'm breaking rules that haven't even made it to the list."

"Like what?" I ask, gathering jars and bottles of hair stuff in my arms, trying to balance without dropping.

"This." Is all I hear, of course before I look.

Now, to say I expected to look at him and see his penis hanging outside of his pants. Like a baseball player's finger dangling from his mit, would be overstating. To say I was caught off guard, would be understating...dramatically.

"Commando." He said, nonchalantly, putting his man parts away.

"Come on, man!" I say, laughing. "That's it, you're on the list, Bud. You're on the fucking list." I say walking into the bathroom, placing my product back onto the shelf then walking back into the living room. Just as I walk in, he answers his vibrating phone, and tells the person on the other end that he'll meet them *there* in fifteen minutes.

"T.K." He tells me, putting on his long sleeve t-shirt, "I'm going to meet him at Emma's, then we're coming back here."

He leans in to give me a soft but deeply passionate kiss.

"Be careful." I tell him, stepping into his arms.

"Yes ma'am." He whispers to my neck. "Do you want anything while I'm out?" He's backing towards the door pulling his sleeves partially up his arms. I must admit, I feel a little sad at the idea of him going somewhere without me. We haven't separated since *Carrie-gate*. I shake my head and poke my bottom lip out, pouting as he opens the door.

"I'll be back." He assures me, smiling.

"Say hello to Emma." I shouted after him. And with that he leaves.

Giving me nothing to do but change from the T-shirt I'm wearing, to something more comfortable for a studio session. Especially since I plan on goofing off afterwards. I search my closet for my favorite pair of black sweats, the ones with gray trimmings. Somewhere folded on the top shelf above the hangers, I have a black off the shoulder t-shirt with sky blue letters spelling out the words...*MUSIC = FREEDOM*, across the breast. I shuffle through my shoe boxes and find a pair of sky blue, black, gray, and white high tops. It's one of my favorite brands of sneakers, aside from Converse, the weight and fit of them are perfect for my legs and feet. The last thing I find is my matching gray, black and blue DC fitted cap.

Frank called telling me he was only going to be about twenty more minutes and he would be on his way. Eros called asking what I felt like eating for the night, and wondered if Franky was going to stay. Stating that he might as well since T.K. would be there. I told him Chinese food, to which he got mildly excited like he did with the sushi. I'm guessing Asian/Chinese/Japanese style food must be something of a favorite for him. I also remind him that I'll try anything twice so don't be afraid of the menu, and that Frank can stay if he wants to, it's up to him. But just in case, I ask that he order two large chicken fried rice, one with no onions for Frank. It's all he'll eat of Chinese food.

In the music room I look around wondering what to do first. I guess since we'll be singing, I set up the microphones and stands, making sure they're properly plugged into the audio system. Since I'll be...singing (ugh) and Franky's playing, I know he's going to need a guitar since that's the only instrument he plays. I walk over to where I have about eight of them hanging from "clutching fist" ornaments mounted on the wall. Each guitar is just as different from each other, as are the ornaments they hang from. One ornament is a tattered and flesh torn zombie hand holding on to a gray and white marbled acoustic. I start with that one. Testing the shoulder strap. I adjust the machine heads and strike a few chords making sure the sound that I hear is pitch perfect.

Next, I sit on a stool with the guitar, two paper towels, one for dusting and one for oiling, and a spray can of WD-40. I laid the guitar across my lap and fold the towels in half the long way twice. I slide half of the dusting towel under the strings near the bridge, then fold it over the top, covering the top half completely. I begin sliding the paper slowly along the strings, following the length up to the nut and back. Applying downward pressure of lifting the paper accordingly, effectively cleaning the top and bottom of the strings. When I'm satisfied with the results of that process, I spray WD-40 on half of the oil rag and fold it around the strings, just as I did before. Repeating the same downward pressure and lighting method, I watch the strings slowly come to life. Shinning brilliantly, waiting for expert hands to finger them. *'Ha,'* I think to myself, *'that's what she said.'* When the entire process is done, I hold the guitar up to my eye level by the base and neck, admiring the smooth glow the strings now have.

Okay, this one is ready. I return it to its zombie hand and reach for the acoustic hanging from the skeleton hand. Just as I'm about to sit and begin the dusting and oiling process I remember that I'm singing and should probably have something to saturate my mouth. *'That's what she said.'* I thought to myself, giggling again. Before I return to my seat I grab a blow-pop from the candy dish on the coffee table and pop it into my mouth. Most people like hot tea or warm lemon water, or something to that effect, but a lollipop is fine for me. I'm no professional, I just don't want my mouth to go dry. By the time I finish dusting my fourth guitar, I hear the front door open followed by Eros' voice laughing, announcing his and T.K.'s return. I replace the guitar in its onyx hand and head to the front of the house, where I find my soon to be and his bestie in the kitchen unloading box containers on the island counter.

"There she is." Eros said, smiling at me. "Hi." He wraps his big arms around my waist caressing me in his hold, giving my bottom a pat and a squeeze.

'Okay, so we're not behaving ourselves I see.'

"Hi." I repeat, puckering for his kiss. He still smells woodsy.

"Ayo," he says, turning to a very well dressed, very handsome, *very* tall, clean shaven and clean cut T.K., "this guy here has been my very best friend, my brother from another mother since third grade. T.K.," holding up my left hand, "this is the woman that said yes."

T.K.'s eyes widened, and he smiles leaning into my hand clutching it into his palm.

"Damn E.," his smile drops, "It's kind of small ain't it?" *Oh, I instantly like him.*

I pull my hand back into my chest laughing.

"Don't talk about my ring, it's perfect."

"Tell him, baby."

"It's all good." T.K. said laughing, wrapping his muscular arms around my shoulders, "Welcome to the family."

"Thank you." I chuckled, returning his embrace.

"Frank here yet?" Eros asks.

"Not yet." I tell him looking through the carryout boxes, "He should be here any second."

"Who's Frank?" T.K. asks, helping himself to a piece of chicken-on-a-stick. *Oh, I definitely like him.* He doesn't have to be told to make himself at home.

"Frank is my sixth brother. He's coming over to torture me in my music room." I told him dropping a dumpling on my plate. T.K. freezes with the chicken at his lips, "You have a music room?"

"Um-hum." I say reaching for the container with the eggrolls, pointing to my right. "It's back there."

"Babe, is your DVD hooked up?" Eros says from the living room.

"Is it for a movie?" I asked, confused, making my way to where he's standing in front of the t.v.

"No," he says, looking at me. I no longer have the lollipop but the gum from the center still remains. "The game T.K. has is on DVD."

"It's for highlights." T.K. tells me from behind the couch, "I'm trying to get a spot-on ESPN."

I nod my head in approval.

"Good for you, I hope you get it." I open the drawer under the coffee table and pull out a *T* shaped remote and turn it on, walking towards the closet in the hallway outside of the music room. I shout behind me and ask Eros to move the coffee table.

"So you have a choice." I say, walking back towards the front room where Eros and T.K. still stand.

Carefully remote controlling the robot machine a few steps ahead of me. Smiling at the bleeps and blop sounds it's making. They're either going to be really geeked out over this robot, or Eros is going to really be embarrassed. Either way, I don't care. This is one of my most favorite gadgets and as soon as I find it online, I'm going to get it's robot partner.

"You can either watch it on the DVD player." I say coming around the front room corner. "Or you can watch it on this."

Both men stand there with their mouths open. Silent at first.

"What…is that?" Eros asks, walking towards me and my robot.

"It's R2D2." I say.

"I can see that." He said, walking around it, bending low to get a closer look. "I can see that, what does it do?"

"It's a movie projector." I say moving it into its place in front of the couch.

I pressed a button, and the DVD slot slides opened. Eros looks at T.K., who is still standing dumbfounded…I think.

"Where's your disc." I look from Eros to T.K. who remembers suddenly that it's in his back pocket. Taking that, I place it in the slot and push another button on the remote, and the t.v. starts to move backwards into the wall. Both men look in the t.v.'s direction then at each other.

"Okay, so once the t.v. is in place." I push another button, and the three of us look up at the screen that's sliding down from the ceiling. When it's completely stopped, I push another button and close R2's movie slot, push play and watch the top of the machine's head spin around towards the white screen. Settling his wheels in a seated position. Bleeping and blooping the entire time.

"Get…the…fuck…out!" T.K. erupts into laughter, walking over to R2, examining it closer.

"I think I just peed a little." Eros announces laughing, "Where'd you get this?"

"I found it online." I told him. *Why is he giving me his 'I see right through you' look?*

"Bro," T.K. says from the couch.

"Oh wait." I interrupted, walking to the kitchen. I open a drawer and pull out a package, return and hand the package to Eros.

"What's this?" he asks, furrowing his brow, turning the blank package over, only to find no words on the opposite side.

"Mini light saber lasers."

Eros's eyes flick to mine then to his friend, "Want one?" He asks T.K., who moves faster than I can see, and is by Eros side picking his laser out.

"Shit yeah." he says.

I watch them add the small watch batteries to the saber handles and screw the light tube in place. Then wave the beam at the screen, making the lights dance around.

"Dude, your girlfriend is cooler than you."

I chuckle and blow a bubble, looking over at Eros who is watching me. Then burst out laughing when he announces that me *and* my little R2 unit is on the list.

"This is cool, babe." He tells me, just as the doorbell rings. I open it, knowing that it's Franky. He steps in giving me the *three-time hand slap, the finger snap* greeting my brothers and I share. He acknowledges Eros who introduces him to T.K., who gives Frank a two-handed handshake.

'Hum...okay, I noticed that.' Not thinking, I hand the remote to Eros, who reaches for it. I watch his mouth drop then follow his eyes to my hand holding the controller.

I don't get it; all I'm holding is the controller. *Oh shit, my ring!* I pull my hand back, thankful for the conversation between Frank and T.K., pull my ring from my finger and slip it in my pocket. *'Whew.'* Eros whistles a sigh of relief and we both laugh.

"What's so funny?" Frank asks, finally turning to me.

"Nothing." I say giving Eros the remote. Who knows first hands how fast news can travel when Frank is around.

"We got takeout if you're hungry." I told my brother, following him into the kitchen, and pick up my plate. I take a couple of drinks from the fridge for everyone and wait for Frank to fix his plate.

"You see that blue button?" I ask Eros, who's still holding the remote. "If you press and hold it you can switch the projector to voice activated." I watch him push the button and hold.

"R2 play." I command and the screen comes to life.

"R2 pause." Eros commands after a few moments.

"Oh wow." T.K. chuckles.

"You ready, Sis?" Frank asks. Groaning, I blow a bubble, and wink my eye at a laughing Eros.

"That bubble gum is on the list too." He calls after me as I'm headed down the hall behind Frank.

"I'll get right on that." I call back to him, chuckling.

Chapter Fifteen

"Okay, so this is the song." Frank tells me as he's pressing play on the computer. *I'll be damned,* it's the same love song from the radio a couple of days ago. At first, I was against it, but once I started to get more familiar and comfortable with the words, I realized that this song speaks volumes for the love that my parents share. I've seen them go through the roughest and toughest of times. They've been with each other ever since they were teenagers riding their bikes to school. No matter what they went through or how hard things got, they never left each other. Ever. We ran through the song a few times until I'm familiar with the words and melody.

Frank, who's already familiar with his part, is coaching me through an entire series of ups and downs. High notes and low notes, and all kinds of notes I'm positive I'll never be comfortable doing. No matter how much time we have to rehearse. Eventually, once he's pleasantly frustrated enough to let me just do the song the way it is, it all starts coming together. After a couple more run throughs it actually starts to sound good. After about the fourth time running through with no mistakes, we record with his voice, my voice and the skeleton hand acoustic. After the third time trying, we finally recorded a perfect take and call all serious business of the evening to an end, and turned rehearsals into a jam session. I don't know how long we were back there, but eventually one of us remembered we had company. And not a moment too soon, my mouth is dry, and my head is starting to pound a little.

"I'll be back." I tell Franky.

In the kitchen I fetch a bottle of water from the refrigerator.

"How's it going?" Eros asks, coming up behind me.

"The torture is over." I tell him joking, turning to face his half smiling face. "What about you? How's the game?"

"So much better with light saber lasers." He smiles, waving the red beam over the food.

"I figured it would be." I say picking a dumpling from the box. "How was Emma?"

"Much better today." He tells me. I love how his eyes twinkle when he talks about his mom. His commitment to her is worth its weight in gold and then some. "I told her you said hello." He steps closer to me.

"Thank you." I say biting my dumpling, looking up at him as he removes my hat, look at the inside tag, then replace it on my head.

"This goes on the list." He tells me.

"Is that right?" I say smiling, "My hat?"

"Oh yeah, and the matching shoes."

"Your list seems to be growing rapidly, sir."

"Stop being cute." He tells me matter of factly, with one eyebrow raised. My mouth drops and a throaty chuckle slips out.

"I can't help that you think I'm adorable. Besides I'm just being myself."

What in the world, I hope he knows I'm going to be extra cute now. I pull the stick from my chicken, break the meat in chunks and spear a piece with the stick. Using my fingers, I dip a chunk of the meat in the sweet and sour sauce and pop it in my mouth. Sucking the sauce from my fingers and thumb.

"You have a R2D2 film projector." He tells me laughing pulling one of my hair coils. "That's very cute to me."

"Really?" I said. "Hum."

I don't think I should give him his list of infractions yet. Instead, I dip another chunk of chicken and hold it up for him to take. The closer he gets to my hand, the further I pull it away from his mouth. Teasing him until he's close enough to hear me whisper. Jeeze, his eyes are beautiful, and they seem to look through me.

"I love you." I whispered against his lips.

"How much." He whispers biting the meat from my fingers.

"I don't know yet." I tell him licking my fingers, smiling at his one raised eyebrow. "How ever much it is today might not hold a candle to what I'll feel tomorrow."

He shakes his head and moistens his bottom lip.

"You just don't even know do you." Before I could respond his eyes flickered to Franky approaching behind me.

"So is this how it's going to be?" he asks, spooning rice on his plate. "The two you stashed in a corner somewhere making out?"

"Shut up, Frank." I say, smiling and kissing Eros' lips again. "And probably."

****

We all gather in the living room, talking, laughing, still munching on leftovers. T.K. and Franky seem to hit it off well. If that's the correct phrase to use. They talked with each other most of the night…guy stuff, I don't know. I didn't try and listen. I was too busy giggling at Eros whispered impression of Darth Vader. Commentating the game replaying on the screen. Which was a pretty good game. Denver against Washington, at Washington. So far, I've watched Washington's quarterback pass the ball to the runner twice. To which he breaks to the right gaining a down each time. The third time the ball is passed, the runner has to break to the right and for some reason, can't gain as many yards.

"R2 rewind." I command. "R2 stop. R2 play." Something's off with this runner. For one he doesn't gain control over the ball as well on the right break as he does on the left. *Hmm, maybe that's it.*

"R2 rewind," I command again, "R2 stop. R2 play." I'm sitting on the floor between Eros's open knees, who has turned his verbal attention to my brother and his buddy.

Watching it thoroughly I realize, it's nothing the quarterback did. All of his movements are the same, down to the position of his feet just before he releases the ball. The runner breaks to the left, forward two paces. A little more to the left, catches the ball then gains the yards.

Next play. Ball snaps. *'Oh.'* He can't break left because two linebackers block his path, so he has no choice but to fast break to the right. Cut two…wait! That's what it is. I sit up higher straightening my posture and furrowing my eyebrows.

"Hum."

"What is it?" Eros asks, kissing the side of my face.

"Watch this." I tell him lifting my cheek to him but still watching the screen. "R2 rewind. R2 pause." I say reaching for a light saber. I explained what I observed on the right break play.

"Now watch this." I say aiming the beam at the two linebackers.

"These two guys block his path so he can't go left."

"Right."

"When he cuts right, he moves five paces, and is supposed to go forward two paces. But he hesitates."

"Hesitates?" Eros asked, focusing his attention from my cheek to the game.

"Watch. R2 play slow motion." Using the beam I circle the runners' feet, talking my way through what I see. "See. Five paces. Then one, maybe two." I look at Eros who's, of course, is looking at me. "If he can keep count on the right like he does on the left he can gain about five more yards to a run."

He doesn't answer me, but his eyes pour warm chocolate honey all over my body. His fingertips softly graze over the navigational, feather quill and eye scope that's tattooed on my soft forearm. What is he thinking, right now. His eyebrow raises…*wait a min.* I squint my eyes at him and half smirk half smile.

"Is that on the list?' I ask sarcastically. His face screws up in this *you've got it* face.

"Fuck." I say, mouthing wordlessly.

"Abso-fucking-lutely." He laughs. I don't mean a half smile or a throaty chuckle. I mean, from his core in the middle of his stomach kind of laugh.

"What's wrong?" he asks, catching his breath.

"You're putting everything on the list, man."

"I told you," He snuggles his thick, brown face forest against my neck and spoke directly into my ear. My good ear! Knowing exactly what my reaction would be.

"Stop being cute." He said.

The vibrations from his voice traveled my spine and split in two directions. My cheeks and my side. All I can do is laugh and hope I'm playing it off.

"You are so petty for that." I tell him chuckling. He buries himself into the back of the sofa with the cockiest half smile I've seen on him yet. Then he winks at me. I chuckle a very composed, very amused, chuckle. The good thing is that T.K. and Franky had stepped out of the room. When, I have no idea. It could have been while I was watching the game, maybe.

"Where'd they go?"

"In the back." He answered. Now that changes things. I turn to face him, standing between his thighs, on my knees.

"You don't play fair." I say, snaking my arms around his neck, and ruffling my fingers through his hair.

Kissing him right now is the easiest kiss I've given anyone in a very long time. Our bodies are almost lined up, so I don't have to reach or bend. I can just gently curl my fingers through the hair at the nape of his neck and lean my mouth into his. I can enjoy his hands as they slide from my biceps down my back and to my butt. *Okay, that's enough.* I pull away from his mouth but enjoy the butt squeezing a little more.

"Show some restraint, sir." I say pulling his hands up to my waist.

"Hey, Sis." Franky called from the kitchen, startling Eros. He didn't jump, or flinch or anything like that. His eyes widened dramatically and I erupt in unison with his laughter.

"Did you want to work on anything else tonight." Frank said entering the room turning the light on.

"No," I said standing to my feet, "I've had enough of your torture for one day."

"Good because I'm leaving."

"What, why?" I said surprised.

"Because I'm ready to go." Frank said, "Eros, I'll see you Friday."

"Yeah, we'll probably leave out at about 5." Eros tells him, shaking his hand.

"Sounds good," Frank said turning to me, "Walk me out."

Frank is up to something; I can see it on his face.

"So," he said walking towards the driveway, "you're getting married?"

'Shit!'

My mouth drops. I should have told T.K. not to mention anything, but who knew they would hit it off. Damn for sure not me. I reach to my pocket and pull out my ring.

"Don't you say anything, Frank. I mean it! I want to tell everyone myself."

"I'm not going to say nothing. I don't tell everything." he said, looking at my ring and gasping.

"Ayo! Look at that thing. It's little as hell." My brother laughs loudly at first until I sush him. "Girl...why did he get you such a little ring?!"

"It's not little," I say examining my hand, "it's modest and I love it, so be nice."

"Okay, okay I won't say anything else." He tries but fails to hide his smile, "But it is small."

"Shut up!" I say punching his arm. "It's perfect."

"Okay, I promise, I won't say nothing else." He punches me back then immediately makes it better by giving me a gentle hug in true big brother fashion. "Congratulations, Sis."

"Thank you."

He gives me another lingering hug and tells me good-bye. Right after he tells me that he's dropping T.K. off at Golden Heights where he left his car. I gave him my best, *don't mess with this guy's head*, face. I don't know how Franky is in his relationships, that's not something we discuss. But I do know this, I've rarely seen him with the same guy twice. It's happened but not often. T.K. is seemingly a good guy, and is very important to Eros, therefore to me. I don't want things to be awkward because of my brother.

"Be a gentleman." I tell Frank, as he's getting in his car.

"Always." I hear him say as I'm heading back towards the house. Going back up T.K. is headed my way with his huge arms stretched out, repeating Emma's words.

"I'm glad he's found you. Take care of him."

"I will." I promise, hugging him tight.

"Welcome to the family." He tells me kissing my cheek.

"Thanks T.K." I say quietly, "Thanks for coming over, and good luck with ESPN."

"Next time I'm over you'll have to play something for me."

"I will." I say over my shoulder.

I like how different this feels. Having people over, enjoying each other's company. Eating, having a few drinks, taking a few smokes. I've done this before, gone to or hosted get togethers. The difference now is, I don't have to be alone afterwards. Eros is here and he is in a playful mood. He was standing behind me with his arms around my waist, waving. Now his grip has tightened, and he hoists me up carrying me back into the house, slung under his arm, supporting my body with his hip.

"Congratulations." He tells me, toting me to the kitchen, "You survived my family."

"Were you worried?" I ask. The food needs to be put away so I'm searching for proper size containers for everything.

"Not really." He tells me, removing the lid from a bowl, "I knew you would like each other." He dumps the noodles into the bowl then covers it. "I just didn't know if T.K. was going to have a *let's tell embarrassing stories about Eros,* moment."

"Oh, it'll be enough of that going on this weekend from my family. Speaking of," I say covering a bowl of rice. "Franky knows."

"I saw." He responds, "How do you feel about that?"

"I mean, I'm okay with him knowing," I say as I pass him bowls for the refrigerator, "I just want to be the one to tell my family face to face." He nods in agreement, licking sauce from the orange chicken off his thumb.

"So, he's going to keep quiet?"

"He promised he would." I speak. "I don't think it'll be a problem."

"What about with the rest of your family?"

"My brothers are huge Bears fans, so you are in with them before you even meet them. My dad will go along with whatever my mother will say."

"And what will she say?" He asks, pausing for a split second.

"I don't know, she's a lawyer. But she loves me…so." We finish dividing everything into bowls and refrigerating them. Then return R2 to the charge station in the closet, the screen to the ceiling and everything is done.

"Come on." Eros said lifting me off my feet by my waist, "Let's get comfortable."

Moving with exactly no sense of urgency at all, Eros walks with me cradling his face in my arms.

"Light switch." He commands with absolutely no trace of strain in his voice. I reach over to the wall where we stop and flip the switch off. Then he takes a couple more steps, stopping at the kitchen wall for me to flip that switch. The kitchen light is off, but the darkness is illuminated by the light from the music room shinning into the hallway. Without a word Eros walks in that direction.

I can see that Franky has straightened the room, putting everything back in its place. The microphones are back against the wall. The guitars are hanging from the rightful hand again. Everything is good, except one thing. Two of the guitars are hanging from the wrong hand and the OCD in me won't let that go. I shift my body expecting Eros to put me down.

"You know I can walk." I say smiling.

"I've noticed." He chuckles, adjusting me in his arms. "Which way?"

"Two of the guitars are out of place."

"Which ones?"

"The skeleton hand and the Onyx." I tell him watching the wall of hands as he walks me towards it. "Here." I say lifting the gray marble acoustic with the black matte finish. Then a thought occurs, I didn't take the opportunity to play for Eros today. He asked but we got comfortable doing other things.

"Are you tired at all?" I ask.

"Not even a little bit." He answers letting me slide down his body until my feet hit the floor.

"Hold this." I say. Then I walk over to a shelved wall and find a pocket amp and cord. I grab a pick from the fishbowl I keep them in. Pick up a floor stand and look up at Eros who's watching me with the guitar held tight in his fist, and his other hand tucked away in his pocket.

"Okay I'm ready." I say standing in front of him.

When we entered the room, I set the floor stand in front of the bedside table. Turning towards Eros, I hold my hand out for the guitar and find him watching, still.

"Thank you." I say excepting the medium size acoustic.

"You're welcome."

I put the guitar in its place and removed the adaptor cord from around my neck. Plug it into the pocket amp and place it on the night-stand surface. I thread the pick through the strings near the machine heads and wrap the loose end around the top of the headboard post. I turn to remove my hat and notice Eros removing his shirt in front of the mirror watching me through the reflection. I can't help smiling slightly, as I walk over to the closet. It's a super-walk-in so I have enough room for a small bench and vanity without it feeling cluttered. Sitting on the bench I remove my shoes one at a time. Then stand to return them to the waiting box and place my hat on the stand where it belongs.

"I have a hat stand that you can put that on, if you want." I bend back to look and see if Eros heard me.

Lord have mercy, this man is only wearing a towel around his waist. Goodness gracious, that towel does nothing to hide his bulge. I sit on the bench just as he enters the closet and point to the empty Styrofoam style heads lined up on a wall shelf.

"Look how cute your closet is." He chuckles.

"You can keep your hats on those, if you want, so they can keep shape." I say separating my hair down the middle and rolling my eyes at his *cute* comment.

"Why do you have a tool bench?" He asks, leaning his elbow against the bench.

"I thought it was cute." I say sarcastically, corn rolling half of my hair. "Open it." I tell him.

I watch him through the mirror as I rubber band the end of my braid. I want to see his reaction, then count how long it takes him to put that on the list. He chuckles as soon as he has the top drawer open. Looking at me he holds up a string of pearls.

"Jewelry?" He smiles, replacing the necklace.

"In every drawer." I told him, finishing my second and final braid. "All laid out the same. Necklaces, bracelets and watches. Earrings and rings." I pin the loose ends of my braids to each of my corn rolls. Over lapping them just above the hairline at the back of my head.

"All color coordinated."

He opens the drawers randomly, "Oh wow, they are."

"And before you say it," I tell him removing my shirt, "None of this is going on the list." I toss my shirt in the laundry basket for dark colors and remove my bra just as he looks in my direction I chuckle and notice a slight thump in his bulge that triggers the tingling and thump of my clitoris.

Closing the drawer, he leans on his elbow once more. My eyes never leave his and his are bathing me in warm chocolate. Watching my thumbs slide down my thighs bringing my joggers to my ankles. I use my foot to toss them in the basket for light colors. Just as I'm about to remove my panties his eyes gaze up at mine.

"Does it bother you that I watch you?"

"Why would you think that?" I ask removing my panties and tossing them in the light basket.

"I don't want to do anything that you don't like." He is so…different, than any guy that I know. He is confident and bashful at the same time.

A healthy balance of each but still. I walk over to where he's standing, getting close enough for our bodies to touch, and place his hand between my legs and press his finger into my wetness.

"That's what you looking at me does to my body." I say against his lips. "But just in case you need to hear it. It does not bother me at all."

Then I turn and head to the shower. Slowly I might add, so he can get an eyeful of me walking away. I click on the bathroom light, hang my towel on the hook. Turn on and adjust the water then stand at the sink to brush my teeth. Just as I'm finishing up Eros walks in and starts to brush his teeth. Watching as I step inside the shower. My first thought was to leave the shower door open so he can continue watching, but I decided against it. If he wants to see more, he can join me. I know he wants to; he's just debating with himself whether he should or not. *Or not.*

I don't even get the door closed all the way before he stops me and steps in. My shower head is like his, round and wide enough to drench the both of us at the same time. I watch him reach for my bath sponge and squirt my coco-butter body wash, working up a lather.

"I like how this makes your skin smell." Then gently he washes me. Starting at my neck, to both of my arms. My breast, making sure to tease both my soapy nipples before moving down to the roses that decorate half of my rib cage, and trail down to my lower abdomen. Cleaning each flower and leaf and stem thoroughly.

He moves the sponge in circles towards my smooth vagina and starts half washing, half massaging. Completely stimulating me.

"Turn around." He tells me. Then repeats the same process from top to bottom. Covering the full back, carefully washing each branch and limb and root of the winter tree covering my skin. Then he cleans my butt. I don't mean just sponge here, or scrub there. I mean, one minute I'm standing there with my eyes closed, enjoying the attention that he's giving me back, and the next he's in my ear telling me to lean forward against the wall and open my legs.

Then his hands are on my hip tracing the roots of the tree that blends in with my skin on the curve above my buttocks. When he's traced them all, he rubs the sponge over each cheek. Squeezing water so that the bubbles run down my skin. He smooths the sponge between my legs as he leans his weight into my body.

"You have a beautiful body." He tells me kissing my ear. *Goodness gracious*, heaven has nothing on this. I am alive to everything. The warm water beating against my skin. The light residual spray that spritzes my face. The fires burning from deep within that only he can put out.

His lips touching my ear, his breath brushing my cheek. The hairs of his damp beard caressing my neck. The gentle caress of his hand rinsing the soap from every inch of my skin until I'm free of any bubbles. He turns me around to face him and leans his lips into mine. Tasting my mouth, toying with my tongue. I place my hands on both sides of his jaw and hold his face to mine. Returning the kiss, he's giving me. I rub my fingertips through the thickness of his face hair, then let my hands trail down to the slickness of his chest. I reach to my right and grab from the shower basket a pair of shower gloves. I put them on and squirt his mountain fresh body wash in the palm of my hands.

I know he's watching me, so I watch my hands. Though I'm curious *as hell*, as to what his expression is, I don't want to miss a second of what I'm about to do with my hands. I begin at his neck and work my fingers over the feathers that spread from his shoulder, over his biceps. Past his elbow, down his firm forearms and to his hands. Lacing my fingers through his. Gently kissing his lips. Toying with *his* tongue, exploring his mouth. My hands are on his chest, and I rub my palms in circles swirling soap through his hair. I rub down his sides slowly, then over his stomach. Tracing my index finger over the lines of his six pack, circling it around the hair of his belly button. His chest rises with each breath as his hands slide down my back. His penis is pressed between us, thumping my belly the closer I get to it.

Wrapping my soapy gloved hand around it, I stroke and caress it stimulating every inch front to back. I softly kiss his chest and lick his nipple. And he *moans,* a soft, quiet throaty sound but I heard it.

I flicker my tongue and nibble it between my teeth and he squeezes me close, hissing air between his teeth. Oh my gosh, I found his spot! I smile against his skin and nibble his nipple again. He pulls my pelvis tight against his erection, caressing deep slow massages into my thighs. I remove the gloves as the water runs down his chest rinsing the bubbles through his hair, down his erection and thighs. I rub my hands up his chest and around his neck, curling my fingers through his hair.

"I want you." I whisper against his lips, and he leans to turn the water off.

I step out of the shower and head to the bedroom. I don't want a towel; I just want him touching me. Kissing me. Tasting me. This almost reminds me of our first time. Him following me to my bedroom, me slowly walking backward watching his chocolate eyes drink me in. But this time it's different. His eyes are hungry, he knows I'm his but he's in no more of a hurry than I am. I turn and enter the bedroom and head to my charge station and select a song from my tablet. The song from the first night he was here fills the room. I turn and find him leaning his back against the closed door, just as before. His arms are crossed over his chest and his legs are crossed at the ankles.

He's watching me with that half smile on his face. He knows exactly what I'm doing. I step towards him, grazing my fingers across the rose bush that covers the lower half of my belly, until I'm pressed against his body. His hands and feet have separated allowing me to step into his embrace. His face goes straight to my neck. Kissing me, biting me gently on my shoulder. His hands are all over my ass. Squeezing, jiggling, lightly smacking. His mouth is devouring my ear. My skin sparkles with fire as his beard grazes my neck. His grip tightens around my thighs, and I brace myself on his shoulders. With ease, he lifts my legs around his thighs and carries me gracefully to the bed. Sitting me right on the edge, kissing my chin and my neck…forcing a slight moan to slip from my lips.

My collar bones. My nipple. I expect him to stop and fondle around in that area for a second and play around a little, but no, he is on a mission a little further south. And I plan on enjoying every second of it. I lay back with my eyes closed, spreading my arms above my head. Surrendering to whatever is on his mind. His mouth leaves random kisses covering the inside of my thighs and my hips. Every other kiss is a long lingering suck and flick of his tongue across my clitoris. Every kiss there being longer than the kiss before. Every flicker is more intense. His hands are holding my thighs close to my sides leaving me completely exposed and open. Every flicker ignites a short spasm of pleasure over and over and over.

Every suck draws an arch in my back so high I have to scoot away from him, just to take a full breath. I drag myself away from his mouth, damn near panting through my half smile. Eyes still crossed.

"Where you going?" he said chuckling. His hands open my thighs, and his mouth is right back at its task. My mouth gapes but nothing comes out. I can't do anything but rock my hips to his rhythm. Which doesn't stop. I can't stop. I open my mouth to tell him I'm coming but all that comes out is a sort of whine, almost moan.

My back arches and my hands grip his face on both sides, holding him in place. Until my body can't hold on any longer, and I release. Spasm after spasm. Over and over. Before I'm even finished, he's inside of me. Thrusting into that spot like he's trying to bust through.

"*Fuck.*" He growls in my ear. I wrap my legs around his back squeezing him deeper. "Yes, baby."

His voice is doing its usual routine on the fires that have refueled with a vengeance. I pant, and moan in a way that's almost chanting with the rhythm that he's keeping. I can't control my moan. It slides from my mouth in long breathy *oh's*. He doesn't let up and I can't take anymore. My body erupts around him in tight squeezing spasms. He groans long and slow, and I can feel him throbbing inside me, releasing himself to the very last drop. He thrust a couple more times, and his body relaxes into my chest. I cradle his head in my hands as I kiss his forehead, while he kisses my chest between my breasts.

I don't want him to move but he does anyway pulling me with him. Turning us so that I'm lying on top of his chest.

"You didn't get to play your guitar." I turn and look at the instrument standing beside the bed.

"You still want me to?" I ask looking up at him.

"Um-hum."

I sit up and reach for the guitar as he hands me the cord from the post.

"I need that please." I say pointing to the pocket amp. Switching it on I adjust the volume to the lowest setting, then hand it to him. Turning to face him indian style, I position the body of the guitar in my lap until I'm comfortable. As I expect when I focus on him, he's already watching me.

"Any request?" I ask smiling.

"What can you play?"

"Lots of things. Although my fingers might not cooperate at the moment." I tell him. "There's always the classic." I pick through the beginning of Flur Elise. "Then there's always the basics." I pick my way through Yankee Doodle. Chuckling at his smile, as his eyes watch me. "What was the one song you remember hearing around the house the most as a kid?"

"Oh wow." he said, leaning his head back against the headboard thinking.

"Hotel California." He says looking at me.

"The Eagles." I say. "That's an easy one that I learned for a talent show in the eighth grade."

"It was my dad's favorite." He tells me.

Oh...another piece of Henry, which is another piece of Eros.

"Okay then." I say picking a melody out of the strings. "This one will be for Henry."

I start at the beginning blending the notes in with the melody. Pulling and plucking every note perfectly, so that they almost sing every word. His head is back, and his eyes are closed as his lips mouth the chorus, and his hands tap the beat out on my toes. My favorite part of the song leading into the end is coming up and in order to play these notes as fast as I'm supposed to, I have to reposition the guitar to an almost upright hold. My eyes are closed listening to myself rather than seeing. I can feel all ten of my fingers cooperating with each string, note, fret. Every pitch perfectly vibrating through my hands until the very last note is played, and the song is finished. Eros hasn't moved. His head is still against the headboard and his eyes are closed. He's not asleep…I don't think, not the way he's sitting. I want to know what he's thinking but, again, Henry isn't a subject that I want to press.

I unplug the amp, replace the pick to the strings and the guitar to the stand. Leaning up, I attempt to tie the cord back to the bedpost, but he encloses me in his arms. He's warm and his arms are tight, around my thighs. I look down at him as he cradles his head against my hip. Yes, Henry is a very touchy subject. I wrap the cord as best I can, and cradle my body around his, straddling his lap.

"I love you." I say this as if that's the answer for anything. Maybe it is.

"I miss him." He whispers. Not knowing what to say, I hugged him tighter and kissed his forehead, wishing I could absorb his sadness and make it all disappear.

"I'm sorry you lost your dad." I whisper. We adjust our bodies so that he's spooning me as he pulls the covers over our bodies.

"You would have loved him." He whispers in my ear. "He was a great man."

Chapter Sixteen

Dammit, morning came quick! I really hate Mondays. I inhale deeply. That vacation really wasn't long enough. I should consider thinking about quitting my job…or maybe even going to work for myself. I have the credentials to do so. Hell, I'm a whole Nurse Practitioner. It would be as simple as getting myself state approved, a couple of letters of recommendation. Finding a few home care residents to look after, and boom, I'm self-employed. I could even go into real estate. I already own three properties including the home I live in now. It's something to think about. Maybe I'll run the idea across my love when I get home today. In the meantime, I still have a current job that I need to drag my ass out of bed for. I open my eyes and rub the cobwebs away.

Why is it so dark? It's not out of the ordinary for it to be dark, but dang, it's almost pitch black in my room. Well, no wonder, I look over at the clock and it's only 3:45 a.m.…*Sunday.* Wait…is that right? 3:45…a.m.…*Sunday?* The thought of having one more full day before life comes crashing down into our little bubble we've created, makes me smile.

"Um…" and moan. *Why am I moaning?* My legs are thrown in every direction.

"*Oh…*" That moan came out without my consent. One leg is bent and the other is thrown across Eros's thighs. "*Ssss…*" *What the hell?* I'm moaning and my hips are rotating around Eros' fingers that are fondling my pleasure button. Is this what woke me up?

"Baby?" He's whispering in my ear, "Wake up."

"Why?" I ask, my voice is husky with sleep which can't be attractive. "What are you doing?"

"Touching you." He whispers in my ear.

"Why?" I ask touching the side of his face, pulling him closer to my neck.

"Because I dreamed about you."

"Did you?" I ask turning my face to his kisses, "Was it a good dream?" Forget sleeping. Why sleep when there's at least one thing I could be doing that's better. "Was it a good dream?" Forget this man in a good way for touching me like this.

"Um-hum." He breathes. I can feel his fingers slipping in and out of my wetness, and his erection is moist on my hip. Telling me he is ripe and ready for the picking.

"What was I doing?" I asked, rubbing my fingers down his arm to his hand, pushing his fingers deeper inside me.

"Riding me." He answers against my lips. I place my hands on his chest nudging him to his back, and underneath me. His hands rub down my back then come back to my shoulders.

"I like when you squeeze my ass." I tell him against his neck.

My body is cradled against his chest so as his hands slide down to grip both cheeks, I separate my body from his. Just enough to slide my hand down and place the head in.

"Like this?" I ask sliding down slowly until there's no space between us.

"Um-hum." He moans, "Just like that."

"Was I going fast or slow?" My voice is becoming uneven and breathy, and I can feel every single sensation. My skin glistens with pleasure, and my insides awaken. One fire at a time.

"Slow," he tells me lifting his head to suck and kiss my shoulder. "But you asked me to go deep."

Sheesh, I'm a freak in his dreams. Hell, apparently, I'm a freak dreaming or not, because I love when he goes deep.

"Show me, Eros." I say licking his nipple, "Show me how deep you were."

"You want me to?" He asks in my ear, sliding his hands up my back to my shoulders. "Hold me tight."

I curl my hands under his arms up to his shoulders, as he props his knees up behind me, bracing his weight on his feet.

"Hold me tighter."

"Okay." I whispered, holding myself steady for his thrust. Which no matter what, I'm not ready for. It's fucking powerful. I gasp and moan, and whimper at the same time.

"Did I hurt you?" he asks, abandoning his thrust and grinding deep into that volcanic spot.

"No." I whimper...he thrust, "No baby." That last part came out involuntarily.

"No?" He groans, bracing himself. "So, I can go deeper?"

Thrust...fire!

"Yes." I whine, pushing myself into his thrust.

Thrust...fire!

"Go deeper?" he asks, turning me beneath him, still curled around his body. "Don't let me go."

I slide my hands down his back to his butt, and squeeze pulling him into me. He flexes his hips, rotating them in a circle then times his thrust just right. Rocking my body and the bed with each pump, slightly tapping the headboard into the wall.

"*Aaah,*" I whine, and whimper. It's dark and I can't see his face but I'm still watching him feeling his warm coco-stare. "*Aaah.*"

"That's right, Ayo." He whispers, "Let me hear you."

With his last word comes a welcome string of deep thrust one after another, after another. Coaxing a moan slash, groan, slash whimper, slash somewhat yell, rhythmically from my open mouth. Now, though I would love to say I was making the bulk of my noise for *his* benefit, truth be told, I damn for sure was not. Every thrust magnified each fire, forcing them brighter and bigger.

Deep thrust...mangled moan...deep thrust.

My voice is raspy with pleasure. Loud, deep seeded pleasure.

"Don't stop!" I whine, "Please don't stop."

"You want me to stop?" He groans driving deeper inside.

"No." I say, pulling his thrust into me, imagining his eyes in the darkness and holding his gaze. "Don't stop."

"I can't stop." He whispers. He leans his forehead into mine, thrusting powerful spasms through my body. "Say you love me, Ayo."

"Say you love me, Ayo." His whisper is a small groan.

"I love you, Eros." I tell him. Not because he asks me to, or because he needs to hear it but because I mean it and I want him to never forget. "I love you." I say again, and again, until my body explodes into his thrust.

"Oh my god, I'm coming." He growls in my ear, mixing his voice with my mangled moaning screams. A violent wave of satisfaction ripples through my body arching my back as I release.

My body is limp and exhausted, glistening from sweat. Shimmering from pleasure, and happy that he claims my every emotion as his own. He lifts my body from the bed onto his lap, holding me close and rubbing my back. Cradling my head to his shoulder, rocking me side to side, rubbing his warm hands across my lower back and shoulders.

"Are you okay?" I whisper.

"I didn't know I was supposed to love you this much."

*Oh no…*my heart kicks into full speed pump.

"Is it too much?" I whisper, almost too quiet to hear. "Have you changed your mind about me?"

Just that thought of not being able to hold him, or see him, or laugh with him, or smell his beard oil, or touch him. Or talk football or do something ridiculous that gets added to his lengthy list brings a golf ball sized lump that I can't seem to swallow down my throat.

"Baby no." He coos, holding me so he can see my face. "Look at me." I shake my head no. I know a tear has escaped and I'm glad it's too dark for him to see. "Look at me, love." He pulls my body away from him. "I can't get enough of you. It'll never be too much. Ever." His voice is a soft whisper of the truth and honesty that usually radiates from his eyes.

"You said,"

"Baby, I never thought I was supposed to love *anyone* this much." He admits, cutting me off, "No one has ever given me as much freedom as you have. Or excepted my love the way you have. No questions. No excuses. No explanations needed. I might hesitate with a thought, but the moment I say it. Or the moment I do something, I regret ever doubting it because you're so accepting and so open to all possibilities. You...are... my...Queen. Before you, love was just a word."

"And now?" I whisper finding a portion of what voice I have left.

"Now," he said, laying his body flat on his back and pulling me on top of him, cradling my face between his hands. "Love is my state of mind, and it's only at peace because of you."

Then he kisses me, taking the words I was about to speak and swallowing them whole. Hushing me with his tender lips. His words echo through my brain, *you...are...my...Queen. Love is my state of mind. It's only at peace because of you.*

I love this man to LIFE!

******

Bacon...I smell bacon. That is the only scent, that I know of, that can lead a dead man out of hell. And right now, it's pulling me away from an already forgotten dream. I stretch and spread my limbs out long and tight, only to realize I'm in bed alone. I'm sure with the magnificent aroma filling the house, that he's in the kitchen. I slide from under the covers, pulling a tee-shirt and matching shorts from the drawer and slip them on. Stretching and yawning again as I walk to the kitchen. I'm still kind of tired, but I smell bacon.

"Good morning." I say, yawning.

"No!" Eros says pointing his hand stopping me in my tracks. His hair is pulled back in a loose bun and he's barefoot, wearing only those joggers and a half apron. To which I have no idea where it came from.

"No?" I ask, knuckles still pressed into my eyes mid-rub. "It's not a good morning?"

"It's a very beautiful morning," he confirms walking toward me. Even the damn apron hangs just right around his waist. "But you're not supposed to be up yet."

"I'm not?" I ask.

"No." He kisses me quick on the lips and turns me back down the hallway towards the room. Giving me a playful swat on the behind. "Go get back in bed."

I make my way down the hallway reluctantly, stopping halfway and turning towards him.

"Like, all the way in bed?" I say pointing my thumb over my shoulders. "With covers and stuff?"

"Yes." he smiles, "all that stuff." I continued walking backwards smiling at him standing there looking like Chef *Boyareyousexy*.

"But I smell bacon." I say stopping in front of the room door.

"Yes, it's really crispy. Bed." He commands finalizing any future comments I was going to make. Except one.

"Fine." I say playfully pointing my pinky at him, "But that apron's going on the list."

"That's okay, it's your apron." He smiles.

I curl up under covers as instructed and set my t.v. to old seasons of Monk. About ten minutes go past and finally Eros walks in. Smiling, I sit up smoothing the covers over my lap.

"Good morning, beautiful." He smiles, as though we didn't just see each other.

"Breakfast in bed." I say. He's holding a lap tray that's steaming with all kinds of deliciousness. Crispy bacon, warm buttery French toast, scrambled eggs with diced peppers in them. Toast, jam and a small bowl with diced apples and raisins for the oatmeal he's fixed.

"Good morning, future husband." I repeat perking my lips for the kiss he's offering. "You fixed oatmeal."

"Yes, I did." He admits grinning. "Wait, don't touch anything yet." I don't think this man understands what happens when food is put in front of me.

He disappears out of the room in smooth strides, leaving me with my nose hovering over my bowl, and returning with two glasses and shaking a jug of orange juice.

"Can I eat now?" I ask unfolding my spoon from my napkin. "I don't have to eat all of this, do I?"

"No," he said laughing, settling next to me. "The bacon is for us both. Oatmeal and toast are yours. Eggs and French toast is mine." He flipped his napkin, then paused, "Wait. Could you?"

"Could I what?" I ask looking over at him. "Eat all of this?" He nodded his head squeezing syrup over his toast.

"Probably," I say mixing the apples and raisins in my bowl, evaluating the amount of food that's on the tray. Two French toast cut in half. About six pieces of bacon and two eggs. I nod my head. "If you dared me."

"Really?" He laughs.

"Probably." I repeat between chews, "This is really good by the way."

"It's not too sweet?" he asked, biting his bacon.

My mouth is full, so I shake my head, covering my mouth with my hand, "It's perfect."

"Thank you." He says hiding his smile behind his glass.

"Thank you." I say biting my bacon. He's such a beautiful contradiction. One minute he's uber cocky, half smiling his way through my heart, smacking me on my ass and ordering me around. And the next he's hiding his smile behind his beard shying away from my compliments. I really don't get it, but I love every bit of it.

"So, you know we have some things to talk about, right." He announces turning his body to me.

"*Ut-oh*". This doesn't sound good. "Like what?" I say into my glass, apprehensively.

"Our wedding."

Oh, this I can do.

My excitement blossoms and drops at the same time. This should be very interesting, especially since I don't really want to plan a wedding.

"Okay." I say, moving the tray from over my lap and placing it between us, then turning to face him. "Where do we start?"

"I don't know." He says through a full mouth, "The date, I think. Do you want a big wedding, or small? Do you want it in a church or not? What colors do we choose?"

"Okay date." I say drinking my juice, "Do you want a long engagement?"

"Hmm?" He spreads jam on my toast and holds it up for me to bite, "How long is long?"

"A year I guess?" I ask, hoping for a no. There's no way I'm going to wait a year. "How long does it take to plan a wedding?"

"I don't know, I guess a year sounds reasonable." He doesn't sound convinced at all. "With all of the planning and...stuff."

I bite my bacon, watching him chew his eggs.

"You don't want to wait that long, do you?"

"No, I don't." He says looking at me, "But if that's how long it takes then, that's how long it takes."

"You know," I say biting my toast, "Franky can get it done in a month."

"That wouldn't be too soon for you?" He asked. I search his eyes and find only genuine truth as always. He wants this, too, and seeing that makes me smile.

"No." I tell him smiling. Freezing as he reaches over to wipe jam from the corner of my mouth, then licks it off his thumb. "The thing is." I inhaled deeply, taking note of the hint of worry that filled his eyes. "It may take some time to plan a wedding, but all we need to actually get married is a license and a witness."

"True." He smiles.

The worry is slowly fading from his eyes as he catches on to my point. "Only, I don't know your mother, but I'm pretty sure she'll probably kill her only daughter for eloping...and the man she married."

"Not if we set a date and tell her that's when we're getting married. But go to the courthouse before then and get it done. Or vice versa."

"You would do that?" he asks, smiling, chewing the straw from his juice.

"What?" I ask eating the last of my oatmeal. "Trick my mom? Sure, I will."

"No, I mean elope." His eyes have completely lit up.

"Of course." His joy is making me smile. I guess this is something we really did need to discuss. "Listen." I say, "I don't really care about the wedding." His eyebrows shot up.

"I mean, I care about the wedding. Put your eyebrows down. But what comes after is what's more important to me. So be it in front of a preacher or a judge, it's all the same to me. Just so long as you're there with me. But I hope not in a church though."

He doesn't speak. He just stares at me, in…wonder, I think? And there he is hiding that smile behind his glass again. I can't take it anymore.

"What are you thinking about?" I asked him.

"You." He admits, "You really just do what you want to do." That's not a question, and it's not rhetorical.

"Only if it makes me happy." I inhaled deeply, shaking my head, "And you make me happy. Besides, we can have two weddings. One just for us to share secretly and one to celebrate with our families."

"I like that." He tells me.

"Yeah? I just came up with that." I say joking. "So, you're okay with that? We agree? Elope…then a wedding?"

"Completely." He tells me smiling. "You keep surprising me."

"How?" I ask, "Wait." I climb from the bed taking the tray with me to the kitchen then rush back and flop on the bed.

"Okay, how do I keep surprising you?" I stretch out the long way opposite from him, putting his feet by my head.

"You are way too excited." He chuckles lifting my feet to his lap.

"I am." I admit, "First off, I've always been told that I'm intimidating. Not surprising, and no one's ever went into detail. So, I'm interested."

"Alright let's start from yesterday. You play so many instruments and can put together songs and melodies going simply off of what someone is thinking. Confidence draws all the oxygen out of the room when you play, because you're *that good*. But your brother asks you to sing and you damn near pass out." He's smiling at me, halfway furling his mustache upward.

"That surprises you?"

"It does, especially since I'm pretty sure you probably have a beautiful voice."

Oh lord, he just doesn't know...bless his heart.

"Okay, what else?" This is it. This is the inside information; I need to know this stuff and he's so willing. He's always so open and willing.

"Your closet is set up like a backstage dressing room of some theater house...on Broadway or something. But, in that closet, you have a Craftsman tool chest full of jewelry, color coded in each drawer."

He chuckles looking down at me as I try and stiffen my smile, but it's kind of funny listening to him light weight make fun of me. Not to mention, I'm sure he put all these things he's telling me on the list, so I know he likes it.

"Your hat's," he continues, walking into the closet and showing me a style head. "Are sitting on dress up heads, so they don't lose shape. Those heads have make-up painted on them, eyelashes and *earrings*."

I bit my lip trying very hard not to join in with his laughter at my expense. It's really funny though, not only because he's right but because, he hasn't even seen me around my family.

"I don't like my hats getting flat." I laugh.

"I know right, who does." He sarcastically jokes, although I know he's making fun of me, I don't care it's funny. Growing up with the Mitchell boys, this girl learned really quickly that if you can't laugh at yourself then don't laugh at all.

"Then there's your tattoos." He spoke. My smile widens and stretches across my face.

"What about them?" I say looking down at myself. They're interesting, they're huge, and they're detailed.

"They excite me." He tells me, clutching my eyes with his, "They're sexy as hell. You're the girliest tomboy I've ever met."

"That doesn't bother you, does it?" I ask.

"Absolutely not." He tells me. "Because you're so feminine and soft. Like now, you're wearing shorts and a tee-shirt, with batman on them."

"What's wrong with batman?" I asked chuckling, pulling at the hem of my shirt.

"Nothing at all, in fact, I'm very attracted to him right now."

That makes me laugh, harder than I expected. My text alert goes off and since it's closer to Eros he picks it up for me, then hands it to me.

"What's it say?" I ask him waving it off.

"It's from, Mommy. And she says...Oh no." His eyes widen and he repositions himself so that he's lined up next to by body.

"What?" I asked, worried. Instantly coming up with ideas of how to get Frank back for running his big ass mouth. *"Ut-oh* what?"

"Does your dad own guns?" Eros asks. All humor from before has vanished and has been replaced with nothing but pure fear.

"Huh?" I leaned over his arm and read the message out loud. *"Just so you know, your father's cleaning his guns."* Immediately I laughed. His eyebrows have blended with his hairline and his eyes are the size of chocolate coins.

"They're hunting rifles." I say still laughing.

"What's he hunting?" His voice bounces three full octaves, which makes me laugh even harder. I swear I try to stop, but every time I catch my breath, and try to relax my cheeks he asks the same question. "No seriously...what's he hunting?"

"Whatever's in season." I tell him holding my cheeks. I think if I let them go, I may have a giggling fit.

"Besides," I tell him, rolling to my side and tossing my legs over his back. "He's old and his eyesight is horrible now."

"But look at me." He says standing up, "I'm a big target!"

"Aww baby," I say standing on my knees running my fingers through the hair covering his cheeks. "Every year me and Franky go hunting with my dad." I giggle, "It's not for you." His hands slide down my back down to my butt.

"Hunting?" He asks, much more relaxed than a few minutes ago. "With rifles?"

"Um-hum." I say nodding. His eyebrows dip in the center of his face, and his eyes seem to somewhat twinkle with humor.

"You specifically, hunt with rifles?" He asked absolutely failing at hiding his humor.

I think, because I'm giggling, he thinks I'm joking. But I'm so serious. I'm laughing because, for once I know what he's thinking.

"Or knife," I say clasping my hands behind his neck. "But I prefer a bow."

"Do you now?" He chuckles, "And what do you hunt?" Okay, I know exactly where this is leading. It's all over his face. The silly smile, that I'm sure is reflected on mine.

"Deer." My smile widens with his, "This time of year is dear season."

"So let me get this straight."

I nod my head sitting flat on the bed with my legs dangling. Leaning my weight back on my forearms. "You hunt...live deer...with a rifle or a knife, but you prefer the bow and arrow?"

"Um-hum." I agree matter-a-factly. He's standing between my legs with his hands on my thighs.

"How old when you first started?" His hands carresses my thighs in a very casual and massaging way.

"Hum." His question catches me off guard at first. I've never been asked that question, ever. People don't even know that about me.

"Um..." I say thinking, "I started off with small things like rabbits mostly, when I was about ten...I guess."

His mouth is agape oval separating his mustache from his beard. His hands have stopped massaging but still lightly gripping my thighs.

"I didn't shoot my first deet until I was about...fourteen, I think."

"With a bow and arrow?" He starts rubbing again. "Why did you choose the bow and arrow?"

"Well," Here's something else I've never been asked before. I've never even really *thought* about it. "It's quieter, and lighter, and easier to lug around. Guns are so heavy and awkward to handle. And they're loud, even with the cans on. I guess." I lift my shoulders and let them drop, like it's no big deal.

"I guess." He repeats shaking his head.

I can't help chuckling, because I see his focus bouncing right back to his original thought. I can tell by the way his bottom lip tucks beneath his top lip.

"How many deer have you shot?"

"Well," wow, he's really asking some good ones. "I shot my first one at fourteen, so. I guess between then and now, about eleven, maybe. I never kept count."

"And you do this every year?" He asks, raising his eyebrows.

"Um-hum."

"What do you do with the deer?"

I laugh again.

"Um...eat it." I giggle. "We skin it, then divide the meat up between everyone and my dad sells what's left. Well, *they* divide it up. I don't usually bring it home. *Or* he'll make jerky and on Sunday my mom will usually make a stew or something and before everyone heads off, we have dinner."

"Why don't you bring it home?"

"I don't know how to cook it." I admit. Because it's just that simple. "Babe, I really can't cook." I chuckle. "Breakfast I can do...a little. Sandwiches, things like that, yeah."

Looking at him shaking his head at me, scratching his beard smiling. I don't know why he won't just say it.

"So, you're going to bring some home this year, right?" *Here it comes.*

"If you want me to, Eros."

Here it comes.

"Oh, I want you to." He confirms nodding his head.

Here it comes. My smile grows with anticipation. I know it's coming.

"Then yes, I'll bring some home. If I hit anything."

Here it comes.

"Okay, so you're going to bring home, fresh meat, for me to cook."

"Um-hum." I say, nodding my head.

"Anyway, I want?"

"Um-hum."

Here it comes.

"That *you* might have killed."

"Yes." And here it comes.

"Okay, FYI." He tells me, waving his palm in the air making small circles, "*All* of what you just told me is *soooo* on the list."

I knew it! We both cracked up. I drop my back flat on the bed and cradle his head on my stomach where he's rested it.

"I knew it." I say laughing, "I could see it on your face, you couldn't even wait to say it."

"Come on, baby." He says looking at me from my belly, I've propped myself back up on my elbows and is watching him bask in his own humor. "I mean, seriously, you are the most interesting person I've ever had the pleasure of getting to know."

I'm stunned, absolutely stunned. Every time I think I've heard the most from him. He goes the extra mile, and knocks the breath clear out of my lungs.

"You are so…different than anyone I know." I say shaking my head.

"*I'm* different?" he asks, pointing his finger at the center of his chest.

"Yes you." I say nodding my head. "You are *very* different, Eros. You make me think about things I've never thought about before. No one's ever asked me about hunting, in fact, no one even knows about it."

"Really?"

"Yes really." I say.

He looks genuinely surprised, as if he can't believe all guys aren't impressed by six-foot three-inch women drummers. With brown skin, a four-foot five-inch round afro, who's body is eighty-five percent covered in tattoos. "Most guys find me ordinary, I guess. Or just intimidating. But you." I look into his eyes searching for…something. I don't know. I think maybe I just want him to…see me. See all of me even though he's already seen so much. "I don't know, you just don't."

I push myself from my elbows to my hands forcing him to sit up. His eyes wash over my face stop on my mouth, then find my eyes.

"It's because you don't intimidate me."

Then his lips are on mine, proving the point he just made. But as quick as he giveth, he taketh away, and I'm left flushing under my freckles.

"I'm going to have a shower." He tells me planting a kiss on the tip of my nose. "You want to join me?"

"Um." I say thinking, fighting the urge to strip right then. "No thank you." I say smiling, "I'm going to clean the kitchen." I hop off the bed and step around him.

"Are we going to see Emma today?" I asked stopping at the doorway turning just in time to see the back of him disappear into the closet.

"And then go back to your place." I say over my shoulder as I enter the kitchen. I hear him agree from the bathroom. The shower comes on and I can hear him say something else, but I can't make it out, so I don't worry about it. He'll repeat it when he gets out.

The kitchen wasn't as bad as I expected. A quick load to the dish washer, and a good wipe down over all surfaces, faucets and handles. Then sweep and Swiffer mop and I'm done. Eros hasn't even made it out of the shower yet.

"Leave the shower on please." I shout, walking past the bathroom, towards the room. Since we're going to his house I might as well grab a few things to keep over his house. That'll keep me from having to drag things back and forth.

I put together a few outfits according to what I need for tomorrow. Extra work scrubs. Extra sleeping clothes. Relaxing clothes, things like that. Underclothes, and accessories. Just as I'm closing my suitcase, my very own Olympic god comes walking in wearing nothing but boxer briefs, fluffing a towel through his hair. I just shake my head smiling. That's going to take some getting used to. I remove my shorts and tee-shirt, toss them in the baskets, then grab my towel.

"I won't be long." I tell him winking at him.

"Um-hum." He half smiles, rubbing what's left of that magnificent oil down his chest.

"Um-hum." I repeat towards the bathroom. How in the world does casual talking turn into flirting with him.

By the time I finish my shower, Eros is finished and waiting for me. "I'm still not going to be long."

"Um-hum." He repeats with the same half smile.

"So, I think I should drive my car, that way in the morning you won't have to take me to work."

"I don't mind taking you to work." He tells me, watching me lotion my legs. "You want some help?" He asks, just as I stand to lotion my backside. I politely decline. Knowing full well, that if I let that gorgeous man put his hands on me, we'll both be naked and will abandon all plans outside of love making.

"Besides," I tell him pulling on panties to match my bra, "I don't mind you taking me to work, except, you're not really an early morning kind of person."

"What?" he asked, leaning back on his elbows just as I did a little while ago. I spritz my body with my cocoa butter after bath splash and slip on my dark denim jeans.

"Really babe." I say smiling through my skeptical glance. "The ceiling could fall in around you and you wouldn't know."

I sit down and put on my white low top converse and adjust the cuffs to my boyfriend jeans.

"Well fine. Since I can't take you to work, I can at least make you breakfast and lunch."

I look over at him from the full-length mirror where I'm standing and pulling my hair into a low ponytail.

"You would wake up that early just to make me lunch?" He's sitting up and watching me pull on my blue and white horizontal striped cardigan.

"And breakfast." He confirms. I put on a white paperboy style hat and give my ponytail one last fluff.

"You're so beautiful." He tells me, scratching his jawline.

"Why thank you, Mr. Apollo." I say smiling, walking over to him. "You're the sweetest soon-to-be husband I've ever had."

"I mean it." He tells me again. "Even when you're not trying, you take my breath away."

I lean back and search his eyes for that familiar look that I've loved since day one.

"What?" He questions, inhaling deeply through his nose.

"You." I say, rubbing my hands over his white thermal up to the soft skin of his neck. "You're the most honest person that I know. It's refreshing to not have to guess."

"You don't think it's…overbearing?"

It's a strange question for him to ask, but I suppose I'd rather him ask than hold it in. That could become a problem.

"Not even a little bit." I tell him, "Having to try and figure out what a person's thinking, or how they feel can be tiresome. And I don't know about anyone else but for me, it can get kind of boring."

His hands snake around my waist under my cardigan, squeezing my lower back, as I pull his face close to my neck.

"Don't ever stop talking to me or telling me anything. I'll never get tired of hearing it."

It's sort of a natural stimulant for me, just like his hands smoothing over and squeezing my ass. Or his oil that enters my brain through my nose. Filling my mind with images of the woods that stretch behind my parents' house. Surrounding my treehouse castle, with green and brown and golden leaves. Whistling and ruffling as the wind dances through the branches. It's my favorite place to be. Well, at least it was. Right now, it's running a close second to being in his arms. The feel of his firm shoulders beneath my hands. His soft neck to my lips, and tongue. I want to feel his tongue. I want his beard to tickle my face and prickle my skin.

But…I can't. Not right now, we have to go. Although…it's just afternoon, we actually have plenty of time. I glide my hands down his back and up the front of his thermal, grazing my nails lightly through his smooth soft hairiness. I smile against his neck at the feel of his nipples pressing, coming to life against my circling thumbs.

"Um-hum." His throat growls, "We need to go." He quickly kisses my ear, and gives my bottom his signature *two-tap-pat*.

"We do need to go." I say giving his neck one last kiss as I smooth my hands down the front of his shirt. Returning it to its original place, somewhat clinging to his torso.

I need to refocus and find something else to put my hands on. Like my suitcase, which, as I look around, I can't find. It's not on the bed, the floor or closet. I'm quite sure of that. Eros must've taken it to the car, he's very thoughtful which is a really huge turn on for me. So...I guess I'll just tuck my hands in my pockets because if I stay in this room and touch him one more time his shirt's coming off. Or his pants...something. Whatever it'll take to seduce him.

"You ready?" Eros ask tugging at the back of my sweater.

"Yup." I say backing up as I turn to walk in his direction as he strolls backwards down the hall.

He's put on a sweater and is pulling the sleeves partially up his arms. Then, and I think he's doing this on purpose because of his cocky half smile and the *keep watching me if you want to* look in his eyes. He adjusts the hem of his shirt around the belt loops of his pants, tucking the front of his shirt down the crotch for me to see. I'm really, really trying to conceal this very sheepish grin on my face. So, I bite my bottom lip hard.

"What are you thinking right now?" he asked, holding the door open for me. I stop toe to toe in front of him, look at him square in his honestly gentle eyes and place my hand over his almost erection.

"That this," I say, giving it a quick poke, "Is going in my mouth later."

His mouth drops. I smile and wink then stroll to my car. It's a beautiful day out, the sun is shining but a slight bite is in the air. I can tell fall is approaching with winter following close behind.

"We'll drop your car off at my house first, since it's on the way." He tells me. His eyes are liquid brown, glazing my soul. I swear I don't know, and I don't care, where in the exact heavens did this man drop from. I just thank the universe for dropping him in my path.

Chapter Seventeen

The drive to Eros house reminded me that I hadn't been here since *Carriegate* and that I was going to have to start referring to this as *home*.

"You coming in?" Eros asks as I get in his truck.

"No, I can wait." He nods his head smiling then gets out of the truck headed towards the house. Our house now. Carrying two of my bags in each arm. How many times a week are we going to have to do this? Traveling from one house to the next? And what happens if we do end up making a little crib midget? Do we keep moving him back and forth every other day? Poor kid will be confused as hell trying to keep up with his addresses.

We're going to have to revisit the subject of selling, and which property would we sell? His would bring more money, its value being well above mine. Not to mention it's a subterranean, so that's a nice perk. Now, my house on the other hand, has two levels. Four bedrooms, two bathrooms. It's in a residential area. Fifteen minutes outside of town, and ten minutes from some junior high, I never bothered learning which one. It's more ideal for a family and may sell faster. On top of that he's been in his house for eleven years. I've only been in mine for six. I own three residential properties; I can stand to part with one.

"You're quiet." Eros tells me, pulling me into the present.

We're stopped at a traffic light and the music is low to background level. Trey Songs singing about Love faces whispers from the speakers. My legs are crossed, and his hand is lightly rubbing my knee.

"What are you thinking about?" He asks, reaching for my hand that dangles over the arm console.

"I was thinking about something you bought up before." I tell him. His eyes are focused on the road ahead, watching the traffic.

"What's that?" He asks, checking the mirror and switching to the left lane, stopping again as the light turns red.

"Where we should live."

He leans his head against the head rest, as he turns to face me.

"Oh yeah?" he asks, lacing his fingers through mine. "And what were you thinking?"

"Well...what if we do end up making a crib midget? We can't go dragging him back and forth."

"Or her." He adds in, chuckling at crib midget.

"Or they." I say laughing at the drop of his mouth, as he makes the left turn into Golden Heights parking lot.

"They?" He says, turning his shocked face to me.

"It's a possibility." I say shrugging my shoulders. "My mother did it twice."

"Hum." He says kissing my hand.

"Anyway," I say getting back to my thoughts, "It may make more sense to put mine on the market. It might not sell at first but, I don't think it'll be out there as long as yours."

"Hum."

I raise my eyebrows at his lack of words and wait. He must have more to say than *hum*. He's at least looking at me, so I know he's paying attention. "So, you're willing to sell your house and move in with me?"

"Yes." I say plainly. "I mean, I guess we wouldn't have to think about it until a third person comes along but...yeah. I would."

"Okay well, why not just sell both places and get somewhere new."

"And then there's that." I say, "But you've been in your house since your first super bowl, that's pretty special." I say quietly.

His mustache curls to one side of his face. "But I'm going to be with you for the rest of my life. We're going to start a family...together.

I think we should do that in a place that has a little bit of both of us in it." I smile as he kisses my hand again.

"That would be pretty special." I agree, smiling bigger against his lips. *Oh, why did he kiss me?* I reach my hand up to his face just as the song switches. I know it's Hozier by the richness of his voice. I'd know his tone anywhere. His hand closes around my arm, squeezing gently. No! Nope, stop, before I get carried away. I pull away from his mouth licking my lips, just as Hozier's sweet voice chimes in telling of how his baby gives him toothaches just from kissing him.

"That's for damn sure." Eros boasts, smiling as big as his face would allow. I couldn't help laughing. The timing was perfect, as was Eros comment. I do believe I'm flushing in my cheeks. I can feel them warm. I wonder if he notices, or if he can tell. I watched him walk around the car to my door. Smooth, long confident strides. That's the man I'm going to marry.

Hum.

****

Emma seems a lot better than the last time I saw her. She is much more talkative than before, and much more alert. She almost has a glow about her, as she tells us about the young students that came to sing for them.

"The voices of angles." She said they had.

"That sounds nice momma." Eros tells her.

"Emma," I say remembering my parents' anniversary. "My parents live in Henderson County."

"I know Henderson," She said raising her hands off the table, "Henry took me to a bed and breakfast there."

Bed and Breakfast? I look at Eros, who's already looking at me with his confused eyes.

"It was on the street named after a president." She said looking at Eros for the answer.

A president?

"Roosevelt?" I say out loud.

"That's it." Emma starts, "That's the street."

"Emmerson House." I say remembering the place well. "I went on a field trip there every year in grade school." I tell her, looking at Eros. His eyes are warm again, almost dripping as he winks at me.

"Well Emma," I say refocusing and clearing my throat. "My parents are having an anniversary dinner and I'd love it if you would come to meet them."

"Oh Dear, I wouldn't want to impose."

"It would be no imposition at all, I promise." I assure her.

"You know," She says looking into my eyes, "I wonder if it's still around."

"It is." I tell her referring to the bed and breakfast. "It's a historical landmark now."

"It would be nice to see it again." She says smiling.

"So, mom, is that a, yes?" Eros asks.

"Sure, that's a yes." She pats her hands against Eros face, "I always said I'd like to revisit, now's my chance."

Eros smile is huge. He is very satisfied with his mother's presence today. He holds her hand, he fetches her tea, and a sweater when she complains of being cold. And when the afternoon grew into evening and Emma became tired, he didn't hesitate to escort her to her room. Only returning after she's settled for her nap.

"I didn't take too long, did I?" he asked, holding his hand out for me to stand.

"Of course not." I object, "She looked really good."

"Yeah, today's a good day." He agrees.

We sign out, and in no time at all we pull into his, *our* driveway, with the sound track to our relationship whispering through his speakers.

"It's still early, do you want to get some dinner, or go to a movie…or something?" He shakes his head slowly, with a look that I've never seen.

"You've got a long day ahead of you tomorrow." He tells me.

"It's only 5:30, Eros." I say raising my eyebrows at the digital clock.

"You've got a long night ahead of you too."

My face stills, and my eyes follow him out of the SUV and around to my side.

"What are you up to?" I ask squinting my eyes at him playfully, when he opens my door.

"I don't know what you're talking about ma'am." He states plainly. "Don't forget your keys." He points at the middle console just as I stand up. Which makes me have to lean over the wide passenger seat. Giving him the opportunity that he takes, to step behind me pressing his groin against my backside. I smile to myself, unnecessarily stretching further into the car so that my back slightly arches against his pelvis.

"Excuse me, sir." I say playfully, pushing myself backwards against him until I'm clear from the car and standing in front of him. "Excuse me, but what are you doing?"

"I was helping."

"Is that so?" I say stepping around him and retrieving my bag from the backseat of my car. Looking over my shoulder just as his head angles to one side for a better view. Until he notices me watching.

"We're going to have to establish some kind of personal space and boundaries." I tell him backing out of the car just as before, turning to stand toe to toe with him.

"Why?" He asks taking my last duffle bag from my hand. "I know exactly where your personal space and boundaries lie." Oh, he is extra cocky today. Standing there oozing chocolate into my soul through my eyes.

"Come on." He tells me, tilting his head towards the house.

He spoke so quietly, I swear, had I not been looking at his mouth I wouldn't have heard him. His hand smoothes over my waist as I closed the car door. As per the new norm, I'm aware of everything about him right now. How he's watching me take off my shoes. He walks over to the huge fireplace and sits my bag down by the wall leading to the back bedroom, next to the others. How he never takes his eyes off of me as he removes his cardigan and shirt. The way he slowly strolls over to me unbuttoning his fly. He stops in front of me, removes my sweater and tosses it to the floor, adding my shirt that he's pulled over my head, to the sweater.

"Take your pants off." He tells me quietly, as he uncages his erection.

Without saying a word, he spins me around and leads me over to half-moon sofa. Guides my legs so that my knees are pressed into the crease separating the seat of the plush couch. My front is pressed into the back of the couch and my skin lights up under his soft gentle touch sliding up my back to unhook my bra. Pushing it down my arms, he tosses it to the pile of my clothes.

"You drive me insane." He tells me. With one hand he's caressing the bend of my hip and with the other he's rubbing his two fingers into my wetness, swirling it around in circles. My body is on fire, my scalp is tingling with anticipation. His lips are a moist contrast in comparison to the warm brushes of his beard as he kisses his way up my spine to my neck.

Damnit. My body is aching for him. Urging him, rocking with his naked grind against me.

"You drive me *fucking* insane." He growls in my ear. "Even when I'm with you my body misses you." His voice travels directly to that spot deep within me as he continues with his circles. "Hold still." He tells me over my moan. "No, turn around." I do as he asks and turn to face him.

Balancing himself on his knees he separates my legs so that they straddle his thighs.

"It's getting harder and harder to control myself when I'm near you." His hands are on my hips pulling me up his thighs closer to his groin. I watch him, watch himself position at my opening then look at me, as he fills my walls. Entering me slowly, then pulling back at the same speed. I watch him, glistening with my wetness, enter and exit my body. Lightly tapping my inner spot. I look up at him still watching me.

"You like this?" He asks through easy breaths. Holding my hip with one hand and cupping my breast with the other.

"I love it." I say softly, rotating my hips.

"Be still." He instructs me again, thrusting into my spot harder.

"AAhh." I gasped.

"You love it?" He asks thrusting again, two times.

"Yes." I moan, "Oh yes."

He places both hands on my hips, hold me firmly in place, and moves vigorously. I don't know how many times, but that spot is quickly disintegrating from within my walls. Making its way to the surface of my skin. Just when I think my body can't take anymore pleasure. He grinds himself into that spot like he's trying to rub a hole in it. Rocking my hips, driving himself deeper still.

"Did you love that?" He asks, sliding in and out of me with ease again.

"Um-hum." I tell him. His eyes are brown holes of smoke, steaming with passion…for me. Only for me.

"You want it again?" He asks, bending to kiss me, "You want it again."

Before I can answer he is pounding away at that spot, and my composure or control is lost. Actually, it's not lost. I know exactly where it is. On the backburner just where I put it. I don't want it right now. I want to let go. I want to feel every pump, thrust and grind he's giving me, and I want it to erupt from my lips like the quiet sounds of an overactive volcano.

"You love it."

"Yes." I manage, "Don't stop."

"Don't stop?" He asks, "What makes you think I'm going to stop?" He thrusts harder as if he had a pocket of energy on reserve, like an extra gas tank.

"Fuck." I squealed, still not moving. I'm about to erupt. "Fuck." I squeal again.

"There it is." He tells me. Or, maybe, not necessarily to me but to the universe that is ours. "There it is."

"Give it to me." He groans, "Give it to me. I can feel it. It's right there."

How does he know? *Pump, thrust, grind.*

"Oh my god." I moan.

How can he tell? *Pump, thrust, grind.*

"Oh my god." I breath.

"I know love."

Pump, thrust, grind.

Our voices are a mangled chorus of pleasure. His grunting, "Give it to me", between each pump, thrust and grind. Mine saying nothing that makes since, responding to his pump, thrust and grind. Until neither of us can hold on any longer.

"How about that?" I say smiling at him, excepting the kiss he's offering me.

"I told you." He said smiling through his beard, "Controlling myself isn't easy anymore."

"Welp," I say, grabbing my suitcase handle, "Anytime you want to lose control, you know where to find me."

"Um-hum." He tells me pulling his under wear up, "Don't go too far, I'm not done yet."

My face goes still as I blank stare at him, smiling when he winks at me, shaking my head. Much of the rest of the evening went pretty smoothly. We work out a space arrangement for my clothes and shoes and other things. Then Eros sets to making dinner, while I fuss and argue with my hair. I managed, finally, to work my way through the tangles, oil it from roots to ends and braid it in five medium plaits. I thought about wrapping my hair in a scarf, making it somewhat sexy. But let's face it, they're *plaits*...they're never sexy. Ever. I'm wearing my Superman pajama shorts with the matching tee-shirt, and as an extra added touch a pair of blue, yellow and red knee-high matching socks.

I feel like Toucan Sam, following the delicious aromas with my nose towards the kitchen. Staring, as I walk through the living room area, at the makeshift picnic area he's set up in front of the fire place. That has a beautiful fire crackling. The kitchen on the other hand is a different story. To say he's made a mess would be putting it lightly. I automatically head to the sink and start on the dish water.

"You hungry?" He asked, watching my movements.

"I am." I respond, "You finished with this?"

I reach for the skillet, still on the stove that he used to ground the hamburger. I'm not a big fan of dish washing, but as long as I'm not doing the cooking, I'm more than willing to do anything.

"You excited about going back to work?"

"No." I tell him shaking my head, laughing. "I've gotten pretty comfortable with the way things have been going." I look over my shoulder at him wiping his hands on the towel dangling from his shoulder, "I'm going to miss hanging out with you."

"Me too." He says smiling, "Here taste this." He feeds me a bit of sauce on a spoon, then wipes the excess drip from my chin with his thumb. "How's that?" He asks, sucking the sauce from his thumb.

"It's really perfect." I say smiling, smacking my lips. "I'm really impressed, Eros, you're an excellent chef."

"Thank you." He's blushing again.

"Eros," I say smiling, as he turns his attention to the garlic toast, "You are so cute." *Oh my gosh* he's getting redder. Why is he so embarrassed.

"Why do you say things that?" He asks me. The confidence I see in his eyes as he stares at me is a direct contradiction to the crimson of his ears and cheeks.

"Because" I tell him crossing my arms over my chest. "One minute you're bending me over the back of the sofa, claiming things. And the next, you're blushing like a bashful six-year-old…It's adorable."

"I'm adorable?" He chuckles placing the pan of garlic bread on the middle oven rack. "Which part?" Closing the oven, tosses the towel from his shoulder to the countertop. Then stalks over to where I'm standing, hovers over my body surrounding me with his arms and legs. "The claiming things, or the blushing part?"

"See," I say grinning, "Look at these muscles." My hands firmly squeeze his biceps. "You make me feel small and delicate. I'm really enjoying not being the bigger half of the relationship for once."

"Just like me. I'm really enjoying having someone that I can hold on to without feeling like I'm going to break them." He palms both sides of my butt and squeezes firmly. It's so casual I don't even bother turning around to acknowledge the gesture. *But*, as I'm reaching to place the last dirty dish on the rack, I stretch a little further than I need to giving him more to hold on to. Then for no reason at all, other than turning him on, I tighten and loosen my thigh muscles making my cheeks jiggle in his hands.

"Oh my god." He gasps stepping back, "What the?" His tone switches so dramatically that I turned a little too fast and accidently smacked his side.

"What?" I gasped automatically grabbing my crotch thinking I'd find undetected menstrual cycle. Then I noticed that he stepped back and was staring at my socks. I can't help laughing.

"Don't even say it." I choke out through my giggles, "These are not on the list." He steps back and pulls the toast from the oven.

"Of course, they are." He tells me laughing, pulling the strainer of ziti pasta from the boiling water. "They have capes on them!" He chuckles shaking his head. "And you think *I'm* cute."

I take a couple of plates from the cabinet, along with forks from the drawer beside the sink and take them to the table. While he stores some of the noodles, sauce and garlic bread in storage containers.

"Here's your lunch." He announces. "Now for dinner." I watched him divide the pasta and sauce between the two of us. I know the meal he's prepared is going to be delicious. The mixture of tomatoes and garlic teases my sense of smell and flirts with my taste buds. But in all honesty, all I see are his muscles. He's so relaxed and casual right now.

"So how do you think it's going to be tomorrow?" He asks sitting next to me.

"It's Monday." I say between chews, "It's going to absolutely suck. Not to mention, I've been gone for an entire week. There's no telling how much has changed."

"Really?" He asks wiping his mouth on his napkin. "What do you do?"

"What do you mean?" I ask pulling my bread apart. "I'm a nurse?"

"Um-hum." He hums chewing. "But what do you do?"

"*Really?* You mean like blow by blow?" I say taking another bite of bread. "Okay But let me go ahead and tell you now, this is about to be really boring." He tilts his head to one side wiping his mouth again.

"I'll take my chances."

"Okay." I say between chews, noticing how his biceps flex every time he moves his arm, guiding his fork from his plate to his mouth. "I'll wake you when I finish."

"Well, first off," I begin, "The night shift has to clock out by 7:15. My shift starts at 6:30, so I have to be there by 6:15 in the morning, so I can get report and count my cart."

His eyebrows furrow and I can tell he's confused. "The night shift will give me all accounts on any issues or changes that may have occurred while I was away."

"Like what?" he asks, forking pasta into the hole in his beard.

"Do you really wanna hear this?" I asked disbelievingly.

"Yes ma'am." He answers biting his bread. "I really do."

I lift my shoulders and let them drop listlessly. Then begin to tell him, play by play, how my day goes. Med counts, accu-cheks. Med-passes, nurses notes, behavior charting. On top of dealing with arrogant doctors, supervising CNA's, activities, appointments, combative residents. Demanding residents. Residents that used to be junkies, who only have their prescription pain pills as a source for getting high. People that refuse to comply with the nutritional guidelines for their diabetes. Family members that only seem to come around just to see if their loved ones passed away overnight, so they can take them for everything they're worth.

This he couldn't believe, and I have to explain to him that not everyone cares for their family member out of love and respect the way he does with Emma. Some of them do it simply because of duty and to count the days when they don't have too anymore. I tell him that his devotion to Emma is one of the first things that I loved about him. Before I can completely change the subject, he asks me why I got into nursing. To which I explain that my mother's aunt, My Grandmother's sister, lived here and had fallen ill and needed someone to care for her.

My mother, because of who she fell in love with had long been disowned and refused to be subjected to my great-aunts...way of thinking. I on the other hand, could care less about what she thought. Or what she said. All I saw was an opportunity to...go somewhere. Or do something.

"Was she as bad as she sounds?" He asks, finishing the last of his pasta.

"Every single day." I tell him lying my fork across my plate, nodding my head. "Every day, until she died, I was a thief. A free loader. A nigger." I admitted quietly. His eyes widened at that last thing.

"Really?" he asked, shocked. "Your aunt called you that?

"Really." I tell him. "My father was a nigger. My brothers were little nigger boys, and my mother was a nigger lover. Every...single...day." I strongly enunciate the last three words.

"So why did you keep doing it?" He asked stretching my legs across his lap and removing my socks.

"Because" I say, leaning against the chair back, "No matter how mean or rotten she was to me, she was family. And I needed her."

His attention was on my feet until I said that last part, then he shifted to my face.

"Why would you need that?" He asked confused.

"Because" I tell him nonchalantly. Once again, he and I are engaging in a conversation that I've never had with anyone. Not even my parents. During the time I took care of my Great Aunt, my mother was either angry at me for not telling her what was going on. Or she was pissed because sometimes I would show up at her house and just hug her. To this day we've still never talked about it. "She was one of the strongest women I knew. No matter what. She never complained. Throughout all of her discomfort and pain. Behind the racial slurs and name calling and accusations...she was afraid. She knew she was dying and from the very end she remained true to who she was. I admired that about her. She didn't let her fear take over who she really was. And at the end of the day, I had to admit that this was my mother's side of the family. Whether I liked it or not, I shared that blood. I never had to see my mother be that strong. My father was always there for her. But Great Aunt Alice didn't have anyone...and she never faltered. That taught me something."

"Baby," He coos, as I stand and remove our plates, "I'm sorry."

"Don't be." I say smiling, "There were times, although she never remembered afterwards, when she would be confused and forget who

I was. She'd call me by Grandma's name and make me sit and talk for hours with her. About…stuff. And I didn't have the heart to tell her who I was, so I'd just lay there until the morphine put her to sleep."

"She didn't remember?" He asks drying the dishes I finished washing.

"Nope," I say leaning against the counter, "And I'll never forget."

"Okay." He said leaning against the counter catacorner to me, "So I know the *why* you got into nursing. Now what about *how*?" This man truly makes me smile. Standing there with his arms folded across his bare chest and his legs crossed at the ankles. His pants are unbuttoned at the top revealing the band of his boxer briefs.

"When Great-Aunt-Alice, which is what she made me call her."

"That's a mouthful." He said smiling, separating his limbs and excepting my body into his embrace.

"Tell me about it." I said, remembering a promise I made, earlier this morning, about what I was going to fill my mouth with. "Anyway. The entire time that I took care of her I was working as a nursing assistant. I paid for my own food, and anything else that I needed. Once a month I even deposited four hundred dollars for rent into her bank account."

"Really?" He asked, draping his arms around my shoulders. "She charged you rent?"

"No." I said plainly. I'm a bit distracted now and have shifted my focus to the tattooed feathers that bend over the muscles of his forearms. "But she already thought of me as a thief and a freeloader, and I saw no reason to make those thoughts true."

"Um-hum." He hummed.

"Towards the end, she had a fulltime nurse that visited her three times a day. She also had an attorney that visited once a month, but I never thought to ask what that was about."

"He never asked or told you anything?" he asked, shifting his body allowing me to turn so that my backside is against his front.

"No, I think he was too embarrassed." I say rubbing my fingers up and down the soft skin of his arms. "A lot of her verbal comments came out when he was around, and I don't think he was too happy about that."

"Why is that?" he asked softly, leaning his face into my neck and squeezing his arms around my waist.

"Well for one he was Jewish, and a lot of her belittling was directed towards him. Also, because, when she died he was way too excited to inform me that everything that she owned had been liquified, into cash and left to me. Minus his fee and the nurses pay. I almost felt like his way of revenge was immediately signing the money over to me. Stating that her stipulations were that I either gained a trade or degree, and as far as he was concerned my Certificate as a Nursing Assistant *was* a trade and he saw no reason to withhold the money." His tiny, furry kisses on my neck stop instantly.

"She left you everything?" he asked shocked, smiling against my skin as I pout and tilt my head further to the side for him to continue his sensual mouth play.

"Yup, nine hundred, fifty thousand and six hundred dollars." I say closing my eyes. "Roughly."

Once again, his magical kisses stopped and this time he drew his head back.

"That's a lot of money, what did you do with it?"

"I invested it." I said, reaching back for his face.

"In what?"

Slowly and very tenderly, Eros kisses my neck, then pushes my body away from his guiding me out of the kitchen and into the living room. The fire had died down some, but still provided a warm glow within the area.

"Real estate." I watch him walk the length of the half-moon sofa tossing every pillow and cushion to the floor.

"I bought a condo in the city. Lived in it for two years then leased it out."

"Hold that thought, babe." He tells me just as I'm sitting on the floor lounging against the chair. "I'll be back."

Not even ten minutes later Eros returned wearing a pair of gym shorts perfectly fitted around his waist. *Damn*, he's a gorgeous man, and he's all mine. I hold my arms up, open for him to join me on the floor.

"Okay," he says fitting his body between my legs. "You were saying?"

"That I lived in a condo for two years then leased it out."

Just as he leans his back against my chest I stop him, pull my shirt over my head and drop it on the floor next to me. Then guide his bare back against my chest.

"So, where'd you go then?" he asked, turning his face back towards me. I like looking at him from this angle. His beautiful eyes are hooded by thick smooth eyebrows, unarched...unkept. Which is more than okay by me. For some reason men, now a days seem to think that us women want them just as clipped, cut, styled and groomed as much as we are. I guess, it's true, some women *may* go for that sort of thing. I myself, like my men as natural as I am.

"I bought four-plex apartment building." I tell him tracing my finger down the bridge of his nose. "By the time I sold the first condo, I'd graduated and taken my boards for my LPN. So, I worked as an LPN and went to school for my Masters in Registered Nursing. It should have taken me two years, but I'd already completed enough courses to be done in eighteen months. I took my boards, graduated and here I am."

I lift my shoulders and let them drop as if it was nothing. "The stipulation to receiving Alice's inheritance was that I go to school. I was already in the medical field, so I figured why not stick with it. Technically my title is Nurse Practitioner. I work at the nursing home because I want to."

"All for an aunt that treated you like nothing." He smiled sweetly, in a way that clouded his already smiley eyes.

"Like shit." I say tracing my finger along the outline of his sideburns into his beard. "She treated me like shit."

"So why did you do it?" He asked tracing his fingers in circles around my skin.

"Because I understood her."

His eyebrows furrowed together, and I smoothed my index finger down the center of his brow, "Some of us don't know how to be anyone else but who we are." Eros twisted his body so that he faced me, placing both his hands on either side of me on the edge of the sofa.

"I love everything about you." He said nuzzling his nose against mine. Taking that as a hint that his session of one hundred questions was over. I place my hands on both sides of his face and pull his lips gently to mine. And he tastes magnificent. Soft and warm and strong. His lips kissed my chin while his hands rub up and down my open thighs. So soft and so tender, my body immediately begins to heat beneath his touch. I lift my chin giving him access to my throat, which tickles as he kisses his way to my breast.

Eagerly I watch his mouth fondle and play with my nipple, urging it to swell and harden.

"Um, excuse me sir." I whispered, lifting his face to mine. "I do remember making a promise about what I wanted to do to you." His tongue snakes into my mouth and I gently suck, moving with him as he lay flat on the soft carpet, pulling me on top of his hard body.

"I'm all yours." He tells me, propping a pillow beneath his head. Watching as I kiss my way down his body. "I love when you touch me." He whispers.

I kiss around his belly button. Then over to his side nibbling and kissing remembering that he's ticklish there. Smiling against his skin as he flinches every time my tongue and teeth touch his body.

"You love me touching you?" I ask seductively, "How about this?" I lick my tongue around his erection, watching his eyes melt over me as he nods his head. He leans up on his elbows and traces his hand up and down my arms urging goose bumps to surface on my skin. I can feel myself getting moist between my legs, but I'm not finished with him yet.

My head is bobbing up and down in slow circles working my lips around his shaft.

"Ssss," He hisses through his teeth, "Shit." His words are slow and long, and his hips begin to move with my rhythm. His hand moves to the back of my head pushing me down urging him deeper into my throat. I, on the other hand, can feel what's happening to my own body, but I'm not ready until he either explodes in my mouth or turns me over and takes me right here on the carpet in front of the fireplace. I pull my mouth from his part and continue with everything I've learned over the years. Pleasing him as much as he pleases me. He loves it. All of it. "Fuck...wait, wait, wait." He breaths pushing me back, stopping me, "Oh, you almost got me." He chuckles, turning our bodies so that he's on top of me.

"I wasn't finished." I tell him wiping the corners of my mouth.

"Oh no, my love, it's my turn." He's smiling and looking at me as he kisses his way down my chest. "Tit for tat, remember."

He made his way down my belly lifting my legs to pull my shorts off by the backs of my thighs. Wasting no time with his tongue play, fondling me like he did my tongue. The purr that escapes my mouth oozes through the warm atmosphere created by the fire. Oh, he is kissing me, and sucking me, and licking all over me. I want to rock with his movement but his hands are holding my thighs close to my chest so I can't do anything but take it. Every slurp, and hum and kiss he unleashes on my delicate spot. My legs are trembling and a thin trickle of sweat trails down my thigh. My body twitches at every turn. Moans hiss through my mouth as I bite down hard on my bottom lip.

"Baby please." I moan, pulling at his shoulders coaxing his glossy face up to mine. "Baby please." I whispered, kissing him hard.

I'm so into the kiss that I'm taken by surprise at the fullness of him inside of me.

"Um-hum." He grunts, thrusting softly into our favorite spot. The spasm that runs through me is so smooth, I can barely keep still. I rock with his thrust. Snaking my long legs around his lower back. My gasp softly exits my mouth and enters his.

"Um-hum." He softly grunts into my mouth, and I swear I can feel it rumble through me. His hands slide up my thigh, stopping on my butt to pull me into his thrust. Then he's up. Pulling away from me. Separating his mouth from mine. I groan my objections as his hair slips through my fingers.

"Come here." He tells me, stretching his hand out to mine. Reaching up, I stand to my feet, stretching into his embrace. Locking my mouth into his and relacing my fingers through his hair.

His hands are cupped around the backs of my thighs, squeezing, pulling my pelvis into his hardness. I brace my weight onto his shoulders and lift my legs around his waist, balancing myself in his arms.

"Am I heavy?" I ask, pulling back to bathe myself in his gaze. His adorable half smile is back.

"I'll manage." He tells me, squeezing my thighs.

"You'll manage?" I say against his lips.

"I think so." He answers back, as I slide my hand between our bodies.

"How's this?" I ask pushing his hardness inside me.

"You tell me." He whispers pulling me onto him as close as our bodies will allow. Once again, I purr into his mouth, as I suck on his bottom lip.

"Um-hum." He grunts walking me easily to his bedroom. Excuse me...*our* bedroom.

Well almost. We make it as far as the hallway and he leans me into the wall. Thrusting...deep. A jolt runs through me, and I gasp, once again into his mouth. He thrust again and I grip his hair tighter and tighten my hold around his neck. Bracing myself for his next thrust, remembering that he likes having someone that he won't break. He grips my thighs and supports my weight in his hands, lifting me off the wall.

Yes! Yes! Yes! Hell yes! This man can have me inside and out! Every piece of me is being given to him through our mouths. I don't even realize that we've entered the room until he's placing me on the bed. Moving with me as I crawl backwards towards the pillows.

"Don't run." He tells me.

"Oh baby, I'm not running." I say opening my legs inviting him into me.

"No?" He says leaning into my kiss.

"Not even a little bit." I say, pulling him closer to me. "I want it."

"Oh yeah." He asks. I can feel his hand position himself at my opening as I twist his face from my mouth to my good ear.

"Oh okay," he says thrusting into me, smiling against my cheek. "I know what you want."

And just like that, with those few words he gives it to me. His voice travels through my nervous system like sound waves over telephone wires.

"Again." I gasp, almost begging.

"Look at that." He manages to say around my ear lobe he's sucking on. "You love it."

His thrusts are long, even strokes, rocking the bed. Tapping the wall with each movement.

"How do you want it, babe?" I hear him talking, but I feel it more. His voice shoots currents throughout my body, electrifying every pleasure point my nerves possess.

"How do you want it?" He asks again. And again, I try to answer but only a moan escapes my mouth, as he continues to thrust. Then he stops and leans away from me. Looking down, half smiling.

"No!" I groan. I snake my hand around his waist and pull his butt into me. He gets the hint and without hesitating thrust long and deep. Over and over and over again. Finally, I can let myself go. Lay my head back, close my eyes and just let go. I can enjoy the sound of his moans, and grunts and tantalizing words that help me escape to a realm where my body is taken over by him, given to him. Possessed by him.

My scalp is tingling like a thousand fingertips massaging and scratching tiny little fires that blossom throughout my body. Winding me up tighter and tighter. Pleasure escapes my mouth as I squeeze my body tighter around his.

"Eros." I moan, rocking with his motion, grinding with his thrust. I start moving my body harder arching my back, "Eros." I say, listening for his response.

"Yes love. I feel it, too." He tells me, "Come for me, Ayo." He whispers, looking down at me, holding my eyes with his. "Come for me, Ayo."

I reach for his face, and he starts moving faster and harder. The headboard is beating a steady rhythm into the wall, keeping time with our passion. I can feel him swelling inside of me, filling me, telling me that he's ready. And frankly so am I. I pull his face close to mine kissing him soft, and tender.

"I'm ready, baby." I whisper against his face.

"Yeah?"

"Yeah." I squeal, "Yes." My head falls slack into the pillow and all I can do is feed my moans to him through our mouths and whisper my release against his lips. The sensation grows bigger, brighter, harder, softer. He groans and I gasp in his ear, and with that my body convulses in spasms all around him. His hand tugs my braid lifting my mouth up to his, for him to swallow the breathy sounds that escape from me. Muffling them. Stealing them from me, claiming them for his own.

His body is still, except for the last few thrusts, emptying into me. When the spasms have stopped and the convulsions are over, and our voices have silenced, and the headboard no longer thumps our movements into the wall. I shift and turn my front into his front, burying my body almost under his.

"Don't ever stop loving me." I whispered into his neck.

"I couldn't stop loving you even if I wanted to." He whispers into the top of my head. "You have taken over my soul."

"What if this gets old?" I say quietly, "What if you grow tired of me?"

I can feel his head shift as he looks down at me and I shift so I can see his face. Caressing my cheek, he smoothes his thumb over my freckles.

"I love that you still think that." he whispers, "But God made you for me. You...are...mine." He kisses my forehead, "And I am yours."

Chapter Eighteen

"It's about time you got back!" Mary tells me sternly.

"What?" I asked plainly. I put my lunch and work bag in the chair at the nurse's station and hung my jacket on its back.

"What?" She gasps spinning in the office chair next to where I'm standing, to face me. Her fingers are still poised over the keyboard keys, mid-type, of the notes she's charting. "You have been working here for six years, Ayo, six years. And every year, you don't hesitate to bug the hell out of us with your phone calls. And your questions, and crap."

I laugh out loud to hide my...embarrassment, I guess. I completely did not think about this place. Nor anyone that had anything to do with this place. Not to mention, I do get bored and think of dumb things to do. And she's right, I will call up here and ask all sorts of questions. Nothing important. Just random questions to get on their nerves, simply because I ran out of things to do, and I'm bored. Once I called, and had Mary go to a resident's room and search under the bed for a pair of socks that I dropped. It took her ten minutes to realize I was just messing with her. This year I didn't even bother.

"I got busy." I said standing next to the medicine cart, laughing to myself about the unintentional pun. "Let's count."

Maybe if I can distract her, I won't have to continue with this conversation, and she'll go home and forget about it. At least it'll give me time to figure out what to tell her. Because I know exactly where she's going with this.

"We're counting this one." She tells me, pointing to the second cart to my right, "I switched to days." *Shit, she's not going to let this go.* "And I know you got busy."

She opens the cart and, one by one, starts calling out the numbers for each prescription. Indicating the exact number of every pill, on every card. In every bottle. For both the regular prescription and narcotic medications. Once I'm sure everything is correct and accounted for, I began with my normal routine.

"Any changes since I've been gone?" I ask, avoiding Mary's widening eyes.

"Oh yes," she tells me nodding her head sarcastically. "But first, Arthur is still out. They went to do surgery on his hip, but he had some complications and think they may have found cancer."

"Oh wow." I gasped. One thing that's true, and all nurses in long term care will attest to this. We always seem to know who's going to be the next to go. We have to admit these things so that we can begin to mentally prepare ourselves and do our jobs effectively. Sometimes we have one or two residents where we just connect with, and Arthur was that to Mary.

"They don't think he's coming back. The resident with the wound on his back was taken out by his family and taken to another facility. So, he's gone."

"Wow, that was fast." I say locking my cart and slipping the keys in my pocket. I check my watch and see that it's seven-fifteen, and log into the laptop to begin my morning med-pass.

Without having to look at her I see Mary walk back to her seat and start again on her computer notes. *Whew*, it worked. Now I just need to keep this tactical redirection up until it's time to go home. Which will be a new experience for me, since it's going to be at a different home. And for once, someone's going to be there waiting for me. A very handsome, and kind, and loving someone that just so happens to love and adore me. *No*, move on from that thought, Ayo.

"So, I got an email from, Tom." She tells me, still staring at the computer screen.

"Who's Tom?" I ask dropping a pill into a plastic packet and smash it in the pill crusher.

"He was in charge of the convention."

I look up from my task, remembering the chatty man with glasses that was very fond of shaking hands.

"And what did he say?" I ask, dumping the crushed pill into the medicine cup and mixing a spoon of apple sauce with it. Mary spins in her chair, crossing her legs in the process.

"That he was very impressed with the knowledge of our nurse." I nod my head and turn to go to my first resident. "And her very tall, *plus one*."

I stop in my tracks automatically close my mouth that has popped open. I'm...so very glad that Mary can't see the smile *plastered* on my face. I continued to my resident, feed her apple sauce pill then return to my cart.

"Hey, did everyone get their in-service points?" I ask, checking for my next residents' pills?

"Um, yes we did." Mary said looking at me, bobbing her head smiling expectantly. Waiting, I suspect for an explanation. She really is a nice person, and not a bad looking woman. She'd probably be better looking if she were to stop smoking and maybe even cut her hair a little. I nod my head and smile, mirroring her bobbing movements, then escape to my next resident. She is not going to let this go. She's going to hound me all day until I tell her something. Now that I think about it, I've been a pretty private person as far as work goes. Not because I'm antisocial or anything like that. I just didn't have anything interesting to tell...but now.

"So, who's *Mr. Very Tall Plus One?*" Mary asked when I returned to my cart. I smile knowingly at her, and the returning grin she gives tells me she knows.

"It's him isn't it." She laughs, "I knew it. I...knew it."

"Ahem. He..."

"Who is he?" She said cutting me off. "What the *hell* did you do all week. And just how tall is he?"

Before I can answer a CNA lets me know that one of my residents complained of trouble breathing.

"Want me to get it?" Mary asks, turning back to her computer notes. She didn't even bother looking up and pretending like she wanted to help.

"No," I say grabbing my oxygen monitor and stethoscope. "I got it."

I follow the CNA to Margie's room and find her sitting in her wheelchair, gasping for small breaths of air. I explain to her as I apply the oxygen meter to her finger, then listen to her lungs. Her oxygen level is at eighty-five percent and anything below ninety could be cause for alarm but can be solved by giving her oxygen through a concentrator. The rattling I hear in her chest, however, tells me that she should probably be sent out to a hospital.

"Okay Margie." I start, hooking my stethoscope around my neck, "Here's the thing. I'm a little concerned about how your lungs sound so I want to send you to the hospital. Is that okay?"

Knowing that she's unable to speak, I exit the room without waiting for a response.

"Do me a favor." I say to the CNA, "Make sure she's dry, for me. And if she'll let you, change her shirt, if she doesn't let you, it's cool."

"Should I do anything else?" The assistant asks. I know she's new to the facility, but I just realized that she's new to the profession.

"How old are you?" I ask.

"Nineteen."

"How long have you been a CNA?"

"A few months."

"You going to school?" Her eyes grow wide, for some reason, with embarrassment.

"No." she tells me quietly. "I thought I'd work as a Nursing Assistant for a while first."

"No worries." I tell her, trying to sound as assuring as I can. "How long has it been, again?"

"Three months."

"I see."

"I'm sorry," she blurts out apologetically, "I tend to ask too many questions."

"Don't be sorry," I say smiling, "This is the one profession where questions are welcome."

She smiles shyly and mouses out a very small, but relieved okay. I told her not to worry. To start with what I just told her, and kind of hang around when EMS shows up in case, they need anything. This girl is very *green*, and by the end of the year she's going to be very corrupted. I go to the desk, pull up everything I need on the computer and print all the necessary paperwork. By the time I'm finished, EMS has arrived and is ready to haul Margie off.

When she's gone, I find Katrina and tell her that she did a good job. Hey, what can I say, everyone needs high praise for doing great sometimes. I call the hospital and give them a brief report on my residents' condition and start on my computer notes. The rest of the morning goes about as smooth as it possibly can. Not too many major catastrophes happen. My assistants are more than dutiful, and helpful at every turn. I even got a moment or two to help my aides out with their work. In the meantime, Mary is asking any and every question she can possible think of. So, out of sheer habit I answer with the most basic answers I can.

"He's six foot eight."

"He's retired from the NFL."

"We spent the entire week together, and…" I say standing from my computer, "Though I'm leaving a *bunch* of stuff out, he's asked me to marry him, and I said yes."

I held my hand up and waved my fingers for her to see my emerald.

"So, wait." Mary says, "In the last week, you met someone. Dated *and* got engaged?"

"Yup." I state.

"Just like that?" she asks.

"Yup." I say again. Smiling at how simple everything sounds when you put it like she did.

"When else am I going to meet a six-foot eight, handsome ex NFL player. That welcomes commitment and loves like a speeding freight train?"

"I don't know." Mary shakes her head slowly chuckling, "But I swear, only you would. Wait a second. I need to call Frances." She picks up the desk phone, dials a number. "Um Ma'am. You need to get over here ASAP...code *G* for gossip." Then very politely hangs up. Moments later our director of nursing is waddling in our direction, smiling before she even reaches the desk.

"So, what's the scoop?" She asks pulling a chair out to sit.

"Well?" Mary said looking at me, "You want to tell her...or shall I?"

"Well, you seem to be busting at the seams, so, knock yourself out." I told her laughing.

"Um-hum."

She nods her head matter of factly, stalks over to me. Lifts my hand and waves my knuckles at Frances.

"Take a look at this." She speaks.

"Um *hum*...that's a nice hand." Frances states confused, "I have two of them, so do you in fact."

"What?" Mary said, not satisfied with her response, "No...this!" She slightly pinches my ring finger and bends it so Frances can see it better.

"Aw... that's nice." Frances looks at me, smirks her face then laughs. Still confused about what's happening.

"Dammit Frances," Mary said thumping Frances in her forehead, "She got engaged!"

Finally getting it, Frances' eyes grow three times their size as she's rubbing the thump spot of her forehead. Her mouth drops and she bounces back and forth from one foot to the other. Then pauses mid motion.

"Hang on," she blurts out, "Eric asked you to marry him?" The confusion on her face resembles the way a toddler might look should anyone ask them to figure out the secret nuclear codes.

"Not..."

"Not Eric," Mary said cutting me off, "Mr. Steamy conversation from last week!"

"Mr. Steamy Conversation!" Frances said continuing her bouncing. "What the hell? Seriously?"

"Seriously." I said laughing at their excitement. "It's happening Friday, which by the way, I need the day off."

"FRIDAY?!" They both said in unison.

"This Friday?" Mary asked. "Like...the end of the week?"

"Yes, you wanna work for me?"

"No, I'm already working." she said quickly, "Are you shitting us? She's kidding, Frances. She didn't play any jokes this year because she was planning this crap."

"Oh, that's not funny." Mary said, oozing disappointment. "That's not funny at all."

"I know." I say laughing, "Which is why I'm not kidding. Friday morning before we go to my parents' house, we're going to pick up his mom. Go to the courthouse and stand in front of the...well I don't know who will perform the ceremony. But we're going to drive to my parents' house for their anniversary weekend afterwards."

"Well, I'll be dammed." Frances said as Mary shakes her head. "I can't believe it."

"I can." Mary states. "Somehow, this makes perfect since."

"Wait a minute." Frances said, "You said courthouse."

"Um-hum." I respond.

"*Then*...your parents' house?"

"Yes."

"So, your parents aren't going to be there?" She asks.

"No not for this. But my brother will plan a different wedding in a year or so and they'll be there for that."

Frances tosses her hand up and shakes her head as she heads back in the direction of her office, mumbling something about the amount of stress she suffered from all of her wedding plans. Leaving me laughing, and Mary agreeing with her by telling her version of horror stories that surrounded the many months of planning her own wedding. Which, most definitely, solidified my decision to stay far away from planning my own nuptials.

So...just to put it out there. If I haven't said it before...*I hate Monday's.* I hate it when I come back to work from a nice, long, seven-day vacation. I'm completely thrown. I mentioned before the morning went well. Now the afternoon is a different story. I have four very good nursing assistants, including one brand new one. So, the residents are being cared for without question. The only problem was, we had what we like to call *bed swaps.* Which basically consist of transferring a resident from one room to another. The nursing assistant would gather the resident and their belongings and take them to their new room. All of their belongings and personal items, including the bed (for some), will be transferred to the new location. In the meantime, I, the nurse, will be busy transferring every medication this person is on, as well as all physical and computer charts and notes.

Okay? Sound easy enough? Well, it would be if we were moving the resident to an empty location. If it's not an empty location, I would have to repeat the entire process and transfer these other people to their new bedrooms. And the CNAs would have to do the same with the other residents and all of *their* belongings. It's not very hard to do, it's just time consuming, and honestly, there's no room for error. No time for any other thoughts outside of the task at hand. Hopefully the residents aren't combative in any way. Or moving to another floor. It could make for a very busy and fast-paced day.

In my case, I not only had to switch two residents to two different rooms. I also had to swap two more. To not only different rooms but to two different floors. Talk about head spinning. At some point throughout the day, though remaining calm on the outside, I just wanted to toss my keys on the desk and say, "I'm done. I've had enough for the day." But I can't. The one thing I'm good at is time management. And my director, Frances, knows this about me. So, when I realized that time might be getting a little past me, I sent her a quick text message, telling her that her assistance is needed. She came right away.

My big mistake was texting in the first place. I should have overhead paged her or dialed her telephone extension. That would have kept me from looking at my phone in the first place. And opening the picture mail from Eros, Emma and Blind Joe. All having tea together in the dining hall at Golden Heights. Emma is all bright eyes and smiles. She even seems to be fluffing her hair, while Joe is very coolly tipping his hat. Had I not looked at my phone, I wouldn't have been so surprised that I sort of...laugh yelped. I guess I should call it. I wouldn't have shown Mary the picture and I wouldn't be trying to explain to her about who Blind Joe is. Or how I met him, and the wonderful date we had. Or how Eros picked him out for me, because he knew how much I would have enjoyed meeting a blues legend. I definitely wouldn't be trying to ignore the intense eyes that smile at me, softly like he can see me.

Good thing, Frances came to help out. Together we were able to transfer all four residents and complete my afternoon med-pass. Before I knew it, the second shift nurse had arrived and was ready to count, get a report on the mornings activities and take these mother-loving keys out of my hands. And *I* was ready to *go*. I didn't even bother mentioning the resident that got sick and projectile vomited on my scrub pants. As a side note, in my mind, I feel like I'm covered in throw-up from head to toe. Like back-in-the-day on Nickelodeon when people got slimed. The worst part about *that* situation is, all I could do was wash it off. Dry it the best way I can and keep it moving.

I didn't mention the resident that will, on occasion, get confused and dramatically refuse his medicine. Today, he decided to smack it back at me. One: I'm very glad my mouth was closed, and two...I must say, in my mind, I feel a little bit like I've had acid thrown in my face. Because, the thing is, during all of the transfer hoopla, I still have to perform everyday tasks. So, giving a report, turning over the cart keys and clocking out to go home was the best way to end a workday and start to my new life.

It's only about four-forty, so when I pulled into the horseshoe drive-way and Eros' car wasn't there. I figure he's still with Emma. Which is okay for me. The first thing I want to do when I see him, is press my body so close to his, we practically share a lung. I want to take a moment and savor the feel of his lips and warm feel that's going to flush through my body.

But first, I need to step out of these shoes, which I do on the front porch before I even go in. Just inside the door I remove my pants and top and stuff them in one of the waste basket liners I keep in my work bag. Then drop them in the garbage bin in the backyard. Next is a shower. All I want now is a nice, long, hot shower to wash off the sweat. And vomit, and medicine and everything else that contributed to this shitty day. I want to feel the water beating into my back, and the soft bubbles that rinse down my skin.

I feel...*so* much better. Relaxed. Refreshed and rejuvenated. The effects of a horrible, *horrible* Monday absolutely washed away. And the smooth, hypnotic aroma of what has become my life has taken over. By the time I'm done in the shower, lotioning my body and dressing myself in a pair of track shorts and oversized tee-shirt. Eros is walking through the front door. He's here. The one thing I've been waiting for since I opened my eyes this morning. I enter the living room just as he's removing his jacket, and step as close to him as I possibly can. I reach behind his head and find the tail of the rubber tie holding his hair bun together and pull. Loosening his hair by scratching my fingertips through it.

"Hi." He tells me, smiling down at me.

"Hey." I respond, tip toeing my face into his. "I missed you."

I breathe in that familiar woodsy aroma as I press my lips into his. It's all I've wanted all day. The one thing I wouldn't allow myself to think about. Now I can finally give in to the feel of his wavy hair between my fingers. His soft face curls against my cheek. Those strong, firm hands that caress my back, then smooth down and squeeze my ass. All of the things I've welcomed since day one. I breath in deeply and softly exhale, welcoming the official start of my very new life.

"I've been thinking about that all day."

"Baby," I say smiling against his lips, "It's been a *long* day."

"Come on." He says smiling, towing me by the hand into the kitchen.

"I got turkey burgers and fries. You can tell me all about it."

The burgers were huge, but juicy and delicious, and just what I needed. We didn't even bother sitting at the table. I cleared a spot ontop of the island and hopped up with my food on a plate next to me. Eros's hands me a glass and a Heineken then stands between my legs as we dig into our meals.

"So, tell me about your first day back." My handsome love commands between chews.

"Long story short." I say as I put my glass down.

"No." He objected, supporting a jaw full of fries. Politely hiding his full mouth behind his closed fist. "I haven't seen or talked to you all day; I want to know everything."

"Okay." I say and lay it all on him. All of it. Starting with Mary, the person he spoke to last Monday and her endless questions about him. Which brought a smile to his face and prompted another question.

"What made her ask that question in the first place?"

I couldn't help the smile and chuckle that I tried to hide behind my napkin as I wiped my mouth.

"You're blushing." He tells me laughing.

"It seems," I begin, sipping from my beer glass. "Every year, for the last six years I've been employed there, I call in and play some kind of prank on her."

"Like what?" He asks laughing.

"Well," I say echoing his laugh, "One year I had her searching from the front doors to the loading dock for me. Only thing is, I disguised my voice and told her that I was a residents family member."

We shared a hardy laugh about that. I told him how I was curled up in bed, all cozy under covers listening to her huff and puff as she traveled back and forth from door to door. Searching for a person that didn't exist. I also told him about how I had her go door to door searching residents' room for a sample of urine that I left behind.

"Which she never found, right?" He asked, stuffing fries into his mouth.

"Oh no she found something." I say chuckling, "I put a specimen cup with a few drops of Mountain Dew mixed with a little bit of orange juice and liquid thickener in it on the nightstand of a resident that's notorious for drinking *anything*. I left the top off, next to the cup so it would look more obvious that the resident drank it. She *freaked* out."

We both erupted, leaning into each other much like we were that night in the Pennington. Giggling like two high school kids, deep in puppy love.

"Oh my god." he said still giggling, wiping moisture from his eyes. "You are stupid."

"Well, this year I forgot." I say leaning back on my hands.

"You forgot, huh?" His hands smooth up my thighs, as I snake my legs around his waist.

"I got a little distracted." I tell him, mirroring his half smile. "She knew right away something was up. Not to mention the email she got from Tom."

"Tom?" He asks, just as confused as I was this morning.

"Yes. Tom." I say, sipping the last of my Heineken, "He told her that he was very impressed with her co-worker."

I bit my bottom lip and dramatically pointed my thumbs at my chest, "And her very tall plus one, *Guess*." Eros gasps loudly, and once again we're leaning into each other laughing.

"I completely forgot about Tom." He tells me, still laughing. I wonder if he notices that, he has a habit of talking in my ear. Even if it's just casual, like now, the results are still the same. Except this time the vibrations travel down my side, slightly making me flinch. But good news, I was able to maintain my composure. Twenty-five much needed composure points for me.

"So of course." I say, taking his attention away from my earlobe he's kissing on, and back to my eyes. "Her first question was about who this *Guess* person was."

"Was it now?" he asks, leaning in to kiss me, almost paralyzing me with dark brown, somewhat chestnut gaze. "What did you tell her?"

"Nothing. I just showed her my ring."

"You did?"

"Um-hum." I lift my chin as his soft kiss trail one by one along my jaw line.

"And what did she say?" Down my neck to my collar bone.

"That I must be some kind of lucky."

To my bare shoulder, softly tickling my skin where his beard has touched.

"I think I might be the lucky one."

His mouth is at my ear again, kissing…teasing. Bringing me to life. My body begins to heat as I close my eyes and welcome his touch. My fingers skim under his shirt, up his smooth sides, to his firm back.

"I missed being here with you." I say against his neck. I smooth my hands from his shoulders to his chest. Brushing across his nipples to the thick bed of smooth hair that my fingers have become so familiar with.

His hands, that are still massaging my thighs, reach behind his back and pull his shirt over his head. I can feel his eyes gazing over me as I press my cheek into his chest where my hands just were.

"I missed feeling this on my skin." My hands smooth down his back until I'm able to tuck my fingers beneath the band of his boxer briefs. His skin is soft and warm and smooth. It still has the lovely, earthy scent that I love so much. I kiss his chest softly. Tenderly. As gentle as his hands are touching my thighs. He grips me and pulls me closer to the edge of the island, spreading my legs wider. Allowing him to press his erection between my legs.

This isn't enough. I want to be closer to him. I want to feel his skin against my skin.

"I want you to take me to bed." I say, kissing the side of his face. My feet softly hit the floor as I slid from the island counter. Looking into his eyes, I pull my shirt over my head and arms revealing my bare breast for him. He doesn't miss a beat.

"And what do you want me to do?" he asks, kissing the space between my breasts.

"Kiss me." I tell him, smoothing my hands over his shoulders and the back of his neck. "And touch me." I close my eyes and breathe as his lips and tongue stretch and nibble to the other. Treating both with equal passion. I can barely breath, or stand, or think.

Look at him. His eyes are closed, fanning his short, dark lashes across his cheeks like thick shadows, *oh my*. His lips curled around my small breast gently sucking like he was trying to swallow it. Just watching his jaws flex back and forth, as his tongue quickly flicking my nipple, starts fires under my skin. I close my eyes, tilting my head back and softly hum my approval. This is what I love the most. Feeling like he's enjoying himself, *more* than he's trying to please me. It's almost like he knows that teasing me this way is more of a visual stimulation, so he's giving me something to look at. Putting on a show for me. He opens his smokey brown eyes and I smile down as he brings his lips up to mine.

"Does that count as a kiss?" He asks close to my face, moving backwards, at the same time pulling me with him. We're going towards the bedroom and my anticipation is fueling the fires within. Along with his hands, that are moving so tenderly around my back. Massaging my muscles, firmly, accurately, slowly turning my body into long limbs of mush. I back into the room and turned towards my tablet on the charge station, flipping the light switch in the process.

I want him to see me. Watch my every move as I slide my shorts down my legs, and off my feet. Hopefully, if I play my MP3 on shuffle playing whatever is playing will be a good one. *Meh*, it's not a bad one. I turn and find him leaning against the foot of the bed, still holding the tablet in front of my breast.

"How's this?" I say, referring to a remix of a well know song, known for its seductive lyrics. He wastes no time shaking his head no.

"Not this time."

"*Really?*" I say, smiling around a chuckle, pressing the next arrow. "How about this one?"

It's a nice beat, a tad bit slow. As a matter of fact, it's very slow. A little too slow, it doesn't match the mood at all. The song is nice, so I can see why his expression changes with his ready approval.

"Nah," I say, smiling returning the tablet to the charge station. "Not this time." *Okay Ayo, third time's a charm.* I shuffled the playlist one last time, crossing my fingers and wishing for something decent. Because no matter what it's going on repeat. A slow, seductive rhythm takes over the air space accompanied by the sweetest toned voice. I press repeat smiling to myself. I know this song and it will do just fine. Now I can focus on him, and the things we undoubtedly want to do to each other. Turning, I find Eros leaning on the foot of the bed still, smiling at me. Watching me.

"*Tsk, tsk, tsk.*" I say smiling at the question of his raised eyebrows. "Well, it would seem," I say stepping towards him. "That you're still wearing your pants."

"Um-hum." He agreed, looking down at me. His eyes are warm shades of coco, dripping into tiny pools of beautiful brown. "What do you want to do about that?" His chest rose and fell with his even breaths against my soft touch. Before I could answer or respond, his warm hands left their place on my hips, and moved towards the buckle of his pants. But I smacked them both away playfully, giggling at his expression of mock offense.

"I'm sorry, Eros, my love." I say, holding his eyes with mine and trailing my fingertips down his chest to the top button of his fly. "But I've had a very long, and very busy day away from you." I say kissing his half smiling lips. I release the first button revealing the band of his boxer briefs. I love the way his soft, smooth hair leads from his chest, down his rippled abs disappearing into the crotch of his jeans.

"All I thought about today was you." He tells me brushing his fingers against my cheek. "How you smelled."

I lean into his hands and perch up to kiss him tenderly again. "How you taste." That last part came out a whisper against my good ear, and a slight moan of agreement escapes my lips. His hand reaches around and firmly grip one side of my ass, pulling me closer to his body as I pop the second and third button of his fly.

"Well lucky you." I say removing his hand and replacing it back to his side. "I was so busy; I didn't have a chance to even think of you." I released the fourth button and separated the ends showing more of his black briefs. "When I did allow myself to think of you," I tell him lowering the bottom half of his clothes to his knees, purring as he stepped from his shoes. "I had to cut it short," I hold his pant legs still while he steps free of them. "I tend to be easily distracted when it comes to thoughts of you."

I lift his still soft penis, pleased at the fact that even in its non-erect state…it is still the length of my outstretched hand, to my warm, moist mouth.

"Um." he hummed, pleased by my touch, "I wonder why that is?" I know the question was rhetorical, but I still wanted to answer. Using my hand, I remove his stiffening erection from my jaws.

"It's because I love you." I tell him, circling the tip of his head around my outstretched tongue.

"You love me." It was more of a repeated statement, than it was a question.

"Um-hum." I hummed, closing my mouth around his head. Flexing my neck back and forth, matching the rhythm of my mild sucking. His hand gently moved to the back of my head until my mouth was completely full, slightly heaving as it stretched down my throat. A loud gasp slips out. His penis springs from my lips, and I stroke him. Giving myself time to catch my breath before repeating.

"I'm attracted to you." I tell him after filling my throat with his length and holding it there for as long as my gag reflex would allow.

"Damn." He growls, over my loud gasp, heave and gag, "attracted, hum?"

My eyes are watering tears down my cheeks. My sweet, tingling vagina thumps and throbs and practically drips with readiness. I wipe the tears from my face and continue with my task, lifting him upward.

"So attracted." I agree, before returning every rock-solid inch of him in my mouth. All the way, in my mouth. His grip on the back of my head tightens and his hips thrust once…twice…three times in tune with the music.

Then he holds it there. Challenging me to take it all. Exercising my throat until my reflexes can't take it anymore. I gasp…loudly, pushing his hips back as his grip loosens and air hisses through his teeth.

"Come here." He tells me, voice husky with passion. He lifts me by my shoulders, to his mouth kissing me deeply. Falling back on the bed, he pulls me on top of him. And I waste no time sliding him into my wetness, greedily swallowing every inch of him. I don't need time to adjust to his length or thickness. My walls expand already familiar with the feel of him. I move with the melody of the music and the rock of his hips.

Circling, and grinding. His hands are on my breast and slide them down to my ass. I want to feel him...deep. His mouth is moving but I'm too far gone to focus on what he's saying. Or maybe it's me. I'm supposed to be watching him unfold from my love making. But the truth is, I'm the one that's losing it. He is *murdering* that spot with expert thrust. My fiery body has taken over my mind, and I can no longer focus on holding myself upright. He notices and flips us so that I'm under him. Pushing himself in me, he leans to his favorite ear, "I want you to feel me." he tells me.

He thrust...deep and I bite my lip, to keep the pleasure bottled within me. I scissor my legs open as far as they will go inviting him in as deep as he wants to be.

"Oh yeah?" He tells me biting his lip, accepting my challenge. "That's how you want it?" He thrust harder, keeping the rhythm of the song. My hands touch him all over. His shoulders. His back. His hips. His butt. Pulling him into me, loving every minute of his love making. Blended with his voice vibrating throughout my body, telling me to, *take it*. That he *loves* how good I feel. That he doesn't ever want this to stop. That he loves me. He needs me. I'm his. I'm his. I'm his.

I pull my arms up wrapping them around his back and hold him close. Never wanting to let him go. Ever. My breathing is labored. My body is glowing from the flames that have blossomed into one sensation from head to toe. Erupting from my mouth telling him to not stop.

"Please, don't stop! Please don't stop! Please don't stop!" My voice is a thin whining moan, and he knows just what that means. He starts moving faster, harder. His voice echoes my voice, matching my feeling moan for moan. Thrust for thrust. Until neither of us can stand the pleasure anymore.

I *erupt* around him in moaning, raspy, throaty gasps until every juicy drop from within has been expended.

"God, I love you so much." He whispers in my ear. Somehow, I find my voice and reply that I love him too, as he slips from inside me, and drops to his side pulling me into his arms. "Don't ever leave me." He whispers, gazing into my eyes.

"You think I would ever give another woman the chance to experience you and all that you are?" I asked him curiously. Holding my left hand up and wave my emerald at him. Reminding him of what was to come. "You've got me for this lifetime and any lifetime after this one." I smile apologetically, "Sorry. You're stuck with me."

A worried look crosses his face as he brushes his thumb across my cheeks. Perhaps brushing my freckles. He loves to count them. But the knit in his brow line tells me something bothers him.

"What is it?" I asked smoothing his forehead with my index finger. He takes a deep breath and exhales easily, then licks his lips. His eyes watch my lips, but still, he doesn't speak. This won't do. Not for us. His unknown worry pulls at my heart and for the first time I see the boy that he may have once been. There is a scar just above his right eyebrow. Perhaps from many years of football or maybe a childhood accident.

His eyes are almond shaped with short dark lashes hooded over them. His cheeks are round and somewhat rosy compared to the rest of his lightly tanned skin. His lips were full, and plump and inviting, so I leaned up and lightly kissed them. And brush my fingers through his curly beard. And still, he doesn't speak, instead his eyes float up to mine.

"Do you still want to get married?" he asks quietly. Is that it? Has he changed his mind. Has the intensity that usually push women away from him, pushed him away from me. *Stop it!* It couldn't have. Only moments ago, he instructed me to *never* leave him. Then what was it?

"Of course, I do." Worry vanishes from his face and the crease smooths across his forehead.

"Do you still want to..."

"Elope?" I ask cutting him off. His eyes, which are watching his fingers curl around my sideburns, flick to my eyes. He nods.

"Absolutely." I say smiling.

"When?" he asks, reflecting my smile.

"Well," I tell him, realizing that when I mentioned those same plans to Frances and Mary earlier this morning, I may have been jumping the gun. Rolling my eyes upward, half smiling at the flutter in my belly, I internally cross my fingers. "I was thinking about that today and I figured…Friday morning is as good a time as any." I tell him, "I already took off of work."

"So, Friday morning?" He asks. His smile widening, baring most of his teeth. I giggled at how much more youthful he looks while he's dancing the goofiest dance, I've seen from anyone.

Taking a deep breath, I stretched and stifled a yawn. It must be very late, and with work tomorrow I should be getting some sleep, but it hasn't fallen upon me yet. The time on the bedside table only reads 9:15. Not as late as I thought it was.

"You sleepy?" he asks, curling his long warm body around mine.

"Nope." I answer, giggling at the poke he gives my ribs.

"No?" He repeated.

"No." I said laughing harder, struggling with smacking his arms away from his tickling. He's too big and too strong. I feel like a small child squirming and squiggling in his arms, laughing until my throat is raw. Kicking and wiggling beneath his massive chest, pleading with him to stop. Loving every gentle fingerprint, he leaves on my naked body.

Suddenly, I'm aware that he's completely above me with my hands pinned above my head. My legs are spread, pressed against the warm skin of his outer thighs. The head of his penis rest against my belly button, slightly thumping its growing erection.

"Friday morning." I agree, smiling and arching my back at the fullness of my very soon-to-be husband entering me.

Chapter Nineteen

The week has gone by as slow as time would allow. Only speeding up when my workday ends and real life begins. As the day went past, I found it harder and harder to keep my thoughts away from Eros. What was he doing? What was Emma doing? Was he missing me as much as I was missing him? Sometimes it ached in the pit of my stomach, only being satisfied when he entered me and caressed his spot deep within. Some days I wouldn't allow myself to think of him. The images of him watching himself graze his fingertips across my skin. The way his eyes closed when he tasted me and kissed between my legs. The soft brush of his lips when he kissed my breast.

At times, the memories flooded my mind, clouding my brain. Once I even felt myself moisten between my legs and immediately diverted my thoughts to something else. Anything else. And that evening when I saw him, I wasted no time ripping him free of his pants and relieving my frustrations. That surprised him, pleasantly. Almost as much as it did Thursday when I found him relaxing across the sofa wearing gym shorts and a Chicago Bears tee shirt with the sleeves cut off so that the sides of his ribcage showed. It was the first day since I returned to work that he was home when I walked through the door. Seeing him there fueled the thoughts that I'd been fighting the entire day.

He stood when I entered, walking around the sofa to greet me.

"Wait." I urged, holding up one hand to stop him, and pulling the tie of my scrub pants. Then removing my shirt. We were at my house this time, so I was able to clean my shoes and drop my clothes in the washing machine like normal. We spoke of my day and his day with me ducking and dodging his much wanted, no...needed, touch. The more I refused him, the sadder he grew, and I found myself explaining to him my afternoon ritual. The more he understood the better he felt. Before I do anything, before I allow anyone to touch me, I must shower and wash the nursing home filth away from my body.

My shower seems to take forever, but I manage to clean myself and wash my hair thoroughly. By the time I finish, I decide to dress only in my towel and found Eros sprawled out on the sofa still watching t.v. He was a massive mound of muscle all covered in beautifully designed tattoos. Finally, I'm able to do exactly what I had been fantasizing about all morning and afternoon. I strolled over dropping my towel to the floor and cuddling myself on top of his warm body. His shirt was removed now, and my nipples brushed against the hair of his chest.

"Feel better?" he asked, kissing my forehead.

"Almost." I tell him, kissing the soft skin under his chin.

"You're cold." He said, brushing one hand up and down my free arm and the other around my back.

"Um-hum." I confirmed, kissing my way down his chest to his nipple. His hand freezes, squeezing the soft flesh of my biceps. I continue and tease him the way he teases me at times.

I love and miss this man when I'm away from him and want to show him just how much. I work my way down pulling his shorts over his glorious erection. Then I take him until he finishes in my mouth hard and strong. Then curl up against his chest and nuzzle my face against his soft fur.

"What are we watching?" I ask.

"I don't even know." He says chuckling, "My vision is blurry." We both laughed, and he tells me of our plans for the next day. It's now that I realize just how nervous I really am. Come Friday afternoon I will be Mrs. Ayo Mitchell-Apollo, and we will both be known as the Apollos.

A laugh bubbled from my lips, and explained to him how nervous I am once I notice his slightly confused smile.

"September 11, 2015, will be our true anniversary." I tell him.

"You'll be my wife." He says sweetly. I like that about him. That a man of six feet and eight inches, with arms the size of tree trunks and feet the length of boat paddles can be so gentle and tender.

I have to be completely honest, this night with him had to be hands down one of the most fun nights that I have had in my life. In a very long time at least. When I say, we goofed off like two middle school girls at a birthday sleepover…I mean we *goofed off.* It all started after we ate. Eros had a cheeseburger he whipped up real quick, and *I* ignoring my already very grumpy stomach, ate a bowl of cereal *and* some left over Chinese food from the fridge. Even though the noodles and rice tasted fine, I knew it was a mistake eating it not even thirty minutes after finishing it.

We were curled up in bed watching some comedy I'd never heard of. Well actually, the Netflix original was watching us. I was listening attentively to Eros' story of how badly he played in his first professional game. He was nervous, his stomach was turning, and the crowded stands were so loud that he could barely here the quarterbacks que to snap the ball. Every time, he found himself starting half a second behind everyone else. He was telling me about being so nervous before the start of the game that he vomited everything that he'd eaten in the tunnel leading into the stadium.

That's when my stomach drops. Actually, more so my insides. They twisted and knotted as tight as I felt they could. And the knots inside continued south. *'Oh no.'* I thought shifting uncomfortably, trying to shift pressure on my lower abs. *'Just give it a minute, it'll go away.'* But in truth it's not, it's getting worse, seemingly every nano-second by nano-second. Until I absolutely can't take it anymore. Groaning loudly, I roll over on my back. Then instantly regret it. I roll back to my side gripping my belly and squeezing my eyes shut tight.

"What's wrong?" Eros asks over my unpleasant moaning. He placed his hand on my stomach, and though it is a gentle touch, I push his hand away.

"Please." I say between panting breaths, "Please don't touch my stomach." I lean up and sit on the side of the bed, hoping gravity would work wonders with settling the eruption going on inside me. Nothing is working.

"What's the matter?" Eros turns his body so that his head and back are rested by my thighs.

"I can tell you right now, that is not a good place for your head to be." *'Oh, this is not going to be pretty.'*

I look down at Eros' overly amused face and do my best to smile at him. There's no playing it off, my insides are about to explode through the bottom any second now.

"I shouldn't have eaten that Chinese food." Why is he smiling at me? This isn't funny...at all.

"I told you not to eat it." he said chuckling.

"Oh my god." I grumble, over my turning stomach. Oh wow, he's laughing now. You know what...screw it, let him laugh. I can't take it anymore.

"Ugh!" I say bolting from the bed. Or at least I try.

The moment I move he wraps his tree trunk arms around my waist flopping me backwards onto the bed. In the process, the air inside my body *noisily* escapes me. The smell is extremely eggy.

Eros erupts into loud, thunderous laughter. I shriek with embarrassment and try harder to wiggle away, but only manage to push more gas out.

"No!" I shout slipping away from him. I *really* can't take it any more. I jump from the bed, mushing his face into the pillow on my way up.

"You're such a jerk, E.!" I shout, giggling over his laughter, clutching my stomach with one hand and my butt with the other as I run down to the hall to the bathroom.

Slamming the door behind me. I can't get my shorts down fast enough. I'm bouncing quickly from foot to foot until finally I go. And oh boy do I go! It's very...*very* weird and loud. Eros is outside the door saying the most ridiculous things. Tapping on the door as he speaks.

Tap tap tap. "I can hear you." He chuckles.

"Go away!" I grumble clutching my face in my hands.

Tap tap tap. "I'm glad everything's coming out alright." He said laughing, "Doesn't sound like you have to push at all."

"*Shut up!*" I laugh, "Go away Eros."

"Why?" he asks, trying his best to sound affronted, but failing epically at disguising the smile in his voice.

"Because I'm pooping." I say laughing and dying a lousy and mortifying death. *Oh god.* I look over at the sink, which is just a tad too far away. I can't even turn the water on to cover up the horrible sound.

"*Pooping?*" He said laughing, drawing my attention back to my side of the door. "It sounds more like you're murdering the toilet. I was thinking about pressing charges."

I can't help laughing as I wash my hands.

"Are you coming out now?"

"Not yet." I answer over my shoulder. I strip out of my clothes, strike a match for the candles lined in the window seal, then turn and start the shower. There is no way I'm going to climb back in bed after all of this...mess.

"You feel better?" He asks as I reenter the room.

"Much." I say smiling. There's still a bit of queasiness in my stomach, but not as much as before.

"What are you looking for?" He asks as I riffle through my drawer.

"Something to sleep in." I tell him politely, looking back at him.

He's propped up on pillows with his arms and hands folded behind his head. Expanding his chest even wider than it already is.

"Why?" He half smiles, "We match now." He flips the small corner of covers away from his body flashing his nakedness at me. My mouth slightly gapes open as I absent-mindedly close the drawer. Leaning against the dresser I fold one arm across my waist and use it as a rest for my free elbow and wonder what I should do with all of that wonderfulness.

"Come to me." He tells me softly. But I don't move. I just stand there softly grazing my knuckles across the skin under my chin. "Come to me." He says again, whispering this time.

Still...I don't budge. His penis moves, then jumps as his erection grows longer and harder. I don't know if I'm turning him on by looking at him or if he's getting turned on from looking at me. Hell, to be perfectly honest, I'm not sure which of the two is turning *me* on. All I know is, it's working. I drag my fingertips from my chin to my chest circling my index finger around my nipples. Playing with them. Teasing them. Imagining that they were his hands. I smile sweetly as he begins to mirror my actions on his own body. Rubbing his nipples as I rub mine. Hum, since he wants to play, let's see if he's up for a game of Simon, and how long he can keep it going.

I slide my hand down the center of my chest towards my belly leaving bumpy goose flesh in its trail. He does the same, watching my every move patiently waiting for the next. I slide my hand over the outside of my vagina, slipping a finger through my wetness. He grabs his penis and wave it's hardness at me, stroking it at the same time. My clit begins to throb, so I circle two of my fingers around it to relieve some of the pressure. He strokes his hand to the top and circles his thumb around the tip of his head. I lean further back, balancing my weight on the dresser, spread my feet wider and rotate my hips grinding my fingers. He rotates his hips matching my movements as if he was inside me. He's smiling at me with those smokey brown eyes, watching to see what I'll do next. I can feel my body building, feel my clit getting harder as the pleasure fires grow.

I can't take it anymore. I want *his* hands on me. I want to feel *his* touch. I pull my fingers from my wetness, *'there's something he can't do.'* I think, as I watch him slide from the bed and stalk over to me.

"I love watching you touch yourself." He tells me.

"I love when you touch me better." I respond. His hands trail down my body following the same path as I did just moments ago. Stopping to play in my wetness.

"You like this?" He asks, kissing me, circling me with his two fingers. All I can do is moan my agreement in his mouth.

"Um-hum." He hums, nuzzling his mouth next to my good ear. "I know you like when I talk to you."

I grip my hands in his hair holding his mouth to my ear, waiting for more words to vibrate down my spine.

"I know baby." He tells me hissing air through his teeth. "It's my favorite thing too."

"Umm." I purr grinding against his hand.

"You're going to do three things for me, okay."

"Okay." I breath closing my eyes against his face. My body is building more and more as his two fingers slide in and out of me.

"First you're going to come on my hand." He nibbles my ear lobe and flickers it with his tongue.

"Okay." I tell him, still moving against his hand.

"Then I'm going to lay on the bed..." He circles his thumb over my clit. "You're going to sit on my face until you come...again."

He's nibbling my ear and shoulder and working his two fingers in and out as his thumb circles around and around. Sounds of deep-rooted pleasures are bubbling from my throat and my hands are gripping tighter. My knees are becoming as weak as old dish water, but somehow, along with his help I manage to continue standing. "Um-hum." he hummed, "I can't wait to taste you." I can't wait for him to taste me either.

"The third thing is, I'm going to lay you down, put this inside." I don't know how he did it without using his hands, but on que his penis thumps against the inside of my thigh. "And I'm going to fuck you until we both come ourselves into dehydration." Just the thought of that pushes me over the edge, and my first thing on his list is checked off.

*****

"Wakey wakey, Ayo." Eros was saying. He's kissing my eyes, rubbing my cheeks, and nudging my shoulder. "Ayo." He was sing-songing in my ear.

"Hum." I grumbled, slowly opening my eyes. I can tell he's already showered; the smell of his oil brightens my senses with good morning hugs.

"Good morning." I say stretching and yawning. "What time is it?" Joy is bouncing and ricocheting around his eyes like a ping pong ball trapped in a box.

"It's time to go get hitched." My smile spreads across my face from ear to ear, mirroring the grin on his.

"Let's do it." I say bouncing up and down.

My nervousness has morphed into something more energetic. Something almost uncontrollable. Before I know it, we're standing in front of the officiate holding hands. Repeating the magic words assigned to join the love of two people willing to unite and become one. For richer or for poorer. For better or for worse. To love and to cherish, for ever and ever, until death do us part...and then some.

We each say our *I do's* one after the other, then he bends and kisses his bride with Emma clapping her cheerful approval. My oh my, I am a giddy woman, to say the least. We actually did it. I've known this man for all of eleven days and it seems as though this moment took forever. And it's all ours. With no one to share it with but us and Emma. Who, might I add, is in very high spirits this morning. The entire hour and a half ride to Henderson, all she talked about was Henry and the bed and breakfast he took her too. The difference of how things look now versus before.

She even spoke about how happy she was not to be the only *Mrs. Apollo* anymore. How good it felt to know that her son had finally found happiness. Eros cradles my hand in his warm bear claw with his fingers laced through mine. Absent mindedly skimming his thumb across my skin. Occasionally lifting my knuckles to his lips, releasing my hand only to navigate the left or right turns I instruct him to take. We turn right on Rosevelt Street and find the Emmerson House at the end of the block. Resting at the bend of a cul-de-sac. Surrounded by, although smaller, very old colonial style homes. Emmerson House is mostly true to its 1868 time period. With very subtle conveniences of 2015, thrown in the mix.

A cast iron gate surrounded the yard leading up to the beautiful two-level home. The French doors style gate opened up to a cement staircase leading to white French doors. Two sets of rectangle bay windows stacked one on top of the other sat on both sides of the doors. The porch light, which was housed in a glass box, dangled from a long bronze chain just above the top of the door.

"This is it." Emma stated, from the back seat. Her voice is small and shaky, but her cloudy eyes are strong with delight, as she smiles at some far away memory. "Let's go kids." She said politely.

The establishment is delicate and beautiful. Decorated with old photos and knick-knacks from the old times and new. The lighting is a soft and dim glow from each carefully placed table lamp, complemented by the boldness of daylight beaming through the small picture frame windows. A large wooden stairwell climbed the wall leading to the second and third floors. The only thing out of place that harshly doesn't fit the *era* is a modern design receptionist desk.

"Hello Dear." Emma smiled softly.

"Oh!" The young lady said startled, looking up from her novel as she removed one of her ear buds, "I'm sorry, I didn't hear you walk up."

"It's okay." Emma tells her. She's holding on to my arm and shifting from foot to foot, which makes me very happy that we decided to bring her wheelchair.

"How can I help you?"

"Is this place still a bed and breakfast?" Emma asked looking around.

"No ma'am," the woman said smiling sweetly, "we haven't functioned as a bed and breakfast for about ten years now, I'm sorry."

"That's too bad." Emma said looking around.

The disappointment was thick in her voice and must have pulled at the young woman's heart strings. "I stayed here when I was a young bride with my husband Henry." Her voice became small and shaky, and tiny tears sat in the corners of her eyelids.

"When does the next museum tour start?" Eros asked, turning over a pamphlet he'd picked up from the counter.

"Well," she sighed, flipping through her appointment calendar. "Not for another hour and a half." The disappointment in Emma's face steadily grew.

"Babe," I said to Eros quietly, "You want to take Emma over to those chairs? I want to speak with this woman really quick."

"Sure." He agreed, looking over at the chairs placed in the foyer. "Come on momma, let's go sit over here."

I watch long enough for them to be out of ear range.

"Hi," I said smiling, "I'm sorry, my name is Ayo. Those two over there are my husband Eros and his mother Emma."

"I'm Rebecca." She said shaking my hand. "You have a lovely family."

"Thank you." I say smiling, "Rebecca, is there any way we can walk around and sort of...sight see? Maybe you can walk us around?"

"Well..." she said hesitantly.

"See," I said quickly, "We were married this morning."

"Oh congratulations." she gasped.

"Thank you." I tell her quietly. "The thing is, we don't know how much time we have left with her, and she was really looking forward to seeing this place one more time."

"Well..." she said again.

"Please." I begged. Rebecca looked at Eros and Emma, then back at me. "We really want to make this day about her. I promise we won't touch a thing."

"I guess it'll be fine." She said looking at her watch. "You have about twenty minutes before my boss shows up."

"I understand." I told her smiling, "We won't be long."

"Stay on the first floor, please."

"Thank you." I say nodding as I walk towards Emma and Eros doing a little happy dance. His eyes are on me, and I smile and wink at the love that transfers from him to me.

"Are you ready?" he asks, holding his hand out to me.

"Actually," I say reaching out for him, "She's going to let us walk around and sight see."

"Okay." Eros said half smiling at me.

"We have to stay on the first floor, and we only have about twenty minutes.

"Yes ma'am." Eros says sweetly over Emma's school girl giggles.

Chapter Twenty

"Turn in here." I say, pointing to my left. My parent's yard is ideal for a suburban neighborhood in the front. Beautiful green grass, colorful flowers lining the walkway and trimming the front porch. Huge trees scattered across the front lawn. Picture perfect. The only thing that's missing are the neighbors. The property is well away from civilization, so comfort is a perk that we're all accustomed to when we come here.

"We're here." Eros whispers gazing over at me.

Look at him, peering into my eyes as if he can see through me. It's hard to believe how far we've come in such a short time. The amount of love that radiates between us is so thick I feel like I could reach out and touch it.

"You, okay?" He asks. It's so sweet that I can't stop the half smile spreading across my face.

"I'm perfect." I whisper, leaning my face into his touch. I'm more than perfect. I don't know what this feeling I have would be called. It's something so new, I find it hard to believe that the English dictionary has a word that could define it...because love sure doesn't say enough.

"Um..." I begin, as I watch Eros hoist Emma's wheelchair from the SUV, "Just so you know, my parents can be a little...abrasive." I nod my head, thinking over the meaning of the word. "Yeah, I think that's the word I want to use."

"Really?" He chuckles, "Anything else?"

"I don't know. I'll point it out as we go." My smile is wide and bright. I'm pretty sure tonight is going to be some kind of disaster, but it's going to have to happen.

"Hey," I whisper pulling his attention from the trunk to my face, "I love you." He smiles his sweet smile, then leans in and tenderly kisses my forehead.

"I love you, too." He whispers against my skin.

"You're finally here!" I hear my mother say from the porch.

"Here we go." I mumble. "Hey mommy." I say louder walking around the back of the truck, to open Emma's door.

"What can I help with?" she asks, walking up to my side wrapping her arm around my waist. "And who might this be?"

"I am Emma Rose Apollo." Emma said, gripping our hands as she carefully steps from the vehicle. "And that big one there, is my son, Eros."

"Well, Emma," Mom said smiling, "I'm Katherine and I'm very happy to have you here."

"Eros," I say stepping next to him, "This is my mother, Kathy. Ma, Eros."

My mother looks from me to Eros, and curiously looks him up and down.

"Well, they sure don't make them small where you're from."

"Depends on who you're standing next to." He jokes. Leaning in, he embraces my mother, engulfing her entire body within his arms. "It's nice to meet you." He tells her.

"Thank you for having us."

"Leave your bags, we'll get them later. Let's go meet everyone."

"Where's Daddy?"

"He's out back with Frank. The twins are inside doing…something, Nate and Danny, that is. Phi and Phil are still at the office but will be here soon. You know how they are."

She laughs, and it's the sweetest sound. I realized then that it's something I just don't hear enough of in my day-to-day life. I wrap my arms around her waist and bend to nuzzle my face in her powder scented neck.

"I missed you, momma."

"Aw my only baby girl." She cooed, rubbing her hand across my back, "I missed you too."

"Hey young man." My father called. He was walking towards us already dressed in his hunting camos, "You want to get away from all this girlie hugging shit and do some man stuff."

"Daddy this is Eros and his mother Emma."

"I'm Maxwell, welcome to our home." He and Eros shake hands and Emma receives a gentle kiss on the back of her hand.

"Let's get you inside, Emma." My mother tells her stepping to the back of her chair. "I'm sure you'd like to freshen up some."

"Yes, I would, thank you." Emma agrees. "It was a nice ride, but a bit long I'm afraid."

Looking back, I realize Eros is watching us, smiling. I give him a quick wink and turn my attention back to the two women in my company.

"Emma, your room will be right here." Mom tells her once we're inside. "It has a door joining you to the bathroom. I hope it's comfortable enough."

"I'm sure it'll be fine, Dear." Emma tells her looking around, "You have a lovely home."

"Thank you," mom says smiling, "The more I look around the more I realize this room is filled with years and years of clutter."

"And memories." Emma chuckles.

"Something smells delicious." I say to mom.

"Meatloaf and pot roast."

"My favorite." I say to Emma.

"Are you going out with your father, Ayo."

"I was going to." I say, pulling out a chair next to Emma, "But I can stay here with Emma while you cook."

"Nonsense." Emma tells me, "I'll be perfectly fine. You go see your father, dear. I'll look after things here."

This lady really makes me smile. Here she is, in a perfectly new place. Around perfectly new people, behaving as though she's been here a thousand times. I glance up and catch Katherine smiling, probably thinking the same thing as I am.

"Yes ma'am." I say to Emma.

"Hey Kat?" my father calls from the front, "Can I have my hunting partner, or do you still need her?"

"She's all yours."

"We're going to take this young man out in the woods and show him the land."

"You sure you'll be, okay?" I say placing my hand on top of Emma's.

"Bye Ayo." Mom tells me, putting a stop to any of my fussing.

"Bye." I say jokingly. I stand and kiss her full on her lips, and Emma on the cheek, "I've been kicked outta better places anyway." I shout over my shoulder as I leave the kitchen and head through the living room towards the back door.

My parents' backyard in comparison to the front, is in a completely different dimension. I'm convinced, though the grass is going through its transition from bright summer green fluff to hard, cold precipitation. It still has a beautiful fall hue to it. Just past the perimeter of the yard, the ground changes from soft green to a concrete slab. Large enough to hold four average size tool sheds. One for bigger lawn equipment and the second for lawn equipment and tools, including two chainsaws and three leaf blowers, things like that. Seeing as how my brothers live closer, they're always over helping my father build something or cut something. The third was my father's *man cave*. He called it his "doghouse", even painted it red and put a *welcome home* mat in front of the door. He always said with a name like that it had to live up to the hype.

The fourth was a sort of workshop for my dad. Anything that needed fixing, repairing, taken apart or anything of that nature, this was the place. The doghouse is where we hung out. As kids, my brothers and I were always getting into trouble and getting put out of the house for the day. Either for rough housing, making too much noise or simply just getting on my mother's nerves. Over time we stopped waiting until we were told to get out. We somehow, at some point in the day ended up here…in this shed.

At first it was just a tin hot box, with a stuffed dear head and a few random posters. Now there were mini-industrial fans mounted on shelves, in each corner of the ceiling, and a picnic table and bench in front of the entrance. A refrigerator, fully stocked with everything from cold beer to diabetic insulin for the twins, Phe and Phil.

"There she is!" Jeffery shouts, smiling with his arms open wide, as I walk up to the shed. My brother encloses his arms around me.

"Jeffery!" I say excitedly.

"I missed you, Sis." He said patting my back extra hard. Next came the twins Nate and Danny, both embracing me. Both kissing my cheeks and telling me how much they missed me. I love my brothers; they are always there for me whenever I need them. At the moment though they're doing a bit much. Laying it on mighty thick.

Then I see him. Leaning casually against the industrial sink. Legs crossed at the ankles. Holding a bottle of beer in his fingers.

"Oh yeah…" Frank said over the mouthpiece of his cell, "before you get comfortable, *Jay-Eff* is in the building."

"What?!" I said shocked, stepping over his legs, making my way towards Eros. "That dream's still alive?"

"And kicking." *Jay-Eff* began rapping, "Judging by the words that I be spittin."

Jeffery's dream, or fantasy, so to speak, was to be a *"famous rapper"*. It's all he talked about as a kid. And then life kicked in. He grew up and decided that we…his family…were the only audience he'd ever need.

"He's been doing this shit all day." Nate said, handing me a bottle from the fridge.

"Hey babe." I say to Eros, leaning in to kiss him.

"Hey." He whispers back. "I love your brothers."

"Good." I chuckle, "You can have them."

"What's that?" Jay-Eff began, "You talkin' bout us? Say the wrong thing, I'm gonna kick yo butt."

"Oh my god!" I say, walking to the picnic table, hoisting myself up. "Somebody please shoot me in the face."

The thing that made everyone fall over laughing is Jeffery is still spitting his rhymes. They're not even clever. As long as the words sound the same, he's good. On top of that, he's abandoned all logic of modern and trendy sound, for the nostalgic flow of eighties hip hop. You know the sound. That Kool Moe Dee, meets Sugar Hill Gang, meets Curtis Blow kind of sound. It's ridiculous and simple and completely over the top. But I laugh every time. Sometimes, like now, I hype him up and encourage him. I turn from Eros and start clapping to the beat of his rhyme, which only makes him rap harder. It's hilarious and horrible, and pretty soon everyone has joined in. Nate, Danny, Eros. Me. All except for Frank, who is stretched out on the fold out sofa. Quietly conversating on his cell phone. Breaking a major...*major* weekend rule.

"Hang it up, Frank." I say over the laughter, "Hang it up!"

"Hang it up." Nate chimed in. Daniel, being himself and not wanting to be left out, hoisted himself over the back of the sofa and onto Franky's side. Trying his best to remove the phone from his hand.

"Stop!" Frank shouted through his laughter.

"Get it Nate!" Danny shouted, laughing, "Take his phone."

Frank frantically waved his arm left and right. To and frow. Back and forth. Attempting, very successfully, to keep Nate away from his phone. They were rolling around, wrestling and sucker punching each other, all in the name of obeying the rules. We were all laughing hysterically and instigating the situation more. Including Eros, though he was mostly laughing.

"Leave the boy alone." A loud voice boomed. It was my father. His voice was very demanding, and we all halted whatever we were doing, except laughing. But. Me being me, I seized the moment and snatched the phone from his hand.

"No!" he shouted, still laughing.

"Hello, whoever this is. I'm sorry to inform you..."

"Give me my phone!" Frank shouted, jumping up from the dingy sofa. The moment I see his feet hit the floor; I dart to the other side.

"Get him daddy!" I said, pointing. "I'm sorry to inform you," I continued, to the unknown other half of Frank's conversation. "That

Franklin is with his family this weekend and we have a very strict *no phones* rule."

"*Very strict.*" Nate loudly added.

"So, if you want to talk to him any further you're going to have to wait for Sunday night. Or Monday morning. Depends on how much he likes you."

"Hello Ayo." The voice on the other end of the phone said.

"Um…hello." I respond, stopping in my tracks. "Who is this?" I ask, looking at Frank.

"It's T.K." The voice *and* my brother both said.

My mouth dropped and my eyes flicked to Eros. Who's shocked and confused expression mirrored my own.

"Hey T.K."

"Hey." He chuckled, "How've you been?"

"I've been perfect. Hey how'd the interview go?"

"Oh." he said, as the excitement in his voice grew. "Eros didn't tell you. It went perfect, thanks to you."

"Thanks to me?" I repeated.

"Yes you." He said, "If it wasn't for your close observation. Pointing out that players inability to fast break to the right. I don't think we would have had anything to talk about."

"Well," I say smiling, "Glad I could help."

"Where's Eros?" He asked.

"He's right here." I tell him, winking at Eros.

"Can I talk to him?"

"Sure, you can." I say smiling, "*If* you drive up here."

"Oh, is that how you're going to do me?"

I laugh at his fake disappointment. "Like I said, strict no phone policy this weekend."

"Text me the address."

"Absolutely." I say smiling. Once I hang up, I text the address then pitch the phone to Nate. "Hold on to this. Don't let him have it."

"I'm getting my phone back." Frank said pointing his pinky finger at me.

"Yep, eventually." I said winking. "Hey daddy." I wrap my arms around his waist and squeeze.

"Hey baby girl." He leaned back, arms still around my shoulders. "How about this guy?" He nudged his chin in Eros direction.

"How about him?" I asked, reversing the question. He looked at Eros, who was now more interested in whatever Nate and Danny were discussing, to listen to us.

"He seems like a good guy." He said smiling at me.

"Yeah, he's a keeper."

My father smiled, nodded his head and said, "Okay." And that was it. There would be no more discussion on Eros position in my life. At least not between him and I. That's what I love about my father. He doesn't require a boatload of explanations or excuses. Things were just that simple. Either it was going to be...or it wasn't. And right now, his peaceful smile tells me that he accepts whatever Eros and I share.

"So, you heading out with us?" The *us* he was referring to was he and Franky.

"Of course." Hell, if I'm not mistaken, I haven't gotten a kill in the last five years that I've been out.

"Well, I thought since you have your special friend with you, you wouldn't want to go." I looked at Eros whose attention was now on me. My goodness, even in a room full of people his eyes can still burn a hole through my soul.

"Hey," I say half smiling, "You want to go with us."

"Absolutely." He said standing from the shelf he was leaning on.

"There you go." My father said turning away from us.

"Yo," I say tapping Frank, who was still trying to negotiate getting his phone back, "Let's go."

"Right behind you." He said smiling. "I want my phone back."

"You ready?" I said to Eros.

"I guess I am."

At first glance, Eros seems to be a massive specimen of a man. Tall, muscular. Even through his beard you can see the sternness in his face. To some people, he may even seem a bit scary or intimidating. For me, all

I see at this moment is the kindness in his eyes, and all I feel is the gentleness in his touch. I wrap my arms around his neck and pull him close.

"You don't have to go if you're not comfortable." I say into his eyes.

"Oh no babe." He tells me. His voice is soft and smooth, and his eyes seem to drink in every unspoken thought that runs through my mind. "I wouldn't miss this for the world."

"Okay." I say softly, smiling.

"So, what should I do?"

"Well," I tell him, pulling his face close enough to softly kiss his bottom lip. "You head out with them; they'll tell you everything you need to know. And I'll meet you back here."

"Um-hum." He hummed low. "You married me."

It was a random and unexpected thing to say, but I completely understand why he said it. I've been thinking about it since it was made official.

"I did didn't I."

"Come...on." Frank shouted from the back door.

"Shut up Frank." We both said in unison. Danny and the other Nate exploded into laughter, as Eros walked in Frank and my father's direction and I in the other.

"Where you going?" Eros asks.

"To my castle." I say over my shoulder, laughing at yet one more thing that I'm sure will be added to his *list*.

Chapter Twenty-one

"You ready?" My father asks as I approach the entrance of the woods where they were standing. Holding up my bow, I fell into step with my father, my brother and my *husband*.

"So, all you have to do this time around," Daddy was saying to Eros, "is be as quiet as you can…and have fun." We stop, form a circle and join hands. Bow our heads with our eyes closed. Listening as my dad recites a prayer of protection for us and our prey. We say amen, tell each other good luck, then they head in one direction and I in the other.

This is my home. This is where I love to be. Outdoors, surrounded by solid, strong forms of life. Changing colors with the turn of the season. The smell of soft, moist earth saturating the air. The sound of the wind rustling through the soft autumn leaves. The dirt path under my soft steps soon turns to scattered grass. Fallen leaves. Broken limbs and branches that have either died or was struck down. It's no matter to me. I've been in these woods my whole life, so a trail isn't needed. I've embedded in my memory each bush and tree trunk that I see. I am very much aware of what lies ahead of me. I know exactly how far I need to go before I reach the stream.

A sudden sound forced my feet motionless just as I was about to step over a long ago fallen tree. The sound was quick. Had my mind been elsewhere, I would have missed it all together. Delicately, I lowered my foot from midair to the moist debris of earth. There it is again! This time it sounded like it came from behind me. If I turn around, or make any kind of sudden movement, I'll spook it. And it'll probably bolt away whatever it is. Rushing to run back to its little home. So, he can tell his little animal friends, family and neighbors not to go by the stream... hunters are lurking.

There it is again! This time, moving right next to me. *'Easy breathing, Ayo.'* I think, *'easy breathing. You've been through this countless times. True, it's never been as close as you think it is, but it's not new.'* Just as I'm exhaling a deep breath, a slow, brown shape focuses into my line of eyesight. She's beautiful. Tall, lean. From the looks of it she's not pregnant. At least not as far as my eyesight can tell. I am dumb founded. I know she can feel my presence. The wind has shifted putting her down wind of my scent, so I know she can smell me. Probably can hear my heart racing too.

'What are you going to do, girl?' I wonder to myself. *'What do you hear?'* Her ears perk up and her head turns in my direction. Looking me directly in my eyes. We stand there. Starring at each other for what seems like forever but was probably more like a few seconds. Then something unheard and unseen startled her attention and she bolted. With me on her heels, as close and as quick as I can. I reach behind me and pull free an arrow.

The sound of the stream is closer now, but she doesn't stop. *'What are you doing girl.'* She slows her sprint down to a trot, then a slow walk. Stopping only for a quick nibble on a low growing bush. I notch my arrow knowing that if I was meant to get her, I'd better do it now before whatever spooked her before, spooks her again. Breath Ayo. Listen to the leaves. Feel the breeze. Hear the water coast downstream. The doe is about fifty feet away from me, but a broken branch is hanging low about halfway between us. All I need to do is step about fifteen paces to my right and my shot will be clear.

'Move slow, Ayo.' Calculate your steps. I move four steps, over a bed of soft leaves, then stop. Her ears perk and rotate but she continues her snack, until whatever green leaves are gone.

She sniffs around then slowly walks to the water, with me quietly stepping behind her. Whatever is going to be done will be done at her pace, and I don't mind waiting. She's filled her belly now I don't mind waiting for her to finish washing it down. I watch her, bow and arrow positioned and ready, as she delicately tests the water by sniffing it. She's so regal, almost like she knows what's about to happen, and refuses to go out with anything less than dignity. Breath, Ayo, breath.

I tighten my fist around the grip of the bow, willing the slight tremble of my wrist to stop. The fingers holding the bow string arched are protected by my glove for now. But my shoulder muscles are beginning to burn from lack of practice. I have to hold on. Not too much longer. Not too much longer. Time creeps along, slowly, but we both hold our position. Me ready to release my arrow and her having herself a healthy drink. I watched until my eyes began to water. Then I noticed her back leg step backwards and I let go, automatically releasing and docking another arrow, then releasing again.

The first arrow missed as she ran along the riverside, but the second one was spot on. Straight through the throat. Taking no time to celebrate, I quickly approached the doe and cautiously kneeled by her side. Her head flopped and her legs flailed as she strained her strength, struggling to get up.

"Ssssh." I tell her, lifting her head to my lap and rubbing my hand over the smooth crown of her head. "Ssssh, girl. Ssssh." Her low painful bleats calmed as I pulled the knife from my boot and placed it to the soft flesh of her shin and slowly lifted her head, giving my knife more room.

I close my eyes and quietly thank God for the creation of this creature. Thank the doe for the gift of its flesh, and nourishment that it will provide. Then I cut smoothly across the jugular and waited as her warm blood saturated the thighs of my camos.

Voices and laughter caught my attention, and I look over my shoulder to see my father, brother and husband approaching.

"Did you see that?" I asked as they knelt beside me.

"That was exciting." Eros bragged.

"Is it finished?" My dad asks, referring to the prayer of thanks he taught us. I nodded my head, lifted the doe from my lap and stood taking a much-needed deep breath.

"What?" I asked, returning the glare of the three faces staring up at me. I look down at myself and realize what they're looking at. The thighs of my pants are so saturated that they no longer look camouflage.

"Oh." I say chuckling. I hand my knife to my brother and began rinsing my pants with stream water and mud.

"How'd you know the first one was going to miss?" Eros asks.

"I didn't." I told him, "No more than I knew the second one would hit." I stood and dried my hands on the backs of my pants.

"We need a long stick." My father says. "Something long and sturdy. This one's a big one."

I look around trying to remember which direction we ran from. Then I spot what I'm looking for. Digging in the backpack Franky's wearing, I find a small hand saw, and go to work removing the low hanging branch. Sometime later the deer is secured by the front and hind legs and tied to the branch, ready to be carried home.

"Everybody all set?" After confirmation from everyone we headed home. "We'll tie her up at the forest edge." My father called back over his shoulder, "You clean yourself before you go indoors, or your mother is going to kill you."

Franklin looked over his shoulder, back to where Eros and I were walking. "Oh Pop," he said, smiling devilishly, "I think a killing is coming no matter what." I flipped Frank the bird, but quickly played it off by brushing my hands down my shirt the moment my father turned his questioning face towards me. The rest of the hike was spent with Eros answering my father's many pro football questions, and me answering Eros questions about hunting.

Chapter Twenty-two

"Ayo!" My mother shrieked as we approached the back porch. "What in the world?!" She stood, placing the teacup on the table between her chair and Emma's. "Did you have to come back looking like a savage?" She stood on the bottom step with her arms folded over her chest, shielding her from the cool wind.

"But Momma," I said skipping up to her with my arms spread wide, "Gimmie a hug." She smacked my hands away, laughing and trying to quickly back her way up the steps.

"Don't touch me, girl." she said, turning her back to me and holding her arm out to keep me at bay.

"Come on, gimmie a hug!" We were all laughing. She knew I wasn't going to touch her with my bloody body. But the sound of her shrieking laughter pleases me. I've missed it. I miss being a part of her day to day.

"Fine." I say pouting around a smile, "I'll just hug Emma. Come on, Emma. Let's hug." Eros sat on the top step of the porch, leaning to one side so I could slip by.

"No ma'am." Emma said proudly, "If your own mother won't hug you, I may be wise to take her lead." My mouth dropped. Everyone that heard exploded into laughter.

"I guess that's it." I say dropping my arms to my side. "If anyone needs me, I'll be on the side of the house washing my savage behind."

"Side of the house?" Eros asked.

"There's *no way* she is stepping in my house, looking like a bloody nightmare." My mother stated. Eros looked at me and I smile.

"I'm a savage." I say looking at my stained camos then back at him. "I shall return when I'm civilized again."

"You might as well go help. She'll need extra hands." I heard Kat say, assumingly to Eros. "Burn those clothes!" she shouted.

Chapter Twenty-three

"So." I say to Eros. He was sitting on a tree stump watching me wash myself behind a roofless, wooden enclosure. "How's your day been so far?"

"I think," he said draping the towel he held over his knee. "Today is the best day of my life."

"Really?" I say smiling at his eyes. His expression is calm, and relaxed and his eyes never leave mine. "That's a pretty big statement."

"It's been a pretty big day." he said half smiling. "You've made me a very happy man." I can only smile as I turn the water off.

"Now all I have do is tell the rest of my family."

"How's that going to go?" he asks, handing my towel over the shower wall.

"Are you nervous?" I ask, teasing.

"A little bit." He rests his chin on his hands, on top of the shower wall edge. Watching me dry my body.

"Babe," I say giggling at his confession. "You're standing in my parents' backyard. Watching me bathe…naked."

His head slightly tilted to the side, but his eyes never left mine. His mouth didn't even flinch, let alone curl up in that adorable half smile that I love so much. And still…his eyes never left mine.

"You're serious?" I ask, tucking the towel corner across my chest.

"What if they don't see things the way we do?"

And there he was. Honest Eros. Standing there staring, back at me with those mahogany eyes. Close enough for me to touch my fingertips to the nest of chestnut hair on his cheek. And touch my lips softly over the surface of his. Pausing a moment to feel his lips respond.

"What if my family doesn't see things...the way we see things?" Not the response I was waiting for but, okay. I leaned my face away from his and search his eyes. While his eyes scan the tingling trail of goose bumps that his fingertips leave behind, as they trace my collar bone.

"Would that make you change the way *you* see things?" I must have stopped breathing because his eyes seem to remember that I was watching him, watch me.

"Change the way *I see* things?" I repeat.

I wanted to laugh and roll my eyes and tell him how silly he was being. But I guess that wouldn't be fair. I've not only met but have been except by his family. Seeing as how that was only two people, it was fairly easy. He's got my parents, my six brothers, their kids *and* spouses. I can see how that could stress a person out. But...he has absolutely nothing to worry about. "Then...we'll make them see." I say sliding the door open.

Stepping onto my slides I stop and stand in front of him. Pressing my tall body against his clothes. Half smiling at his apprehension. "We'll make them see." I say again, curling my fingers through his beard.

"And if they don't?" He said slipping a lock of hair behind my ear. He looks *so* genuinely worried and sweet at the same time.

"Nothing will make me change the way I see things. I told you. I don't really care about how anyone else feels. All I care about is how you make me feel, and how I make you feel. That's all my family's...my bad." I say correcting myself. "*Our* family is going to care about too." I have to get used to saying that...*our family*. "Besides," I can't help but smile as I pull him close. "They kind of don't have a choice, babe. We've already tied the knot, so, you're stuck with me. Whether they like it or not." This time I don't wait for him to respond to my lips. I wrap his arms around my toweled waist, and my arms around his neck and pull his face to my lips.

I can feel the muscles in his neck slightly relax and his arms began to tighten around my waist, but I know he's still worried. I also know... there's nothing I can do about it. I have to let him see for himself. He's a trusting man, he'll get there. *Holy...shit.* He's *my* trusting man...*my* husband. This is going to be something else.

Chapter Twenty-four

"Somebody pass the rolls?" One of my brothers asked.

We were a full house now, every Mitchell, minus three. Phelix and Phillip showed up at some point while I was in the shower. Alone. Apparently, Phillips girlfriend wasn't his girlfriend anymore...again. I guess. They're so on again off again, I don't even ask any more. Whenever he shows up with her, they're on again. Tonight...they're off. And Phe's girlfriend was never a girlfriend in the first place, so she doesn't even get an invitation. And supposedly *she's* okay with that, *if* you listen to the story *he* tells. His problem was, *we* were listening, and he wasn't. It took myself, my mother and Danny's wife Melanie to point out to him that the argument he and his girlfriend *that's not his girlfriend* got into days before this weekend, was *not* because he was coming here for the weekend.

It may seem like she doesn't want him around his family, but that's only because she knows that it's actually the other way around, he doesn't want to bring her. Now, according to him she's more than welcome to come with him. He just never thought to actually ask and she never volunteered. I couldn't help but laugh at him, because he was so serious and saw nothing wrong with that logic.

The point I was trying to make was if he never thought to ask, then she really wasn't welcome. He wasn't getting it. He couldn't or wouldn't understand.

"If she wanted to come, why didn't she just say so."

It was my mother who told him. "Because she wants you to ask on your own."

"If she don't say that…then she don't want it."

"Lord have mercy." My mom sighed, defeated.

"She can't be happy with being your," Melanie looked over her shoulder to where her twin boys and Nate and Deedra's twin son and daughter sat, then back at Phe, "special friend."

"Why not? She knows she's not that special." Everybody burst out laughing. Everyone that heard that is. Like we thought, the kids were being nosey, so they laughed. My father, on the other hand, looked up just in time to see my mother smack Phe in the back of the head and tell him for the ump-tenth time how much he gets on her nerves. So, he laughed.

"What happened, Kat?" He asked.

"Nothing, your son is crazy." She couldn't help giggling, "He gets on my nerves." Or help hitting him again. Even Emma was laughing. Now that I think about it, she seems to be in great spirits today. She's been up longer than she has in days. She also looked happier.

"Emma, please forgive my family." My mother said, "I tried to teach them manners, but it just didn't work."

She plopped down in her seat, then smiled as if exhausted. I hadn't really looked at her since I've been here, until now. She wasn't what people would call *beautiful*, more like super cute. Especially since she got her hair cut into a pixie style. It's cute the way her blond snips frame her forehead. Her face was rounder, but her smile was a thousand times brighter and her eyes sparkled like a grey sky on a sunny day.

"Don't apologize to me, honey." She said smiling back at Katherine. "I haven't laughed this much in a long time." She looked across the table and held her hand out to me just as Eros' hand slid across my thigh.

Since it was still evening when I finished my shower, I saw no point in dressing back up, so all I had on was a pair of yoga pants, a slightly oversized vee-neck tee and a pair of flaps. The warmth from his hand as it lingered and lightly squeezed, made me smile.

"I want to thank you for sharing your family with me." Emma continued. Eros leaned in, with everyone watching, and kissed the top of my head. "It's nice to see everybody so happy and I'm glad to be a part of it." I was going to tell her that she was welcome, but she yawned just as I was about to speak.

She's tired, I can tell now. Her eyes were glossy, and her smile just didn't seem to go that high anymore.

"You tired, momma?" Eros asked, removing hand from my thigh to wipe his mouth with his napkin.

"Well son, I'll tell you." She said leaning back into the chair, "When you get to my age, your body has a way of telling you when it's time to go."

"Of course, momma." Eros smiled.

"Ayo, why don't you show Emma to her room." Katherine told me. She spoke in a quieter voice now. In fact, everyone did. The chatter picked back up, but it stayed at a low murmur.

I stood, placing my hand on Eros' back just as Nate, who was sitting beside Emma, stood and pulled her chair out for her. Then walked her around the end of the table to where I was standing. Waiting. Making quick note of the slight flex of my husband's back muscles where I touched him.

"Good night, Ms. Emma." The children all recited.

"Oh," she said, smiling back at them, "good night, children. Don't stay up too late, you'll get bags under your eyes."

"That's what you say, Nan." Trey, Nate and Melanie's son, said.

"Good night, everybody." she said again.

"I'll be in there in a few, momma." Eros told her softly.

Chapter Twenty-Five

It was different helping Emma for bed this time. Usually, just in case she has an accident, she waits for morning to have her shower. Tonight, because of the long drive here and being outside for most of the day. Along with helping out with the cooking she insisted on having it now… and doing it herself. No matter what I said, or how tired she was, she would have no help from me other than, standing in the bathroom with her. Any other time, after she's dressed in her bed clothes, I or someone depending on who she is with would brush her hair for her. Tonight, though her hands were stiff, and the closer I look…a little too shaky, she insisted on doing it alone.

Almost too shaky to hold on to the brush. She made a couple attempts at the sides but fumbled both times. The second time, I offered to help but she declined. She did, however, ask that I open the window and close the vents.

"Sure." I told her.

"And if you don't mind," she said as I lifted the window and tested the screen, making sure it was secure, "I have some blouses in my suitcase that should be hanging. If I leave them any longer, they'll wrinkle, and lord knows I hate ironing."

"Okay, I'll hang them for you."

"It's alright, dear." she said smiling at me through the mirror, "I can hang them myself; I'll just need the hangers."

"Okay." I answered, spinning on my heels towards the closet. "How many hangers will you need?"

"Four will do."

"You sure you don't need me to hang your shirts for you?" I asked after sliding open the closet door and seeing how jam packed the clothes were. She'll never be able to move anything over. Not only because of her lack of strength, but also because she's short as shit.

This closet has some of everything in it. My parents' clothes. Some of my grandmother's clothes from before she passed. Quilts. Shoes, some in boxes, some not. Some of this stuff needs to go.

"Momma?" I said into my cell phone, "Is it okay if I move some of these clothes into another room so I can make space for Emma's things?"

"Yeah." she responded, "Wait where are you?"

"I'm in Emma's room hanging up some of her blouses, well trying to." I said, pulling clothes from the rack two hangers at a time. "It's too much stuff in here."

"I know, baby." She said, "I've been meaning to get some of those old things together for Goodwill, but I just hadn't gotten around to it yet."

"I see." I told her bending to pick up a shoe box.

"Well, sweetheart, me and your daddy is about to go to bed. You need anything else?"

"No momma, that was it." I said opening the shoebox lid. "I'll just put this stuff...*what in the world?*"

This box of nude, slingback princess heels turned out to not be that at all. Instead, it was my old Yahtzee game. *Which* was just a magical decoy box of goodness. Inside of that, was me and my brother's old herbal stash, some rolling papers and about five lighters.

"What in the world, what?" I heard my mother say. She actually repeated herself maybe three times, but I was too mesmerized by what I'd found to answer.

"What in the world, what?"

"Oh nothing, momma." I said quickly closing the box lid as if she was looking over my shoulder. "It's just too much junk in this closet, that's all." I lied. I know it's wrong, blah blah blah...it was necessary. It's not like I was going to say, *yeah ma, I just found an old stash of weed from last year.* There's no point in telling on anyone, after tonight it's going to be gone anyway. Besides, if my parents knew about it, they'd probably smoke it and we'd have nothing left for next year.

"Okay, love." She said yawning, "We're going to sleep. I'll see you in the morning."

"Tell her I like her boyfriend." My father said on the other end. *'My husband.'* I corrected silently.

"Hey before you go to sleep." I told her as I flopped Emma's suitcase on the bed, "I want to come up and say goodnight."

"Well come on," Momma said, yawning, "we're already laying down."

"Okay, five minutes." I said carefully placing the shoe box on the bedside table. "I'm going to bring these clothes up too."

"Okay." Emma said, also yawning, "I think I've done about all I'm going to do. I'm ready to lay down now."

"As you wish, ma'am." I smiled scooping the Goodwill clothes from the bed into my arms. "Let me just…" Looking around, I realize that the recliner that used to sit by the window was no longer there. So, I was left with my arms stuffed with clothes, turning a slow circle trying to find a place to drop the load.

"Can I come in?" Eros asked, peeking from behind the door. Perfect!

"Yes!" I say smiling.

His eyebrows arched to the top of his hairline in confusion. He looked at Emma sitting on the bed and bounced his eyebrows up and down at her. Looking at me as he fully steps into the room. Smooth striding in my direction. Six foot, eight inches and still he is every bit as graceful as a delicate ballet dancer…and he's all mine. Those mahogany eyes. That chestnut hair that now brushed his shoulders. The thermal style tee-shirt that I love so much, that seemed to be giving his biceps and abs the most affectionate hug possible…and he's all mine.

"I need you." I said to him, smiling at the slight drop of his chin.

"You need me?" He repeated softly. He stopped in front of me and slid his long, muscular arms around my waist. Pulling me and the bundle of clothes I held into his body.

"Yes, I do." I said, smiling at the soft kiss he planted on my lips. "But, for now," I smiled, "Will you hold on to this for me. I have to move them to another room."

"Of course." he said, "Anything else?"

"That box," I told him, unfolding the shirts and slipping them onto the hangers. "But I'll grab that myself."

I gave him the clothes, hung the blouses on the rack. Helped Emma get settled into bed. Said our goodnights. Then headed upstairs, with my husband following behind me. The closet upstairs was way more forgiving with space than the previous one. So, hanging the clothes was as simple as dropping them on the rack.

"Okay." I said looking through the full-length door mirror at Eros graze his lips over the surface of my neck from behind. "We have to tell my parents." His eyes popped open wide and stared back at me.

"Tell your parents what?" He asked.

"About our wedding. Well actually..." I pulled my phone from my pocket, tapped open the camera and snapped a mirror image of his eyes closed with his face softly buried in my neck. "Not today's wedding but the wedding we plan to have."

"Um-hum." He hummed. His hands smoothed from my belly up to my breast. "We should tell them."

Just a simple touch from this man sets my blood to boiling, and now was no different. It took no effort to tilt my head back against his chest and allow him to make sweet tender love to the surface of my skin. No fight, whatsoever, to reach back and weave my fingers through his thick curls. "Yes, we should." Gently clenching my fist and pulling him closer into the curve of my neck. His tender lips gently moved up to my ear.

"When?" He asks. I turned to face him, wrapped my arms around his neck and pulled his face into mine.

His lips were smooth. His beard, as thick as it was, softly prickles against my face. Tickling my skin as his face moved, matching the rhythm of mine. My body began to stir. Heat began to radiate from my pores. Electricity began to spark from his soul to mine. Before I knew it, I'm hoisted up to cradle his waist with my long legs. Crossing my ankles around his back, as his magnificently large hands gripped my ass. As easy as it was for my spirit to merge with his, and get lost in every second of the moment, *seventy-five composure points to me for resisting the urge.*

"Now." I whispered, pulling away from his delicious lips.

"Really?"

"Yes." I answered unlocking my legs from around him and placing my feet on the carpeted floor. He sighed heavily, then trailed his lips and tongue up the surface of my throat to my chin. He cradled my face in his hands, tilted my head up to his and tenderly bit my bottom.

"I love you so much more than I thought ever possible for any human."

"I love you too." I smiled. "I still can't believe you let me marry you."

"Let you?" He chuckled, stepping aside so I could slide past him. "I can't believe I got this lucky. Look at all of that."

He smacks me on my butt, then groans at the jiggling response of my cheek. I can't help but giggle. He sounds like a kid in a candy store that was given permission to roam free, pick out anything they want, only to grab the piece they weren't allowed to eat. My parents' room was directly across the hall. I could see the soft glow from the television flickering under the door frame. Hopefully I wasn't too late, and they were still awake.

"Mommy." I said knocking softly. My goodness, the pit of my stomach feels just as flat and empty as it did every Christmas morning, when I was a little girl trying impatiently to wake them up. Eros on the other hand seemed to be as easy as pie. Caressing his hand over the curve of my hip.

"I swear." He whispered in my ear, "You and these yoga pants."

"Mommy?" I said a little louder, smiling over my shoulder.

"I thought we had a talk about wearing these?"

"We did." I whispered, "That's why I keep wearing them."

"Come in, Ayo." Momma's voice called out. Eros firm jaw dropped in mock fear, as I opened the door. *Oh, my stomach.*

"Can we talk for a minute?" I asked curling up on top of the covers next to her.

"Is that one of our children in bed with us?" My father's muffled sleepy voice asked. He adjusted the pillow that covered his face and peeked out around my mother.

"Yes." My mother yawned, "It's the girl. Now come on, they have something to talk to us about."

"I can hear, woman."

"Maxwell, sit up and pay attention, now. It's important."

He sighed heavily, removing his pillow.

"It better be important." He said, "It's ten-thirty at night."

My father sat up and focused his eyes on the massive man that hulked over the foot of their bed.

"Katherine." He whispered, "There's two of them in here, what are we going to do?"

"We're going to listen to what they have to say."

He looked at my mother, "You promised me I wouldn't have to do that once they moved out."

"Maxwell, shut up." she said, chuckling and looking at me...smiling. "Anyway."

My father leaned into his wife's side, close to her ear, "You lied." He whispered loudly, chuckling as she pushed his face away with the palm of her hand.

"What were you saying?"

"I was saying."

"This better be good." Daddy said cutting me off.

"Daddy..."

"Maxwell." My mother and I said simultaneously.

"I'm trying to tell you something serious."

"Look at that. You have three minutes."

"We're getting married." I blurted out. The back-and-forth banter between mom and dad stopped mid-breath and they both stared at me. Jaws dropped. Hum, this is something new. *Both* my parents rendered speechless. I smiled and mentally closed my eyes and enjoyed the sound of parental silence.

"Are you pregnant?" Momma asked.

Silence took its turn and fell upon me, this time. *Was I?* I guess I could be, we haven't been using any protection. *No*, I couldn't be. I looked back at Eros and briefly imagined myself holding a baby with a head full of mahogany hair and chocolate, twinkling eyes.

"I don't think so." I said, returning my attention to momma. "No, I'm not."

"Are you sure?" she asked.

"No." I said blankly. "I guess I could be." *Maybe I am.* "I don't feel like I am."

"But you could be?"

"I suppose so, yes." Now I'm confused. *Am I?* Wow, this conversation took a strange, unexpected turn. "But that's not why we're getting married." I said quickly, before she could ask any more pregnant questions.

"Then why?" my father asked.

"Because we want to." In my mind I sighed heavily. It may not be a good enough reason, but it's the only reason I could come up with. Besides it was a good enough for us so it'll have to be good enough for them.

"Why not?" I said adjusting my seating on the bed.

"We're not getting any younger. It doesn't get any better than him for me. And if I am pregnant. Well then," I hunched my shoulders, "then that just makes things all the better."

Maxwells eyes cut to Eros, "You're awful quiet over there, son. Are you hearing this?"

"Yes sir, I am." He half smiled.

"And you agree with this?"

"Yes sir, I do." He smiled bigger, flashing his pearly whites, and I completely dripped away into a warm puddle of satisfaction.

"Marriage?" My father asked chuckling a little harder than necessary.

"Yes sir."

"To her." He pointed his long boney pinky finger at me and laughed. Much harder than I wanted to appreciate.

"I like him, Kat." He said, still laughing as he slid the sheet up to his shoulder and the pillow over his face. "He wants to keep one." And that was my father in a nutshell, always quick to tell a joke.

I remember when, I guess, I was about eleven. I had been cranky all week. Everything pissed me off or made me sad enough to cry. My brothers were aggravating me beyond repair. My mother kept telling me something about premature PMS, whatever that was. Scaring me half to fucking death. Telling me that, at some point in the near future, I was going to basically bleed to death. And that the only thing I was going to feel was the need to throw up and cramps.

At least that's the understanding I walked away with. All day I was whining and crying about why I couldn't have been born a boy. So, needless to say, I was getting on Maxwells nerves. Danny and Nate had the chicken pox and wouldn't quit whining about itching. Being allergic to oatmeal. I know it's a stupid allergy, but it's true…oats. Anyway, every few minutes my father was dabbing calamine lotion on random pox marks on one twin while holding the waste basket to the other. Trying his best to keep them from making *another* mess on the floor. My mother got lucky. She'd never had the pox before, so she didn't have to deal with Nate *or* Danny. She did, however, have her hands full with me.

With both parents being occupied, that left Jeff in charge of Phelix and Phillip. Who wasn't in any way trying to listen to anything Jeff had to say. They were fighting and wrestling. Keeping such a racket that by midafternoon, Jeff, Phi *and* Phill were kicked out of the house. They weren't allowed to leave the yard that day because it was raining, but you can best believe they made the best out of a game of one-on-one touch football. Which almost always ended up with someone being tackled, pushed or drug through the mud. By the end of the day my father took a shower and flopped his entire weight across the foot of his and my mother's bed, the same bed I'm sitting on now, sighing heavily.

My mother was propped up with her back up against the wall, holding me against her almost not there bosom.

"Un-unh." she urged, nudging him with her foot. "You can't sleep in here."

"I don't see why not, it's my room. I pay for it."

"I'm not sleeping with you and your chicken pox germs. Go sleep on the couch."

"I ain't sleeping on no damn couch in my own house...that *I* pay for." He stood up and began snatching pillows and covers, mumbling under his breath and stomping around until he had all he needed. "It's a damn shame." He said snatching open the door, "Man can't even sleep in his own bed."

Pre-mature PMS or not, that shit was funny to me. "Listen at her laughing." he said to my mom, "She thinks it's funny. That's okay...don't say nothing." He mumbled, "It won't be funny when I sell all seven of them to China so they can get jobs and start earning their keep." We rarely ever took his threats seriously, especially the funny threats. Except on that rare occasion where his threats made since. Then, we all knew that if he had to *get up, pull this car over,* or *stop what he was doing...* he was going to tear some butts up. It was never the harsh words that warned us, but the stern expressionless stare into our eyes that made us fall back and rethink our actions.

Tonight, there was none of that. His smile pushed the corners of my own smile further into my cheeks.

"To her?" He said moving the pillow peeking up at my secret husband, "You sure? You know it's for the rest of your life, right."

"Till death do us part." Eros said repeating a quote from our pre-scripted vows.

"Okay." Daddy said, "Suit yourself."

"Oh, shut up, Maxwell." Momma told him, "You're so silly."

"This man don't know what he's getting himself into. I'm trying to warn him."

"He stays starting stuff." I joked, standing from the bed. "That's why you're paying for the wedding." I laughed, kissing my mother's cheek and leaning to kiss his.

"I guess it'll be a cookout in the backyard then."

"Ummm...cookout food." Eros smiled. Then chuckled at the three faces that whipped around him. "He said cookout food." He's blushing and his cheeks are flushing. "I like cookout food, it looks good. It smells good. It's cooked over an open flame." And he's rambling.

"Okay there, champ." I said reaching for his hand, "Time to go."

"See he gets it." My father said over my mother's fussing. I closed the door behind us and let out a loud whisper of a sigh.

"That went…" I was going to say well, but those eyes stole the breath right out of my lungs. He was standing with one hand halfway in his jeans pocket and the other under the hem of his shirt. Exposing the puff of hair that swirled around his navel.

"What?" I asked, biting my bottom lip.

"You want to hang out with me?"

Well look at that. Mr. Concrete Chest has succeeded in asking yet another question that I've never been asked before. And I am completely flustered. My smile is stretched tighter than any human should be allowed. Plus, I'm pretty sure a stupid sounding giggle bubbled from my lips. Yep, it did and it's official, I'm an idiot. *Pull yourself together, Ayo.*

"And do what?"

"Whatever." he smiled, "First I was hoping to see this castle you kept mentioning but it's gotten dark. Now I just want to go somewhere and make out with you."

"Yeah?" I said smiling even harder…as if that was possible. "Okay."

I know I probably look stupid, standing here nodding my head slowly. I know I sound stupid; I heard the giggle that fell from my lips. I'm losing all kinds of composure points. But this is my husband, and I'm his wife. And this is our wedding night. For the first time today, we can finally be by ourselves. As husband and wife…whatever that means.

"You're so cute." He said stepping closer to me, sliding his hands to the small of my back.

"Really?" I smiled, stepping into his hold. "Because I feel like I look a little silly."

"Of course, you look silly." he said smiling, lifting his chin to the touch of my fingers. But his eyes never left mine. I don't know if it was the way the light was shining from the bedroom into the hall where we stood, but, his eyes were molten chocolate. "That's what I love about you…silly looks good on you."

"Coming through." Jeffery said loud whispering from behind me, announcing himself and his wife Kelly. Who was slowly but surely climbing the steps behind him. "Just to let you know, Franky got his phone back." he said, patting me on my back and Eros on his arm as he strolled past, stopping just at the doorway of the extra room.

"How'd that happen?" I asked, amused.

"Good night, guys." Kelly sighed, finally reaching the top of the stairs. Sighing loudly, as she bent backwards to stretch herself. "I'm so glad there's a bathroom up here."

"He's had it for about an hour now." Jeffery said holding his hand out to help his pregnant wife.

Now, a couple of things happened at the same time. Jeffery stoops down to remove Kelly's shoes from her swollen feet. When he lowers himself, I spot the decoy shoe box in the other room on the bed where I left it. When I saw it, my eyes opened wide, and I immediately move around Jeffs body towards the bed to retrieve it. Just as I was leaving the room with the box in hand, my parents' door pops open causing us all to jump, startled. Which in turn startles my dad. He clutches his chest with one hand, calling for the lord to keep him until the end. And the door frame with the other.

Rolling his eyes up towards the ceiling. Rambling about people lurking in the halls while other people were trying to sleep. Myself, Jeffery and my father bantered back and forth in a whisper match about what was really going on.

During the process, daddy makes his way to the bathroom. Jeffery stands and helps his wife into the room to get her off her feet. Now I, with my magical box of goodness, make my way around my brother to my husband. So, we can make our way down the steps and out the door. We have some making out to do.

I take Eros by his bear paw hand and lead him down the stairs.

"Hey..." Jeffery whispered after us. I look up to my eldest brother leaning over the railing smiling down at me. Eros had stopped on the steps above me.

"What?" I whispered, stepping up to see him better. The good part about that was, it gave me a chance to press my body against my love's solid chest.

"What are y'all about to do?"

"Play Yahtzee." I said smiling, knowing full well he understood, the bulge in his eyeballs told it all.

"We're playing Yahtzee?" Eros asked.

"Wait for me." Jeff whispered.

"No!" Kelly whispered loudly. With, I might add, a very generous amount of sarcasm. "If you think..." I couldn't see kelly, but I imagine her finger pointed in the air, stamping an accent on every whisper that came out of her mouth. "Do you *know* how many *hours*, I'm on my feet a day. Carrying this load..."

Eros and I should have walked away, but we were too tickled to just leave it be. "And don't get me started on the other three. All day long it's *momma* this...and *momma* that and *momma I need*. Now I finally have an entire weekend..."

"But baby listen." Jeffery couldn't help laughing, he knew it was a long shot in the first place.

"And you want to go play *YAHTZEE*?!"

"But babe,"

"No." She whispered.

Humor was evident in her tone, but neither of us thought for one second that she was joking. Jeffery kept peeking over the railing at us. Eye signaling for the giggling to stop and for us to wait.

"Just one game." he pleaded. Eros placed his hand on my back and leaned into my shoulder muffling his laugh.

"All this over Yahtzee?" He whispered, catching his breath. I'm just going to wink at him, he'll find out in a minute.

"No," Kelly whispered, "The only game you're going to play is *hide the sausage*." At that she finally broke. Her giggling triggered Eros and Jeff, which triggered me. I can't believe she said that. But then again, it was Kelly, and one of the reasons I like her is that she isn't afraid to say what was on her mind. "Sorry guys," she whispered again, looking over the rail smiling and laughing, "Jeffery can't come out tonight. He's got a job to do." And on that note, Eros and I say goodnight one final time and leave...

P.S. - Stay tuned for volume 2...BECAUSE I HAVE TO: his side.

Printed in the United States
by Baker & Taylor Publisher Services